Tested by Fate

Historical Fiction Published by McBooks Press

BY ALEXANDER KENT
Midshipman Bolitho
Stand Into Danger
In Gallant Company
Sloop of War
To Glory We Steer
Command a King's Ship
Passage to Mutiny
With All Despatch
Form Line of Battle!
Enemy in Sight!
The Flag Captain
Signal–Close Action!
The Inshore Squadron
A Tradition of Victory
Success to the Brave
Colours Aloft!
Honour This Day
The Only Victor
Beyond the Reef
The Darkening Sea
For My Country's Freedom
Cross of St George
Sword of Honour
Second to None
Relentless Pursuit
Man of War

BY DOUGLAS REEMAN
Badge of Glory
First to Land
The Horizon
Dust on the Sea
Twelve Seconds to Live
Battlecruiser

BY DAVID DONACHIE
The Devil's Own Luck
The Dying Trade
A Hanging Matter
An Element of Chance
The Scent of Betrayal
A Game of Bones
On a Making Tide
Tested by Fate

BY DUDLEY POPE
Ramage
Ramage & The Drumbeat
Ramage & The Freebooters
Governor Ramage R.N.
Ramage's Prize
Ramage & The Guillotine
Ramage's Diamond
Ramage's Mutiny
Ramage & The Rebels
The Ramage Touch
Ramage's Signal
Ramage & The Renegades
Ramage's Devil
Ramage's Trial
Ramage's Challenge
Ramage at Trafalgar
Ramage & The Saracens
Ramage & The Dido

BY V.A. STUART
Victors and Lords
The Sepoy Mutiny
Massacre at Cawnpore
The Cannons of Lucknow
The Heroic Garrison
The Valiant Sailors
The Brave Captains
Hazard's Command
Hazard of Huntress

BY R.F. DELDERFIELD
Too Few for Drums
Seven Men of Gascony

BY DEWEY LAMBDIN
The French Admiral
Jester's Fortune

BY C.N. PARKINSON
The Guernseyman
Devil to Pay
The Fireship
Touch and Go
So Near So Far
Dead Reckoning

BY JAN NEEDLE
A Fine Boy for Killing
The Wicked Trade

BY IRV C. ROGERS
Motoo Eetee

BY NICHOLAS NICASTRO
The Eighteenth Captain
Between Two Fires

BY FREDERICK MARRYAT
Frank Mildmay OR *The Naval Officer*
The King's Own
Mr Midshipman Easy
Newton Forster OR *The Merchant Service*
Snarleyyow OR *The Dog Fiend*
The Privateersman
The Phantom Ship

BY W. CLARK RUSSELL
Wreck of the Grosvenor
Yarn of Old Harbour Town

BY RAFAEL SABATINI
Captain Blood

BY MICHAEL SCOTT
Tom Cringle's Log

BY A.D. HOWDEN SMITH
Porto Bello Gold

Tested by Fate

DAVID DONACHIE

THE NELSON AND EMMA TRILOGY,
PART TWO

McBOOKS PRESS, INC.
ITHACA, NEW YORK

Published by McBooks Press, Inc. 2004

First published in Great Britain in 2000 by Orion, an imprint of
The Orion Publishing Group Ltd.

Cover: *The Rhinebeck Panorama of London, c.* 1810, The Museum of London. Courtesy of The Bridgeman Art Library.

Library of Congress Cataloging-in-Publication Data

Donachie, David, 1944-
Tested by fate / David Donachie.
p. cm. — (The Nelson and Emma trilogy ; pt. 2)
1. Nelson, Horatio Nelson, Viscount, 1758-1805—Fiction. 2. Hamilton, Emma, Lady, 1761?-1815—Fiction. 3. London (England)—Fiction. 4. Naples (Italy)—Fiction. 5. Mistresses—Fiction. 6. Admirals—Fiction. I. Title.
PR6053.O483T47 2004
823'.914—dc22

2003022226

Distributed to the trade by National Book Network, Inc.,
15200 NBN Way, Blue Ridge Summit, PA 17214
800-462-6420

Additional copies of this book may be ordered from any bookstore or directly from McBooks Press, Inc., ID Booth Building, 520 North Meadow St., Ithaca, NY 14850. Please include $4.00 postage and handling with mail orders. New York State residents must add sales tax to total remittance (books & shipping). All McBooks Press publications can also be ordered by calling toll-free 1-888-BOOKS11 (1-888-266-5711).
Please call to request a free catalog.

Visit the McBooks Press website at www.mcbooks.com.

Printed in the United States of America

9 8 7 6 5 4 3 2 1

To Andrew
The newest member
of the family

List of Ships

Raisonable
Victory
Triumph
Dreadnought
Swanborough
Seahorse
Racehorse
Carcass
Ramilles
Vixen
Euraylus
Dolphin
Worcester
Lowestoffe
Torbay Lass
Ardent
Hinchingbrooke
Badger
Victor
Albemarle
Daedalus
Harmony
Iris
Barfleur
Boreas
Bristol
Agamemnon

Battle of St Vincent

Captain
Santissima Trinidad
Culloden
Orion
Excellent
Diadem
Blenheim
Prince George
San Salvador
San Nicholas
San Josef
Theseus
Fox
Vanguard
Alexander
Goliath
Mutine

Battle of the Nile

Swiftsure
Zealous
Minotaur
L'Orient
Le Guerrier
Audacious
Le Spartiate
Guillaume Tell
Généraux
Bellerophon
Le Peuple Souverain

Prologue

GIVEN THAT THE NAME Horatio Nelson resonates down the ages, it is hard to imagine that same person as a small thirteen-year-old boy, the son of an impecunious parson, leaving his Norfolk home to join a Navy in which he would be required to daily risk life and limb. Equally difficult is the notion that a small grubby lass called Emma Lyons, who had hawked lumps of sea coal by the side of a country road, could at the opening of this book, be sitting as a model for one of the most famous painters of the age.

The first book of the trilogy *On a Making Tide* covered the time from Nelson joining the Navy and ended with his service in the War of American Independence, fourteen years in which he rose from midshipman to the rank of Post Captain. At that time his unique qualities were known only to a very few people—those who had served with him in the land campaign against the Spanish in Central America, and the officers and men of the various ships which he commanded. That he had unique gifts was not in doubt—many who served with him spoke of his common touch, the ability to connect with men of any rank from lower deck to officer's wardroom.

Having learnt his trade as a sailor aboard a merchant vessel, Nelson never lost sight of the life led by those he commanded. And, unusually for his time, he was also an avid student of his profession, taking as much interest in gunnery, carpentry, sail making, and pursery as he did in the skills necessary to sail and fight a ship of war. He fought on land with the same tenacity he employed at sea, nearly forfeiting his life to gain victory. And his enemies in the American War would attest to his honourable behaviour.

Nelson could, and did, converse with everyone without a hint of condescension. It was not forced—it was natural, as was his concern for the welfare of his crew. This made him popular amongst the lower decks, though he was less appreciated by those who shared his rank; some of his fellow captains thought him odd—

other reckoned him dangerous, few rated him as an equal, let alone a superior intelligence.

The same book told the story of Emma Lyons, who grew up to be a famous beauty, though not without the vicissitudes brought on by her own wayward personality. Bonded as a housemaid first in Cheshire and then in London, Emma failed to adhere to the rules her station demanded—to be quiet, servile, and well behaved. Instead, she rebelled, and followed in her mother's footsteps to end up as a hostess at the well-known establishment of a lady called Mrs Kelly. That she sold sexual favours in return for comfort is without doubt, but Emma would always deny in later life that she had been a whore, for in her mind and that of the age there was a distinction between those girls who worked the streets and bawdy houses, and the more favoured and refined ladies who staffed "respectable" places of entertainment.

Taken as a mistress by a famous rake, Emma fooled herself into believing that their relationship was more than that of kept woman and master. The disillusionment brought about by the reality of her situation, the abandonment of both her and the child she was carrying, was tempered by a new association with the Honourable Charles Greville, who undertook to provide for the child and set her up in small but comfortable London house, with Emma's mother as housekeeper and chaperone. But by now Emma was a beauty, much sought after by men of parts, including the Prince Regent. Greville's parsimony and jealousy, in contrast to Emma's openness and gaiety, led to many a spat, but the relationship survived, mainly due to what Greville called Emma's sweet nature.

These two people, who formed one of the great romantic attachments of history had yet to meet. Emma's life was to change dramatically, and put her in a place where that first acquaintance would occur. When she met Nelson he was but one captain amongst many in King George's Navy, but that was about to change.

Tested by Fate tells the story of how Horatio Nelson, the small boy from Norfolk became the nation's hero, and of the attachment he formed for that coal-vending urchin girl, who was, by the time they met, Lady Emma Hamilton.

BOOK 1

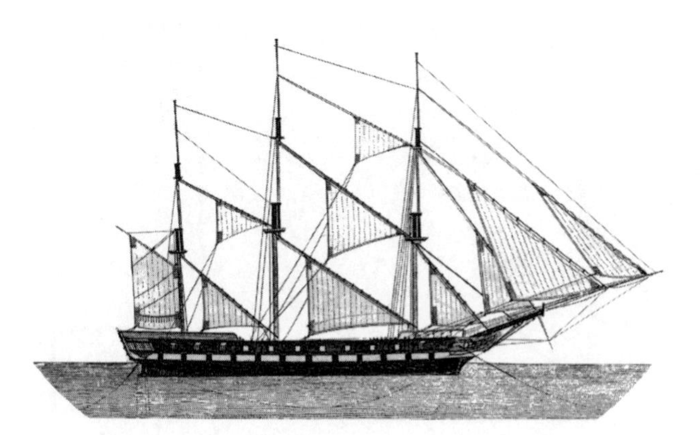

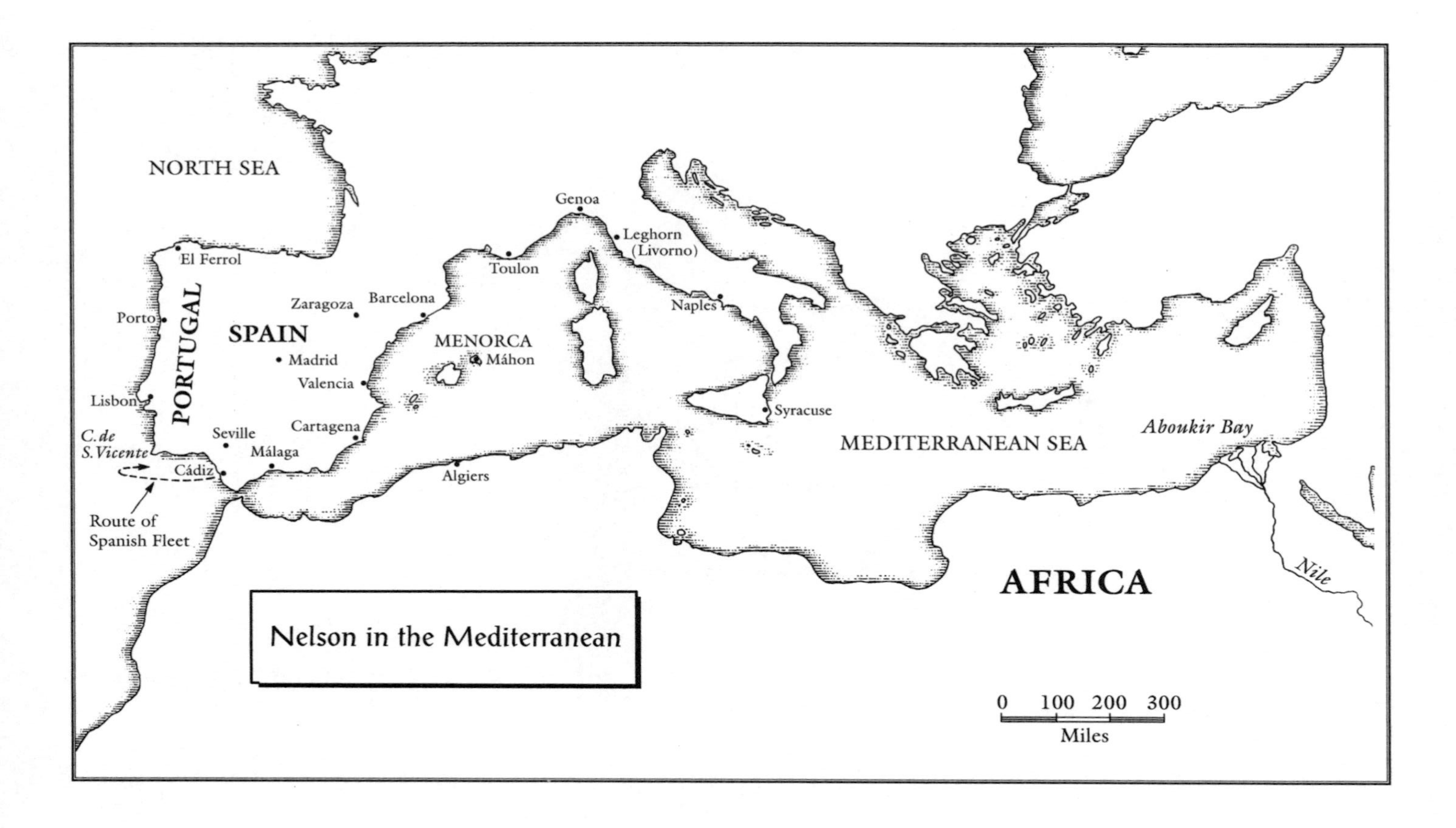
Nelson in the Mediterranean
NORTH SEA
El Ferrol
Porto
PORTUGAL
SPAIN
Lisbon
C. de
S. Vicente
Route of
Spanish Fleet
Cádiz
Seville
Málaga
Madrid
Zaragoza
Barcelona
Valencia
Cartagena
MENORCA
Máhon
Algiers
Toulon
Genoa
Leghorn
(Livorno)
Naples
Syracuse
MEDITERRANEAN SEA
Aboukir Bay
Nile
AFRICA
0
100
200
300
Miles

Chapter One

1784

"LOOK LIVELY, LADS," said Giddings, at the sight of the hatless midshipman who was desperate to reach the quayside before Captain Nelson's carriage appeared.

All but two of the barge crew slipped down the slimy wooden stairway, taking their allotted places in the boat, clasping and raising their oars till they stood, regulation fashion, pointing towards the grey sky. The rattle of iron-hooped wheels set up a steady tattoo as the coach bounced on to the cobbled hard of Sheerness dockyard. Midshipman George Andrews skidded to a halt and jammed his hat back on his head. He had just enough time to raise it again as the door opened. His hair was whipped to one side by the steady wind, which also carried his high-pitched voice to the waiting sailors' ears.

"Mr Andrews, sir, at your service."

Nelson returned the salute with a smile that carried more than his normal ration of paternalistic good humour. He had met the Andrews family in St Omer, in what now seemed like a futile attempt to better his French. The clerical father had been happy to entertain a naval officer bent on improving himself. Once he met the parson's daughters his studies had lost their lustre. Kate Andrews, at eighteen the elder of the pair, had occupied his waking thoughts, filling his mind with imaginings of the blessings of matrimony, even if, as an officer on half pay, he couldn't afford it.

Letters to relatives had not produced the desired financial assistance, probably due to Nelson's inability to guarantee that the object of his affections held him in the same regard. It was the kind of bind from which it seemed impossible to escape: he couldn't propose marriage because he lacked the means, but couldn't acquire the means without some indication of commitment from the object of his affections.

That short exchange with young George brought the memories flooding back: sweet Kate, who sang like an angel and played the piano with grace; the secret glances they had exchanged to fool those present. Jealousy surfaced in Nelson when any other seemed to occupy Kate's attentions and he recalled the way her lips pursed with annoyance at the sharper tone his voice took on in such circumstances. It was love of the truest and purest kind, painful in an almost physical way.

And here before him stood Kate's sibling brother, who had been at school in England while the rest of his family had been in France. He had the same corn-coloured hair, blue eyes, and fair complexion, features that produced a physical reaction that ran through his entire frame. Nelson had a ship on foreign service, with every hope that his fortune might improve; at the end of this commission he might well find himself in a position to call on Kate with the means to make a proposal. Having returned the salute, he stuck out his hand. "Why, Mr Andrews. I am happy to make your acquaintance. Might I be permitted to enquire after your family?"

"My father asked particularly to be remembered to you, sir. Both he and I are conscious of the honour you do us by taking me on board."

"How could I refuse?" he replied. "Was it not Kate who requested it?"

The boy's eyes opened wide in surprise. "Why, no, sir. If anything she's dead set against it."

That made his new commander frown; it indicated that his pursuit of Kate Andrews was stalled. "Did she say why?"

"My sister thinks me too young, sir."

"Did your father not inform you that is exactly the same age at which I came to sea?"

"Why, sir, that is amazing."

The wonder on George Andrews's face, the startled look in his cornflower-blue eyes, restored Nelson's dented spirits. He, too, could recall the impossibility of the thought that his seniors had once been just like him: young, gauche, and inexperienced. He looked up to see Giddings approaching, reminding him that the midshipman, in his enthusiasm, had forgotten to attend to his duties. And Frank Lepée, never one to shirk in articulating his displeasure, was frowning, though whether at the boy for his failure or the master for his indulgence was impossible to say. Giddings saw the look, observed that the servant was about to speak out, and solved the problem by acting as though the order had just been given.

"Aye, aye, sir," he barked, turning back towards the hands who had yet to take their place in the barge. "Sharp now, an' see to the Captain's dunnage."

Andrews's whole frame shook, in a manner that reminded Nelson of the charlatan Graham's electric therapy. He sought words to cover his lapse.

"Holy Christ in heaven," growled Lepée, which earned him a stern look of reproach from his captain.

"You must ask me to step into the barge, young man," Nelson whispered. "That is, once the sea chests are loaded."

"Aye, aye, sir." The boy gulped.

His voice was restored by the time they came alongside. The way he yelled "*Boreas,*" to inform the crew that their captain was coming aboard, would have been heard halfway across the Medway. It was also quite unnecessary, since the first lieutenant had given the lookout orders to keep his telescope trained on the shore.

The barge crew hooked on to the chains and Nelson leapt for the rope ladder that rose towards the gangway. As his head appeared above the level of the deck, the pipes blew and the marines crashed their boots on to the planking, producing a resounding salute. Ralph Millar was the premier. A florid-faced American Loyalist, he had served as a midshipman aboard Sir Richard Parker's flagship, HMS *Bristol,* when Nelson was first made Post Captain and had never ceased to correspond with a man he openly admired. The last time he had seen Nelson was as an invalid being shipped home after the San Juan river fiasco. Millar stepped forward as Nelson's foot made contact with the deck, hat raised, his round face showing with subdued pleasure. "Welcome aboard, sir. It does my heart good to see you fit and well."

Nelson raised his own hat in return, both to his first lieutenant and, facing the quarterdeck, to his new command. "Assemble the men aft, Mr Millar, so that I may read myself in."

As he glanced up from a document he knew by heart the eager faces cheered him mightily. Giddings had volunteered; Thorpe was there, as well as Nichols, and Bromwich, standing head and shoulders above the rest—still not promoted, despite Nelson's best efforts—had agreed to serve him as a master's mate. There were numerous others, who had formerly served on *Albemarle* and had now volunteered for his new 36-gun frigate and a return to the Caribbean. Nothing made coming back aboard a ship as pleasant as this.

Nelson glared at the stack of papers on his dining table. It served as a desk as well, a piece of fine mahogany on bare planking in a wooden-walled space painted pale green. There wasn't much else: a wine cooler, the gleaming brass instruments he used for navigation, two Harrison chronometers, which would give him his latitude, and enough chairs to host a decent dinner.

"A summary, Millar, if you please." Millar rattled off the facts, in his twangy Yankee accent, which covered myriad items: sails, spars, rope, tar, nails, turpentine, even bales of tow. "Combustibles?"

"Fully loaded, sir. Deficient only in wood and water."

"Powder and shot?"

"Your predecessor was all husbandry in that department, sir. The hinges on the shot store hatches are rusty."

"And likely to remain so, Millar." The premier's thick black eyes betrayed just a hint of what must have been deep surprise. Nelson pulled a second oilskin pouch from his pocket. "We have become a mere postal packet. If you peruse that you will see that we are to be burdened with passengers." Millar reached forward to take it, as Nelson continued. "Twenty-five midshipmen, enough to man every vessel on the whole Leeward Island station, with a few to spare for Jamaica. Added to that we shall be carrying the wife and daughter, no less, of our future commander, Admiral Sir Richard Hughes. I doubt they'll take kindly to their repose being shattered by daily gunfire."

"The lady is a sailor's wife, sir."

"Wrong!" said Nelson, with a grin. "She's an admiral's wife."

"Should I be a-continuing, your honour?" Lepée, busy unpacking, had a face to match his grumbling voice. "If we has an admiral's wife aboard, she'll have the use of most of the cabin."

"As like as not I shall have to shift my cot into the privy."

"So, no gunnery, sir?" asked Millar.

Nelson grinned even wider. "Let us see how she shapes up. Maybe she will love the smell of powder as much as we do."

The sound of the marine sentry, coming noisily to attention, made both look to the door, which opened abruptly at Nelson's command to reveal the swarthy, handsome face of the second lieutenant, Edward Berry.

"Pilot coming aboard, sir."

"Good. Mr Millar, stand by to weigh at first light tomorrow morning."

Spithead, 18th April
To Mr Stephens,
Secretary to the Admiralty,

Dear Sir,

I have the honour to acquaint you that His Majesty's *ship, under my command, arrived at this place yesterday, and enclosed is her state and condition.*

Yours,
Captain H. Nelson

"And damned lucky we are, Millar," he added, putting down his quill. He sanded, folded, and sealed his letter to the Port Admiral at Portsmouth.

"The man was clearly drunk, sir," Millar replied. He referred to the Nore pilot who had run them fast aground in water so shallow when the tide went out that an audience had gathered to walk round the ship. He got her off at the next high water, only to be bound to the shore by a gale and a blinding snowstorm. In the Downs, still suffering from seasickness, he had got into a quarrel with a Dutch captain, who laid a complaint at the Admiralty about his behaviour. Unusually to Nelson's way of thinking, they had backed him up.

A knock and the sudden appearance of Andrews disturbed his thoughts. "We've been hailed by a whole fleet of bum-boats, sir. They're full of women and servants who claim that one is the wife to Admiral Hughes."

"The lady is sharp, sir," said Millar. "We've barely made our number."

"Perhaps she fears I'll sail without her," replied Nelson.

"You are most gracious, Captain," said Lady Hughes, for the tenth time.

"The offer of my table is trifling enough, madam," Nelson replied. "The food, as well as the plate, is all yours."

Aboard three days now, she had dressed for the occasion, head turbaned in silk, jewels flashing each time she moved her head and neck. From the little he knew, she had been a beauty when young, and some of that had stayed with her into middle age. But the line of her jaw had hardened, spoiling what might otherwise have been an elegant, if matronly, countenance.

"I do so think there is nothing like an occasion for making proper acquaintance. Especially, sir, with members of the gentler sex."

The great cabin was full to overflowing. Practically every officer and midshipman aboard *Boreas,* including Lady Hughes's own son, was present to consume the ample dinner. Naturally she had yielded the head of the table to the commanding officer, but she had taken station to his immediate right and showed equal care in the way she placed her daughter, Rosy. The girl, plain, plump, and pitifully shy, had been sat within full view of the Captain, her position close enough to the lieutenants to ensure that, should Lady Hughes's premier stratagem fail, these junior officers were there to fall back on.

Almost her first words on coming aboard had been a polite enquiry after Mrs Nelson. The predatory gleam in her eye as he replied that he had no wife had troubled Nelson. Trapped at table, with George Andrews a visible reminder of his hopes, he was brusque with both. This wounded the girl and bounced harmlessly off the mother. Her "butterfly," as she so inappropriately called Rosy, was off to the West Indies unattached. Clearly, Lady Hughes had no intention that she should return to England in that same estate.

"You're sure the hour of dinner is not too early for you, madam?" he asked, seeking to shift the conversation towards alimentary rather than matrimonial pursuits.

For once his passenger replied precisely to the point. "A trifle. I reckon my disposition, after long abuse, will bear it. Your three of the clock dinner is a naval habit that the Admiral insists on when he's ashore. My butterfly greets his determination to dine early with much grief, claiming it plays havoc with her digestion, which is, I may say, as delicate as her manners."

"Then she must take care to avoid sailors, madam," snapped Nelson. "We engage in a rough trade and perforce make poor husbands."

It had been too good an opportunity to miss, but he had spoken with more force than necessary. Lady Hughes might be single-minded, but she was far from stupid. More than that, she was not one to suffer so without retaliating. Her glance strayed down the table to where Midshipman Andrews sat opposite her own son, Edward. She had noticed that among the ship's youngsters the Captain had afforded this blond child extra attention.

"You do not hold with officers marrying, sir? Perhaps you find it unnatural."

The inference was evident. He had to fight the temptation to administer a public rebuke at such a charge. Only her position as the Admiral's wife saved her. But his reaction clearly alarmed the lady since she sat back abruptly—anyone who had seen his face at that point would have recoiled: his eyes were as hard as gemstones, the skin round his jaw was fully stretched, and his reply was delivered in a subdued hiss so at odds with his normal manner. "You will oblige me, madam, by leaving off with your matchmaking. I expect you to apply this injunction to both myself and my officers. Your position affords you many advantages, but trapping your husband's inferiors is not one of them."

"I dislike your tone, sir!"

Nelson deliberately looked at Andrews. "And I, Lady Hughes, dislike your insinuations. I will have you know that I have an arrangement with that young man's sister."

She didn't flinch, being of the type who didn't require her husband's position to provide a defence. Lady Hughes was formidable in her own right, quite strong enough to examine Nelson with open curiosity, as if seeking to determine whether his words were true. He, on the other hand, could not respond in kind: he was well aware of the flaws in his forthright rejoinder and he was obliged to concentrate on his plate to hide his thoughts. He was contemplating putting the Admiral's family ashore, with a "goddamn" to the professional consequences.

When he looked up again Lady Hughes had turned away. Her eyes were roaming the table and when she spoke Nelson knew that, despite his clear injunction against it, her attention had shifted to a new target.

"Lieutenant Millar, I've scarce been afforded a chance to make a proper acquaintance." Nelson's premier bowed his head in acknowledgement. "I am sure your duties have precluded it. You're from the Americas, I'm informed, that melancholy country. My boy tells me you keep them to their tasks. Rest assured that my husband will be made aware of your zealous endeavour."

"You are most gracious, milady."

"Did you know that my husband once had this ship?"

His reply, when he took in the look on his captain's face, was nervous: "No, madam, I did not."

"And very fond of her we were. To me she will always be dear *Boreas*. Why, I felt as though I was stepping aboard a private yacht when I came on to the deck." The hiss beside her, from the present commander, did nothing to deflect her. "Perhaps, Mr Millar, with your captain's permission, you will escort me in a turn around the deck after dinner."

Millar could not refuse: to a man of his rank the lady's expressed wish was as good as a command. And his captain could not intercede for the sake of good manners. But it was gratifying to him, at least, to see Rosy Hughes drop her head into her napkin in a vain attempt to hide the embarrassment. At that moment Lepée, leaning close to whisper in his ear, distracted him.

"Mr Berry's compliments, your honour. The Port Admiral has made our number and sent us a signal to weigh."

"Mr Millar will be relieved when he hears that," replied Nelson softly.

The forward half of Nelson's cabin was partitioned so that he occupied his own sleeping and working quarters. The Hughes family had the day cabin as theirs, though they were obliged to shift to the coach during daylight hours. Despite his respect for Lady Hughes's position, Nelson did not set aside the midshipmen's lessons to accommodate her presence. A class of twenty-five, of whom all but five would shift to different ships when they raised Barbados, required space to learn their lessons. In truth, when it came to the majority their education was none of his concern, but if anything cheered him it was imparting knowledge to youngsters. To him, Edward Hughes was no different from the rest, and suffered not one jot from his mother's poor relations with the Captain.

Nelson was also on deck at midday to oversee the noon observation, where the young men would learn to use their quadrants. They studied mathematics, trigonometry, and navigation with the master. At night they were lectured on the stars, so that they could read their way around the world by merely looking aloft. Then there were their duties as young gentlemen.

Though not commissioned, they were officers as far as the ship was concerned. Fencing lessons would be given daily. There was gunnery and sail drill; how to recognise which knot to use and when, then instructions in the actual tying. In calm weather, each mid in turn would be given command of a ship's boat, with Giddings and an experienced master's mate on board for company, their primary task to sail in strict station on the mother ship.

This manoeuvre called for seamanship. The run of the sea and the play of the wind on the frigate's larger area of sail ensured different rates of progress. In time they would be ordered away to identify some imaginary sail on the horizon, with a rendezvous provided for the following day. These orders would be delivered by an officer standing on the poop, speaking trumpet in hand, yelling a stream of instructions, none repeated, which the candidate had to memorise without benefit of pen or paper.

Nelson's greatest concern was for the youngest of his charges, an eleven-year-old child whose small build exaggerated his lack of years. Called Henry Blackwood, he was under four foot tall and so scrawny he looked like an eight-year-old. Nelson had paid particular attention to him from the first day, knowing that his appearance would leave him open to abuse from his fellows. Words with the gunner's wife had him removed from the mid's berth after dark, to be accommodated in the gunner's own quarters, as Nelson had once been.

But that only protected the lad at night. During the day he was exposed to all the perils of his peers. The Navy required each young gentleman to progress at the same pace, and being the runt of the litter afforded the boy no special privilege. The first time he was ordered to go to the masthead nearly proved his undoing. *Boreas* was making around six knots, pitching and rolling evenly on what, for the coast of Brittany, was a calm sea. Nelson, pacing the windward side of the quarterdeck, well away from Lady Hughes taking the air on the poop, was watching the noisy group of mids out of the corner of his eye.

Each in turn was required to climb to the tops. He observed

the way little Blackwood eased himself back into the crowd, hoping that Berry would fail to notice him. But the second lieutenant knew his duty. He had 25 mids to send aloft, and only 24 had performed the task. When he enquired as to who had ducked their duty, every eye turned to the stripling boy, and a path was cleared between him and Berry, leaving the miscreant nowhere to hide.

"Mr Blackwood, you are required to proceed in a like manner to your fellows, that is, to the masthead." The boy, who had never been further than the main cap, began to shake from head to foot, the image of terrified reluctance, which made Berry snarl, "It is your duty, young man!"

"Aye, aye, sir," he piped, though his feet remained rooted to the spot.

"Then proceed."

"With respect, sir, I can't."

Berry's already swarthy face went two shades darker as he shouted his response, a bark that stopped Lady Hughes in her tracks. "Can't, sir? You are in receipt of a direct order. You must and will obey."

One foot moved but not the other. Blackwood, looking aloft to a point one hundred and twenty feet in the air, tried to suppress a sob, but it came out nevertheless. Nelson stepped forward on to the gangway, which immediately brought the entire party to attention. Berry whipped off his hat in a respectful salute, but his expression showed his true feelings: this was a situation in which his captain had no right to interfere.

Nelson couldn't fault him: he had every right to require obedience to his orders. But this child was so small, and clearly so frightened, that he was in mortal danger. He would go aloft eventually. Berry, and the fear of derision from his peers, would ensure that. But would he reach his destination? In his terror he might slip. Luck, if it could be termed that, would take him overboard, to the chancy hazard of a difficult rescue from the cold sea, but if he mistimed his fall, he would land on the deck. That would see him entered in the ship's log as "discharged, dead in the execution of his duties."

"Mr Blackwood," Nelson said, moving forward.

"Sir," the boy squeaked, spinning to look at the Captain.

"I am about to go aloft myself. I'd be obliged if you would join me."

With that Nelson stepped on to a barrel to aid his ascent to the bulwarks. He turned and smiled at Blackwood. "As you will observe, I am not as nimble as you. Why, I daresay you could leap to my side without the aid of that cask."

The eye-contact produced the desired result. Blackwood's expression changed from fear to something akin to trust. He did as he was bidden, and jumped up on to the bulwark, grabbing at the shrouds to steady himself.

"I see I shall need to be quick, Mr Blackwood. You're even more lively than I supposed."

He started to climb, slowly at first, but with increasing speed as he sensed the boy following. The shrouds stretched like a long rope-ladder all the way to a point just below the mainmast cap, every movement of both ship and climber combining to alter the shape. After some forty feet the shrouds presented two avenues. One took the climber on, through the lubbers' hole, on to the spacious platform of the mainmast cap. The others rose vertically, skirting the rim to rise even higher. Nelson had no need to hesitate. He increased his pace, arching backwards as he gripped the ropes. He slipped past the edge with ease, leaning forward again to ascend this narrower set of shrouds.

Up he went, fifty, sixty, seventy feet from the deck. Out again, this time as *Boreas* dipped into a trough, which left his back in line with the sea below. The slim strip of ropes led on past the tops. He knew Blackwood was with him; not close but there, his eyes fixed on the Captain before him, rather than the frightening panorama below. Once at the crosstrees, Nelson threw his leg over on to the yard, easing his back till it rested against the upper mast.

"Come along, Mr Blackwood," he called. "There's no need for you to favour an old man in this fashion." As the boy's head came level he held out his hand to help him up. "Mind, respect to the Captain is a very necessary notion, I suppose. It would never do to show me up. Bad for discipline, eh! Now, young sir, clap on hard to this rope and sit yourself down. Then we will have the leisure to look about us, and the chance to talk for a while."

"Aye, aye, sir," gasped Blackwood.

"Is it not a fine place to be?" Nelson saw the boy's face pale as he looked down towards the deck, where the assembled mids now looked like a colony of ants. "I remember when I was a shaver, just like you, an old tar, who had sailed with Anson, brought me up here. I remember him saying that once you was above ten feet, it don't signify. As long as you clapped on in a like manner."

"Aye, aye, sir."

"Now, Mr Blackwood, being a captain has its advantages. But one of the drawbacks is this, sir. You rarely get a chance to be alone with anyone. Now that we're up here, just the two of us, it will give you a chance to tell me all about yourself."

The boy's mouth opened and closed, but no sound came. Nelson had to prompt him with a direct question. The tale the boy told was a depressingly familiar one. As the younger son to a middling family there had been little prospect that he would receive a decent education. Nor did the Army, with its bought commissions, present a realistic prospect of advancement. The family had few connections and, lacking interest as well as money, could not place their son in any milieu other than the King's Navy. But as the story emerged, Nelson couldn't help but wonder, for the hundredth time, whether some sort of age limit should not be placed on entry, so that boys like Blackwood were not exposed too early to the rigours of life afloat.

Nelson felt like a youngster again as he grabbed for the backstay and slid down to the deck, wondering halfway if his dignity as a captain would be impaired by such behaviour. But it had the desired effect, Blackwood following him down in a heartening sailorly fashion, to be greeted by a grinning Nelson.

The arch look Nelson received from Lady Hughes, still on the poop as he turned to return to the quarterdeck, made his blood boil: it was nothing less than a repetition of her insinuation that his interest in youngsters was at best misplaced, at worst impure.

Chapter Two

THIS MORNING, Emma felt she was at loggerheads with everyone, not least George Romney, who was sketching her for yet another portrait, this time in the pose of wild-eyed Medea, classical slayer of children. The clothes she wore were tattered and revealing, her hair teased out wildly with twigs, face streaked with dark lines of heavy makeup. It was her eyes he needed most, that look of near madness he had struggled hard to create, which Emma kept discarding.

Old Romney, with his lined, walnut-coloured face and unruly grey hair looked up from the pad on his lap and glared. They had already had words about her inability to sit still, Romney pretending he had no idea of what triggered her fidgety behaviour. Yet he had seen Greville's face that morning, when he had delivered her to the studio: the black looks and stiff bearing that had characterised their exchanges, he all formality, Emma all meekness, until Greville departed.

Emma had spent the last half-hour locked in an internal argument in which she naturally cast herself as the aggrieved party. Playing both roles, her face was animated by point and counterpoint. She was winning of course, an imagined Charles Greville being easier to deal with than the real person, especially as she was of the opinion that the previous night's behaviour had been due to nothing more than high spirits. How dare Greville insist that if she couldn't learn to contain herself he would never take her out again!

As ever, when he was working, Romney's grey hair stood on his head, giving him the appearance of an elderly monkey, the impression heightened by his large, dark brown eyes. The old man was kindness itself, and Greville's black mood of this morning was no fault of his, so Emma worked to put the mad stare back in place. Romney nodded and went back to his frenzied sketching.

She should be angry with her lover about this too, being sold like a carcass. Greville had an arrangement with the artist: he provided the model, Romney provided the oils and the talent; the money from the sale of the resulting portrait was split between them, Greville's portion to set off the cost of keeping her. Romney had painted her a dozen times now; every picture had found an eager buyer.

Romney's eyes darted back and forth, boring into her. Did he, with his artist's insight, see how she felt? She loved Charles with a passion that had grown deeper through three years of attachment, and enjoyed their domestic harmony. Yet certain losses rankled, like the social life she had enjoyed on first arriving at Edgware Road, which had been slowly choked off. Her life now seemed sober and confined. After a year, Greville had moved into Edgware Road permanently, imposing his fussy bachelor habits on what had been an easy-going household; he had let the townhouse he had built in Portman Square to ease his debts. However, it had obviously not eased them enough: only the week before he had scolded her for giving a halfpenny to a beggar.

Excursions from the house had been rare of late. She could never be brought to the notion that her own natural vivacity was in part responsible for this. Was it her fault that when they went to a ball or a rout nearly every man in the room sought to engage her attention? Was she to blame if powerful and well-connected men cared not a whit if their outrageous gallantries offended her lover? It was not her fault that Greville was so jealous and insecure, unable to accept her repeated assurances that he had no cause for concern.

He had insisted that she had made an exhibition of herself the previous night. To Emma, singing and dancing were the stuff of life, and a glass or two of champagne encouraged her. She knew that Greville had cause to celebrate. As a collector he acquired only to sell, and was careful in the way he built up collections to make sure that the whole was always vastly superior to the sum of its parts. Many a time quick disposal had saved him from ruin. He had been corresponding with his uncle in Naples, using his good offices to amass a set of Roman and Etruscan artefacts that he had already sold at a substantial profit. The news that his virtu, in the company of his uncle, had arrived in England had sent him into raptures of delight, and loosened his normally tight purse strings to such a degree that he had insisted on taking Emma to the Ranelagh Pleasure Gardens.

Could Greville not see the joy she felt in wearing a fine dress, having her hair tended for a night of entertainment, and crossing the portal for pleasure not duty? This was the first time in an age that Greville had offered to take her out to somewhere fashionable.

"Rumour has it," Romney said, "that you were the *belle amusement* at last night's rout."

"I greatly enjoyed myself, I admit," she replied defiantly, wondering how he knew.

"More than you have on previous visits?"

"Who said I have visited the Ranelagh before?" Emma demanded.

Her mother had told her she had a duty to deny her previous existence, even to those who must know it well. She was the semi-respectable Mrs Hart now, not the wild, promiscuous person of her former incarnation.

The old man grinned, laid aside his pad and ran a hand though his spiky grey hair. "The two different faces of the gardens have always fascinated me, Emma—the decorum of the early evening contrasted with the riot of the later night. It seems that two different worlds occupy the same space. Reynolds captures the first, Hogarth the second."

"With some men in both," Emma replied firmly. Having been lectured by Greville she was in no mood to take the same from Romney.

But it was true what he said, just as it was true that she had misread the place, never having been there at what Romney called the Reynolds time. Then the prostitutes who plied for trade were still outside the gates. The gardens in the early evening were patronised by respectable London, who admired the carefully arranged plants, listened to good music and short, amusing dramas. They were not a scene of riot, with couples cavorting in the bushes, lewd songs, and risque plays, all aided by the consumption of vast amounts of wine.

"All I did was stand to sing," she insisted.

"With a much admired voice, I'm sure." Emma blushed and dropped her head. "Take the compliment, my dear. You do have a sweet voice and the lessons Greville arranged for you have made it sweeter yet."

"If I'd seen his face I would have stopped."

He might have been scandalised, but others weren't. Compliments and drinks arrived before her in equal measure and she knew she had become drunk on both, the depth of her inebriation only serving to deepen her lover's disgust. She had seen that go skywards when she had got up, acceding to a request to dance. He demanded that they leave and the atmosphere on the way home had been icy. Once inside his own house Greville blew up like the volcanoes he was fond of describing.

Her mother, roused by the clamour, had advised Emma to apologise, grovel a bit if necessary to appease the man who kept them. Emma had taken a great deal of persuading, especially when Mary Cadogan had insisted she change into a drab grey dress to indicate penitence. It had been in vain. Her lover had even refused to share her bed, retiring to his study for the night, and in the morning, still under the burden of his anger, he had delivered her to this studio.

"I begged him to forgive me, even changed out of my finery to do so. You should have seen me, Romney, in that drab outfit, on my knees weeping in despair."

"Show me the pose you adopted."

Emma sank to her knees, her hands joined in supplication. The old man gazed on her shaking his head. "Too biblical for my taste. I prefer the Greeks, though it would be a charming notion to paint you in a more modern pose."

"But would that sell?" she asked sarcastically.

"An artist does not always toil for money."

Their shared look was proof enough that such a sentiment did not apply to Greville. "The mood you saw him in this morning was evidence that I am still not forgiven," she said.

"You shall be, Emma, never fear."

"How can you be so certain?"

The large brown eyes, normally so expressive, took on a certain blandness. The truth was that she was a beautiful bargain, a woman who might have commanded a much more puissant lover if she had so decided, might have moved in the grandest circles with a little education. There was a touch of love in Romney, old as he was, for the best model he had ever had. Greville kept her out of sight as much for fear of loss as he did to save coin. He had seethed with anger when the Prince of Wales had waxed lyrical on Emma's beauty, since his admiration was bound to be followed by an attempt at seduction. What Greville could never accept was that while male attention flattered her, and she responded, Emma wasn't interested.

"Greville will forgive you because he is so very fond of you, Emma."

"Is he, Romney?" she whispered.

"Most decidedly so. He values you so very highly."

Visitors to Romney's studio were frequent, and people who might become clients took a chair to watch the artist at work. His ever-attentive son, who was also the person charged with encouraging commissions, served refreshments. Emma had witnessed much of this, and was normally unconcerned by others' presence. But this day she was less than happy, given the pose she had been asked to adopt. It wasn't Greville who bothered her, it was the person she suspected to be his uncle William, as she reprised her wide-eyed and unattractive pose.

Greville had seen her in such a state of *dé shabillé,* wrapped in their shared bed sheets, but for a total stranger to see her so was a different matter, especially one whom he esteemed so much. As soon as Romney declared the session closed Emma dashed to a private room to repair her appearance, then emerged with her hair brushed, face clean, and properly dressed.

"Allow me, Emma, to name my uncle William," Greville said. "He is, as you know, His Majesty King George's ambassador and minister plenipotentiary at the court of Naples."

"How you load me with honours, Charles."

"They are yours by right, sir. Or should I say Chevalier?"

"But they are also much less impressive than they sound. Mere trifles, I would say, of some use in the Two Sicilies but of small account in a London full of grand titles."

Charles had been talking about his uncle for days, with an increasing excitement that was hard to fathom in one so naturally reserved, yet nothing in either voice now suggested the kind of blood tie that would hint at an emotional attachment. Certainly the uncle was a kindly looking soul, soft voiced with an ease of manner that came from having mixed from birth with the cream of society. Greville had told her more than once of his connections, of the fact that, as a child, he had been a playmate of King George.

"I confess, my dear, to being quite startled when I entered. The face you presented to the world then was frightening in the extreme. Now I find myself gazing at untrammelled beauty."

Emma smiled sweetly but without sincerity, recognising in the voice the muted tone of dalliance with which, in the past, she had been so familiar. Compliments would come easily to Sir William Hamilton, as would the desire to seduce her should the chance present itself. His manner stayed in that vein on their return to Edgware Road, to a supper prepared for them by Emma's mother, who was introduced and treated to as fine a piece of noblesse as Emma could remember. While they ate, Sir William and his nephew talked of family, politics, land, inheritances, and the older man's recent widowhood.

It was in the latter that he showed real emotion, his sadness at the loss of his late wife, who had been for many years an invalid. But, for all that, the conversation carried little resonance for Emma.

Greville's hint that she should retire and leave them to talk was made abruptly enough to stir her rebellious spirit, but only in her breast: she had enough sense with Uncle William in attendance to suppress comment. To answer back would have made her Ranelagh misdemeanours look tame. But at least the Ambassador knew his manners. When she rose he leapt to his feet and came to hold her hand.

"Mrs Hart, I cannot say how much I have enjoyed the pleasure of your company." The eyes that held hers were blue, steady, slightly watery, and benign. "I intend to presume upon my nephew's good graces to see you again—that is, if the prospect of such does not repel you."

"How could it, sir?" Emma replied, in a lilting voice of which her singing teacher would have approved heartily. "I revel in good company."

"Revel?"

Sir William rolled the word around in his mouth, as if it was a sweetmeat he had never tasted. Out of the corner of her eye she could see Greville watching this exchange, a slight smile playing on his lips. When other men had tried the same, he had been furious.

"My nephew tells me you like to sing."

"I do."

"Then may I be permitted to visit when you are in a mood to do so?"

"Of course, Uncle," Greville barked. "You must come and see Emma at any time of your choosing. I'm sure she will enrapture you."

"My dear Charles, she has done that already."

"Good night, sir," Emma said, curtsying.

Sir William kissed her hand and then she left. Greville's words followed her, and as she closed the door, she pressed her ear to the panel.

"I see that you approve of her."

"That is understatement, Charles. Were she not in your care I swear that, old as I am, I would set my cap in her direction. She is a rare creature, and her manners are of the highest."

"She's decorous now, I grant you, sir. But you have no idea how many rough elements had to be polished to produce the diamond you now observe."

"Emerald, Charles! With such eyes she can be nothing less than that."

"Then it is, no doubt, with some reluctance, Uncle, that you must once more turn your mind to Wales."

After that first visit Sir William came often, accepting with pleasure the way that Emma called him uncle. He called her "the fair tea-maker of Edgware Row," alluding without the least trace of restraint to his appreciation of her beauty. She returned his affection in full measure, happy to spend time with a man so congenial, who was not just urbane but could take and give a quip in equal measure. In that he showed up his nephew, who was wont to examine raillery aimed at him for an insult, and to include in his own attempted witticisms a degree of cruelty that robbed them of their humour.

Uncle William was an easy man to be with, and the occasional gallantry did not seem amiss from a man who still had his good looks. It was rare for Greville to leave Emma alone with any man, but he seemed to have no fear of his relative. Though in his mid-fifties, the Ambassador looked younger, which, when she remarked upon it, he ascribed to his love of walking.

"And you shall walk with me, Emma, should you and Charles come to Naples. I'll take you to Pompeii and Herculaneum, and show you what beauty lies under the mountain of ash that Vesuvius spewed forth to cover them."

Seeing her confusion, he smiled. "These names mean nothing to you?"

"No, Uncle William, they do not."

His patient explanation was similar to that undertaken by Greville when he had first made her acquaintance. He described the volcano and the destruction it had caused, spoke of how he and others initiated digs to extract objects of great beauty and antiquity that had been wholly preserved by the ash.

"There's a fine collection of such virtu, many of the pieces acquired by me, in the house of a friend. Should you desire it, I will take you to his gallery for a private viewing."

"I'd like that very much, Uncle, though if this volcano is still a danger, a visit to Naples is something I might not greet with the same joy."

"I would never say not to fear it, but it can be approached as easily as I approach you, my dear. And the effect is somewhat similar. I got so close to the summit one day that I singed the soles of my boots."

"Then for all you're a clever fellow, Uncle William, you have a streak of foolishness."

Sir William was as good as his word: he took her not only to his friend's gallery but to any place she chose to visit. He escorted her to the Pantheon in Oxford Street, where society gathered in the daylight hours to gossip, exchange pleasantries, and indulge in attempts at seduction. Sir William Hamilton commanded attention in his own right, but he clearly enjoyed the extra consideration he received with a beautiful woman on his arm. And Emma responded by behaving with becoming grace, commanded by Greville to be on her best behaviour, determined not to let down either him or the uncle they both admired.

There was a changed feeling in the household with Hamilton a frequent visitor. He came for tea most days and supper many nights, either at Edgware Road or at the house of a friend, singing round the harpsichord, games of Blind Man's Buff, and the like. Life was once more the charmed existence Emma had enjoyed on first arrival. The Chevalier, as Greville called him, made no secret of his admiration for Emma, but never once did he overstep the bounds of good taste.

Occasionally, Greville would look at her with that hunger she knew so well, which never failed to produce a corresponding response in her breast. In the bedroom, he seemed restored, more relaxed, the Charles Greville she had known from her days at Uppark. He laughed more, his sallies lost their cruelty and Emma's love for him deepened accordingly, while gratitude was boundless to Sir William, who had brought this transformation.

There were worries, she knew, to do with Sir William's estates and what would happen to them after his death, undercurrents of anxiety that still troubled Greville. He greeted his uncle's suggestion that he and Emma visit Naples enthusiastically one day, with a frown the next. And Emma nursed her own hope to use this new household mood: she wished to advance the notion that her child, now three years old, should be brought to London. Greville wouldn't hear of it, but Sir William, when she mentioned it privately, saw no objection, and undertook to broach the subject with his nephew at an appropriate moment.

"Perhaps he will be more amenable when we are on our travels."

"Travels?" Emma asked.

"You go to Chester, I believe?"

Sir William saw the confusion on Emma's face, and had the good grace to show embarrassment. "Charles has not told you?"

"He hinted," she lied, to recover her poise.

"We go to Wales on Friday, my dear, to look over my estates, while you journey to see your relations in Chester, including your child. You will travel with us as far as Cheltenham. I suggest the timing for what you desire could not be more appropriate, you with the child, me nudging Charles to agree."

Emma was still confused, and her response showed it clearly. "How long are we to be away?"

"A month."

The last time Emma had seen her daughter she had been in swaddling clothes. To gaze on her now, a child of three years, induced the most unwelcome sensations. The large eyes held her smile in place for a lot longer than she had intended, but there was no change in the little one's expression when Emma spoke her name, nor when she held out her arms to enfold her.

"Say a welcome to your mother, Little Emma," encouraged Grandma Kidd. The old lady was now so bent that her head was almost at the same level as that of the suspicious child. But there was no doubting the deep affection in the look, even if it was from a face lined like tree bark. Her smile exposed that what few teeth she had had left were now gone. "She's come all the way from London Town just to see you."

It required a gentle push to get Little Emma any closer and a tug from her mother to make enough contact to complete the hug. But the ice of greeting had been broken and the little girl, a lively child, soon began to chatter, first to her great grandmother, then slowly including this stranger called mother. Emma found the transition harder than her daughter, and constantly referred to her grandmother for clarification of the child's unformed speech.

"You'll get used to it, girl. She's a rare one when it comes to tattle, bit like you was when you were a bairn."

That induced a rare silence in Emma. Grandma Kidd was one of the few people who could mention her past and evoke unpleasant thoughts. Her life had not turned out in a way that anyone in the family wanted. Her grandmother was an upright, honest woman, though not a hypocrite when it came to accepting money help from whichever source provided it.

Yet the old lady must have been saddened to see the way her brood had gone, first her daughter, Mary, then her granddaughter, not settled but living off the good grace of men who thought them too lowly to marry. The way she was looking at the child now, as she played with and talked to her doll, carried with it some of that sadness, as though she was seeing Little Emma grown and in the same predicament.

"How do you cope with the burden?"

"Bairns ain't no burden, Emma. They is a joy, least at that age."

"It may be that the child can come and reside with me."

"In London?"

"Yes. With my mother as well, a proper family."

"That would be good," Grandma Kidd said, without conviction.

Emma imbued her voice with as much enthusiasm as she could muster. "I have engaged in this the good offices of Mr Greville's uncle, the one I wrote to you about."

"Old Tom Fort reads for me. He says it be called Napoli where this uncle comes from, not Naples as you wrote, and with him being an old sailor, well, happen he knows."

The way it was said implied some lack of honesty in the man who had lived there, though Emma struggled to find what difference it made.

"Old Tom Fort is just showing away 'cause he's been there. I've yet to meet a sailor who don't boast. Stands to reason the locals term it different to we English." That earned a loud sniff, as if the matter was to be considered but not too readily accepted. "Tom would have doffed his hat soon enough to our uncle William."

"He ain't your blood."

"It is a liberty he allows, in fact positively encourages. He is, Grandma, the most gracious of men, with a smile that would have you over in no time."

"Wed? Only you didn't mention."

"Widowed, with a heart still bruised from the loss. Not that it depresses his spirits. He loves to be gay and has a ready wit as well as stories you would scarce believe about the scrapes some of our English folk get up to abroad."

"There's not a lot he could tell me about folks, and that's without ever leaving my own parish."

Grandma Kidd was disposed not to like Sir William Hamilton, that was clear, but then she had not much good to say for Charles Greville either, even if he did foot the bills for Little Emma. To the old woman they were cut from the same cloth: the kind that had exploited the girls she had raised.

"Uncle Hamilton has undertaken to seek permission for Little Emma to move to Edgware." Hearing her name, the child stopped talking to her doll, and raised a pair of large green eyes to stare at her mother. Emma addressed her directly. "You would like it there I am sure, for Mr Greville is a kinder person than he will at times let show. I'm sure a few of your smiles would melt his heart just as quick as they have mine."

"Whatever's best for the child," said Grandma Kidd. "That's all I care for. That's all I ever cared for."

. . .

Charles Greville was reading, silently, Emma's first letter since their parting, as usual half amused, half despairing of the breathless way in which it had been composed. But the "Damn!" he hissed was loud enough to make Sir William Hamilton look up from his labours.

"She has given that old woman, her grandmother, near a full fifth of the money I allowed her for the month."

"That is bad?" Sir William's reply was halfway between a statement and a question. Greville was clearly displeased, but that didn't signify since his nephew was prone to disapproval of many things, something he found trying at times.

"Apparently Mrs Kidd bought the child a coat she couldn't afford." He spoke brightly now, because he had read the words that followed. "Emma promises to make good the loss. She tells me she has taken cheaper seaside lodgings and is eating frugally."

"Does she mention her health?" asked Sir William.

"Blooming, Uncle, as is that of the child."

"Then that at least is good news."

"Sea bathing, both of them," Greville added, tossing the letter aside. He went back to his own set of books, the accounts for the present year that would have to be checked before being passed to his uncle. Greville was the man responsible for the stewardship of these Welsh estates, an obligation to which he devoted considerable time. "Do you really believe such immersion can be efficacious?"

"Not in these northern waters. But I have a small villa at Posillipo in the Bay of Naples. In summer, when the sea is warm and the body is robust enough to withstand the power of the waves, it does wonders for the ague."

The voice drifted into silence, and the older man had a wistful look in his eyes. It was hard to compare in any favourable way this house, this dark, oak-panelled room and its musty, unoccupied smell with either Posillipo or his apartments in the Palazzo Sessa and the freshness of the Mediterranean sea breeze that wafted through them. Nor could he conjure up much affection for the green Pembrokeshire countryside that rolled away from the windows. He yearned for the warmth of the sun, and the smell of lemons and abundant flora that filled his rooms, for the sight of his collections, and the excitement of a dig when the first sign of some artefact emerged from the ash.

Absence kept him from recalling the smell of the city when the wind blew from the east, the beggars and the light-fingered, noisy inhabitants—the court, too, which was full of intrigues that seemed so petty they might be amusing, had they not been so deadly. Neapolitans loved to sing and dance the *saltarella*. They loved food, wine, and blatant carnality. But, most of all, they loved to hate. There were family feuds, political enmity, and a visceral hatred of all other nationalities: Spanish the most, Austrians the next. His duty was to ensure that Britannia retained if not affection at least no increase in animosity.

He had a duty here too: to pass the accounts with which Greville had presented him, books that covered the years he had been away. These showed he had well-managed assets that yielded him an income, without any effort on his part, of some five thousand pounds per annum. Not that he was unaware of the profit: spending it wisely was a major concern.

"I cannot bring myself to decide whether to be pleased or angry with Emma." Sir William looked at the bent head, knowing that the face he could not see wore a frown. "I suppose I should be sanguine about the way she has behaved. I have to tell you, Uncle, there was a time, and not so very long ago, when she would not have shown the sense necessary to make good the loss."

"Hardly a loss, Charles. It went to the child."

"I make provision enough for the child. Little Emma wants for nothing."

Sir William forbore to say that his nephew was clearly wrong, since the purchase of a coat, in a Cheshire winter, would be a necessity. "There is the matter of parental affection."

That made Greville look up. "I didn't have you as a lover of Rousseau."

"The fact that I do not have children of my own . . ." His uncle had to pause and look away to avoid the avarice in Charles Greville's eyes. "It does not mean that I do not ponder on the proper course of raising and educating them."

"And?"

"I look to my own past. I was put out to a wet-nurse on the very day of my birth."

"With a king for a companion on the other teat."

"A prince then. But that is to digress. What I mean is that Rousseau has identified this as an unsatisfactory way of rearing infants. And it is not just he. The Duchess of Leinster I consider a friend, and she in her letters cannot be brought to think of child rearing in any other way than by the natural mother."

Greville favoured him with a thin smile. "I sense a reason for the route of this conversation, Uncle William."

"I doubt it is a secret to you that Emma herself inclines that way."

"The books bore you, I fear."

"They do, nephew, they do. You have carried out your stewardship in a splendid fashion. Were it not that you insist, I could scarce be brought to check the figures you produce."

"A turn round the garden?"

There had been a shower earlier, so although the grass was damp, the air had a clear odour to it that was pleasing. Less engaging was the turn the conversation had taken, with Greville's point blank refusal to consider that Little Emma should live with her mother. His reasons, though they sounded practical, were based on selfish motives. He was a fastidious man, a lover of order who would find the accommodation of a child's needs, the sheer disruption, impossible to cope with.

"You only see Emma, Uncle, as she is now. You do not see the wild, untamed creature she once was. Keeping that which has been achieved intact is paramount."

"If what you say is true, that is so."

"Yet you admire her."

"It would be hard not to, Charles. She is, even you admit, a rare creature. Were she not under your protection I doubt I could be saved from a foolish attempt at dalliance."

"Hardly foolish, sir, and do not fear that any attentions you paid to Emma would evoke a jealous reaction in me."

Sir William looked sideways at his nephew's profile, the set of the jaw, the look into the far distance meant to convey sincerity. Perhaps he did mean what he said, but his uncle had seen him react to the presence of other men around Emma Hart, and nothing he had observed had led him to believe that he took kindly any form of attention to her.

"The foolishness would stem from my age. Besides, it would scarce be fitting. Suffice to say, Charles, that I consider the obligation of family."

Greville tried to suppress the combination of anxiety and excitement in his voice. "Do you truly think of me as family, Uncle?"

"How can you doubt it, since you're my blood nephew and I consider you my heir?"

That was an amusing moment for Sir William, who was too wise and urbane ever to be fooled by his nephew. He didn't dislike Charles, quite the reverse, but there were traits in his character, the most notable his endless calculation, which he found reprehensible. As a younger son himself he knew what it was to lack an inheritance. And there was the clear memory of his own marriage which, while founded on a degree of regard, had had as much, if not more, to do with the stipend produced by the very estates they were now inspecting, property that had come to him through his late wife.

Charles worried that he would not succeed to the income. He knew that his mother had been Sir William's favourite sister, and that once she had realised her brother was childless, she had pleaded eloquently on behalf of her younger son. Sir William had been happy to oblige, with the caveat that should he predecease his wife the estates would not be in his gift. He considered it a point of honour that, having made that promise and having survived Lady Catherine Hamilton, he could not go back on it.

Yet he couldn't help teasing his too-serious nephew with hints that he might remarry. Such talk, though Greville tried to disguise it, threw the young man into a frenzy of doubt. With a shaky concept of honour himself, he could not ascribe unselfish motives to others, and constantly saw barriers to his inheritance where none existed.

"There is some pity in the fact of our blood ties," said Greville, holding up his hand to feel for the first spots of rain.

"In what way?" Sir William had already turned towards the house, thinking that the rain, a cause for some celebration in Naples because of its rarity, was all too commonplace here.

"I speak of Emma, of course. She is, I must tell you, the sweetest bedfellow a man could crave, as capable of gentility as she is of abandon. Had you been afforded a chance to discover her charms, I assure you, no barrier of age would have ruined your pleasure."

Hurrying for shelter now, Sir William noted the words but not the expression that accompanied them.

However, over the next week, as the subject of Emma and her obliging nature came up again and again, it was not difficult to see which way his nephew's mind was moving. Sir William was unsure whether to be offended or pleased, to anticipate delight or ridicule, to agree to what was being hinted at or scoff at it: the proposition that a man of his age should investigate the possibility of housing, and quite possibly bedding, a lively creature considerably less than half his age.

Trained as he was in diplomacy, Sir William did nothing to commit himself to any course of action. But he was not immune to imagination, and he had to admit that though the thought didn't entirely please him, it didn't appal him either.

A month with Little Emma had not only affected the child, it had had a deep impact on her mother as well. There were tantrums, of course, times when Emma's patience was sorely tested, such as when she encountered her daughter's reluctance to put more than one foot out of the bathing machine and into the sea, or to go to bed when the appropriate hour had struck. Hunger made the child fractious, as did tiredness, and it was plain that Grandma Kidd had over-indulged her. But on the whole she was a joy to be with, a source of endless wonder with her chatter and her childish view of events and objects.

There were moments that would live with Emma for ever: the first voluntary taking of her hand, the morning when a sunny smile greeted her, the look in those green eyes, so like her own, when she read her daughter a story, the peals of laughter that accompanied a session on a swing. But, most of all, she loved that moment when Little Emma, tired after a day on the beach collecting shells or searching for crabs, fell sound asleep on her mother's breast, the gentle pounding of her own heartbeat timed exactly to coincide with that of the child.

In Southport Emma was anonymous, just a mother with her child, a Mrs Hart whom everyone assumed had a Mr Hart in the background. Hints of a man serving at sea were accepted without question by the lady owners of the lodging house, who were too polite to enquire after an excess of detail. She was nodded to by strangers as a decent woman, and eventually engaged in conversation about matters domestic that had her falling back on her years in service. It was so long since Emma had experienced respectability that she was disinclined to give it up.

Against that she missed Greville, even his moods. She had sense to see that this seaside interlude was just that: a short break from the life she had chosen; a chance to play the part that might have been hers, had she not allowed her life to take the course it had. Having corresponded with her lover before, she knew better than to look for affection from his pen, but the coldness of his writing, especially on the subject of her daughter and Edgware, still wounded.

That absence of emotion served to rekindle her natural spirit, the need to challenge, rather than just accede to the wishes of others. Her growing attachment to Little Emma made the thought of giving up her daughter more and more difficult to bear. Emma swung between confidence in her own ideas and a fear of the reaction they would provoke, but finally, with no one present to check her, she determined to act as her conscience dictated. The first thing to do was to get both of them to London and installed before Greville returned.

"If she is already here, then it would be a stone heart that had the inclination to turn her out."

Mary Cadogan watched her granddaughter playing on the floor with the same affection Emma had experienced at the Steps. It wasn't just the blood tie either: the child had a winning way as well as an open, trusting gaze and ready smile that was heart-melting. The surprise of the child's arrival had faded in her, but not the notion that Greville would ever stand for it. He was a man who liked the house tidy. You only had to look at his choice of furnishings, which inclined towards the dainty rather than the robust, and to observe how he checked them continually for position and cleanliness to understand how finicky he was.

Greville liked things just so, and however sweet Little Emma was, she was still a child, prone to speak when not asked, cry when hurt, demand attention when inappropriate and leave her playthings wherever they fell when she tired of them. Though Mary suppressed these thoughts in order not to spoil a happy interlude, she had good reason to feel vindicated when the master returned.

"If anything, Emma, I am more vexed now than I was when I read your letter."

Greville was pacing back and forth, hands behind his back, in the master-of-the-house pose that had become an increasing feature of his behaviour since he had moved in. Emma sat, head down, careful to avoid adding an eye challenge to a domestic one.

"Did you tell your uncle?"

"How could I not when you'd engaged him as advocate on your behalf?"

"I believe he shared my view that it would do no harm."

"A stand of which I would take more cognisance if he would be obliged to suffer the consequences of such an arrangement."

"Suffer, Charles? She's only a child."

"The only is singular, Emma, given that her being an infant is the whole point of my objections. The household is simply not suitable . . ."

"She has her own room, and both my mother's and mine when matters permit. She need never come downstairs at all when you are about. You won't even know she's with us."

"Nonsense," he replied, impatiently, his voice rising as he spoke. "And what I do and do not know is hardly the point. Do not tell me that in some crisis you will not put her needs as paramount. Do not tell me that when I have friends in my own house some act of the child will not be noticed."

"Who can object to the sound of a child?"

"I can!"

Mary Cadogan was listening behind the door, and when she heard Emma reply to that, she noted there was real steel in her daughter's voice. It wasn't anger but determination, and for once her mother, who feared to be cast out on the street more than any other fate, was with her.

"I require you to indulge me in this, Charles."

"Require? Am I to be required of?"

The answer to that was no. Pleading, tears, tentative intercessions from an uncle who knew the bounds placed on interference had had no effect. Charles Greville ordered his life just so, and would not stand to see it altered.

Returning Little Emma to Grandma Kidd was heart-wrenching for Emma and ultimately sad, too, for the old lady, given that Greville had decided that the child must be placed with some respectable family to secure her future. That his notion had wisdom attached did not detract from the melancholy such a suggestion provoked. If the child stayed at the Steps, she would grow up in the same manner as her mother and grandmother before her. Who was to say that she would not turn out to follow the same occupation? It was a notion that Greville, for very good reasons, could not countenance.

"The choice will be yours, Grandma," said Emma, the offending letter in her hand, her eyes, like those of her grandmother, red with tears, "though Mr Greville's approval will be most essential."

"It should fall to you, Emma, not me," croaked Grandma Kidd.

"I would not pick someone close by. You will, so that at least you can see her when you want. It sounds cruel I know, but I cannot abide the way I feel. I would send her to a family so far away that even should I come to visit you I would not have the chance to see Little Emma."

"I never thought you'd turn your back on your own child."

"I do it for her," Emma sobbed, her eyes turning to the curtain behind which her daughter slept, "so that she will not see tears every time she beholds her mother's face. Let her grow up thinking someone else her true parent."

Grandma Kidd stood up, if her bent frame could qualify for such a description, and both her face and the tone of her voice showed her anger. "I was never one for falsehood, Emma, and I reckoned you the same. But all this 'doing it for the little 'un' is stuff and nonsense. You'se doing it like this for your own ends. It's your heart that is uppermost, not the bairn's."

"I—"

"Say no more, Emma. Go to the Post House, where you took care to leave your possessions, and wait for your coach to London."

"You speak as though I have a choice."

"You do, child," Grandma Kidd replied wearily. "You could stay put and raise your own. But you're too like your own mother, always looking for others to fend for you."

Emma tried to embrace her grandmother, but was foiled as she moved away. "I'd like to part in harmony."

"You could stay in that, Emma, but as to parting I can't see how. Tell your man to write his conditions for the child. Rest easy that I will place her where she will be happy."

Chapter Three

1785

A LIVELY SIXTEEN-YEAR-OLD, Miss Parry Herbert, daughter of the Governor of Barbados, was enthralled by the approach to the island of Nevis, St Kitts just visible beyond it, beautiful Montserrat over the stern. Conical in the clear blue sky and water, with the tip of the old volcano topped by a ring of mist, the high cirrus clouds of a Caribbean dawn formed a perfect backdrop. Whatever doubts she had had about taking passage from Antigua on HMS *Boreas* had long since evaporated. She had discovered very quickly that the supposed ogre, Captain Horatio Nelson, who was standing with her now, was nothing of the sort. He was a kind, considerate man who ran a ship that defied everything she had ever heard about naval service: it was clean, free of fear, and crewed by men who treated her as if she were a princess.

It was hard to credit that this man who never raised his voice was, according to his servant, a real Tartar when it came to a scrap; that he was so in love with trouble that if it didn't present itself he went out of his way to find it. Frank Lepée was often a trifle inebriated when imparting this information, indiscreet in the way he talked about his master and the troubles he brought on his own head, both with the ladies and authority.

Not long after arriving on the station Captain Nelson had fallen out with his commanding officer, Admiral Hughes, though some put that down to his relationship with Lady Hughes. Then there had been his unfortunate association with the wife of a fellow naval officer, which had set tongues wagging all over the region. Captain Moutray, retired from the active list and in some ill health, was married to a woman twenty years his junior. Mother of two children, she was reputed to be a beauty, though of a rather faded kind.

Gossip had it that Mary Moutray was a flirt, always keen to ensnare any passing young officer in the web of her vanity, managing to keep several gullible swains on tenterhooks at any one time. At worst, Nelson had been a fool among many, perhaps a greater one for the depth of his attraction and the directness of his method. He had made matters worse by entering into a dispute with the lady's husband to do with the prerogatives of serving officers as compared to those afforded to a man who'd retired, some nonsense about a commodore's pennant, which many ascribed to jealousy more than professional pride.

It was all stuff to a girl of her age, and that included the most boring subject of all: Navigation Acts. Nelson had set the sugar islands on their ears by insisting on an adherence to the laws, which obliged British subjects to buy British goods solely from goods shipped in British-owned bottoms. Anything brought in by foreign ships, especially Americans, might be cheaper but, in the eyes of the law he represented, it was contraband and would be seized as such.

Nelson watched her face, noting the excitement, responding as she pointed out some feature of the island that had caught her attention. Miss Parry Herbert was an engaging creature, full of the enthusiasm of youth that Nelson so admired yet could not but feel had long departed from him. For Nelson the Caribbean was a sea of troubles. Mary Moutray had gone home to England a few months before, leaving an aching void. With her corn-coloured hair, flawless skin, deep blue eyes, and winsome manner, she had led him to believe that all was possible, then broken his heart.

Frank Lepée reckoned he had been a fool, and in his drunken ramblings told him unwelcome truths: that the barbed remarks from his commanding officer about Nelson's responsibilities, the gentle nudges of friends, and the warnings to desist, had sprung from genuine concern, and not, as he had supposed, from envy. Now, in his prayers, he begged forgiveness for having conjured up a base vision of Mary Moutray as a widow, her sick husband dead, and himself inheriting both her and the couple's two young children.

Heartbreak was not his only trouble: having risen to become

second-in-command on the station, he was at loggerheads with his admiral, one-eyed Sir Richard Hughes, who would not support him in obliging the island traders to abide by the law. He claimed that if Nelson persisted, he would ruin the economy of the islands. Nelson had been forced to go over his head and appeal for support from the Admiralty, which had soured relations even more and did nothing to ease his present difficulties: they could not respond from London in less than three months. Nearly everyone in the islands cursed him as an infernal nuisance, and that included many of his fellow officers. But he had right on his side, and he was determined to prevail.

A puff of white smoke emerged from the bastion covering the anchorage, followed by the first of several booms from *Boreas*'s signal cannon. Nelson insisted to Miss Herbert that the courtesies exchanged between the shore batteries and his frigate were a salute to her, not him. That had pleased her mightily, and underlined to her how wrong she had been to listen to those who had advised her against requesting this passage. How could this gentle fellow, with his shy manner, threaten the very fabric of society?

She did not know that she herself had been a boon to the ship's captain: her lively nature and genuine interest in all things nautical served to keep his mind off the worries that assailed him.

"Mr Berry, my barge," he said, "and Mr Hardy to join me ashore when he has completed his lessons."

Martha Herbert, daughter of the household and a year older than her cousin, was on the porch to greet them. There was a moment of appraisal between the two girls, who were strangers to each other: Miss Parry was fair-haired, bright-eyed, and pretty, while Martha, no beauty with her pinched face, had hair that was near black and contrasting almost translucent pale skin. Nelson observed them, and could see that while Miss Parry was happy to be visiting, her cousin was not so outgoing. Beside Martha stood the youngest member of the household, Josiah Nisbet, and Nelson's glance in his direction broke the contact between the cousins.

"This, Miss Herbert," said Martha, stepping to one side, "is Master Josiah Nisbet, son of Mrs Fanny Nisbet, your cousin, whom I'm sure you know is held in high esteem by my father."

The boy didn't move, but concentrated on not meeting her eye. Miss Parry Herbert moved forward and held out her hand. "Captain Nelson has mentioned your mother many times since we left Barbados."

"Have I?" asked Nelson. He was as surprised by this as Martha Herbert, who raised a quizzical eyebrow.

Miss Parry continued, "All praise, sir, I do assure you. I believe you even went so far as to advise me to model myself on the lady in my relations with my uncle."

"Wise advice, cousin," said Martha, rather formally. "Mrs Nisbet runs Montpelier on my father's behalf, removing the care of domesticity from his shoulders, allowing him ample freedom to attend to his more pressing affairs. Is that not correct, Josiah?"

The reply was halfway between a grunt and a hiss. Josiah was clearly determined to give away nothing in front of this strange girl. Nelson, though smiling at the boy, was thinking about those "pressing affairs." John Richardson Herbert, president of the Island Council, was the wealthiest man on the island, so rich that half of the other planters annually mortgaged their property to him. Certainly he behaved with great generosity, scattering gifts with little regard to depth of acquaintance or cost. He carried himself well, as befitted the grandson of the Earl of Pembroke, and this house, Montpelier, white and imposing, stood as testimony to his taste.

The floor of fine English oak was highly polished and all about them in the hallway was evidence of a high appreciation of fine objects and furniture. At night, when the chandeliers were ablaze, they combined with the decoration to create an almost magical effect, which was enhanced by a steady stream of visitors whom Herbert seated, dined, and entertained, his only complaint being that the business of playing host fatigued him.

Martha, having informed the visitors that her father was still at his toilet, offered to take her cousin to her room. As they disappeared up the grand open staircase, Nelson turned to the boy, whose mood had changed abruptly: with the females gone he was looking at Nelson with open affection, which was not reciprocated.

"I have to say to you, Josh, that you did not acquit yourself well with your cousin." The boy's eyes dropped, and Nelson felt a bit of a scrub, especially since the child was not his to chastise. "But she is near enough in age to you to understand, so no harm will be done."

"Thank you, sir," Josiah said, abashed.

Nelson could never be stern with a youngster for more than a few seconds, so he adopted a pleasanter tone. "You look a bit peaked. How have you occupied yourself since I was last here?"

The boy gave an exaggerated sigh. "At my books, sir, which is tedious, though Uncle Herbert has promised me that I shall have a pony if I do well."

"You must do well, Josh," Nelson insisted, "otherwise I will not be able to ride out with you when I next sail this way."

"*Will* you ride out with me?" Josiah Nisbet asked eagerly, taking Nelson's hand.

"Most assuredly, young sir. It will be a pleasure."

The tug to demand attention was unnecessary, since Nelson was looking right into the boy's eyes, and smiling. "Can I come aboard your ship again?"

"If time and your mother permit. Indeed, when you are a little older, perhaps you may spend a spell with us, take a trip around the islands as my guest, as your cousin Miss Parry has done."

"Why sir, that would be splendid."

"Where is your mother?"

"Off the island, sir, at present, visiting on Montserrat."

"That is a great pity," Nelson replied, his smile evaporating.

"She will be back before nightfall, Captain Nelson. It will please her that you have called. I know for certain that she esteems you."

That made Nelson smile again. "Does she, Josh?"

"Highly, sir."

"Then that is gratifying to know."

"Will you play with me?" the boy asked, tugging again.

"How can I refuse, when there is nothing to distract me?"

"If you run down the stairs, sir, the floor here provides the most satisfying slide." Seeing the raised eyebrows, Josiah added, "That is, if you can be brought to remove your footwear."

"It's a good notion, but I fear for my stockings."

"Tear them, if you must, sir. Uncle Herbert has pairs by the hundred."

They were under one of the hall tables, quite oblivious to his presence when John Herbert appeared. He was a small round man, balding, with tidy features who cultivated his movements in the same way that he carefully modulated his voice. Fastidious of dress and behaviour, he had been caught out by the sudden arrival of his niece, forced to make a hastier than usual toilet. What he saw before him did little to restore his equanimity.

Josiah Nisbet was squealing mightily, emitting almost endlessly a high-pitched, childish yell. Nelson manoeuvred through the table legs, growling like some great jungle beast, grabbing him and snarling then letting the boy's foot slip through his fingers. The queue that tied back the Captain's hair had come loose, and so had his stock. But that was not what alarmed John Herbert most.

"Captain Nelson, sir. Do I find you my guest and in disarray?"

Their sudden awareness of the owner of the house had a great effect on both man and child. Josiah Nisbet scurried away, looking for a place to hide, while Nelson, caught only half dressed, sought to rise and fetched his head up hard against the top of the table with an audible thud.

"Mr Herbert," he said. He crawled out, pulled himself to his feet and straightened his coat, stock, and hair. "Forgive my appearance. I could not refuse a request to play from a youngster. He is a sprightly fellow, as I'm sure you know."

Herbert was looking at his feet, at the stockings that now had holes at the toes. He could scarcely credit the dishevelled apparition before him: this man sent shafts of fear running through all of the islands, with his accursed enforcement of the Navigation Acts threatening ruin to many. Herbert's fat face was a mask of controlled anger. "The boy can be a damned nuisance, sir. I have often had occasion to remind my niece that, if she is absent, there is no one here at Montpelier to hold him in check."

"He is no pest to me, sir," Nelson responded. "Indeed, being a hearty young fellow I enjoy his company. He reminds me of my midshipmen."

That brought a frown to Herbert's face, as though what Nelson had said edged the bounds of good manners. "You enjoy the company of the young, I perceive."

Nelson looked hard at Herbert, before deciding to treat his remark as an innocent one. "Of course."

"That, sir, is singular. I find children a bore. Those misguided modern nostrums as to their care are all stuff and nonsense. I was wet nursed, fostered, and left to the care of my father's black servants and it has done me naught but good." He continued to look at Nelson as, voice raised, he said, "Josiah, if you have not breakfasted, do so. If you have, go to the schoolroom and await your tutor there. And do so in silence."

He looked Nelson up and down once more. "As for you, Captain, I think you need some privacy to compose yourself. That, and a new pair of stockings."

"They have suffered, sir, but in a good cause."

"The room you occupied on your last visit is empty. Might I recommend that? I will send someone to you with the means to effect a toilet."

"Thank you, sir."

He was moving away before another thought struck him. "How did you find Miss Parry? Her parents tell me she is a joy, which I hope to establish as being true. I am, as you know, Nelson, plagued by female relations as it is. It would grieve me if she were to prove tiresome."

"My acquaintance is of short duration, but I certainly found her an entertaining companion."

The look on his host's face told Nelson that someone he found good company would not necessarily find the same favour with Herbert.

"You must join me at the breakfast table, and acquaint me with her nature," said Herbert, in his troubled, fussy way. "I am so often at a loss with the younger family members, fearing to open my mouth lest I offend some unknown sensibility."

Nelson knew that to be the opposite of the truth and was confirmed in this opinion that evening just before dinner when, rum punch in hand, he sat in silence, while Herbert monopolised the conversation. It was the typical planter statement: about sugar, its price and position in the creation of a strong British nation; the way West Indian traders were ignored in the councils of government. He made the obligatory slash at the fools who would abolish slavery, with an aside to the effect that if they knew the black man better, they would be less forceful about freedoms.

Midshipman Hardy, lessons and duties completed, had arrived in the early afternoon, it being Nelson's policy to introduce his youngsters to polite society as often as possible. Thus he rarely went ashore without one in tow, or ordered them to join him when he was being entertained, in the hope that by example and exposure to non-naval company they would improve their manners, as well as the quality of their conversation.

Hardy now sat rigidly on a hard chair as Herbert droned on, bored by all of this, his stomach rumbling for the food he could smell already, his eye fixed on a glass he had long emptied and hoped to see refilled. But Herbert rarely even flicked an eye towards the youngster. To him the lad was just one of Nelson's foibles, one of that group of spotty midshipmen he always seemed to have in tow.

For all that conversational dominance, and his host's utter determination not to acknowledge Hardy, Nelson had to admit that John Herbert had a kindly streak. Most planters did, with their easy come, easy go attitude to money, which would have been seen as reckless in colder climes. They gave gifts with a freedom that staggered new arrivals, and expected nothing in return. Herbert was exceptional only in that the base of his wealth was so secure that he did not, unlike most sugar planters, run into debt on an annual basis.

"Ah! Fanny," Herbert exclaimed, caught in mid-flow as his niece entered. Nelson had no idea that she had returned, but he was aware that he was happy to see her. "You have come most carefully upon your hour, as the bard said. I must visit your aunt Sarah in her sick bed, so for the next quarter of an hour I would ask you to entertain Captain Nelson."

Just then Josiah Nisbet appeared from behind his mother, which made his great uncle frown. He then glanced at the rigid midshipman. "Josiah. You are much of an age with Mr . . ."

"Hardy, sir," the midshipman replied, in his Devon lilt, his voice betraying the cracks, wheezes and strains of puberty. Spotty-faced, with thick lips that were designed never to smile, he was a big youth, broad, heavy jowled, and slow thinking.

"Quite. Take him out into the garden to work up an appetite."

Thomas Masterman Hardy's face was a picture of self-control that amused his captain. Was that ire due to being thrown into the company of a five-year-old, or the host's failure to recognise his near starvation? Nelson reckoned on a combination of both.

"I will send a servant to sit with you and Captain Nelson, Fanny," Herbert stated. He never forgot the need for propriety.

"Run along, Josh," said Fanny. "That is, if Mr Hardy does not mind?"

"Ma'am," Hardy replied, in a strangled tone.

Her voice was soft and melodious, reminding Nelson instantly of Mary Moutray, an impression that was strengthened by the elegant way in which she moved towards the fireplace to pull a bell rope.

"I shall summon a servant myself, since I suspect that between the door of this room and another my dear uncle will have quite forgotten. Believe me his many cares make him unmindful. You only see the obliging host, never the much put upon plantation owner. Might I request for you another rum punch, Captain?"

"Thank you, no, Mrs Nisbet. I fear my head is swimming enough with what I have taken in."

He was only aware then that he had been staring hard at her, giving a *double entendre* to his words that was unintentional. She blushed and dropped her eyes. He took the opportunity to admire the slim figure beneath the light muslin dress she wore.

"I must say I like your boy," Nelson stammered.

She gave an engaging and musical laugh. "Not half as much, sir, as he esteems you. I cannot thank you enough for the kindness you have shown him. He insists that you are the only person to whom he would issue an invitation if the right lay with him."

"Then perhaps a turn in the garden, Mrs Nisbet, to see how he and Mr Hardy are faring."

He held out an arm, which she accepted and they made their way out into the warm evening air.

Chapter Four

THE GARDEN was like the house, exquisite in the way each of the plants, shrubs and trees had been placed to provide gentle promenades. They soon came upon Josiah, who had persuaded Hardy to push him on the swing, the cry of "Higher!" repeated several times. Nelson felt her tense beside him as Hardy responded positively to the request, sending her son so far in the air that the tension broke on the ropes.

"Have no fear for him, Mrs Nisbet," he said reassuringly. "Observe the grip of his hands. Josiah has clapped on like a true topman and nothing will dislodge him."

"I cannot pretend to share your faith," she replied with a slight gasp.

Nelson inclined his head towards hers, enjoying the gentle aroma of her lemon verbena scent. "That is, dear lady, because you have never yourself been aloft in a gale of wind. I do assure you he is in no danger."

The tiniest squeeze she administered to his forearm as she replied to that was as pleasing as the sentiment she expressed. "I must accept your word, Captain. Josh wouldn't thank me for interfering in a situation that his father would have let stand. I cannot tell you how the boy needs a man to help raise him."

"Mr Hardy," he called, aware that the authority he was about to show was designed to impress.

"Sir," the midshipman replied, standing to attention then skipping smartly sideways to avoid a blow from the returning swing.

"I would request that you ease up on young Master Josiah. Not that I believe him at any risk, but it does no good to worry his mother."

"Mamma," Josiah wailed.

"It is my injunction, young man," Nelson said, coming closer. "Though I expect your mother to be worried she has made no move to interfere."

"Thank you, Captain," said Fanny Nisbet, softly.

"I fancy you for a future sailor, sir," Nelson continued, "like Mr Hardy here. Should you be lucky enough to be accepted into a King's ship, I hope the first thing you would learn is that good manners towards the gentler sex are of primary importance. Is that not so, Mr Hardy?"

"Aye, aye, sir."

A gong rang out from the hallway to announce dinner. Nelson escorted Josiah's mother back into the house, bowed to both Miss Martha and Miss Parry, then took up his place at Herbert's right hand, several places up the table from Fanny. But as he ate and listened to Herbert, he watched her carefully. Fanny Nisbet was younger than Mary Moutray and pale of complexion, a tribute to the care she took to stay out of the fierce Caribbean sun. She had fine, if quiet manners and a cultivated mode of speech, peppered with enough French to let any listener know of her fluency in the tongue. The linen napkins they were using had fine embroidery at the edges, all Fanny's handiwork, according to her uncle.

"I can't think how I would manage without her, Nelson," he insisted, after both ladies and youngsters had withdrawn, and his guest had alluded to her capabilities. "Montpelier is never run half as well in her absence, which I cannot help but notice as I am dragged away from some task to deal with domestic disputes. I swear she's dearer to me than my own daughter."

"I believe I have already said I can see ample cause for your esteem."

"Then, sir, we shall drink to the lady, you and I."

"Most heartily, sir," Nelson replied, his mind suddenly a turmoil of future possibilities. Fanny Nisbet was not only attractive as a person, she was in all respects sensible. And as a favoured niece of a rich man, the lack of funds that had restrained him from proposals of matrimony in the past might be removed.

Young, vibrant creatures were all very well, but a sober spouse might serve him better. He could see her as an admiral's wife, able to entertain the very best of society with an ease born of long experience. And she had shown her fecundity in the production of a son already, so that his potent desire to be a father would be likely to be satisfied.

"You would not, however, stand in the way of Fanny's happiness, sir?"

"Of course not, Nelson," Herbert replied, seeking to relight his pipe.

"Damn the man to perdition," said Nelson, having read the latest letter from Admiral Sir Richard Hughes.

He was looking through the casement windows of his cabin to the packed anchorage of St John's harbour, Antigua, the busiest port in the Caribbean, scene of his own first landfall in these waters as a mere child. If he recalled it as welcoming then, it was less so now.

He threw the letter aside. It was a reminder from on high that regardless of Nelson's view on illicit trading into the islands, his commanding officer was not minded to act by ordering every ship in his squadron to intercept foreign vessels and seize their goods, nor to impound whatever they landed. The trouble was that Nelson had with him on his quarterdeck a whole posse of representatives from half a dozen islands, who wished to ensure that he followed the same course.

"Our visitors, sir?" asked Lieutenant Millar, anxiously.

In the silence that followed Millar reflected on the relations he had with Nelson, an intimacy he had never enjoyed with any other captain. No one had ever taken him into their confidence in a like manner, not just in a professional way but almost as a friend. Yet, while harbouring nothing but admiration for Nelson as a seaman, Millar often wondered if he knew what a fool of himself he made when he stepped ashore. This desire to take on the established order and turn it on its head was just one example. Right was only one of Nelson's motivations, the other being an almost visceral need for conflict, a trait often to be found in men of small physical stature. Sir Richard Hughes disgusted Nelson, with his fiddle-playing indolence and his fear of confrontation, a man who would agree with the last person he spoke to, who was very often his wife. Yet he had the prestige of his office, powerful friends and supporters at home, and was a person it was unwise to cross.

But that was as nothing to the Captain's romantic attachments, Millar mused. Nelson had offered him many confidences for he saw the premier as a good and compliant friend. And Millar knew he would back him, even if it blighted his own career. He spoke to remind him of the need to act. "Sir!"

"Hold them for just another minute."

"They have all said most forcefully that they have business to attend to, that they are civilians, and are not subject to the arbitrary power of the service."

Nelson didn't reply. He wanted his minute to make up his mind as to what to do. His inclinations were to ignore the Admiral and continue. But for once he heeded the advice of others and, instead of charging like a bull at a gate, stopped to consider the consequences. Taking on Sir Richard meant taking on the entire West Indian establishment: planters, traders, corrupt officials, and even a number of his fellow naval officers, happy to accept gifts in lieu of action. The only help he could muster was an authority three thousand miles away, which was scant comfort, especially since Admiralty support was not guaranteed. Against that, though, he was faced with withdrawal from a position that was, without doubt, right. No matter what opposition he could imagine, nothing was worth that. He looked into his premier's florid face, a man who had stood by King George when his countrymen wouldn't, and had lost everything because of it. How could he relent before such a man?

"Send them in, Millar." He turned to Lepée, who was already glassy-eyed and it was only ten of the clock. "Start pouring, man. When they hear what I have to say to them they'll need strong liquor to stay upright."

It was a noisy, quarrelsome group who entered the great cabin of *Boreas*, yet they were overly polite in the way they gave precedence to each other, as if to underline to this upstart naval fellow that they were all men of position. Nelson looked hard for his host from Nevis, and was relieved to see that Herbert wasn't present. He stood to greet them, indicating that Lepée was standing by with refreshments, and waited until they all had a glass in their hands before raising his own. "Gentlemen, the King!"

"The King," they replied in unison, drinking and talking noisily to each other. To their rear Lepée joined in the toast and downed another glass.

"Who is our anointed Sovereign, gentleman," Nelson continued. "He has, through his ministers, instituted a series of laws known as the Navigation Acts." That rendered the group silent and wary. "You know what these are so I won't bore you with repetition. What I will say is this. That a *laissez faire* attitude to the landing of illicit cargoes falls without those laws. I will therefore see it as my duty to clap a stopper on such activity. From now on any foreign vessel claiming the need to land a cargo, may do so."

That made a few, the more foolish ones, nod. Other wiser minds were staring at him as though he was some kind of animal to hunt. "That cargo will be seized by His Majesty's customs officials and destroyed. It will *not* be sold through the back door. Any customs officer colluding in such an act will end up in my cable tier, there to repent his sins."

The cabin erupted, each man shouting in an attempt to overcome his neighbour. Hughes was mentioned somewhere in that cacophony, as were justice, poverty, local rights, and the inadvisability of such high-handed tactics. Nelson stood in the face of this barrage, thinking it worse than cannon fire, until it began to subside.

"The law rules in these islands, as elsewhere. If you wish it changed I suggest that my cabin is not the place to make your representations."

"You will regret this, Captain!" shouted one voice, exciting a general murmur of agreement.

"How can I, sir, regret doing what is right?"

. . .

"I cannot do other than agree with you, Captain Nelson," said John Herbert, apprised of what had happened, though surprised to receive another visit so soon from Nelson, "though it is like to cost me dear."

They were walking in his gardens again, with Fanny Nisbet and Midshipman Andrews several paces to the rear, Josiah between them holding a hand of each. A sudden laugh from George Andrews caused the face of the boy's sister to come to Nelson's mind, which he suppressed quickly and guiltily. How long ago that seemed, St Omer and the beautiful Kate, yet it was only eighteen months.

"I am grateful for that, sir," Nelson said, aware that Herbert was expecting a reply.

Herbert stopped, frowning, closing the gap between themselves and those bringing up the rear. "But you will struggle, Nelson, to persuade others of the rightness of what you do. You fail to understand the nature of the beast you attempt to control. As men they suffer from all the follies and vanities that are prevalent. They make vast sums after the harvest, yet spend even more to display the extent of their wealth. Every year most are obliged to mortgage their land to find the money to carry out planting, which they pay back from their crop before frittering the residue on outdoing each other once more. They drink heavily, gamble to excess, and purchase luxuries with an abandon that would shame a sultan."

"You do not fall into that trap, sir," Nelson replied, with some feeling.

"I have better land and I have husbanded my resources when times are lean. I must say, most of my fellow sugar planters do the opposite."

"I cannot lay aside the law to oblige the profligate."

"No. But do not think for one moment that reason will affect their opinions."

The group behind had caught up and, to Herbert's annoyance, Nelson offered his hand in place of Andrews's to swing young Josiah.

He hadn't finished lecturing his guest about the ways of the plantation fraternity.

"I fear you have vexed my uncle, sir," said Fanny. Andrews had moved on, as politeness demanded, to walk beside Herbert. "You leave him in the company of enthusiastic youth, in which he finds scant comfort."

"I would not upset him for the world, Mrs Nisbet, only for you."

That reply lost some of its gallantry through Josiah's insistence on continued swinging. But the look in the grey eyes told Nelson he had struck home, that if he chose to pay attention to her it wouldn't be unwelcome. They chatted happily, assessing each other's antecedents in a way that caused no offence. He mentioned his Walpole relations and his father's clerical lineage, while she alluded to her connection to the Scottish Earldom of Moray. Her late husband, from a good Ayrshire family, had qualified as a doctor, though he found practice in Nevis hard due to his propensity to suffer from sunstroke.

Their sparring reassured her suitor. Nelson knew that she would not have volunteered such information without at least a passing interest in some future connection between them.

Lieutenant Ralph Millar put as much emphasis as he could into his latest set of objections, though it signified little to the recipient, his captain, lost as he was in the throes of yet another romantic attachment.

"Sir, how can you even consider such matters when you are confined to your ship and in danger of being clapped in gaol should you step ashore?"

To Millar's mind, Nelson replied like a spoilt child. "There is a lady on Nevis to whom I can only communicate by letter, while I have to stay here in St John's harbour to ensure that these damned planters do not humbug me with the first enterprising American trader."

His premier wanted to mention Mary Moutray, not six months gone from the islands, who had so affected his captain that he had claimed to be unable to breathe. But then he recalled the way Nelson had talked about Kate Andrews, when they had first become close enough to share intimacies. And he had heard from others, mutual acquaintances, of his attachment to the Saunders girl in Québec. He just had to conclude that his commanding officer was an incurable romantic, a slave to his passions, inclined to fall in love at the drop of a hat, never having succeeded enough in any of his suits to be exposed to the unhappy consequences of his actions.

The troubles he had now outweighed anything he had faced before, with the entire Leeward Islands establishment combining to sue him in their own courts for the cost incurred in his enforcement of the Navigation Acts. They claimed the loss of £100,000, and demanded that Nelson make redress. Millar had offered to take on some of the responsibility, even though he was as poor as his captain, only to be rebuffed with a reminder that Nelson's rank demanded that it was he who had to face them down.

How he was going to do that, with few means, wasn't clear. He couldn't afford the lawyers necessary to defend himself and was at present confined to *Boreas* for fear of arrest if he stepped ashore. Yet with all that hanging over his head it was hard enough to get him even to consider the subject, so taken was he with the idea of matrimony and the occupants of Montpelier.

"Herbert is a man after my own heart, Millar, able to go against the herd. He offered to post bail for me to the value of ten thousand pounds. Ain't that the finest thing?"

"Of course, sir," said Millar, who had met Herbert and found him a fussy old goat. "But does that mean he sees you as a future relative by marriage?"

Nelson frowned. "I cannot read him. One minute he is all encouragement, the next as cool as a glacier. I have no real certainty that he is not toying with me."

Millar had another vision of the wistful Mary Moutray. "As long as the lady is not toying with you."

Nelson put his head in his hands. "I cannot believe she is,

though I admit that my letters have yet to receive a reply."

"Have you asked for one?"

Nelson fixed Millar with a petulant stare. "I don't see the need."

Millar might be half the sailor Nelson was, but when it came to the fair sex he had a better idea of procedure. He tried to keep his exasperation out of his voice. "She is a widow, sir, dependent on her uncle, who is stiff when it comes to doing what he perceives to be right, and mindful of the opinion of others. She cannot volunteer herself to you without you requesting it."

Nelson's blue eyes opened wide with revelation, though inwardly he felt foolish. "I never saw that, Millar. How could I be so blind?"

His premier denied himself the pleasure of telling him that in matters of the heart his blindness was as complete as it was when it came to his servant. Millar had often hinted that Nelson should remove Lepée, who grew more drunk and less respectful in equal measure. Nelson couldn't see that the man who had nursed him down the San Juan river was not the same person now. He was a thieving rogue and rude with it. But this was no time to ruminate on that: there were more pressing matters to attend to.

"That, at least, you can repair, sir, but I beg you to allow yourself time. The most pressing thing is to see off this suit from the planters."

"The most pressing thing is for you to take over here, Millar, while I have Giddings get the cutter rigged and head for Nevis."

"Nevis?"

Again Nelson showed the petulance of a man who hated to be thwarted. "How can I be idle in such a matter?"

"You'll end up in a debtor's cell."

Nelson brightened then, looking for all the world like a mischievous boy. "Only if they know I am ashore. But since I shall depart and return in the dark, I shall confound them."

John Herbert loved to worry and he did not confine his anxieties to his own cares. With Captain Horatio Nelson a frequent visitor in the last two months he had taken on the burden of his concerns too, though it didn't take precedence over the care of his garden, which they were, at that moment, walking through. "It must be another several weeks yet, Nelson, before you can hope for any reply from London."

Nelson nodded agreement, though the subject bored him and he did not want to talk about it. He half suspected that Herbert had deliberately brought it up to avoid engaging in the one his visitor desired. It had been a strange interlude, these last few months, with the planters huffing and puffing yet fearful to go too far until Nelson heard from the Admiralty, a message they feared might praise his high-handed actions.

Even more odd was the way he had to skulk about in his cutter, leaving ship and returning in the dark, sneaking ashore on Nevis and making his way to Montpelier in secret. But if things had gone badly on water, they could be said to have progressed on dry land. He was far from having an arrangement with Fanny Nisbet, but enough had been imparted in a dozen meetings and over fifty letters to convince him that a formal request for her hand in marriage would not founder on an objection from that quarter. He was desperate to pin down Herbert, who was eel-like in his determination to avoid being ensnared.

Now good manners overrode Nelson's impatience and forced him to reply. He acknowledged the truth of what Herbert had said. They talked of Admiral Hughes, due to be relieved, too taken with imminent departure to bother with his second-in-command.

"He is determined to get away before the hurricane season makes it too dangerous. I think he's only awaiting the arrival of Prince William."

At that name Herbert lifted his head. "You know the King's son, do you not?"

This was a question he had asked before. The prospect of royalty being present in the islands excited him. But that was not what animated Nelson, and his exasperation was evident in his voice. "You may recall me saying I served with him in Lord Hood's fleet during the American War. I—"

"He will come here, won't he, Nelson?

Nelson looked away for a second so that his sigh would not be obvious. "Nevis is high on the list of places His Royal Highness must visit. Naturally, as president of the council, the task of greeting him will fall to you."

An already puffed chest swelled even more. "Most satisfactory."

"I have," Nelson said nervously, "come here upon another matter. That which I wrote to you about."

"Quite," Herbert replied, noncommittally, pausing to examine a brightly coloured flower.

Exasperation finally broke the bonds of politeness, and Nelson spoke quite sharply. "Do my attentions to your niece offend you?"

"Never, Captain Nelson," Herbert said calmly, still fingering his flower. "As a man I esteem you, though I would never allow personal taste to interfere with my duties as the head of the family. Your own family connections raise you to the rank of suitor, regardless of my opinions."

"I must advise you, sir, that I am poor as a church mouse."

Herbert laughed. "Never fear, sir. I have seen many an officer arrive out here penniless, only to return home as rich as Croesus."

"That would apply only in wartime. I am obliged, before pressing forward in any way, to ask of Mrs Nisbet's circumstances."

Herbert's small eyes were on him. "She hasn't a penny to her name, sir."

Nelson felt his chest constrict and he struggled to hide the shock. This news flew in the face of all that he had observed of her here at Montpelier. Frances Nisbet played the hostess to such perfection, in this grand mansion on an island crowned with wealth, that the idea that she had no money of her own was ridiculous.

"And her expectations?" he asked, breath held.

Herbert waved an airy hand. "Without my good offices she has none."

For the first time they locked eyes. "Then I must ask you, sir, if you intend to endow her?"

Herbert held the stare. "And I must ask if you are intent on pressing your suit."

Nelson had to hesitate then, faced by a Rubicon that, once crossed, would provide no retreat. "I have expressed certain sentiments to the lady by letter, Mr Herbert, that make the subject of income delicate."

The words were burning in his brain: that he would as happily occupy with her a cottage as a palace; that esteem founded on sound reasons was more to him than money. He was forced by these surprising revelations to ask if such statements were true. But as he conjured up a vision of wedded bliss, of young Josiah running riot in some well tended cottage garden, he was happy to acknowledge the warmth of his feelings.

Besides, he was convinced that Herbert was just being coy, a wise move for a man who, for all his display of generosity, had had the sense to be careful of his money. He esteemed his niece, that was certain, rarely missing an opportunity to praise her. When the time came to show how much he cared, Nelson was sure that his bounteous purse would be loosened.

"I have set my heart on a course of action, sir, from which I would be desperately disappointed to be deflected."

Herbert nodded sagely, forcing his chin back into his chest. "You propose to take on a heavy burden. And I propose to think on the matter if that answer satisfies you."

"Only a wedding will satisfy me, sir."

"So ardent, Nelson, so damned ardent."

Herbert nearly blurted out his concern then; that this suitor was a man who made trouble wherever he went, and none of Herbert's fellow planters would take kindly to him being welcomed into the Montpelier household. Yet clearly Fanny was smitten. He had heard that Nelson was as mercurial in a fight as he was as a suitor, as determined to succeed professionally as he was to dun him out of a dowry. And what then? He had just as likely get his head blown off in some action and leave him, John Herbert, to take on the burden of a niece who had been widowed twice.

"I have told you, sir," he said, "these are matters to be thought on."

In the face of that Nelson had to be content.

Chapter Five

1786

MARY CADOGAN'S relations with Charles Greville were based on one principle: he was the master and she, though of the superior sort, was his servant. It was an arrangement she worked hard to keep in place, never assuming as Emma's mother any prerogative that didn't come naturally to her through her position. Never once did she presume to comment on their relationship, content to accept that, despite occasional disputes, it satisfied something for both parties. In so much as he was capable of affection Greville cherished her daughter. Emma, emotional always, veered between submissive love and occasional bouts of intense fury, but on the whole seemed content with her lot.

That Emma loved him mystified her mother, but she had seen too many unlikely couplings in her varied life to indulge in any deep reasoning. When he was absent Emma praised Greville to the skies, quite forgetting that her mother saw nearly as much of the man. Even the pain of Little Emma's removal, which had come closest to breaking their connection, faded within weeks of the child's departure, leaving an atmosphere once more calm, as though she had never been a resident.

Mary Cadogan was too wise to try to comprehend the ways of love. The most inappropriate pairing often lasted longest and perhaps this was one of them. Her interest was to keep them in the house, in relative comfort, to satisfy the fussy Greville, and smooth the odd bouts of rebellion in her daughter. She and Greville talked often, of course, since the maintenance of the house required it. There were menus to discuss, guests to accommodate as well as the mundane costs and quality of the keeping of the house.

No meeting was an occasion for comfort. Greville lacked that ease of manner with servants that made for a simple exchange. He tended to bark his enquiries rather than speak them. He worried over the smallest amounts of money but insisted that when he entertained nothing should be left aside that his guests had a right to expect from a host.

He was constantly on the cusp of ruin, speculating here and dealing there to keep himself and his way of living afloat. The building of a collection for future sale and keeping Emma Hart ate up money that had to come from somewhere. The annual five hundred pounds allowance from his father didn't go far, so he tried to make up the shortfall by dealing in pictures, acting as his uncle's agent, and accepting commissions to act for others. The rental of his house in Portman Square failed to produce the required income, leading to a sale, which resulted in losses once he had paid the builders.

His endless search for a rich wife was no secret, though it was never openly discussed. Nor was it a cause for much anxiety. If Greville did land an heiress the match would be for money, not love. It was tacitly accepted that success was not intended to affect the arrangements at Edgware Road. They would continue, albeit without the permanent presence of the master.

So Charles Greville existed in a financial and social circle whose ends couldn't meet. But his housekeeper, a clever woman, manipulated his moods and her expenses in an attempt to satisfy both his purse and his aspirations. The knowledge that this was so did little to temper his moods at their weekly meetings.

Mary Cadogan sensed that this interview was to be different when Greville invited her to sit. It was not the normal day for their perusal of the accounts and the commitments for the coming week; that had already taken place. And he was nervous rather than cranky, fiddling with papers or moving the candles, occasionally jumping up to poke the fire before throwing himself back on to his chair. The opening remarks had the general quality of gossip, as if he was in some doubt as to how to proceed.

"Tell me, Mrs Cadogan, what did you think of my uncle William?"

"A fine gentleman, sir."

She meant it, but considered it a daft question. How could she say any different? Uncle William, as both Greville and Emma called him, had been a breath of fresh air in the house, with his worldly manners, ready wit and lack of side. He was a man who found the lower orders easy company, was of the type to make them feel comfortable attending on him—that evidenced by the genuine tears that had accompanied his departure. Yet she had heard his name damned only two days previously on receipt of his latest letter by the very nephew who claimed to esteem him most.

"It seemed to me that Emma was exceedingly fond of him."

"She was and still is, sir."

"Has she spoken to you of this?"

He had turned away to poke the fire again, but his voice gave a lie to the impression he was trying to create, that the question was of little import.

"Emma talks of him often, sir, to you as well as me, I'll wager. He was kindness itself and not above an excess of flattery to please her. It wouldn't be going too far to say she misses him. We all do in the house, from scullery to attic."

"What you term flattery was nothing more than the plain truth, Mrs Cadogan. My uncle regarded your daughter in the highest possible light, not only for her beauty but for her manner and her accomplishments."

Mary Cadogan wanted to say that that was obvious, as obvious as the attentions paid to Emma by everyone Greville introduced her to. How many times had he come back from some event railing against some poltroon for his forwardness? Mary Cadogan reckoned that through usage, Greville had lost sight of what a prize he had captured.

"It is pleasing as her mother to hear that, sir."

"I have arranged for Emma to visit him in Naples," Greville said abruptly, sending up a shower of bright orange sparks as he poked at the coals. "Naturally I would like you to accompany her."

The obvious question to follow that was a request to know what he was going to do, since there was no "we" in the proposal. But that was one she felt it would be unwise to ask. Mary Cadogan knew, or at least formed judgements on, more than Charles Greville imagined. It was one of the advantages of being a servant that you were free to observe what others involved in such exchanges failed to see: the pitch of a voice, the undertones of a statement, the look the listener couldn't see were all objects of acute interest to a person rarely included in the conversation.

Little could be hidden from someone who occupied and supervised the house. It was her task to take in and pay for the post, so even if the contents of any letter were unknown to her, the name and location of the correspondent were not. If a verbal message came when the master was absent it fell to her to take it. With her daughter the mistress of the house, Mary Cadogan had more than a passing interest in the relationship between her and Greville. Having suffered so many changes in her life she was attuned to the atmosphere that preceded a shift. And right now that extra sense was at full stretch.

"I must go to Edinburgh for six months," Greville said finally, a slight growl in his tone, evidence to Mary Cadogan that he had been waiting for her to ask. He threw the poker at the fire and himself into his chair. "I had considered taking Emma with me, but it won't answer. Nor, as I'm sure you will agree, would leaving her here."

Again Mary Cadogan didn't respond. There was a sniff of finality in the way he was speaking. Was Greville the type to cast Emma out like Uppark Harry before him? A vision of her and her daughter on the street again was hard to keep out of her mind.

"Sir William has written to say he is happy to accept you both into his household until I can join you." There was a vague wave of the hand. "Some time in September or October, I would say."

It wasn't that which had caused the shouted goddamns she heard from the outside of the parlour door. The invitation from Sir William that the trio of nephew, mistress, and mother should visit Naples had been made often in this very room.

"You have told Emma this?"

"No," he said slowly. "I fear that after our last parting, as well as the loss of Little Emma, she will take it badly."

With another man it might have been easy to accept his every word at face value, but not with Greville. He surely didn't want her to tell her daughter of his plans. That was a task he could not pass to another. So why tell her first? There would be scenes for sure, tantrums from Emma, the kind of tears and wailing that wouldn't go amiss in a stage tragedy.

"I want her to be happy, Mrs Cadogan. I hope you know that."

"I do, sir," she replied. Once more, what else could she say?

"If I do anything, I do it for her own sake."

The word "liar" was in her mind but not on her lips as he continued, forced jollity evident in his voice, his words jumbled. "My uncle has painted such an enchanting picture of Naples, I am afire to see the place. Emma will share a similar excitement, I'm sure, and he is so fond of her and she of him, they are so very easy in each other's company, that the visit is bound to be a success. I must in truth tell you I am already suffering pangs of both loss and jealousy."

"For six months?"

"Quite," he replied, avoiding her eye. Then, warming to his theme, he spoke with calculated enthusiasm. "Think of it. He will be able to take her to dig for his treasures. She has often said she would enjoy that. And Naples is not London. My uncle remarked on the ease of manners. I daresay Emma will meet the very cream of Neapolitan society."

"That will be very nice," Mary Cadogan replied, in a voice that earned her a sharp look.

"You do not agree?"

"Why, sir," conjuring up an expression of false innocence, "whatever gave you that idea?"

"I have arranged for a fellow to accompany you, David Gifford, a pupil of Romney, who is charged to visit Rome to improve his skills. He has French and Italian, so will be useful."

So Romney knows, Mary Cadogan thought, and this pupil knows. It must be that Uncle William knows. How come Emma don't know?

There was something afoot that she couldn't fathom right off. But it was there and a clear mind was needed to discern it. She was tempted to challenge him, to demand outright what he was up to. But there was no point. He wouldn't oblige her with the truth.

"When do you intend to tell Emma, sir?"

That made him look exceedingly uncomfortable, causing him suddenly to shift his body in the chair as though he itched all over. "As soon as she returns from her singing lesson."

"Would I be permitted to enquire how far your plans are advanced, sir?"

That made him shoot out of the chair again, so that he could turn his back and avoid her eye. "The decision is made."

"And when would you be expecting us to travel?"

Another vague wave, as though that part of what must occur was a fresh thought. "The middle of the month."

"No more'n a week away."

"Matters have come to a head in less time than I allowed."

"Best prepare for a squall then, sir, for my Emma will not take kindly to your notion."

"I cannot see why," he insisted, more to convince himself than her. "Naples, in the company of a man she is fond of. It's an exotic place, you know, very exotic. Emma has been entranced to hear my uncle describe it. I've seen the look in her eye when he tells his tales. I cannot see how it can fail to appeal to her sense of adventure."

"Change is never as welcome to those doing it as it is to them that proposes."

In the end, Mary Cadogan was surprised by the meek way in which Emma reacted to news of the arrangements. Perhaps Greville had persuaded her that there was some advantage in his proposals, benefits he had not vouchsafed to herself. Also, she knew that Greville had cowed Emma's spirit somewhat, but only realised now how much. An earlier Emma would have raised Cain at his plans and rightly so. Mary Cadogan, for all the strictures she herself had employed with her daughter, wasn't sure that she was as fond of this humble apparition as she was of the old contrary one.

Since a storm-tossed crossing and that first night in the inn at Montreuil, the journey had represented six weeks of sights, sounds and smells larded with discomfort and misery. The latter, in Emma's case, stemmed from the need for a six-month parting between her and the man she loved. For her mother it was the need to listen to the endless expectations her daughter espoused that Greville would fly to her side long before the due period was complete.

That served to keep David Gifford at bay. He was a handsome young man, with an enthusiasm for art so profound it could be wearing. And charged with looking after Emma, he didn't see his responsibility as any bar to an attempt at seduction. Neither did the object of his desire entirely accept the need to discourage him. But however far he proceeded, Gifford ran into the wall of affection Emma carried for the man who had paid his passage.

Off the subject of art Emma did find Gifford attractive. He had an open, honest face, made engaging conversation, and had a pealing, infectious laugh. To flirt with him would have been easy, yet the determination to be good overrode that; Emma needed to prove to her absent lover that her attachment to him was total, that she knew what Greville required and was determined to abide by the principles he had laid down. She must avoid becoming the object of gossip or speculation both on the journey and in Naples.

She was convinced that Greville was putting her through some form of test, an extended parting in what would be seductive society. The cost of failure was one she dreaded so much that it was pushed to the back of her mind. The lack of someone to confide in was a burden: she needed a person in whom she could trust and to whom she might relate the happy memories that raised her spirits. Her mother was no good in that respect: she didn't like Greville, much as she tried to disguise it. All she saw was his public face, serious and a bit self-righteous, which exasperated Emma as much as anyone.

Mary never saw the private Charles, the person on the other side of that bedchamber door, who was capable of being boyish, light-hearted, and wickedly funny, a gentle but potent lover still intent on improving Emma's mind as well as enjoying her body. Alone, provided she had not upset him in some way, his demeanour changed, and he became the man that Emma so much wanted to please. The thought that she would, by some inadvertent act, cause Greville to break from her filled her with apprehension.

Besides memory and inner fears, there was the futile attempt to avoid discomfort on the coach, which bucked and rattled across roads too rough for its springs. Stops were frequent, the cacophony of languages barely comprehensible even to Gifford, who spoke them. This left Emma and her mother adrift and helpless when he was absent, seemingly intent on searching every church, monastic building, or nearby chateau for a work of art. The simplest request without him, the water to wash, a pan to warm a bed, drink, food, gave cause for an elaborate mime. Emma, never having feared the need to perform, overcame this, and by the time they reached the Italian border she excelled in her ability to garner proper attention without a word being exchanged.

The smells were not all foreign: the odour of an open sewer, a French barnyard or cow stall was the same as it was in England, likewise rain on grass, though the further south they travelled the more that turned to the unfamiliar smell of baked earth. Mary Cadogan, not deeply religious, maintained that the locals, all the way from Picardy to Calabria, gave off the stench of Papist heathens. Every inn they stopped at on the well-travelled route saw a battle over price and what was provided for coin expended, clean linen, always at a premium—especially in the Italian inns—and some way of dealing with the fleas that infested the horsehair mattresses.

Emma found the sights astounding: Paris, with its teeming narrow streets and rookeries cheek by jowl with the great aristocratic hotels; the vast expanse of Versailles, teeming with those dependent on the King's favour; great cathedrals in towns that seemed too small for their towering campaniles. The vineyards of Burgundy, stretching away on red-soiled hillsides, became real villages with real people instead of half-remembered names from some dusty bottle on Greville's table. In this part of the world towns, even a city like Lyon, were built on the tops of hills, what buildings stood now, Gifford explained, resting on what had once been the great hill forts of a Celtic France subdued by Julius Caesar. They rose to the Alpine pass at Mont Cenis in tolerable heat, alongside a rushing torrent of icy water that could be gathered to cool the brow and spent nights in inns where the air was crisp and clear. There was ample snow still left at the peak of the route, which had the whole coach party engaged in a snowball fight.

Little pleasure was afforded in the steep drop down to the Lombardy plain, a cauldron even in the late spring that left the party near ill with heat exhaustion. Turin heralded a two-day delay while Gifford, with Emma on his arm, scoured the ducal palaces, likewise in Genoa, Lucca, Parma, and the Medici fortresses in Florence, she turning heads with the radiance of her beauty and her smile.

Gifford left them in Rome, and Emma and her mother, now seasoned travellers, continued south on their own, staying in inns on the Via Latina where the level of filth increased as the latitude fell. A full month of travel in a coach gives such an existence an air of permanence: it comes to seem like a natural state instead of an uncommon one. Beside that was the notion that it was here in Naples that Emma risked the kind of gaffe that, reported to Greville, might alter their relationship. Was Sir William Hamilton her friend, as he had appeared in London, or an uncle so conscious of his nephew's wishes that he would act for him, not her? As a consequence of these thoughts Emma had mixed feelings when the end of the journey arrived.

Sir William was there with his servants to greet them as the coach, having struggled up the steep hill, turned into the open gates of the

Palazzo Sessa, his handsome face and kind smile helping to wash away some of the recent, less pleasant memories. The sunlight, till then a glare to be avoided, mellowed to a welcome choice between heat and shadow.

"My dear Emma," he said, in his familiar baritone, as he bent to kiss her hand, "welcome to my meagre lodgings."

Mary Cadogan was forced to mind her manners when he turned to greet her, realising that the look on her face was less than friendly—a fact attested to by the alteration in Sir William's own expression. After near six weeks of speculation she found herself looking at their host as if the answer to all her disquiet lay in his face. A curtsy took that out of view, and it was a countenance of due deference that appeared as he raised her up. "Mrs Cadogan, how good of you to accompany your daughter. I know only too well the discomforts of the journey. Allow me to commend you for being so intrepid as to undertake it."

Greeted with such easy familiarity Emma felt herself relax. How could good, kind Sir William ever be a threat to her position with Greville? He took her hand and escorted her up the broad staircase to his first-floor apartments, a spacious residence full of light and shade, littered with vases, ampoules, and archaic statues set off by motes of dust hanging in the sunbeams. The floors shone with the beeswax, and the view from the windows, across the Bay of Naples to the distant offshore islands, took Emma's breath away.

"This," Sir William said, "will be your private drawing room. There is a comfortable apartment for you, Mrs Cadogan, which adjoins the music room. The bedchamber I have made ready for Emma is across from that, likewise overlooking the bay."

If he knew how closely Mary Cadogan was examining him, he gave no sign, and it was a moot point as to whether the thoughts she harboured would have pleased or disturbed him. Now there was a solicitous air about the Chevalier quite at odds with his previous persona. He seemed too much the supplicant. Perhaps it was the charge of being host instead of guest, or even Emma's mood. She had mentioned Greville when they came through the gates and her mother wondered, for all her daughter's smiles and gracious acceptance, if that thought was still with her.

"You will find much to occupy you, my dear," Sir William continued, addressing Emma. "I have engaged both a music and a singing teacher to continue the lessons you had in London. Since you are to be here for some time I have also taken the liberty of asking a few of my friends to converse with you in the language. That, I find, is the best way to learn."

"I must write to Charles, to tell him of our arrival," said Emma, brightly.

Sir William seemed rather crestfallen as he pointed to a set of double doors and said, "The materials you require are on the escritoire in the music room."

"Thank you."

Emma headed for the doors, which were opened and closed behind her by one of the servants. Only then did Sir William give Mary Cadogan any real attention. And when he spoke to her, the tenderness he had shown Emma slipped somewhat, to be replaced by a hurt tone. "A letter to Charles could surely wait awhile."

"Not for a second, Sir William. Scarce an hour has passed since we departed London that he was not mentioned."

He waved a hand towards the large windows, and the Bay of Naples beyond, gleaming in the sunlight. "This generally gives people pause. Their arrival in Naples and first sight of the view is held to be an occasion to remember."

"There's little doubt she would rather spend any occasion with your nephew than here, pretty aspects notwithstanding."

The expression on the Chevalier's face was a mixture of perplexity and disappointment. Quite clearly he had built up to the moment of arrival, only to find his hopes dashed by Emma's behaviour. But that only lasted a second or two, his cheery air returning, although it was probably a mask. His hands waved elegantly once more towards the blue bay. "She will come to love those pretty aspects, Mrs Cadogan, as much as I do, I am sure of it."

The temptation to issue a challenge, a demand to be let into whatever was going on, was as strong as it had been when she had talked to Greville. But Mary Cadogan resisted it. Happen it would emerge naturally. If not, she would ask in time, once Emma had settled in and she had her own feet well under the table. She had noticed that the Chevalier's servants spoke good English. Quizzing them might produce something. Servants always knew what was going on.

Sir William Hamilton was an easy man to admire. He knew that Emma thrived in company, and made every effort to ensure that she was never without it. Into the apartments came an endless stream of visitors to add to the teachers. Count This and Baron That, visitors from home as well as half the countries of Europe, courtiers, doctors, writers, scientific thinkers, and artists, who begged to be allowed to paint her. All, whatever their speciality, paid court to her, which was hardly surprising since her radiant beauty was enhanced by the sunlight and warmth of the city, yet never did anyone go beyond the bounds of proper behaviour, for which Emma was grateful.

Then there was the Chevalier himself, dancing on her as much attendance as his duties would allow. The residence of the King was close to the Palazzo Sessa; a short walk away the Palazzo Reale hugged the shoreline. The journey there and back was one he made several times a day, so ensuring that his beautiful guest was rarely, if ever, alone.

Being an ambassador required frequent attendance on the King, even more upon his wife, Queen Maria Carolina. She was the daughter of the formidable Maria Theresa of Austria, sister to the French Queen Marie Antoinette. Ferdinand, her husband, was a simple oaf, though in truth his lack of dignity was not entirely his fault. When his eldest brother had gone mad it was decided that education of any sort might have a deleterious effect on the unformed mind of this future sovereign. So, instead of being taught those things necessary to run a kingdom, martial skills, financial acumen, shrewd evaluation of advice given, and a degree of manners, he had been left to his own devices and passions. The centre of these was hunting, both wild animals and ladies of the court, closely followed by an appetite that bordered on gluttony.

Tall and imposing, with a direct demeanour, he looked at a distance every inch the King. Close to, the corpulence was less impressive, the vacuous look in the eye and the lack of intellect obvious. He was a buffoon, but an amiable one, a combination that had great appeal to his fickle subjects. They saw a man who looked like a monarch and behaved like a peasant, a fellow who was not above relieving himself over the walls of his various palaces, spraying his subjects with a generous dose of royal piss.

Emma was fascinated by the regal goings-on. The Queen was as much an object of interest as her husband: mother of a dozen children, the voice of power on the Royal Council, the real ruler of the Kingdom of the Two Sicilies. When he spoke of her Sir William praised her sharp mind and deep intellect, her sense of duty and purpose, as well as her devotion to her husband. This not only saw her forever brought to the delivery couch, but extended to ensuring that when he strayed, which he did often, the women she chose for him were either poor and clean, or well born and already married, so of no risk to her position.

Emma's mother watched all of this with an acute eye and, when she was reasonably certain of her suspicions, on a day when Emma was out of the Palazzo Sessa visiting a dressmaker, asked the Chevalier if she could have words with him.

Chapter Six

THE MEETING took place in Sir William's apartments, which were crammed with the results of his digging and his purchases. It was difficult to move without knocking over some valuable object or bumping into a case full of antique coinage. Seated, Sir William enquired as to what she required.

"Little, sir, 'cept enlightenment. I would like to know, Sir William, why there's not a soul in the town who does not, by look and deed, think my Emma your mistress." Mary Cadogan received a dismissive wave. The air of the professional diplomat was more obvious in this setting: the bland face and slight smile meant to convey friendship without commitment, the slow use of the hands to ward off anything unpleasant. "And I has the further impression that such an opinion has been held since we arrived here three months past."

"Idle tongues, madam. Neapolitans love to gossip."

"They were not the source, sir, since I've yet to comprehend the *lingua*."

Sir William responded, in a bluff manner, "Our English visitors are equally afflicted with that particular disease, Mrs Cadogan. They chatter and they write letters home, few of which contain a single grain of truth. It is the bane of my existence mollifying both a court and a ministry that choose to give their ravings credence."

"I asked for this interview, sir, with the intention of speaking plain. Not gossip or ravings but open, and I wish to know if in doing so I will be indulged with the true state of things."

He didn't reply immediately. Instead, he held her gaze for several seconds, wondering whether to allow her to proceed or to point out politely that she did not have the right to challenge him. To open himself to her scrutiny would lead to certain admissions: one being that things were not proceeding as had been hoped. Could he face that?

Sir William thought Mary Cadogan a good woman, a beauty herself once, though not in comparison with Emma. In any exchanges they had had he had been happy to acknowledge her good sense, as well as the wry wit that never exceeded the bounds of her position. She had even managed to impress his irascible nephew. Here, in his establishment, she had fitted seamlessly into the domestic arrangements, undertaking tasks his own servants were happy to surrender, never interfering in duties that didn't concern her.

"It would grieve me to be treated as just a stupid woman."

"And I, madam, would be a fool to do that, for you are very far from it."

"Then I'd be obliged if you would tell me what is going on, sir, not that I ain't formed a notion of my own."

"I'd be interested to hear it."

"Folk hereabouts have Emma as your mistress. That you make no attempt to deny them leads me to believe that you would wish that was true."

"She is attached to my nephew."

"Would that he was attached to her," she replied briskly. "You don't see it, 'cause my Emma hides it from you. She writes sometimes more than one letter in a day. In three months not one reply has come from Mr Greville."

"He is a poor correspondent."

"He has found time to pen several letters to you."

A flash of annoyance crossed the Chevalier's face. The quizzical expression on that of Mary Cadogan was evidence that she had noticed it.

"You get a lot of letters from Greville," she continued. "Your man was happy to save his legs and let me bring them up."

"A glass of wine?" said Sir William, standing up quickly. He manoeuvred his slim frame between the statue of a bearded ancient and a large decorated pot, poured from the decanter and returned to present her with the glass. "What is it you want?"

"The truth, sir. I expect you have an arrangement with Mr Greville. What I see is my own girl near to despair sometimes, she loves him so."

"I doubt you approve."

She took a deep drink of wine before replying. "I learnt long ago, sir, an' in a hard school, that the heart don't often adjoin to the head. Whether I approve of your nephew is neither here nor there. What my Emma suffers because of it is. If she is to be cast out I need to know of it."

Sir William helped himself to a glass of wine and sat down again. "There is no intention to cast her out, I do assure you. She'll always have my protection, should she want it."

"The question is sir, does she need it?"

Again, he had the temptation to dismiss her, to say that what she was asking might be her business but she was being above herself in demanding to know. But he had a nagging thought that would not go away: matters were stalled with no sign of a way to break the deadlock. Was the key to that sitting before him? The natural diplomat in him rebelled at revelation; the frustrated suitor in him demanded that something happen.

"Would I be allowed to tell you a story, Mrs Cadogan?"

"I judge it to be a long one, so I'd be obliged to see my glass recharged."

That made him laugh and he rose to accommodate the request. There was a moment when their hands touched, as he took her glass, a moment when he thought he saw the woman she had once been, the lively eyes that could hold humour so easily, the notion that in her mind there was judgement, but rarely condemnation.

"Your Emma is quite remarkable, but so are you. You'll be aware of my nephew's prospects, but I doubt you've any inkling of his inability to indulge in decisions that would materially advance them."

"He always seems in a stew about money, that I do know."

"The solution lies within him. There are people who esteem his gifts, not least those who'd help him to achieve office within the ministry. Opposition can lead to advancement too, yet Charles dithers, says that he cannot support either Fox and the Prince of Wales or Pitt and the King."

"I thought he had it in mind to marry well."

"In his mind, yes, Mrs Cadogan," Sir William growled. "But his aim is so inept that if he were a hunter needing to live off his kill he'd starve. But you must let me tell you what happened in England or, to be more precise, in Wales."

He paused for a moment to gather his thoughts. "It's no secret that I had tender feelings for my late wife, attachments based on those most solid foundations, trust and esteem. In short, Mrs Cadogan, though not accomplished in any startling way, my late wife was a good woman."

"Everyone below stairs says so, sir."

"They talk too much below stairs," he snapped.

"Funny that, Sir William," Mary Cadogan replied, dipping her head to her glass. "That's what folk attending usually say about those they serve."

"Something tells me that I have just been humbugged," Sir William admitted, before continuing. "My late wife's estates, bequeathed to my nephew, will ease his burdens. But, being Charles Greville, he will not come out and say so. He's a schemer even when such behaviour is unnecessary. He seeks to tie me to what my inclinations direct me towards, notwithstanding the fact that I may, at some future date, decide to marry again."

Mary Cadogan smiled. "It would be a lucky woman who got you, sir."

"Thank you for that," he replied, genuinely touched. "I have named Charles as my heir and that makes him happy, though the notion that I might take another wife renders him anxious. Matters came to a head on my return to Naples. I travelled part of the way with the widowed Lady Clarges. In a moment of madness, in Rome, after a good supper and much wine, I let my tongue slip enough to emit what might have been construed as a proposal of marriage."

The Chevalier told a good story, describing both the supper and the conversation, his face animated enough to convey the depth of the shock at his own stupidity, plus the nature of the farce that had followed.

"Luckily the lady either missed the nature of the allusion or chose to ignore it. I wrote to Charles recounting this vignette in the most light-hearted vein, presenting myself as a buffoon who had, by sheer serendipity, managed a narrow escape. I need hardly tell you of the effect on him."

"He offered you Emma?"

"Quite," he responded, uncomfortable again at being so rudely reminded of the point. "I doubt to a woman of your sagacity that much more explanation is required. The regard I have for your daughter's beauty must be plain to the dimmest eye. I made no secret of it in London, though she, besotted with my nephew, chose to see it as mere gallantry."

"Understand, sir, she receives that kind of attention all the time."

"Don't I know it!" Sir William replied. He stood up suddenly and fingered the motif around the rim of a tall Roman vase. It was sad to see his shoulders sag a little and his voice, though not weak, was melancholy. "You forget, Mrs Cadogan, that I have been out on the town with her. It has been my duty to confound the attentions of those who know both my nephew and Emma, even the Prince of Wales himself. I also confess myself flattered that those who did not know her thought her attached to me. And I can assure you that delivering her back to Charles Greville was often the occasion for a sad reflection on the burden of age."

"You was telling me about Wales."

"It was there, while we were touring my estates, that Charles first mooted that I might take on responsibility for your daughter." He ignored Mary's loud sniff of satisfaction, the certain knowledge that she had been right, and carried on, gently turning the tall vase to admire the artwork. "I believe I had said to him many times that her beauty was so classical. Do you know how often I have seen her face on objects such as this?"

That made Mary Cadogan look more closely at the decorative friezes that adorned the vase he was fingering, at the reclining beauties holding lyres or grapes. In profile they were, indeed, like Emma.

"From my point of observation," Sir William continued, "the idea has obvious attractions, as well as uncertainties. To Charles it is all advantage. Don't think he doesn't esteem Emma, he does. But love is not an emotion to which his heart is open. My nephew is a man so practical that it is sometimes necessary to wonder if he is actually flesh and blood."

The look he gave her then, as he turned to face her, was unblinking. "The rest you can guess. If I take on responsibility for Emma, Charles has less to fear in the article of my marrying again. He also offloads the cost of keeping a household for her and, as a *quid pro quo,* he has a lever on which he can work to get me, publicly and legally, to name him my heir."

"You have not done so?"

"No, Mrs Cadogan, I have not!" he replied, the snap back in his voice. "I will not see everything I own entailed by some extravagance, for he would be bound to borrow on his expectations. He plagues me in the letters you deliver to stand surety for a bond, which I will refuse to do. Should he inherit, which is my intention barring the caveats I have already stated, then I want that bequest to be that which was left to me, not the residue of his speculations."

"One of which is Emma."

"I'm very fond of her, I hope you acknowledge that."

"It's our lot to be used, sir. I had decades of it, and had hoped for better for my only child."

"That was wounding, madam."

"Then forgive me for my honesty. And forgive me for observing that I had your nephew as less the rogue than you."

"I think it a bit high to term him a rogue."

Mary Cadogan lost some of her reserve then. Her voice was emphatic. "He has sought to profit from Emma since the day he moved her to London. How many times has Romney painted her and how many pictures do you see? Sold, near every one, not kept to gaze on in admiration. And now that he tires of her he barters her off in order to maintain a grip on your good intentions."

"It is not as mean-spirited as you make it sound. He observed my attraction to Emma and thought he saw that it was mutual in its potency. And I do not think that he has the capacity to return the level of affection she demonstrates for him."

"So he'll break her heart?"

"I seek to mend it."

"Without success." That sharp rejoinder caused Sir William to respond with a curt, unhappy nod. "It was the attentions you paid her that caused me to ask for this chance to talk."

"I am more concerned with what your daughter thinks, Mrs Cadogan."

"Why, sir, if she notices at all, she ascribes it to kindness, not desire. My Emma does not think of you as a gallant."

"That is the unkindest cut of all," he replied, crestfallen. "It is true to say that I am aware of being well past the first flush of youth, but the prospect of never being anything other than an uncle is not one to savour."

"What would happen if Emma and I were to return to London?"

"The true answer madam is that I have no idea."

Mary Cadogan suspected that he was lying. If they had discussed Emma coming to Naples, they must also have talked about what would happen if the hoped-for result didn't materialise. Set against that would be Sir William's reluctance, having invested so much, to admit to failure. No man would embark on such a deep-laid plan of seduction contemplating outright defeat.

Sir William Hamilton, harbouring that very thought, had been made uncomfortable by Mary Cadogan's question, the assumption that failure would see Emma and her mother back in Edgware Road. Every time he had mentioned it to his nephew the idea had been swept aside as absurd. He realised just how much Charles had flattered him, playing on his vanity to achieve an object that, in truth, held more advantage for the proposer than it did for the supposed beneficiary. Had he been alone he might have voiced the thought that there was no fool like an old one.

"The question, sir, is where we go on from here?"

"I confess myself at a stand. I am unable to offer any solid opinion."

"What would you offer Emma?"

That made him look at her sharply. She dropped her head to examine the back of one of her hands.

"I cannot be certain I know what you are saying, madam."

She looked at him, her eyes hard. "Then you are not the clever man I think you are, sir. It be simple enough, Sir William. Does my Emma have a better prospect of happiness here than elsewhere?"

"And if she does?"

"Then I'd see it as my duty to help persuade her of it. And I might add that, given your nephew has gone to such lengths to create such a situation, no doubt he will take a mighty unkind view of a contrary outcome."

"He will meet his obligations, madam, I will insist on it."

"I know you will forgive me the liberty I take when I say that don't reassure me." She ignored his flash of irritation and carried on talking. "You know something of my life, sir, and can guess what you don't, just as you know all about Emma's. I want for her now what I have wanted from the day she was born. That she should not have to bend to the will of any man who—"

"I have no desire to bend her to my will," he interrupted. "What I desire I would want to be surrendered willingly."

"And having won that, what then?"

"Security and the knowledge that as long as I live Emma will be a charge upon my honour. And I would add this, I am not like my nephew."

Mary Cadogan stood up. There was little more to say, except, "I will not assure you that all will work out as required, but if Emma is to be persuaded to see where her advantage lies, then I am the one she will listen to."

• • •

Months of carefully dropped hints and allusions to betrayal did not dent Emma's attachment to Greville. Throughout the summer and early autumn she still spoke of him as if he was just about to walk through the door, and in such an obsessive way that her mother sometimes wondered if the oppressive heat had addled her brain.

Mary Cadogan had experienced love in her own life, as well as infatuation and all the shades of regard in between. She had also been part of a society of women where the ability to hold on to a fantasy, despite ample contrary evidence, was endemic. But never had she come across something of the depth of Emma's enthusiasm. It took the transfer from comfortable, warm Naples to cold, lonely Caserta, to bring matters to a head.

Sir William attended the King's annual hunting expedition, for which he had been allotted what he liked to call his cottage near the Winter Palace, a stab at humour that had some merit since it could accommodate over forty souls. Occupied for two months of the year, it lacked any sense of permanence, but what was worse for those not engaged in blasting every living thing that crossed the landscape, was the lack of company.

Sir William would set off every morning clad in ample clothes to ward off the chill, weapons cleaned and gleaming with fresh oil, several flasks of ardent spirits in his servant's saddlebags. The hunt would last all day, Ferdinand leading furious charges over his land in pursuit of wolves, foxes, bears, stags, and, when none of those larger creatures would oblige, any small bird demented enough to fly within the range of his weaponry.

At night they consumed the day's bag, long feasts well oiled with drink, all-male affairs at which the hunters would eat to excess, drink bumper after bumper in endless toasts, sing vulgar songs, exchange lewd anecdotes, and end up in furious arguments regarding the claims of rival noble families. At some point several of Ferdinand's courtiers, having watched him eat for four men, would be required to accompany him to the privy, there to wait patiently while he burbled on in his nonsensical way and eased the pressure on his bowels.

Back at the cottage, Emma and her mother were left with a few servants, to sit in a draughty house in which every doorway required a bolster, every room and passageway a blazing fire. During the day, if the sky was clear, the aspect of distant snow-capped Apennine peaks was pleasant, but there were rain-filled days, when the landscape seemed to close in on the royal enclosures, making the place feel like a prison.

There were few visitors for Emma, no teachers or aristocrats to sit at her feet and admire her beauty. Outdoors it was nothing like teeming Naples, where the *lazzaroni,* the peasant class of the city, on seeing her face would seek to touch her hem and hail her as the living embodiment of the Madonna. Good rider though she was, Emma was forbidden to join in the Royal Hunt, her status forbidding attendance at an event often observed by the Queen. With no recognisable social standing, she couldn't be presented to royalty. Indeed, if she was out riding and saw the hunt heading in her direction, she had to turn and flee lest she cause a scandal. Accustomed to better treatment, this led to many a tantrum, stormy sessions during which Italy was cursed, the weather likewise, and Sir William castigated for his ill-treatment of a guest he often admitted as his favourite person.

"I shall tell him as soon as he walks through that door, Mother. I have had enough of his damned Italy."

"And what d'you reckon his response will be, Emma?"

The surprise was genuine, the way she treated the answer seen as obvious. "Why, he will arrange for us to return to London, of course."

In all the three months since that talk with Sir William, Mary Cadogan had tired of the game she had been playing with Emma. She was also irritated by the ague, brought on by the draughty residence she was forced to occupy. Her joints were stiff, and the morning and evening chill had her sniffing and wiping an almost constant drip from her nose. It was no preparation for a game requiring patience, and neither Sir William nor any of the endless stream of guests who attended her daughter in Naples was here to restrain her.

"So you've finally given up on your Greville ever coming here to you?"

"No!"

"Then you're a fool, girl. If you still hold a candle for Charles Greville you're worse than that."

"How can you say such a thing?"

"Cos it be right. How many letters have you penned these last months?" Eliciting no reply Mary Cadogan continued, in a harsh voice that had as much to do with her condition as it had with her daughter's stupidity. "Dozens, and not so much as one word to say he's even read them."

"It's his way. It was the same when he was with his uncle in Wales."

"His way is to ignore you, then, lest you be right by his side."

Emma threw herself into a chair, hand over her brow like a lovelorn stage heroine. "You cannot fathom how much I miss him."

"Ain't hard, girl," Mary Cadogan replied, with scant concern to be polite, "since you never leave off telling me."

"You must want to go home as well, Mother. This house, and this particular climate, little suits you."

"Cold air suits better than cold charity," Mary Cadogan snapped.

"What does that mean?"

That was the moment at which maternal patience fractured, for reasons numerous and manifest: but especially Emma's blindness to the fact that Sir William was, and had been since their arrival, paying court to her. How could she not see his endless attention to her and her education, his occasional salacious sallies, for what they were?

Personal discomfort also played a part to shorten Mary's temper, the aches and pains that racked her body, but most of all it was the weight of keeping a secret from someone who had every right to her support. It was as if a dam had been breached, and a torrent of words told Emma just what arrangements had been made for her, and just how she stood in regard to the man she professed to love.

"She fled the room in tears."

"I wish she had been made aware more gently," Sir William replied. His voice was slightly slurred from the drink he had consumed in the King's company and his face was flushed, but what was most striking was his air of depression.

"You're more'n fond of her, aren't you, sir?" asked Mary Cadogan gently.

"I won't deny it," he said sadly. "I made no secret to you or my nephew how attracted I was to Emma. But it was an appreciation of her beauty you saw in London. My doubts as to the wisdom of her coming to Italy you must be able to guess at, leaving the bed of a young and virile fellow to go to that of an old and somewhat diminished man."

"That, I sense, has changed."

"Do you look at her, Mrs Cadogan, and see what I see?"

"I see my girl, your honour. I see beauty and her lively nature. I see her make you and other men laugh. I see the look of lust that your friends take care you should not notice."

"I notice, madam," he replied, staring at the burning logs, adding a small, humourless laugh. "You have no idea how it pleases me to do so. I am flattered by it, especially since Emma seems so ingenuous as to positively encourage the notion that I am her lover."

"She wants to touch often those she is fond of."

"If I didn't know better I would think she was teasing me, flattering my vanity as Charles did my mind, leading me towards an indiscretion so that she could play the shocked innocent and embarrass me."

"My bones ache for the chill, Sir William. I am about to help myself to that ardent spirit you recommended. Might I be so bold as to suggest that you would benefit from the same?"

"Let it be so."

Half of the bottle of grappa disappeared while they talked of the spectre in the background, a distraught young woman, who might at this very moment be sobbing herself to sleep. Mary Cadogan wiped a maudlin tear from her eye, then took another stiff drink to kill the temptation to weep.

"It just came out, what with her on yet again about going home."

Sir William had a lump in his throat. The open admission that Emma had captured his heart had escaped suddenly.

"It is, you must understand, an expression of feeling I thought to leave behind in callow youth. To be moonstruck at my age is to be made ridiculous."

"Only if it is not requited, your honour," sniffed Mary Cadogan.

"What chance is there that it might be?"

"You must own that I know my Emma better than you, sir. She might seem to you just a flighty creature whose heart has been won by an undeserving knave. But she is far from that, albeit in her mind's eye she has a vision of a future that cannot be."

"What are you telling me, madam?" Sir William demanded.

Mary Cadogan drained her glass, as if by doing so she would fortify her train of thought. "You must offer her better, sir."

"I cannot compete with Charles Greville."

"I don't mean in the bedchamber," Mary Cadogan replied testily. "I will not say it is a place where Emma cares naught for who she's with, but you must know that your nephew was not the first man to bed her."

"I cannot hold that against her."

"Nor should you, sir, never having had to make your way in our world. It's not the same as yours."

"It is not so very different, Mrs Cadogan."

"Two things must be done, sir and the first is to persuade her that there is no future for her with your nephew."

"That is not something of which I am certain."

"But I am, sir," Mary Cadogan protested. "The next thing to

do is to present her with a picture more rosy than the one she harbours now."

"I have no assurance I can do that."

"Then send us home."

"What cruel alternatives."

"Which be the lesser of twin evils?"

Chapter Seven

SIR WILLIAM was out hunting again the following day, so was spared Emma's ranting and the need to listen to the words used about him and his nephew, language so coarse that even her mother pretended to be shocked. It wasn't the cursing that upset Mary Cadogan, so much as the effect of her daughter's shouting on a head suffering from the previous night's excess.

Greville was a lecherous, penny-pinching arse, his uncle a spavined old goat, her mother a snake in the grass. Rogue, scoundrel, villain, cheat were spattered about among swearwords that would have shamed a sailor, the whole tirade liberally sprinkled with bouts of weeping and demands to be taken back to the arms of the man she loved. There were endless dashes to the escritoire to start angry letters that ended up as balls of parchment on the floor. Mary Cadogan held her tongue, waiting for the storm to pass. But, with less of a sore head as the day progressed she offered some wise words regarding the good of flogging a dead horse, which reduced Emma to another bout of weeping.

Mary Cadogan was glad now that she had spoken out. The matter was in the open, there to be discussed when Emma calmed down. And she flattered herself that she understood her daughter, passionate and less versed in the application of wisdom to any predicament. When the time came to make a decision, she could rely on Emma's good sense. In that she was too sanguine by half.

Even back in Naples, a less glamorous location in midwinter, Emma refused to give up on Greville, and brooding on that made her a less engaging companion for those who called at the Palazzo Sessa. Sir William was the first to drop away, happier at the gimcrack Neapolitan court—anything to be spared the accusatory looks of his beautiful young guest. Others who had that summer sat at Emma's feet found her sudden recourse to tears, without any indication as to what had triggered them, tiresome, especially since she made no move to enlighten them.

Matters were scarcely improved by the arrival of letters and gifts from Greville, finally stung into a response by Emma's anguished pleas. The blue hat and a pair of gloves were well received. The enclosed cold missive, which advised Emma to "Oblige my uncle," was enough to near break her heart.

It took the festivities of the Nativity, a weeklong orgy of celebration of the Birth of Christ, before even the glimmer of a chink showed in her longing. It was a time to be out in the streets, to see the endless processions with hand-carried tableaux—three wise men, the shepherds in the stable, the Virgin holding her child under a glowing star, made by rich clans determined to display their wealth. The singing of Christmas hymns in the crowded squares of Naples was uplifting to Emma, but not to Mary Cadogan, who dismissed it as Papist nonsense.

The effect on Emma was marked. She was much taken by the natural theatricality of the people, which lifted her mood. Perhaps it was the commemoration of that birth, when she had been denied a life with her own child, that finally made Emma realise the connection was broken: that a man who could sever so cruelly his relationship with a child who might be his daughter could steel himself to deny anyone.

Drink helped, and her mother encouraged her, knowing that wine-induced moods, though tending towards the maudlin, at least contained an acknowledgement of the facts. When she felt it would serve, Mary Cadogan encouraged Sir William to resume his courtship, glad to see that although Emma struggled she did so to accommodate not discourage him. Another man might have stumbled, but Sir William had the bedrock skills of his diplomacy. Emma gave silent acknowledgement, in mood not words, which indicated to Sir William that she was prepared to go further than mere gallantry.

All that was needed now was the moment.

. . .

"It is a rare thing, Mrs Cadogan, yet pleasant all the same."

Mary Cadogan nodded to accept the compliment. It had been her idea that, after all the mad revelry of the last three weeks, masques, balls, and open-air festivities, a private supper would be a blessing. Thus, instead of the usual nightly throng that graced the Ambassador's table, or a coach trip through the crowded streets to dine at another board, they were having a quiet, intimate meal, just the three of them, in his private apartments.

Soft candlelight played over the stone statuary and white porcelain vases, blue glass and red, the table a brighter pool in the centre. Servants came and went as silently as ghosts, as if they, too, knew what was afoot and were determined to ensure success. The paintings on the walls, each with a candle to illuminate them, seemed to aid the intention, being composed of cupids and nymphs, or lovers separated by a fate they longed to overcome. Even if she thought herself detached from what was happening, Mary Cadogan knew that she was part of the performance. Her role had been in organising this, her presence adding a veneer of innocence. It was pleasing to see the pretence played to perfection by the two other participants.

Emma was all gaiety, dressed in a gown of light muslin that betrayed the full flower of the figure underneath, drinking a little more quickly than she should, making occasional conversational gaffes that caused her to giggle and Sir William smile. It was the way she had worked for Kathleen Kelly. There was no intimacy of the kind that would occur between friends. It was as though Sir William and Emma had only just met. An unkind observer would say it was a tart's performance but Mary Cadogan didn't care, because it was a damned fine one, so fine that withdrawing, which she had to do, was painful. She longed to be a fly on the wall, to see how Sir William Hamilton would manage the final step from surrogate uncle and detached benefactor to lover.

He used his latest purchase, a large urn dug up by another collector from the ashen mud of Pompeii, to set the mood. It was a vase that carried classicism to a point well beyond the borders of good taste, depicting an orgy of sexual couplings. Men and women were entwined, of course, but there were other images of guests consorting with a variety of animals or with their own sex. Standing behind her, Sir William slowly turned the vase to point out each detail of the frieze.

He was taller than Emma, and the scent of her body, rising on the heat from her skin, was overwhelming. The sight of her exposed shoulders, catching the candlelight, made breathing an effort. With his head by hers, as he leant forward to indicate another point of interest, he brushed her auburn hair. Emma leant back slightly, affording him an alluring view of her voluptuous breasts.

"I fear we are a sorry crew compared to the ancients, but they had their pagan gods as examples." He pointed to a reclining female figure, naked, head back. Even with primitive art it was obvious that she was enjoying the attentions of her lover, on his knees, head between her legs. His voice was soft and hoarse, low enough to vibrate though her head and neck. "And this, Emma, this creature in profile, is so like you. All that is different is the adornment of the hair. I have often wished you would dress your hair like a Roman courtesan."

Emma experienced none of the sensations she had enjoyed with Uppark Harry or Greville at his best, that racing of the blood that made every nerve end tingle. But she did feel flushed, and the languor induced by good food and wine made leaning into Sir William seem natural. Nine months of being denied the company of her lover also had an effect on her, since she enjoyed physical love as much as she longed for emotional security.

And though it was something of which she was unaware of, Emma Hart was honest. The road to this moment had been long and painful, streaked with nocturnal tears. Even though tonight had been a performance, she lacked the duplicity necessary to be a whore with an eye for a prize. The part of her being that longed for gaiety—singing, dancing, and drinking—was balanced against a need to feel secure, to be loved for herself, not just for her accomplishments in the bedchamber. So, having finally acceded to the inevitable, she would not tease the man who offered her that.

There was no resistance as Sir William placed his hand flat on her belly, pulling her backwards so that she could feel him through her thin garment. She closed her eyes for pleasure's sake, not disgust, as he leant to kiss her shoulder. This he did several times, each touch of the lips and gentle movement of his hand interspersed with paeans to her looks, her hair, her body, her accomplishments, and his deep regard for her. He pointed to the reclining courtesan again. "I would give much to see you thus."

To oblige him, and slip out of a thin dress lacking undergarments, was easy. She didn't turn right away, aware that he had stepped away and was silently admiring her back. After several seconds he moved forward, a hand on her elbow to spin her round. She stood, one foot slightly raised while his eyes ranged over her body. He cupped his hand under one breast, lifting it slightly so that the erect nipple pointed straight towards him.

"Truly, Emma, you are fit for an emperor."

The touch had made her shudder, sending a clear signal to her putative lover that she could match his passion. He bent and kissed that same nipple, at the same time taking her hand, so that when he raised his head again he could lead her to his bedchamber. Accustomed to a man who was young and passionate, Emma was surprised and pleased by Sir William's gentility. What he lacked in ardour he more than compensated for in patience and experience. He was adept with hand, tongue, and voice, mixing flattery and touch to achieve his purpose, which was to raise Emma Hart to a pitch of sexual expectation so high that the pleasure she craved must follow. In doing so he worked the same effect upon himself, leaving his new lover with the impression of a man not far from the full flush of youth.

Emma returned to her own apartments halfway through the night, wrapped in Sir William's dressing gown, leaving him to his slumbers. Her mother was asleep too, in a chair, head lolling forward, probably too anxious or curious to go to bed and intent on waiting up for her daughter to return.

Looking at her, mouth open, jaw slack, Emma went through a gamut of emotions: anger at her mother's machinations, gratitude for the concern that had prompted them, a renewed stab of passion for Greville, swiftly followed by a feeling bordering on hate. What had happened tonight she knew was not enough. She could take pleasure from Sir William's company both in bed and out, but one coupling did not make for a commitment. That expression nearly made her laugh out loud. She thought she had that very thing with Uppark Harry and Greville, only to see it snuffed out by indifference.

The balance of what was on offer had been spelt out, albeit with much circumlocution, by her mother. Fine bones and youthful mettle were all very well in a lover, but they did not keep you fed and clothed. Beauty, her only asset in the eyes of most men, was not going to last for ever. If she craved comfort, and she did, then any arrangement that provided it was better than one that promised only passion.

"I must be more like you, Ma," she said, "and look out for what suits me in advance."

Mary Cadogan opened her eyes and, seeing what Emma was wearing, Sir William's patterned dressing gown, she smiled and nodded.

"Did I do right, Ma?"

Her mother's voice had the croaky quality of one who had drunk too much wine and slept badly. "How's to know, child. Only time will tell us that." She heaved herself stiffly out of the chair, a hand going to ease her aching back. "But I will say that what went afore is dead and buried now, even if you find that hard to accept. Take it from one who knows, that pain don't last for ever. A mind on what's to come is worth a ton weight of memory. I take it the Chevalier didn't disappoint?" she added, with arched eyebrows.

"No," Emma replied softly.

She was unable to give the true answer; that however accomplished Sir William seemed, however kind and wise, she was not in love with him. For five years she had shared her bed with a man she loved, and nothing merely physical could compare. She felt empty.

"You do like him?"

"Yes."

Mary Cadogan hooked her daughter's arm to lead her to her own bedchamber. "Then that is where the likes of us start from, Emma. We can ask no more'n a chance, and if what we are faced with ain't too low to contemplate, then we can bear with it."

"I want Greville to pay for this."

"His type don't suffer. Take what you can get and leave the rest to God."

"There should be more."

"Happen there is, girl. And happen you will find it."

Chapter Eight

1787

THOUGH THE DISPUTE over enforcement of the Navigation Acts had been resolved in Nelson's favour, the Admiralty backing him to the hilt, several obstacles still hampered his pursuit of Fanny Nisbet. With Sir Richard Hughes now departed there were his duties, as the commander on station between admirals. Second, there was her uncle, who still seemed to blow hot and cold, sometimes a touch of both on the same day. Would he give her a dowry? He declined to be drawn. Did she have expectations for his estate? Perhaps! How went Nelson's own requests to his family for financial assistance? How could he answer when a reply might be six months in coming?

Then there was the difficulty of explaining his feelings when he was mostly confined to letters, his fulsome and excitable, hers sweet and full of gossip. A dashed visit to Nevis, with a brusque demand for clarification, extracted from Mr Herbert permission that they might become engaged, provided his niece had no objection. That was a difficult moment, one which Nelson dreaded. But Fanny assented to his suit, and even allowed him a gentle kiss to seal their bargain.

But if any cause could be laid at the root of his difficulties it was His Royal Highness, Captain Prince William Henry of Hanover. The slender youth of previous acquaintance, full of respect and wonder for a senior naval officer, had quite gone. Instead, Nelson had to contend with a porcine, gluttonous creature, who could never be brought to admit he was in the wrong profession, a potentially fatal trait in one who, though he commanded a frigate, should never have been entrusted with a coracle; a man who had achieved his rank because of his blood, not his ability. Whoever had chosen his officers had done so on the grounds that seamanship was necessary, and a Germanic background was an asset. Where they had failed was in the notion that in dealing with someone like Prince William, tact was also required.

On arrival at Antigua, Prince William delivered a brusque and rude demand for a court-martial. He wanted his first lieutenant, Schomberg, removed for failure to show due respect to a superior officer. Horatio Nelson wanted to remind the Prince that he was signally failing in that respect himself. Barking at the senior captain on the station was not a right even gifted to a king's blood relative. But the need for tact applied to him as well. It was nothing new for a first lieutenant to fall out with his captain—it happened all the time, the confines of a ship almost inviting conflict between the two senior officers if there was any grit in the oyster of their relationship. Those faced with solving such a confrontation knew that a court was a poor solution, since neither party would emerge unscathed.

Prince William didn't know that Nelson had on his desk a letter from Schomberg detailing his own accusations against his captain: failure to keep proper logs; arbitrary misuse of his power to release rations and accusations of collusion with the purser to deny the rights of his crew; drunkenness; a wanton disregard for the safety of the ship; and a failure to heed the advice of his officers, as well as the ship's master.

The list was endless and, if Nelson recalled his visitor properly from their time spent together in the Caribbean, probably true. When serving under Lord Hood, Nelson had tried to bring on the Prince's nautical education, with little success. The boy was dogged but useless at mathematics, slipshod in his attentions to the needs of his division, an embarrassment at sword practice, and something of a boor at the dining board. In the circle of those who could speak openly to each other, it was agreed that such things mattered little. No royal prince would forsake home for life aboard a man-o'-war. This one had confounded them by pursuing a naval career, though whether the notion had been his or his father's was not known.

"Now, Nelson—"

"Captain Nelson, Your Royal Highness. Or sir, if you prefer."

Unaccustomed to being checked, Prince William managed a stuttering reply. If he blushed, which he should have done, it was not obvious on such a rotund, high-coloured face. "Yes . . . Yes. I wanted to ask you about the tour of the islands."

"Which part in particular?"

"Your suggestion that we use your ship. I'd much rather captain my own. Let my father's subjects see a prince who is not some stuffed affair, but a real man with a job to do."

That was the last thing Nelson wanted. He knew Schomberg and esteemed him as a very competent sailor, honest though somewhat dour of temperament. Added to what he had experienced of the Prince, the accusations he had made were likely to be more truthful than spiteful. Not that it mattered much; no one, least of all Captain Horatio Nelson, was going to bring charges against a member of the royal family. That would be professional suicide even for an Admiral of the Fleet. But he knew if he agreed to sail in Prince William's own ship, he might find himself in the same bind as Schomberg, forced to interfere in the running of the frigate, especially in entering and leaving the difficult West Indian harbours. That was where the Prince's lack of even the rudiments of seamanship would be most exposed.

"I fear you will find the journey exhausting enough, sir, without the need to captain a vessel as well."

"Nonsense, Nelson," Prince William replied, angering his host again with his lack of respect. Yet that turned to amusement as he wondered whether the son of His Majesty could be guilty of *lèse-majesté*. This clearly showed on his face, since his guest enquired with furrowed bow, "Something amuses you, sir?"

"I was anticipating the pleasure you'll bring to your father's subjects."

"Especially in my own ship!"

What followed was pure inspiration. "Even with Lieutenant Schomberg on board?"

"He must be removed, naturally."

"That, as you know, Prince William, is beyond my power to do. Schomberg was appointed by the First Lord. Only he can remove him."

In the weeks that followed, Nelson had constantly to remind himself that he was Christian, and that since he had claimed a kind of friendship with the Prince, it was his duty to forgive his royal passenger a great deal. His misfortune was that William of Hanover would have tested the patience of a whole bevy of saints. Inclined to boorishness when sober, he became a positive menace when inebriated, which was frequent.

On deck when Nelson wasn't present, he interfered in the way the ship was run, which cut down what little time the Captain of the *Boreas* had to himself. He was exhausting, not least in the endless gaffes he committed socially by seeking to seduce every attractive woman he met. Few were unmarried; all the unattached had fathers; princes did not apologise, so it fell to Nelson to mollify the locals this sprig of Hanover offended. He undertook his duty with a sore head, since his guest was addicted to the tavern and the whorehouse. Nelson tried to be abstemious, but that was a hard task in the company of a man determined to prove he had hollow legs, to prove that the Navy could not be bested in the article of consumption by "these damned planters."

Worse, Nelson's duty to visiting royalty threatened to keep him away from Nevis. There was a pecking order in the West Indian islands, though to persuade the inhabitants to agree to a listing would have been impossible. Jamaica was the largest British possession, the jewel of the Caribbean, which must be visited first. But what came next was at Nelson's discretion and, still unpopular over his enforcement of the Navigation Acts, he took advantage of that to push Nevis well up in the itinerary.

John Herbert was thrilled to receive a royal prince in his capacity as president of the council, and by the time they landed Prince William was aware of Nelson's attachment to his niece, which added a *frisson* of deeper excitement to the visit. And the way the Prince flattered Fanny held none of the innuendo for which Nelson had been forced to apologise on other islands. For once acting like a gentleman, Prince William absented himself so that Nelson and Fanny could spend some time together. The gardens at Montpelier were big enough to find a secluded spot where they could sit and talk, though not so cut off from view as to offend propriety.

"He seems to think highly of you, your prince."

"I flatter myself that he thinks me a friend. Indeed he has shown me the content of the letters he sends home to his father, which say so."

"Who could have a better friend than you, Captain Nelson?"

"Fanny," he replied earnestly, "you know my feelings for you."

She dropped her head slightly, in a way that he found enchanting. "I blush to recall some of the things you have written."

"All true, I do assure you. It is my heart that pens my letters."

"Who can doubt that? I fear my replies must seem dull."

Just like his reply regarding the Prince, Nelson had to sacrifice truth to the greater goal. Fanny's letters indeed lacked the depth of passion he had hoped for. In his own daily missives no image of bliss had been excluded: rose bedecked cottages and ebullient children; her on his arm as he accepted the greetings of neighbours that went with his status as a senior naval captain; the fact that he would astound the world with his exploits and that she would find herself betrothed to an admiral and a hero. Even the bliss of conjugality had been gently alluded to, in an attempt to draw her out into admitting that she too craved the physical side of marriage.

Yet for all his passion Nelson admired the sense of proper behaviour that debarred the woman he sought to marry from responding in a like manner. The desire for respectability was strong and what could do more to grant to him that status than a woman of such accomplishments as Fanny, with her French, her music, her embroidery, and her kind, gentle manners?

"Your letters, Fanny, are meat and drink to an aching heart. I own up to my emotional nature, of which you are tolerant. I confess that when we are apart I am afire with curiosity. Where are you? What are you doing? Is some other creature paying court to you in my absence? When you write, and when I receive what you have written, it calms me. I swear it is no secret to my officers and my men, all of whom wish nothing but happiness for you and me and young Josiah. They know that I am a different man after a packet of letters from Nevis. Only the reservation of your uncle stands between me, even us, and bliss."

"You must forgive him, Captain Nelson. It is not that he does not consider you worthy, it is more his concern for my happiness, for which I cannot do other than respect him."

But Nelson harboured the suspicion that Herbert thought him not good enough for his niece. As a direct descendant of an earl of Pembroke perhaps he felt the Nelson bloodline less blue. Or was it just parsimony, the knowledge that by giving permission he would have to open his purse to an unrestricted commitment?

"You do wish for us to be married?" he asked, deliberately sounding doubtful.

"With all my heart."

"Then if you can forgive your uncle, Fanny," he lied, "so can I."

Herbert, happy to receive Prince William, was less than enamoured of the abrupt way in which he departed. Nelson heard all the reasons as they weighed, none of which sounded even remotely like the truth, which was that Nevis did not enjoy much in the way of entertainment. The inhabitants were sober and industrious, and because the island was not a port for ocean-going vessels it lacked the kind of palaces of entertainment so beloved by sailors. In short, there were no whores, no riotous establishments, and few women to whom His Highness could pay court.

So, as they continued their tour, touching at the other Caribbean possessions of the King, it was back to letters to Fanny and attempts to pin down her uncle on the matter of a dowry or some future allowance. Herbert's replies deftly turned that responsibility back on Nelson, reinforcing the feeling that though Herbert had agreed to a match he was not settled as to its entire suitability. Worn down by that and his attendance on his charge, liverish in the extreme from over consumption, Nelson became so melancholy that others saw his distress.

Even the Prince noticed, and quizzed him on the state of his suit. "You are sure that this lady is the one you wish to wed?"

Nelson was thinking two things: first that it was really none of his business, and second, how like a parent Prince William sounded. He might have been the Reverend Edmund Nelson, except that he was round and red, instead of tall and saturnine.

"Because if you are, Nelson," the Prince continued, "I may have the means to effect a conclusion to this affair."

"In what way?"

There was a long pause, and much pacing to and fro designed to convey that Prince William was giving his reply careful thought. "Have you engaged anyone to stand as your best man?"

"I would have hoped for a fellow captain but, failing that, I intended to approach Ralph Millar."

"In listening to you explain the situation and, if you will forgive me from what I have gleaned in conversation with your officers, it seems to me that you require some lever to force Herbert's hand."

"He will consent to it in time."

"I am surprised, Nelson, that you did not see fit to approach me."

"You?"

"Does the thought of a prince of the blood as your guarantor depress you so?"

"I could not have presumed to make such a request."

"I can see how my position might debar you," the Prince replied portentously, "but what if I offer my services, man?"

"It's not an offer any loyal subject of the King could refuse."

That threw the King's son, who had clearly been expecting a more fulsome response. He cleared his throat. "Well the offer is there, Nelson. Take it, if you will, and convey to Mr Herbert that my duties do not allow me much time to act in that capacity. That if he wants to see you wed with me alongside he must make some haste."

When such an offer was put to him Herbert's response was swift. Fanny Nisbet and Captain Horatio Nelson could be married at the Prince's convenience. The financial matters, however, were not dealt with, so Nelson was left with the prospect of the nuptials yet no idea if he would have the means to sustain the married estate. But there was no going back. In his hearty manner Prince William had taken to the notion of a wedding so it was not only his intended bride's feelings he had to consider.

"Come along, sir," cried Prince William, as they landed on the fateful morning. He had hosted a breakfast for the ship's officers and young gentlemen, consuming a couple of bottles of claret with his beefsteak, his high colour, as well as his jolly manner, attesting to that. "I find it hard to believe you are shy, Nelson. I know you to be a warrior, sir, and there is a wench up that hill waiting to be conquered."

Horatio Nelson had never felt less the warrior, never so unsure of his aim, and the sip of wine he had taken at the Prince's bidding had not been enough to grant him any courage. It was the press of his officers, midshipmen, and friends landing behind him that pushed them forward, and once his feet were moving some of his confidence returned. The carriage ride up the hill to Montpelier, through what seemed to be the entire island population, exhilarated Nelson. They were there for the Prince, of course, not him, though they wished the bridegroom well. But it was pleasant indeed to bask in that kind of attention, to be allowed to return the cheers of the crowd with a wave that signified he was the man of the hour.

Naturally John Herbert was fussing before they arrived, darting about, pushing his plantation slaves into something resembling a line, checking that his daughter especially and the rest of the household were in place to receive royalty for an occasion of such magnitude. The clatter of the iron hoops on the roadway sent him into a near faint, the handkerchief he held wiping copious amounts of sweat off his face and absorbing that which ran from his hands.

Nelson had never known the Prince so regal. He handed the bridegroom ahead of him, ceding pride of place, a signal honour that earned a flutter of applause from those who had followed the carriage up the hill. Nelson addressed those assembled in a state that belied his inner nervousness, only relieved when he came to young Josiah. "It will be a grand day, young Josh," Nelson said. "And think on this. Standing as parent to you, I can see to it that you join me aboard ship. How does that sound, sir, a career as a sailor in the King's Navy?"

Prince William Henry, behind him, heard the last sentence, and added, "If your stepfather cannot oblige you, Master Josiah, then rest assured I shall."

There were cooling drinks and a brief sojourn in a shaded part of the garden for the Nelson party as Herbert saw to the final preparations. Nelson noted that his officers and midshipmen had raided Montpelier's flower-beds for a variety of exotic buttonholes. Hardy and Andrews had gone further, and festooned themselves so comprehensively with orchids that their captain had to order them to return to a state of respectability. They were drunk, of course, having started on the claret at the Prince's breakfast and not having stopped till they landed on Nevis, only to resume consumption as soon as they reached this shaded arbour.

Eventually all was ready, a table acting as an altar with a lectern to the side so that the clergyman could read the service. They stood facing a set of high French windows, Nelson and the Prince hemmed in by the crowd, leaving only an avenue to their rear through which the bride and her uncle could enter. The scents of hibiscus, the perfumes of the assembled crowd and the smell of their massed bodies suddenly assailed Nelson. His eyesight and perception seemed very acute, allowing him to see that much of the silk on both men and woman had suffered from being in the Caribbean, a repair here, moth-attacked lace there. Along the base of the veranda a line of ants was at work, carrying off the detritus of the bed of roses that already looked limp, so hot was the air.

As Fanny appeared he was more conscious of the trickle of sweat down the centre of his back than of her appearance, and he had to force himself to concentrate. She was veiled, in a dress of old-fashioned cut that he knew to be an heirloom, the garment in which the late Mrs Herbert had married the uncle who was giving Fanny away. Somehow the veil, which he had expected, annoyed him. He wanted to look at his bride throughout the ceremony. Prey to commonplace doubts himself, he wanted to see if she was likewise, wanted to witness her overcome them as he did.

Beside him, he picked up the faint lemon smell he recalled from their early meetings. It was strong and clean. Fanny wouldn't sweat, she was too good and refined. His doubts were replaced by the heart-warming image of presenting his bride to his king, he having astounded all of England with a great victory, Fanny already well known as a hostess whose good opinion society considered essential.

"We are gathered here today, in the sight of God . . ."

Nelson was aware that he had dreamed throughout the whole ceremony: visions of battles, cannon blazing, sails and masts torn asunder; of the return of the hero, cheers from the rigging of every ship anchored at Spithead. Or of a glorious death, with Fanny and Josiah black clad and weeping before his memorial in Westminster Abbey, placed next to that of James Wolfe. At times he was bleeding on shattered quarterdecks, at others advising a roomful of gold-braided admirals, all of whom nodded with sagacious agreement at his tactical and strategic proposals.

"Captain Nelson."

The ring seemed to make its own way to Fanny's finger, and as the clergyman pronounced them man and wife she lifted her veil to reveal damp eyes but dry cheeks, one of which he kissed, before bestowing another on her lips, and one for good measure on the back of each hand. In his ears, as though from far away, he heard the locals clap and his officers and midshipmen cheer.

Chapter Nine

1790

IT WAS EMMA'S HABIT to recall every date of significance in her life: her birthday; her first employment; the date on which Samuel Linley had died having held her hand throughout the hours in which he wasted away. There was the night she met Uppark Harry, the day she first gave way to the importunities of Charles Greville. The anniversary of her arrival in Naples, on a sunlit April day, was a time for reflection, a time to put together the advantages and drawbacks of her life. Four years on, she relived the moment of stepping into these apartments for the first time, thinking how much she and her circumstances had changed since then.

Slowly her longing for Greville had evolved into something near hatred. The letters they had exchanged grew ever more bitter, sometimes descending into bathos as Emma threatened to kill herself, to return to London and take to the streets, selling herself for a pittance, expiring in the gutter, which would tarnish him with shame for ever. When that failed to move him, she even threatened to marry his uncle and bear a child, though Greville saw through that. Even Emma had to acknowledge that he was *Sir* William Hamilton, with dukes and the like coming out through his ears when it came to relations. Quite apart from that he was the King's Ambassador.

"I sometimes wonder if I'm happy," she said to her mother.

"What brought that on?"

"Thinking of Greville, and of the changes in my life since we came here."

Mary Cadogan was sorting dresses and costumes for the forthcoming performance of Emma's *Attitudes,* the occasion to be celebrated on the date of her arrival in Naples, a day Sir William

Hamilton insisted had been one of the most significant in his life. Not that the Chevalier needed much excuse: he would throw a dozen such balls in a year, inviting several hundred people, more if the calendar of social obligation permitted it. He loved to entertain.

"What looks bleak turns out to be for the best," said Mary.

Her daughter was applying powder to her face, prior to making up her eyes, lips and rouging her cheeks. "I wish I had a gold sovereign for every time you've given me that answer. I swear you'd say it on a sinking ship."

"Said often don't make it wrong. If this ain't clover I can't tell what is."

"I got my feather bed, right enough," said Emma, more to herself than her mother, to whom she had never mentioned her visit to Lady Glynne's bedroom.

"What are you on about, girl?"

Emma just shook her head. Being mistress to Sir William Hamilton now had all the familiarity of habit. It was hard to remember a time when it hadn't been so. Only at such moments could Emma be brought to a position of deep introspection. The benefits she enjoyed far outweighed the sorrows. Half of Naples thought them husband and wife, joined in secret ceremony, though her letters from home told her that others were not fooled. In every respect, she was the lady of the house, acknowledged to be so by everyone who lived within or visited. The list of guests who'd enjoyed her company included the cream of society, aristocrats, painters, writers, thinkers; English, Scottish, Welsh, and Irish fought with French, Germans, Austrians, and the ubiquitous Italians for a moment of her attention.

She had achieved a social pinnacle that would have been denied her anywhere in England. But it wasn't the men who mattered when granting her that—they would have paid court to her for her looks alone. It was their wives. Quite apart from those she counted as close friends, the drawers of her escritoire were filled with letters from women whose station was of the highest, each one committing to paper kind sentiments and flattering references to some or several of what they considered her attributes.

Nor was she merely decorative. Her lover was besotted with her, and included her as much as he could in what he called his "toils." Every discussion with the court was reprised inside the Palazzo Sessa. Emma knew as much about affairs of state as Sir William, and was invited to comment and proffer advice, the sole caveat being that the Ambassador was allowed to ignore it if he chose. In the process she learnt a great deal about politics, not only in Naples, and her conversation, if she chose, rose well above the level of mere chat or gossip. She could now converse in French and Italian as well as in her native tongue. Gone were the days when every meeting had been a trial, where one or two words missed ruined a whole raft of talk. Now Emma could engage in an exchange of ideas, hunt down an allusion, and exercise her wit with whoever came to visit.

When Emma sighed that she was, truly, far from content, her mother said, "Strikes me you've got more'n enough to be going on with. Where does the Chevalier go that he don't take you along?"

"Court," snapped Emma.

That was a constant bone of contention. She had met both the King and the Queen informally, the latter on dozens of occasions. On their first meeting Maria Carolina had been stiff, which befitted their respective stations, but the Austrian-born queen, who surrounded herself in her private life with forty servants from Vienna, was delighted to find that Emma spoke enough German to converse with her haltingly.

Two things grew from that: Emma applied herself to learning the Teutonic tongue and the Queen relaxed the rules of protocol that debarred her from receiving Mrs Hart on unofficial occasions. Lacking colourful people in her life, as well as those who had no thought for personal advantage, the Queen warmed to Emma and the two women became companions. As their friendship deepened, a daily visit to the Palazzo Reale when in Naples, or the Royal Palace when they were in Caserta, formed part of Emma's day. There she would sit with Maria Carolina and engage in gossip, or play with and assist in the English lessons of the numerous brood of royal children.

Sir William, taking both note and advantage of this, began by entrusting messages for Maria Carolina to his young mistress, then sought her help in nudging and persuading the Queen to adopt some particular policy. Because Emma was careful never to carry to her anything too radical, or to protest too loudly in support of any plan hatched in the Palazzo Sessa or the small seaside villa at Posillipo, the attachment had grown to a point where Maria Carolina acknowledged Emma as a confidante.

That made it doubly galling not to be officially received. Every formal court function, from the daily levee to the endless state balls, masques, and entertainments, was barred to her. Emma could engage in games with royal children, sing to them, dance with them, and squeal with them. She could have them as guests at the Palazzo Sessa. But she could not be seen on the arm of Sir William on any official occasion.

"If you're still fretting on that, girl, you're soft in the head. What will be will be, the locals say, and they have the right of it. And it won't do to be miserable, especially not this night."

An anniversary party at the Palazzo Sessa, the cream of Naples in attendance; music, dancing, and an opportunity for her to do what she loved most, to perform. Yet Emma wanted more. Did she really want to be Sir William's wife? It would damn Greville, impress her mother, and she would have official recognition in society. But though she was fond of him, and much as she appreciated the attentions he paid her, it would not be something she would undertake for love.

Her elderly paramour had taught her patience. As a diplomat, especially in such a febrile posting as Naples, he insisted it was a trait required by the ton. Many times Emma had seen him receive what appeared to be terrible news and admired the way he never allowed it to prey on his mind. Equally, when requested by the court to pass on to his own government some stinging rebuke, he would pocket the missive for several days, then quietly dispose of it when the Neapolitan government, alarmed that it might have gone too far, added a conciliatory codicil.

But her patience was on the way to becoming frustration. All that held her back from the inevitable explosion was the simple truth: there were no more options to pursue and no Greville waiting in the wings to carry her back—the only thing that would bring her to break her commitment to Sir William. Was it just as her mother said, "That she always wanted to be on a coach to someplace else"? Was it fear that her lover, now approaching the age of sixty, might die and leave her in limbo? Certainly he was less sprightly, but not much so. He still walked, still climbed Vesuvius, still scrabbled away at his excavations. But there were her looks, which would fade as she aged.

"Aged?" Mary Cadogan said, her voice full of reassurance. "Name of God, child, you're not yet thirty."

"I don't know why I tell you what I'm thinking. All you ever do is tell me to rest content."

"There'll be no rest now," Mary Cadogan replied, ignoring the true import of what her daughter was saying. "There be near two hundred folk out there, as grand as you like, all waiting for you, Emma Hart."

The shouts from the assembled guests were enough to banish Emma's earlier melancholy. Using no more than a pair of shawls and a Greek shield, the pose she struck was immediately recognisable, to an audience with a classical turn of mind, as Andromache mourning the death of Hector. Candles combined with cleverly placed mirrors ensured that light and shade added to the effect. Her mother used a thick black curtain at each change of scene, servants moving lights and mirrors, this accompanied by a clash of cymbals as the curtain was pulled back. Emma had rearranged her clothes to appear in another guise, that of the bronze statue of a dancer, recently excavated from the ruins of Herculaneum. The transformation was so swift and accurate that it drew forth gasps of amazement and a round of applause.

Behind her lay the Bay of Naples, moonlight playing on the water, with the occasional scudding cloud adding a dramatic backdrop to her pose. A trio of musicians played suitable airs, a dirge for Aphrodite, a minuet for the bronze dancer, something light-hearted and gay when she became the Comic Muse.

Abandoning her shawls, and with the use of a staff, Emma changed her attitude to that of the Goddess Circe, daughter of the Sun. A sorceress, she was leaning forward, arm outstretched, her garment low cut and tantalising to lure Odysseus, sailing home from the sack of Troy, on to the rocks of her island.

Emma loved to perform, to enthrall her audience with these *Attitudes*, and in fact this was an extension of her personality: every move she made in company had a tinge of theatricality. She had rehearsed every gesture, every facial expression, many times in her mirror glass. She had an interior and an exterior disposition, the latter a critical eye that judged each act, each phrase and each movement against the aspirations she worked so hard to perfect. That watchful spirit was most active in performance. She could pose in any one of fifty guises, sing in four languages and loved to dance: sometimes stately gavottes, at other times, in the right company, the wild peasant *saltarella* of southern Italy.

She performed other *Attitudes* and executed dances more pagan in origin, embodying notions that Sir William had brought back from his excavations. Since these included the exposure of a great degree of flesh they were reserved for his eyes only. Much of his virtu—lewd vases, cups, and statuary—carried graphic images. In addition Sir William had copies of frescos and drawings from the walls of the ruined houses of Pompeii, all of which Emma was invited to emulate.

Some of that art could not be reproduced, not even by her talent, so scandalous was the nature of the images portrayed. Humans in every kind of sexual congress; women with one man or several; old men with young boys; representations of Sapphic poses, painted lovingly before being sealed by disaster, to survive the passage of near eighteen hundred years thanks to the harsh hot ash of Vesuvius.

Sir William enjoyed these as much as he delighted in Emma's private performances. Early on in their relationship he had openly confessed to being a lover of licentiousness, even to being a great masturbator. He had not only his art, but books as well. Without Latin, Emma could not read them but she barely needed to given that he was only too eager to act as her muse, sure she gained as much gratification as he did from the retelling of these obscene stories.

Sir William Hamilton had grown up in a world in which the acquisition of sexual accomplishments was as much a requirement of his position in society as his undoubtedly polished manners. He had had a dozen mistresses before his marriage, and several after, and when young had been no stranger to the better class of bagnio. Courteous, kind, sometimes fatherly, behind his bedroom door he revelled in vulgarity. The carefully modulated manner, the pose of the diplomat deserted him, to be replaced by a mode of speech that owed much to the whorehouse. A loud fart would reduce him to uncontrollable giggles, and he was even more amused if he was not the perpetrator. Everything he had learnt from experience and his reading he passed on to Emma, happy to find himself attached to a companion who loved ribaldry and physicality as much as he did.

Quite prepared to acknowledge his age and the constraints it placed on his abilities, Sir William more than made up for his waning sexual powers with the sheer variety of his endeavours. He saw innovation as a challenge, and the presence of an uninhibited creature like Emma Hart as a licence to push back the boundaries of his own skills, and to lift to increasing heights the pleasures she should enjoy in his company.

And he continued to fill the house with visitors, determined that either during the daylight hours, or when the sun had faded, Emma should never feel any hankering to return to London.

Mary Cadogan observed them with a judicious eye, keeping her place, never presuming, notching up each point at which the relationship progressed, where it stumbled. She was always there to reassure Emma that what she had now was better than what she had left behind. She had a clear idea of what went on behind the closed door of the bedchamber. No man can keep a secret from his servants, least of all his valet, so Sir William's tastes were well known below stairs.

Only Emma knew the depth of her frustration, only her mother knew it existed. If Sir William guessed she was not unreservedly happy, then he had the good sense to keep it to himself.

Chapter Ten

A DOZEN CHARACTERS LATER Emma rejoined the party to partake of supper, more music, and cards, accepting the compliments thrown in her direction. General Acton was there, the elderly Englishman who was minister to King Ferdinand, but was even closer to the Queen. She engaged pleasantries with the German poet and diplomat Goethe, who would amuse Emma by rustling up a flattering couplet in four languages with consummate ease. The Duchess of Argyll, her good friend, had her usual place by the door. Angelica Kaufmann, the most celebrated artist in Naples, had painted her several times already, yet was still sketching in the background.

There were half a dozen wealthy rakes on the last part of their Grand Tour, all of whom, during the evening, would seek to seduce Emma away from her older lover. They would not succeed, however handsome or well connected. This pleased Sir William mightily: although rumours abounded about his Emma, she showed him nothing but fidelity.

Sir William swore that this endless caravanserai fatigued him and kept him away from his five true loves: Emma Hart, the sea bathing villa at Posillipo, the hot lava flows of Vesuvius, his archaeological digging, and the English garden he had crafted for King Ferdinand and Queen Maria Carolina at Caserta.

While Emma flatly refused to go near it in winter, Sir William's hunting "cottage" provided an oasis of peace in the summer. The air there was clear and cool compared to that of the city, the smell of flowers and cut grass so much more pleasant than the rank odour of the open sewers that ran through the alleyways of Naples into the bay. The draughts that came through the gaps in the doors and windows were welcome, and with the mountains so close, and a great cascade coming straight off the glaciers, chilled water was always available to drink, or to dab on a heated brow.

Even if he wasn't much given to lifting spade or hoe, Sir William sweated as he ordered his gardeners about. They weeded and clipped, trying to keep alive plants accustomed to cooler climes and to check those that would run riot in the sunshine. Even though he spoke the language his minions took pleasure in misunderstanding every word he said to them and it was the frustration of that which brought on the perspiration. Disinclined to interfere, Emma wandered off to find a shady spot where she could sit with sketchbook and charcoal and entertain herself by drawing Vesuvius, smoking away in the distance. A liveried attendant fell in behind her, so that should she require anything, he would be on hand to fetch it.

Sir William had worked hard for over twenty years on his garden and much of it was now mature, small copses and flower-beds, bushes and hedgerows, cut by winding paths. It was a place of peace, a gift to the court of Ferdinand and Maria Carolina, a sanctuary to ease the burdens of statehood. It was pleasant to proceed slowly, to gaze upon the carefully arranged beds, then kneel to sniff the pungent scents that rose from a disturbed flower.

"Buon giorno, Signorina."

The voice made her stand up abruptly. It came from within the small grove of trees, was a deep *basso profundo,* suited to the man who emerged, blinking like some wild animal suddenly exposed to the light. The King of Naples was tall, dark-skinned, and a trifle unkempt, with food stains on his black coat. The hair, jet black and unbrushed, was sticking out in a dozen different directions from under his hat and in his blood-streaked hand he carried two dead rabbits.

Emma was unsure how to react. Incognito, Ferdinand had attended many a ball at the Palazzo Sessa, had watched her perform her *Attitudes* with alarming concentration. In complimenting her on her singing, he had even gone so far as to say that she sang like a king. This, she found out later, was a reference to his known love of his own voice, and in his mind was the highest compliment he could pay her.

The disguise was slight, but respected as far as possible by all those present. Even as a known glutton he never stayed to consume any food or drink, which underlined the fact that he had come to see her. Should she recognise him now, a man who plainly sought to avoid that at other times?

"Signore." That made him grin, and Emma had the relief of knowing she'd chosen the right course. "Do I perceive that you have been hunting?" she asked in Italian.

"I'm still hunting," he replied.

"Is the garden not too cultivated for hunting?"

"There is sport all round for he who's determined enough to pursue it."

It wasn't hard to get the drift of these exchanges. The King was known to lack education, but Emma knew from Sir William that when it came to pursuit of the ladies he was as direct as any hot-blood in Naples. A man who grew tongue tied and bored over affairs of state had great clarity of speech, and no subtlety whatsoever, when it came to fornication. Judging by the bulge in his breeches, which he was making no attempt to hide, that was his aim now. But knowing what he was after did not supply the answer as to how she should react. How do you say no to a king?

"I have admired you often, Signorina Hart," he said.

A maidenly hand went to her mouth, to indicate surprise as well as to cover the incipient smile that threatened to break on her lips. "You know my name?"

"Everybody in my kingdom does," he replied gruffly, completely demolishing the pretence that followed with a look of confusion. Emma curtsied, not the full depth due to a monarch, but certainly enough for a gallant prepared to flatter her.

"I've seen you make magic with just a shawl. There's not a man in the room does not yearn to see what is under so flimsy a garment. I want to see."

"It would scarce do for me to reveal what it is in public, Signore."

"Then let's go somewhere private." He jerked his thumb over his head. "These bushes will do."

"I was in search of some shade, sir," Emma said, thinking, but that bush is not what I had in mind.

"Shade?" he demanded.

"I was heading for the bower at the end of the lane."

"Then I shall join you."

Emma advanced down the path, hearing behind her a whispered exchange, which obliged her to stop and peer. She saw the servant palm a coin, which denoted a bargain struck. But she was on her way again before Ferdinand looked round, forcing His Neapolitan Majesty to scurry so that he could catch up. The bower was close, and within a minute they were under an overgrowing wisteria. Emma sat down without asking, which caused the King a split second of annoyance. Then he joined her, occupying the other end of a rough-hewn bench, his eyes boring into hers. Unable to return that look, Emma laid her parasol across the bench as a not very effective defensive barrier.

She might be sitting opposite a well-known ignoramus who loved to play the buffoon, but he was also a ruler of the most absolute kind and accustomed to getting his own way. Emma sought to find a method by which she could deflect his attentions, without insulting his person.

"Since you know who I am, Signore, you must also know that I have a present attachment."

"I know the gentleman well," he replied, edging closer, his hand on the parasol. "We are good friends, close enough that he would gift me anything I asked for."

"You may say that, Signore. I cannot be sure it is true."

"You are a woman so that makes little difference."

"To you." Emma laid a firm hand on her parasol, to keep it in place. "That gentleman is my protector, on whom I depend for everything."

"What is wrong with me?" he demanded.

"Nothing, Signore," she lied.

"I disgust you, perhaps?"

The truth, that she did not find him attractive, would not serve. But Emma was convinced that, whatever his rank, she was not about to succumb to such a clumsy attempt at seduction. To call it uncouth was by a long mile an understatement. It was positively insulting. The King was treating like a street whore the mistress of the British Ambassador.

"You say that the gentleman who is my protector would agree?"

"He will."

Like a conjuror performing a trick, the sketchpad was open and the thin stick of charcoal offered. "Then write to him. If he is such a friend and he agrees, then I do not risk my position."

Ferdinand looked confused, so Emma continued. "I cannot chance my present comfort, and that of my aged mother, on a whim of desire, Signore. The prospect of what you propose is not unpleasant, but sense informs me I must have permission to accept."

"When?"

"I walk in this garden often and so I think do you."

Ferdinand grabbed the pad and wrote quickly in large, untidy, childish letters. His scrawl, when she looked at it, was hard but not impossible to read. He had written to Sir William without the use of either name, identifying himself as a hunting partner who had, on more than one occasion, given him the kill of a stag. By the time she finished reading the King was gone. All she saw was his broad, retreating back, and two dead rabbits.

The question is this. What do I say to Sir William? Do I mention it at all? And what will he say if I do? Surely he would never suggest that I submit!

The questions multiplied the more Emma gnawed on the problem. A dinner with forty guests, and the social obligations that entailed, did little to ease her disquiet. At worst her keeper would accede to the King's request. At best that equable temper of his would explode. Rare as it was, she had seen it happen, usually when some visitor from home rudely demanded of him a service he was not obliged to provide.

Should she let her mother see it first? She was far more experienced, after all. But Emma was reluctant to do that, wishing for once to act on her own behalf. There was difficulty here but also, perhaps, advantage. This train of thought was interrupted continually by her requirement as the hostess of the evening, and it was the respect shown to her in that role which gave her an indication as to how to proceed.

"You cannot deny that my position is irregular?"

Sir William was reading one of his favourite authors, the Marquis de Sade. He didn't want to look up from the story of innocence corrupted to where Emma was sitting, poking at her teeth with a sharpened piece of hazelwood. There was a slight flash of annoyance as well, because his mistress clearly didn't quite comprehend that at his age he required a degree of stimulation prior to their lovemaking. He would have been doubly annoyed if he had known that Emma was deliberately interrupting him when she knew he needed to concentrate.

"I am at mercy of any number of male vanities."

Justine was at the mercy of two callous monks, which to Sir William was much more important.

"Because I am attached to you in such an irregular fashion every lecher feels he has the right to try his luck."

"I have always thought you liked the attention," Sir William replied, his train of thought broken.

"I sometimes wonder, Sir William, if it is you who derives pleasure from that—the knowledge that while many may make the attempt, none succeed. Perhaps I am the victim of your vanity."

"You are fractious tonight, my dear."

Emma turned round to look into his bright eyes, at the lined face, the nose and the jawbones made more prominent by the passage of time. She composed her own features to convey a dissatisfaction to which he was unaccustomed. In three years Sir William could count on one hand the number of times that his mistress had argued with him. Greville's prediction that she was a sweet and willing bedfellow had been more than borne out. His further observation that Emma had a temper, which would break out occasionally, had not. More importantly, having acceded to the present situation, he had never once heard her complain vocally of her lot. She was too beautiful ever to look shrewish, but those green eyes could convey hurt with little effort.

"Something has happened to bring on this mood."

"Yes."

"Am I to be told what it is, or am I merely to be a gull to the consequences?"

"What is your true opinion of those men who leer over me?"

Sir William smiled. "I admire their taste, my dear, while at the same time pitying their prospects."

"What if I found such approaches offensive?"

"Then, my dear, I would be obliged to demand that those making them desist. But never having observed that and, I may say, trusting your own wit to take what care is required, I have never felt the slightest inclination towards even an ounce of jealousy."

For the second time that day the sketchbook was conjured up. "Then I beg you to look at this."

It was with some reluctance that Sir William put aside de Sade to reach for Emma's sketchbook. Slowly he read the scrawl that requested of him, as a hunting friend, that he surrender his mistress.

"Ferdinand?"

"No less."

"He pressed his attentions upon you?" Emma nodded, and Sir William smiled. "It is not unusual for the King to behave so. Every woman in the court, from noblewoman to skivvy, has had his hand on her arse. You will have observed, if you did not know already, that his behaviour is that of a child."

"If you had seen the stretch on his breeches you wouldn't say that," Emma protested. "'Tis a wonder they didn't rip."

"He is near permanently erect," Sir William replied wistfully. "The only thing that quietens his ardour is hunting, though a kill can often bring forth an unbidden emission."

"Am I to be a kill?"

"From your tone, my dear, I observe the prospect does not entice you."

"He smells to high heaven, and though I may not know I can guess that his attentions would be swift and selfish."

"In that you are likely correct."

"And am I allowed to observe that you are not taking the matter seriously? He will chance upon me again. What am I to do?"

"You must leave it to me, my dear, for it is a matter with which I know how to deal. And you must disrobe so that I gaze upon that which the King will see only in his imaginings."

Emma obliged, as Sir William reached for his book, still open at the page. Then, intermittently raising his eyes to look at her naked body, he began to read aloud the de Sade story of the debauching of the young Justine.

Chapter Eleven

SIR WILLIAM HAMILTON was no booby, even if that was a face he often sought to present to the world. He knew that Emma and his nephew still exchanged letters, suspected that, vitriolic to begin with, they had probably settled down to mere correspondence. While he had never known the depth of Emma's written spat with his nephew, he could certainly guess at some of the contents: if Greville kept insisting that matrimony with Emma would be a disaster, then that had been a subject raised in their letters. That she never mentioned such a desire did not in any way diminish the notion that it was an estate she sought, either for the sake of permanence or to spite her ex-lover.

He had pondered on it often, weighing the pros and cons, aware that he would need royal assent from his own sovereign, let alone the nod from the Court of the Two Sicilies. Resignation would remove that requirement, but that was something he was loath to contemplate, even if his duties fatigued him. He loved Naples, the foothills of Vesuvius, and the diggings that such a natural monster had provided.

There was also his desire to do the right thing. Though he felt fit and well, he could not ignore the difference in their age. Unless Providence dealt Emma a cruel blow, she would outlive him by many years, and without the protection of his name might descend into the hellish pit of poverty. Having already assigned his estates to Charles Greville he had little else to bequeath her. Yet much as he pondered on this, he always shied away from conclusion, reasoning that another day, another week, or another month would make little difference. Ferdinand's behaviour altered that, forced him to concentrate, and also presented a solution to a man who had a brain.

• • •

"The matter is delicate, Your Majesty, since it concerns your husband, the King."

If ever any person lacked a majestic quality in the physical dimension, it was Queen Maria Carolina. She was a small, plump woman, inclined to wear drab costumes. Her face was plain and her eyes dull. She seemed permanently weary, hardly surprising since she had been brought to bed with child seventeen times since her marriage to Ferdinand. Other cares assailed her, as the true ruler of the kingdom, the day-to-day running of which would tax ten men. Events in France bore down on her, as they did on her brother, the Austrian Emperor.

"It is 'ard, Chevalier 'Amilton, to put together those two words, 'husband' and 'delicate.'"

"I think you know how much I esteem His Majesty."

She nodded at the diplomatic remark, aware that the Chevalier liked her husband, going well beyond that required of him in the matter of time spent in the King's company. He was unfailingly polite to her, as well, though she wished she could see the true face he must present when out hunting, for rumour had it that Sir William was a committed killer of game.

"I must pass this to you."

Maria Carolina took Emma's sketchpad, already open, and read it, not once, but twice. Sir William Hamilton watched her face, noting the slight movements: a diminution of the cheeks, the thinning of the lips, the way the heavy eyebrows stretched a fraction. He knew she wouldn't be shocked: Maria Carolina and her husband were a tolerant pair. It was rumoured she had an attachment to General John Acton, though since he was said to be a pederast, too, that was open to question.

"This was written about Miss 'Art?"

"It was."

"You do not approve?"

Sir William executed the tiniest of bows. "It hardly falls to me, when dealing with a king, to entertain such a notion as approval."

The Queen smiled: Sir William had found a neat way of deflecting her question while providing an answer. "Poor Emma."

"Indeed. It gives me no pleasure to admit that it is not an attachment she favours."

"It is not one I favour, Chevalier 'Amilton. I allow his bestial attentions because it is my duty to do so."

Sir William wisely chose to ignore that outburst, uncharacteristic in a woman who normally kept the unpleasant side of her marriage to herself.

"I have the problem of her very public attachment to me. I love His Majesty, and would under most circumstances seek to oblige him. But no gentleman could consent to another cuckolding him with his mistress. Aside from that, I'm aware of the passions to which His Majesty is prone, therefore I've come to the only person who could intercede without causing offence."

"The best method I 'ave found is to distract him."

Sir William Hamilton had encountered some such distractions and been subject to the odd pang of jealousy. Maria Carolina, or the agent she employed on her behalf, had an unsurpassed eye for beauty, of which there was no shortage in the area of Naples. Young peasant girls, with clear olive skin and figures just on the wrong side of being wholly formed, were the Queen's only method of contraception, the only way she could get enough peace to recover from her endless *accouchements*. Ferdinand was happy with a young and luscious bedmate while the girl chosen was happy with a financial reward that gave her the price of a good husband.

It is often the case, in conversation, that the import of a remark only dawns on the recipient after several more exchanges have passed. As Sir William and the Queen discussed how to deflect her husband, he could almost see on that square, unattractive face the notion, the seed of which he had planted, form in her mind.

"You said, Chevalier 'Amilton, that no man could consent to 'anding over possession of his mistress."

"I would find that impossible."

"We both know other men who would not."

"With respect, Your Majesty, I am not other men."

Maria Carolina gave a wry smile. "It would be curious to know how you would react if my dear companion Emma was your wife."

"A man and his wife are different, Your Majesty. Having formed a bond and had it sanctified by holy matrimony, each party enjoys the right to seek pleasure, within the bounds of discretion, where they may."

She was nodding slowly, since her visitor was only stating the obvious. Marriages in the upper layers of society were rarely made for love, but for financial or dynastic reasons. It was not unknown for a woman to leave the bed of her lover, attend church for her nuptials, see out the celebrations and return to her lover, presuming that her new spouse was doing the same.

There was genuine admiration for Maria Carolina, and not only from Sir William Hamilton. The diplomatic community praised her for her sagacity, were at one in naming her the true daughter of the formidable Empress Maria Theresa of Austria. Unlike her sister the Queen of France, Marie Antoinette, who was held to be frivolous, Maria Carolina had a brain, good deductive powers and the ability to take advice. It was such a pity, the same diplomats concluded, that she had to exercise her gifts on such a poor patrimony, and on such a husband.

"You are saying that, were Miss 'Art your wife, His Majesty's attentions would not offend you?"

"Let us say that I would leave it to my wedded wife to make up her own mind as to whether they offended her."

"But you take leave to doubt such a suit would be pressed to the wife of the British Ambassador?"

"Knowing the King as I do, and cognisant of the source from which he receives his advice, I am sure he would see that if such attentions were unwelcome, the interest of the State would ensure that they be discontinued."

She put her fingers to her lips, hands almost in an attitude of prayer, a slight smile hidden, just as were her thoughts. But it took no great powers of deduction to guess at their train.

"Would you wish to marry Miss 'Art?"

"The notion would not displease, Your Majesty, given the pleasure it would afford her. I believe you are aware of how attached I am to the lady."

"I, too, am attached to 'er, Chevalier 'Amilton. She is a presence that brightens my day and my younger children adore 'er."

"Might I say, Your Majesty, that she has, in private, nothing but praise for you, both as a companion and as a monarch."

"It had always caused me much pain not to be able to receive 'er. It is bad that at a time when one often needs a friend to add colour to a dull occasion, a person like Miss 'Art is debarred from attendance."

"Again I would tell you that it grieves her also, though she would bear that and much more to maintain her attachment to you."

"Then marry 'er, Chevalier 'Amilton, and make two women happy."

"Alas," Sir William replied, throwing up his hands, "my position forbids it."

"You require the consent of your king?"

"I do," Sir William replied, his face bland at what was the crux of the problem.

Maria Carolina nodded slowly, engaging in a long pause, as if seeking a way out of an intractable problem—instead of immediately suggesting the solution that had occurred to her when she had sent the conversation in this direction.

"What would His Majesty King George say if you were able to tell him that a refusal to you would offend the Two Sicilies?" That got a raised eyebrow. "What if you were to say to your sovereign that Miss 'Art is a friend to the Queen, a confidante she seeks to 'ave by 'er side as and when she chooses? What would the King of England say when 'e is told that my little princes cry to be told that the Emma they love cannot be with them?"

It took some effort to quell the beating of his heart. "I cannot answer for my master. But I know in my dealing with both kings and queens, that they can rarely be brought to refuse a request from a person of equal rank."

"Chevalier 'Amilton," she said, in grave voice, quite at odds with the beaming face, "I require you, for the sake of the peace of mind of the Queen of Naples, and for the cementing of good relations between the Court of St James and the Court of the Two Sicilies, to marry Miss 'Art."

It took all Sir William Hamilton's skill as a diplomat to keep the triumphant note out of his voice. "And the request to my sovereign?"

"The request to King George, Chevalier 'Amilton, that this should be so, will come from me. Might I suggest that it is one that you, in all duty, should deliver."

The faint tinkling of the harpsichord, and Emma's sweet voice coming through an open window, greeted Sir William on his return. He made for his own apartments first. There, with great care and the assistance of his valet, he repaired his toilet and changed his clothes. He donned a cerise watered-silk coat that he knew Emma was very fond of, ordered that some flowers be formed into a bunch and, once that was in his hand, made for Emma's part of the palazzo.

Below stairs they were abuzz with curiosity at this unusual behaviour, and sensed that something was in the air. Mary Cadogan, with a firmness they had come to expect, made sure that not one of them tried to sneak upstairs. Whatever Sir William had in mind was to be carried out without disturbance.

Emma didn't hear him enter, concentrating on playing the harpsichord part of a Haydn concerto. That allowed Sir William to examine her, which he had done a thousand times these last few years. Dressed for the climate in garments of light material, he could see her breasts moving as she swayed across the keyboard. Her hair moved too, its ends close enough to the sunlight coming through the window to flash red at one second, then burnished gold the next.

Carefully, his silver-buckled shoes making no sound, he approached her back, admiring the way the tendons and bones flexed and moved as she played. Emma must have turned because she sensed him; he was sure she hadn't heard. But turn she did, swiftly, gracefully, her green eyes lighting up with pleasure as she saw him.

"Sir William?"

"My dear Emma."

"Flowers. Is there some occasion that I have missed?"

"No, my dear. But there is, I am happy to say, one that you may anticipate."

The frown of curiosity on such a flawless complexion was delicious, creasing her forehead slightly, moving those full red lips together without ruining their shape. The frown deepened as Sir William went down on one knee and placed the posy he was carrying in her open hand. Then he took the other and lifted it to his lips, holding on to it when he had kissed her hand.

"My dear Emma. You have been companion to me now for near five years, and I am certain my life has been improved by the association. It is my fond hope that the same truth holds for you. With that in mind, and knowing that it is something you desire to come to pass, I have come here, and gone on to one knee in time-honoured fashion, in order to ask you to be my wife."

The green eyes opened wide with shock. "Wife?"

"You would make me the happiest man on earth if you merely said yes."

"Wife?"

Chapter Twelve

1791

"CHARLES, I swear to you, Emma couldn't say anything but 'wife' for several minutes. She kept repeating that one word."

"How amusing," said Charles Greville, though both his tone and the sour look on his pale serious face belied his words.

They were in a coach, heading back from Windsor. Sir William had used his right as a returning ambassador not only to report to his sovereign regarding his Neapolitan mission but to pass over the request from Maria Carolina that King George's Minister Plenipotentiary regularise his position *vis-à-vis* her good friend and *confidante,* Emma Hart. Greville, returning from his family home in Warwickshire, had met him at the royal castle.

"She agreed to a wedding in the end?"

"Most assuredly." Sir William could recall the scene now. Emma had flown around the room in a torrent of excitement, before acceding to his request that she help him back to his feet. Emma had obliged, showered him with kisses, rushed to tell her mother, embraced all the servants, who seemed just as ecstatic, then rushed back up the stairs to embrace him again.

There was pleasure here, too, in almost guying his nephew. Charles Greville should know he had nothing to fear in the matter of his inheritance, yet he was piqued by his uncle's intentions. It was as though he still considered Emma his own; was annoyed that the man he had put in as a surrogate had usurped his prerogative. Now, for the first time in five years, he was on his way to meet her.

"The King was gracious?" Greville asked.

"My old foster-brother George has no knowledge of grace. He sees directness as a quality. It is a good thing that I represent him abroad and not the other way round. We'd be forever at war."

"Any hint of madness?"

"None, unless you count that damned habit he has of saying 'what, what' all the time. He was always a bit of an odd fish, even as a child."

He had been a damned unhappy fish earlier, King George, searching for a way to refuse his ambassador permission to marry. Throughout a deeply uncomfortable interview Sir William had searched in vain for a sign of the child and young man he had known. Whatever his oddities, George had possessed a degree of humorous vulgarity. In the rollicking life they had led as young men he had always been to the fore when it came to causing mayhem. George loved women, married, single, betrothed; high-born, low-born, and anywhere in between. He drank like a fish, sang loudly, badly and frequently, teased any watchman whose path he crossed, and flew in the face of authority. He had also, as a prince, set up house and fathered a bastard by a commoner.

Now he was Farmer George, father of the nation, model husband with a dog of a wife who had raised dullness to a performing art. He preached marital fidelity as if he had never bedded the wife of another man, bore down on his sons in the article of low-born mistresses for behaving exactly as he had himself, and had hummed and hawed to his old friend like the worst kind of pious hypocrite. Sir William, angry at the hypocrisy, had enjoyed his discomfort: the letter from Maria Carolina had made it impossible for him to refuse. He hadn't quite squirmed, but it was a close run thing.

"Brown's Hotel," said Greville, indicating that they had arrived at the place where Sir William and his intended bride had taken rooms.

It was with an attitude of studied calm that Greville ascended the stairs to their suite. It would be a curious reunion, which Emma had known she would have to face, and which she had signally failed to mention on the journey from Naples. Opening the door, Sir William was surprised to see Mrs Cadogan. But that made sense:

Emma must be nervous that by some inadvertent act she would destroy a prospect of the happiness she had come to London to set in stone.

With that air of theatricality that never deserted her, she had taken station by the bow window. The light was nothing like as flattering as that of Naples: indeed, there was scarce any sun to speak of, even on this, a late-spring day. But what there was played across and flattered her features. Emma had dressed carefully too, in a dark blue dress that hinted at sobriety. Yet she had also taken care that it did not hide her magnificent figure, so that Charles Greville should be sure that the creature he had abandoned was even lovelier now.

Sir William had to admire her poise. The slow turn, the look towards him to receive a nod that told her of the King's consent. Then an even slower smile, followed by an advance across the room, both hands outstretched. Emma was every inch the lady.

"Charles."

"Emma," he replied, bending to kiss one of those hands.

This was a moment of truth for Emma, the point at which she would know her feelings. Would there be that *frisson* running through her hand and her arm? She knew she was being watched by her future husband, knew that Charles, if only for the sake of his pride, would be looking for a response. She felt nothing, just the touch of dry flesh on her moist skin. The breath that she had held, in fear of finding the love she had once harboured for Greville still there, was released. Greville saw it and the disappointment was plain in his eyes.

"I arranged to meet Charles at Windsor, my dear," said Sir William, "so that I could fetch him back to see you."

A slight untruth. Greville had suggested meeting at Windsor, taking advantage of the interview to bring himself before royalty. His excuse was that gossip of the worst kind regarding Emma had flowed to the King's ears from every malicious voice in London. If necessary he wanted to be on hand to refute it.

"Then I thank you for that, Sir William," said Emma, voice slightly over-modulated to show Greville she was truly now a lady.

"Your nephew and I have much to catch up on. Letters can never do as much justice to events as conversation. Mother, would you oblige me by ordering for us some tea?"

Sir William was content. The prospect of this meeting had caused him some concern. He disliked the notion of committing himself to Emma without being sure that her previous regard for his nephew had cooled. His concentration, at that moment of contact, had been total: he had seen her response and it had pleased him. But more than that he had observed how stiff Greville had become, like a man rebuffed. He could now leave them alone with an easy mind. And the way she had said "your nephew" was like a deliberate blow aimed to wound Charles's pride.

To take Emma out into society carried many risks, but they had to be borne. Some people, Sir William knew, would slight her without ever allowing themselves the chance to test defamation against experience. Others, ogres to his mind, would come to peer, but with a set view that would not alter whatever Emma did. Yet, even in stuffy London, so different from pleasure-loving Naples, there were those who would receive both the Chevalier and his intended bride and make them welcome.

Sir William Beckford, author of *Vathek* and a famous pederast with a reputation to put Emma's to shame, accommodated them at Fonthill, eagerly discussing the plans for his new house to be built as a seal at the end of his ten-year self-imposed exile. Bath, home to the fashionable world in August, was split. Sir William's old friend the Dowager Countess Spencer fled to Longleat to avoid a meeting; her daughter, Georgiana, Duchess of Devonshire, welcomed the pair with open arms.

Emma sat once more for old Romney, feeling different from the chattel who had been painted so many times before. Now she was there in her own right, as a future ambassadorial bride, posing for pictures that would not be sold off for her keep. It seemed that every artist in London wished to capture her likeness, though time allowed her to accede only to a youngster called Thomas Lawrence.

This came at the behest of his patron Lord Abercorn, Sir William's cousin, who had agreed to stand witness for her, this in a family that was scandalised in the main by the match.

There were parties at the Richmond home of the Marquis of Queensberry, where Emma performed *opera buffa* songs that enchanted all present, one fellow so much that he offered her two thousand pounds to appear in a pair of concerts. That was something to make an old friend laugh when they went to Drury Lane. Jane Powell, Emma's fellow housemaid, was now a famous actress, ever grateful to that rat Gil Tooley, who had engineered her and Emma's dismissal from the Budd household, for forcing her into the profession.

Mary Cadogan went north, first to Hawarden to see her mother and settle some money on the family, then to see Little Emma. She was able to report on her return that the child, now supported by Sir William, was well, that her education progressed at a goodly pace, and that she had no idea that the lady she was talking to was a relation. "Better to let her grow up in ignorance," was the grandmotherly conclusion.

The temptation to send a note to Arlington Street, to Kathleen Kelly, was to be avoided. Besides, she was a woman with her ear to the ground. She would know that Emma Hart was back in London on the arm of a Knight of the Bath. Perhaps, on the day of the wedding at St Marylebone Church, she would be outside to see Emma.

The sun shone as if by command, giving a golden tinge to the stone of the church. Crowds had gathered to watch the nuptials, the usual mob drawn to any hint of scandal, but leavened with more than just the curious. Some members of society might not be able to bring themselves to attend, but they were determined to see a woman famous now, all over Europe, as a beauty.

There was gentle applause mixed with ribald good wishes for Sir William, dressed in cream silk, the sash and brilliant star of his knightly order very prominent. Strangers watched for infirmity, but saw only the sprightly gait of a fit and healthy man, and a face that could only be described as patrician. A hush fell as Emma's carriage approached, open-topped, with the bride in a pale green dress of fine silk, set off by a dark green sash around her waist, both designed to show her fair unblemished skin and highlight her huge green eyes. On her head she wore a high hat of the same colour as the sash, held in place by a silk scarf and topped by a huge curled feather, both of a hue to match the dress. Her rich auburn hair, so beloved of every man she had known, she wore loose and long, the whole ensemble bringing forth from the crowd a spontaneous ripple of acclaim.

From inside the small church they could hear the music and the singing, not a choir, nor a doleful church melody, but musicians hired by Sir William to lend an air of gaiety to the proceedings with light, quick airs from Austrian and Italian composers. She stepped down from the carriage on the arm of Lord Abercorn, and went into the dim interior of the porch.

Few had attended the ceremony, at Sir William's request, and he stood at the end of the short aisle facing Emma, erect, looking proud as she walked slowly towards him, nodding to those present. Greville was facing her, his eyes searching her face, perhaps in the hope of seeing doubt. After a brief glance at him, Emma looked away and produced a dazzling smile aimed at his uncle.

Would Greville see it for what it was—performance? From her earliest days Emma had dreamed of marrying a prince. Sir William wasn't that, but he had a palazzo, he lived in the grand manner and she rode in carriages as fine as any nobleman could muster, and all worshipped at her feet. But she had also dreamed of an all-encompassing love, a depth of passion so profound that her heart would burst at the thought of union. But as she reflected on the life she had led so far, which was different from those childhood dreams, Emma knew that she was lucky. To ask for perfection at a moment like this seemed the height of selfishness.

Sir William bowed to her before turning to face the cleric, who stood ready to carry out the ceremony. As he spoke the words of the service she could hear the soft crying of her mother in the front pew. As a woman who had done much to engineer this moment tears seemed an odd response. Did she wish for better too?

Her future husband's skin felt as dry as parchment as he took her hand to put on the ring. She noticed a slight tremble as he aimed it at her outstretched finger and wondered what doubts he too harboured at this, the final moment, as he bent to kiss her hand.

"I now pronounce you man and wife."

"Lady Hamilton," said Sir William softly.

The musicians, silent throughout the ceremony, burst into a joyous *rondo* of harpsichord, violas, and French horns, and all present applauded as the couple turned to them. At Sir William's bidding, he bowed and she curtsied, before they turned to enter the vestry, there to sign and solemnise their marriage. What doubts Emma had were now gone. Those words Sir William had used chased her demons away. She was now the lawful wedded wife of the Ambassador and Minister Plenipotentiary to the Court of the Two Sicilies.

She was Lady Hamilton.

Sir William, preparing to return to Naples, sent to tell King George of his intentions. That was, by custom, another occasion on which an ambassador was obliged to meet the monarch, also an occasion, if he was married, to present his wife at court. The reply came back from Windsor, couched in terms of no politeness whatsoever, that neither the King nor the Queen recognised Emma as his wife; that while he was welcome to attend and receive his instructions, on no account was he to be accompanied by her. Sir William had no choice but to go, but he used the occasion to tell the man with whom he had shared a nursery what he thought of such behaviour. Their meeting wasn't private, as it should have been, but held publicly at the normal weekly levee.

"I depart at the end of the week, Your Majesty."

"Time to be gone, what, what?" King George replied, with a knowing look aimed at those courtiers close enough to observe and hear the exchange. "I daresay you yearn for the warmer climate of Naples. They allow for things there that would not pass elsewhere."

"We shall stop in Paris, Sire."

Farmer George shook his head. It wasn't a happy prospect for a reigning monarch to look on, the events taking place in the French capital: King Louis and Queen Marie Antoinette had been dragged from Versailles to be kept in the Palace of the Tuileries and denied the freedom to move. Mobs gathered in the *faubourgs* and orators on street corners incited the mob to violence. Would the contagion spread to Farmer George's own realm? "Bad business there, Sir William, what, what?"

That raised a murmur of assent from the eavesdroppers.

"But interesting, Sire."

The bulging Hanoverian eyes bulged a little more. "Interesting?"

"Of course, Sire. It will be instructive to observe how a king goes about his duties when his subjects are in a position to command his behaviour."

Sir William bowed, turned on his heel, and left the audience chamber, which was buzzing with his carefully honed insult.

Emma thought they looked a sad pair, King Louis and Queen Marie Antoinette, as they made their way through the gardens of the Tuileries to attend mass, an absolute precursor of their holding court, a sign of their continued belief that the office they occupied came from God, not man. The nation, or at least the National Assembly, didn't agree, and was just days away from the ceremony that would inaugurate a new constitution.

Louis seemed vague, bereft of that regal air so necessary to command a nation like France. Dress like monarchs they might, but for both himself and his Austrian wife the appearance of their office had deserted them along with their power. After the mass, King Louis's conversation with Sir William and Lady Hamilton was perfunctory. His wife, however, knowing that Emma was a confidante of her sister, was eager for their company.

Observing Marie Antoinette as she talked, Emma could see a family likeness to Maria Carolina in her face, but that was where it ended. The French Queen was taller than her sister, a more willowy creature, had clearly been a beauty, and those physical traits seemed replicated in her behaviour. The eyes betrayed a weak, distracted personality, her conversation was floating and inconsequential, odd given her circumstances. The assurance that the prayers of Naples were with her and her family lifted her spirits somewhat, and she pressed on Emma a letter for delivery to Maria Carolina. The Hamiltons were also presented to her children, who showed punctilious behaviour in the way they greeted these visitors from England. Emma remarked after they left that the Dauphin was "quite the little man."

"More so than his father, I hazard," said Sir William. "If ever I saw a fellow defeated, then it is Louis."

Two days later, Emma and Sir William made their way to the Champs Élysées on foot, all carriages having been banned from the city, to witness the celebrations of the new, constitutional France. A balloon, in the red, white, and blue of the new tricolour, was sent up to a huge clamour of emotion; strangers kissed and embraced as they toasted each other and freedom.

But it was not all bliss. Making their way back to their residence, after a wearying day, the Hamiltons came across a mob surging through the streets, grubby individuals, shoeless, trouserless, wild-eyed creatures egged on by fiery demagogues. When the rabble stopped to listen to the orators, Emma heard threats of death uttered that chilled her blood, threats not just against royalty and aristocrats, but against all men of property, including the most rapacious landowner of them all, the Church.

The scenes of riot continued into the night and Emma watched from the safety of her window. Clutching in her hand the letter from Marie Antoinette to her sister in Naples, she felt more sympathy for King Louis than that evinced by her husband: she had seen in the faces below her and in those they had observed on the way home that he truly had something to fear.

Taking possession of the letter turned out to have been easier than delivering it. The King and Queen of Naples were at Caserta when the Hamiltons returned to the Palazzo Sessa, which occasioned a short stay, a hasty repacking, before they were once more in the coach on the way to the royal country palace. Sir William, as a returning ambassador, had a duty to present his credential, and the more pleasant task of finally presenting Emma at court. Powdered and dressed for the occasion, it was a blow to arrive at the palace only to be informed by the Court Chamberlain that, while Sir William Hamilton was welcome, he had no instructions regarding his wife.

Left outside while others passed through to be presented, for he had refused to enter without Emma, Sir William exploded. His voice, in a mixture of Italian and undiplomatic French, echoed off the high ceiling of the anteroom leading to the audience chamber. That was as nothing to the tirade he produced as, with the levee over, the Neapolitan courtiers departed while he and Emma still waited.

Emma tried to keep a brave face. She had been traduced many times and, even after a wedding that had been the stuff of fairy-tales, still had enough sense to know that her titular elevation left her exposed. She had kept from Sir William her hurt at not being presented at Windsor, laughing it off as the behaviour of people too stuffy to engage her interest anyway. Diminished as the French royal family were, presentation at their court had salved the wound. But she had expected that here, of all places, she would be fully welcome, and that, hard as she tried not to mind, engendered some tears.

Enraged, Sir William insisted he would leave the country, not just Caserta, and court officials were sent scurrying to seek a solution. In an establishment that moved slower than a wounded snail, a hurried compromise was arranged. The King was already gone, gun in hand to shoot any poor bird that flew over his head, but Maria Carolina agreed to return to the audience chamber and take her seat on the throne.

Sir William was tranquillity itself as he entered, Emma in court dress on his hand. He could feel her slight trembling as they made their way up the carpet, which was decorated with the royal coat of arms. She had practised for this a hundred times, dreamt of it a thousand. And here she was at last.

"Your Majesty, I bring you greetings from my Sovereign Lord, George, by the Grace of God King of England, Ireland, Wales, and Scotland, Lord of the Isles, Duke of Hanover." In a calm voice Sir William Hamilton reeled off the endless titles of his king. But the note changed to one of pride as he continued, "And may I, Your Majesty, present to you Lady Emma Hamilton, my wife."

Maria Carolina stood up, came down from the dais, and kissed Emma on both cheeks. "We welcome you, Lady 'Amilton, and pray that you will grace our court often."

Emma responded with a deep curtsy, her heart pounding with an excitement that far outweighed what she had felt at her wedding. Part of her dreams at least had come true.

BOOK 2

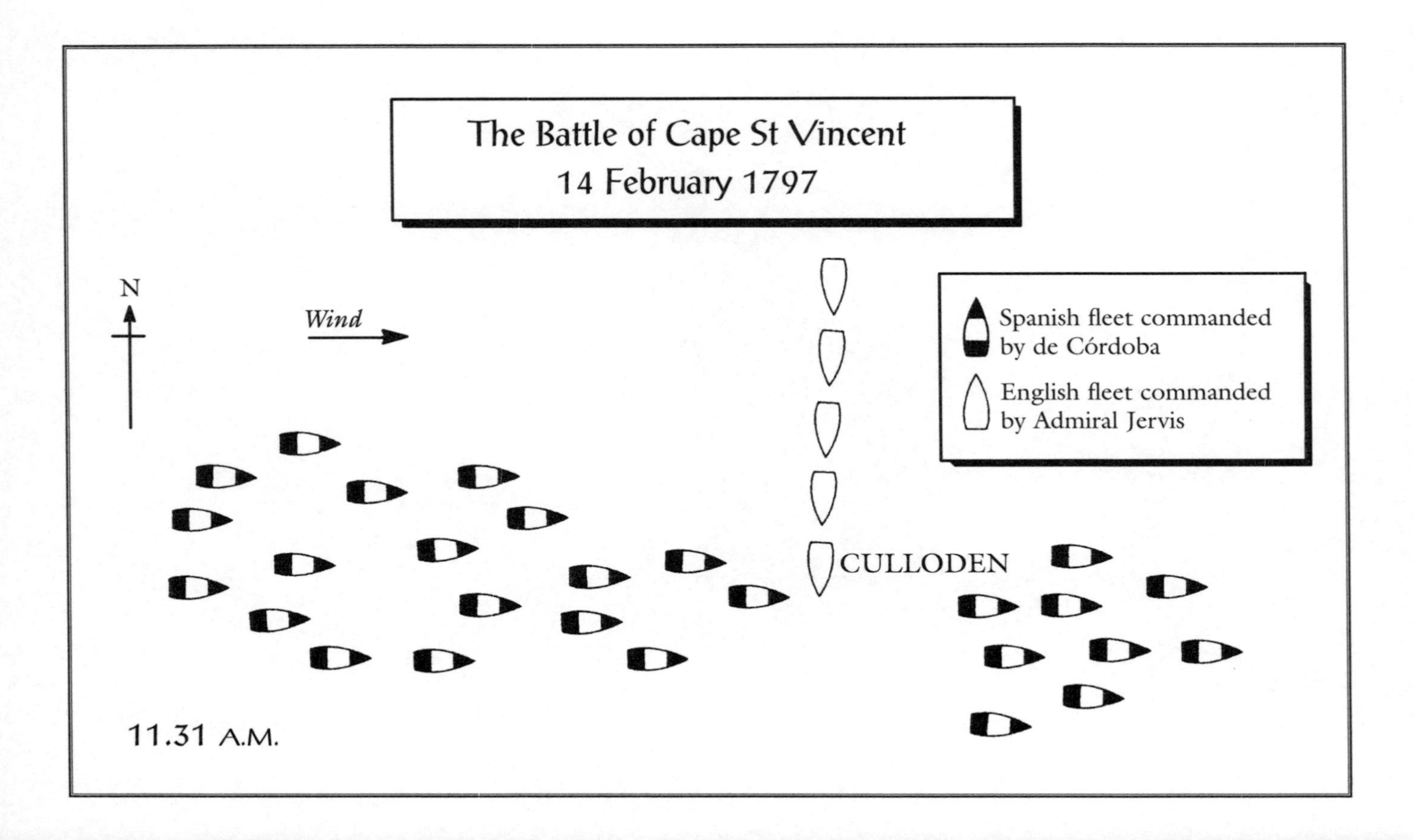
The Battle of Cape St Vincent
14 February 1797
N
Wind
Spanish fleet commanded by de Córdoba
English fleet commanded by Admiral Jervis
CULLODEN
11.31 A.M.

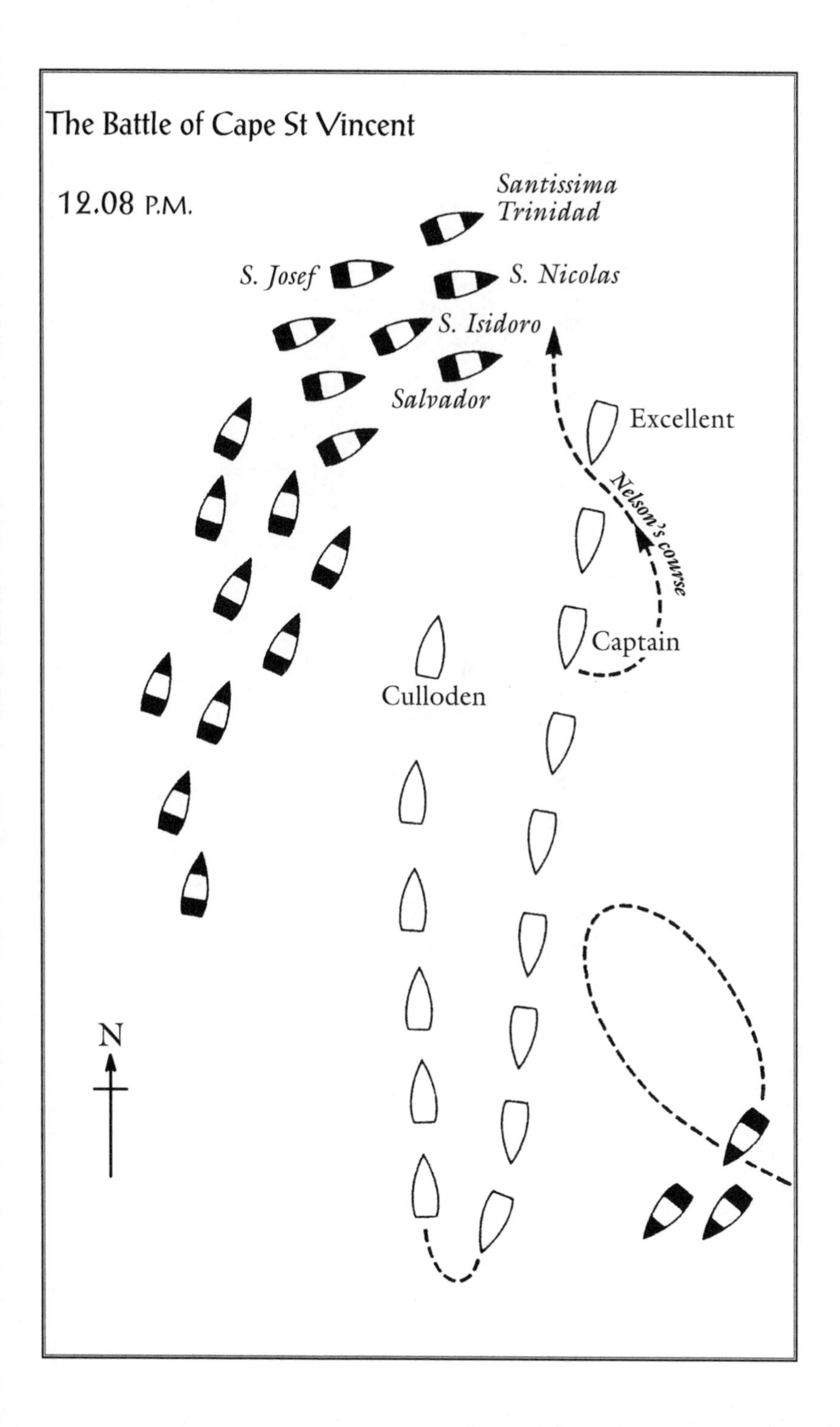
The Battle of Cape St Vincent
12.08 P.M.
Santissima Trinidad
S. Josef
S. Nicolas
S. Isidoro
Salvador
Excellent
Nelson's course
Captain
Culloden
N

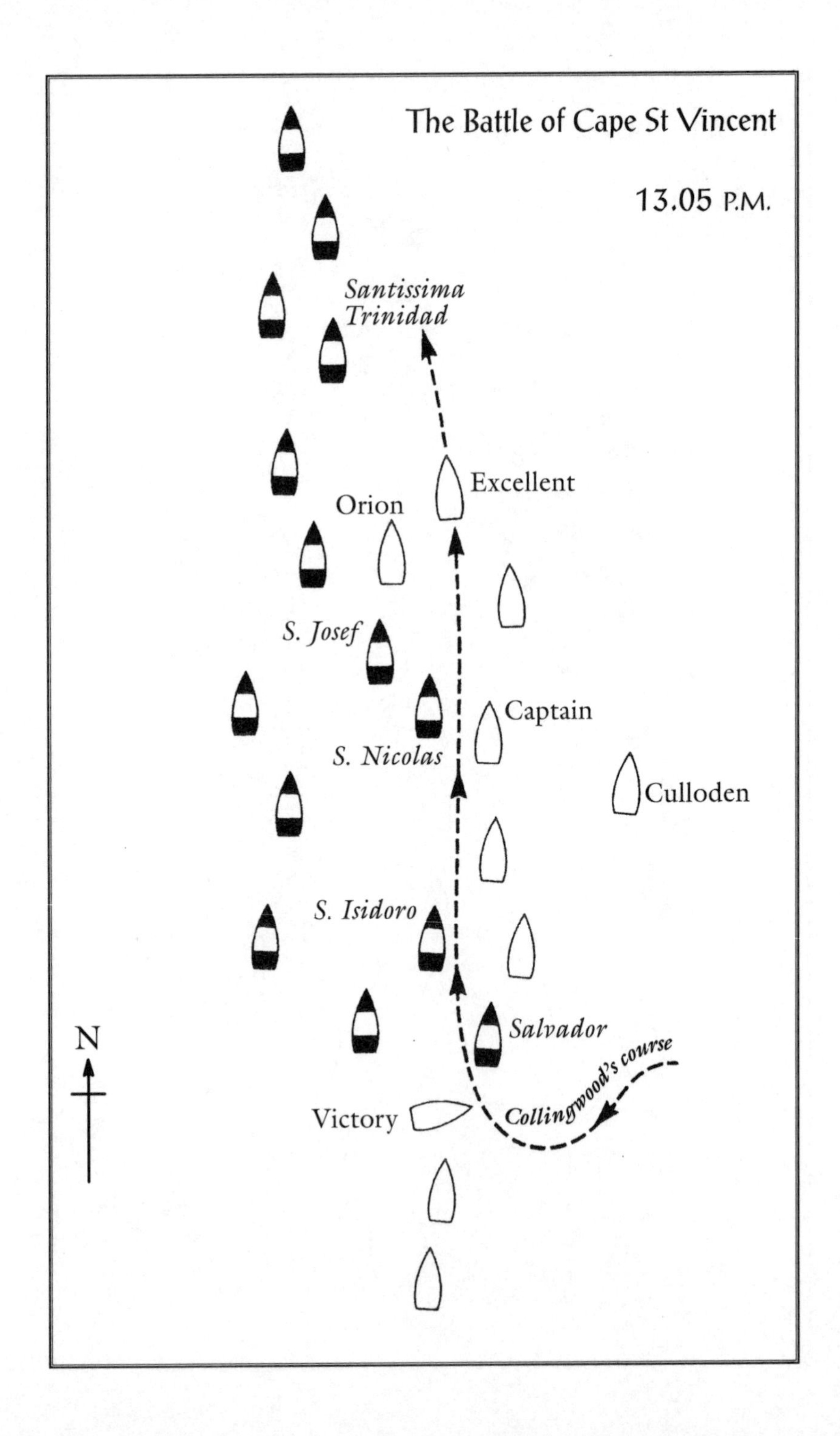

The Battle of Cape St Vincent
13.05 P.M.
Santissima Trinidad
Excellent
Orion
S. Josef
Captain
S. Nicolas
Culloden
S. Isidoro
Salvador
N
Collingwood's course
Victory

Chapter Thirteen

1793

SCRAPING THE ICE off the inside of the window-pane did little to increase the light. The sky was slate grey. Only by peering through the glass could Nelson see the stark outlines of the bare trees in the Parsonage garden, a line of gaunt sentinels that, in fanciful moments, stood like gravestones for his naval career. Halfway up the hill, All Saints Church, grey moss covered stone, stood barely defined against frosty fields. The sneeze, loud enough to penetrate the closed parlour door, reminded him that he was not alone, though it seemed like it at times.

In the grip of a Norfolk winter, it was hard to recall the sublime moment of his wedding: the hot sun, the gardens of Montpelier in the same full bloom as his bride-to-be, the grin on young Josiah's face at the melting of his worries. Prince William Henry, now created Duke of Clarence, had behaved like a *grand seigneur*, and John Herbert fussing as he deferred to a man whose social position dazzled him. Nelson frowned. Herbert would have been less enamoured if he had known the Prince's true character, had had any inkling of the merry dance he had led the bridegroom on their travels round the Caribbean both before the ceremony and afterwards.

That association had done Nelson nothing but harm, which had been made plain to him since paying off *Boreas*. In four annual visits to Windsor to attend a levee, the King hadn't chosen once to engage him in conversation. He was more inclined to scowl at the man who, according to the reports he had received from outraged husbands and dunned tavern keepers, had allowed his son to make an ass of himself and the institution he represented.

It seemed that nothing he had tried to do in the Caribbean had worked in his favour. Admiral Hughes had enough friends on the

Board of Admiralty to place a check on any career and he had not forgiven him, blackening his name at every opportunity, telling all that Nelson was a damned nuisance; that to employ him was to employ trouble. Instead of being grateful, the officials in the departments to which he had reported on the way the planters were bent on cheating the Exchequer were inclined to back up Hughes's opinion, on the grounds that Nelson had done nothing but aggravate their workload and disturb their measured, peaceful existence.

Many spoke for him, William Locker foremost among them, but Nelson knew from his own experience that one negative voice in a situation where employment was scarce could outweigh ten in favour. For some reason, Hood, the senior sea lord, who should have aided him, had turned his face away. The years had gone by: five years on half-pay when his only accomplishment had been to turn the gardens around the Parsonage from his father's untidy desert into something respectable. Five years of annual visits to his noble relation, Lord Walpole, where his wife could see in the broad acres and landscaped lakes what might have been hers had she married better.

Josiah, on his visits home from school, grew more morose and less joyful, the carefree infant rapidly turning into an adolescent irritant. Locally he had seen gawky girls turn from geese into swans, spotty boys grow to be men, and stalwart farmers and their wives shrink into their dotage. His calendar revolved around local feasts and markets, coursing for hares with his dogs, and shooting in the autumn. That was until he learnt that he was a deplorable shot; that his fellow hunters wished to steer clear of him from his habit of walking with his weapon cocked. Firing on sight, without proper aim, was no way to fill the larder.

Alarms and excursions abounded. Spanish bellicosity, revolution in France, even fleets gathered and sent to sea so that Britannia's enemies should know that she was prepared for war. Hopes had been raised that he might stand for Parliament but they, too, had faded away. The list of correspondents to whom he sent pleading letters had grown longer as time passed, but not one had been able to alter his prospects.

He breathed on the window, then traced an outline on the steamed up glass with his finger, a rough drawing of a frigate under bare poles, half a dozen strokes, one from bowsprit to sternpost, the second the deck and the poop. Three masts were added and stroke six was a wave-filled sea. He imagined her as *Boreas* with everything aloft, royals, studdingsails and kites, to see that line of waves below the hull as the deep blue they had been when he had sailed from Barbados for home. He couldn't draw the vision of happiness that had filled his mind then any more than he could understand where it had disappeared.

Those unemployed years had felt like five decades, spent in the company of a wife who had good reason to be more miserable than he. Fanny hadn't taken to England, let alone isolated and windswept Burnham Thorpe, shuddering even when the sun shone and the garden on which he had toiled so assiduously was in bloom. She hated it when it rained, which was frequent, or when the east wind froze her to the marrow even on a day when the sky was blue. Grey skies and icicles reduced her even more, so that she could barely be brought to exchange a civil word with anyone, his father when he called, her husband or the servants, especially Frank Lepée, who was often drunk and always boastful. Her blood was accustomed to the heat of the West Indies while her domestic appetites hankered for the ease and luxury of Montpelier. Often these complaints were vocal and general, but it was with her silences and her personal frigidity that she punished him.

Leaving the window and his drawing, Nelson went through to the parlour, a hurried opening and closing of the door earning him a glare from the figure hunched inside a shawl by the fire. He replaced the bolster laid to keep out the draughts, jamming it hard against the gap at the bottom of the door, then walked past his wife to poke the logs, causing them to flare up and light what he could see of the pallid face.

"I shall need to get Lepée to fetch more wood."

"Is there enough wood to fend off this chill?"

"This weather will pass, my dear."

"To what?" she snapped. "To rain, sleet, to a hint of warmth in the sun blasted to petrifaction by a North Sea gale, with you telling me of storms at sea and how you love a good blow."

The words he wanted to say died on his lips, merely because he had used them before and failed to lift her spirits. For all his desire to secure employment, Nelson could extract some pleasure even from this ice-bound existence. It certainly suited his health. The fevers and agues, which had plagued him in warmer climes, were absent here in this bracing English air. Winter was a time to hunt for game and fowl, to skate upon frozen ponds with young Josiah when he was home from school. This part of Norfolk was blessed with hills, and snow allowed for the manufacture of ice slides, as well as providing the ammunition necessary to indulge in a snowball fight. The fantastic landscape afforded by a sudden thick frost, which covered the branches of the trees and made them into hanging sculptures, delighted him.

Society came from visiting neighbours, relatives, or friends, and a day spent in Burnham Market, where he could share the newspaper in a snug coffee-house. There was a degree of frustration in reading in the *Register* of events outside the borders of the Burnham parishes; of who was received at court, who led fashion, and how his nation stood in the councils of the greater world. Commenting on the news gave him a reason to correspond with people, allowing him a justification for putting his name before them.

He often accompanied his father as he visited his parishioners, all of whom never forgot to include Captain Nelson in their prayers. He would listen as the Rector ministered to their souls, seeing the other side of his parent's doleful nature, the part that could encourage and uplift. Edmund Nelson's sermons, delivered from his trio of pulpits, were stolid rather than inspiring, but they were designed to ease troubled souls, and to remind his flock of the dangers inherent in a lack of scrupulous observance to the teaching of their God.

It was pleasant to stop outside the church and talk to these people; to remember that, but for fate, he might have ended up a farmer himself, obsessed with flukes of wind that presaged a storm, watchful of birds as they migrated and returned, caring for livestock that suffered danger from pestilence, weather, and hunting animals.

And he studied and wrote about the lives of the lowest in the land, the farm labourers. It was no secret that the King was interested in the state in which they, his least blessed subjects, existed. Nelson could report that their lives were close to miserable, that what they ate would not and could not sustain them, and that recourse to the alehouse, their only relief, did naught but beggar them further. These reports were not sent directly to the King, but to Prince William, Duke of Clarence, for onward transmission to his father, as a way of alerting both to his continued existence. He longed to say more since the lives of these wretches depressed him. But tact was required, so the unpleasant truth had to be made palatable. At least he could openly tell their sovereign that they were loyal, that the sedition spreading from France had little influence in the hovels or alehouses of Norfolk.

He relished the feeling of frozen cheeks warmed by a welcoming interior and a blazing fire. The taste of spiced wine, mulled with a red-hot poker, was twice as pleasant outdoors than in. The sight of robins pecking the berries, hard because of deep frosts, could keep him still till his marrow froze. The moment when the weather broke, and the first green shoots of spring emerged through the morning mists, was a perfect joy, making him feel close to his Maker. Activity kept Nelson warm by day, and should have by night, but the lady he had married, in concealing certain things, had hidden most her fear of ardent desire.

Consummation, his wedding night, even after five years, was fresh in the memory, being so swift and dull, almost an agony to Fanny who had made it plain that, while her husband was entitled to his due, it was not to be freely and frequently offered. Nelson lacked the heart to press, to insist, nor was he good at signalling desire, either merely corporeal or his wish to father children, to which out of duty Fanny might have responded. The merest hint of disinclination drove him away. He wanted warmth offered freely, not cold charity, so that aspect of his marriage had now faded to nothing.

"Post on the way," shouted Lepée, who managed to make the passing on of such mundane information seem like an imposition.

"Post my dear," said Nelson, searching his pockets for the means to pay, glad to suppress the disloyal thoughts he had been harbouring.

"Another letter of regret, no doubt, husband." Her voice took on an arch, shrewish tone, meant to convey the heartless tone of officialdom. "'Their Lordships regret to inform Captain Nelson that they cannot oblige him in the matter of a ship. We are sure Captain Nelson will appreciate that there are many deserving officers and a want of opportunities, with the country at peace, to employ them.'"

"We mustn't lose hope, Fanny."

Her voice was weary, her head sinking even deeper into the shawl than hitherto. "Your anticipation fatigues me so, husband. How many letters must you have before you see the truth? How many wasted trips to London and fruitless interviews can that sanguine nature of yours contend with?"

"I can't lose expectation, Fanny. It is all I have to sustain me."

"Half pay is what sustains us both, and in a degree of cold and misery I never thought to experience."

"These are the worst months, January and February. It will soon be spring."

"With you throwing open windows as if what comes through passes for warmth."

"The postman," Nelson said, to avoid having to answer.

Muffled against the wind, the post messenger slithered up the slippery path, between the empty flower-beds, past the white frosted lawn and the frozen pond. His hardest task seemed to consist of keeping his feet on the uneven paving, reminding his recipient that repairing it had been a task he had promised for last summer, but had failed to fulfil.

"Post for thee, your honour," the voice said from under layers of scarves.

Nelson took it, examining the seal, his hope evaporating as he saw that it was not from any official source. There was no crown impressed into the red wax, nor anchors to denote the Admiralty. He paid the fellow his sixpence, bade him God speed, and hurried back indoors. He had to heat his hands by the fire before he could begin to open the letter.

"It's from Davidson, my dear."

"If he offers you a merchant vessel, you must take it."

Nelson declined to reply to that. It was a long-running marital sore, the notion that he should take employment in a merchant ship and at least afford himself the chance of earning a decent stipend. Behind the insistence was the notion that Fanny would benefit too, perhaps to sail in his ship to some warmer shore or, failing that, being able to move to a less isolated spot, perhaps even to a house that might be said to be comfortable. He knew he could not oblige. It was one of the catch-all tenets of naval service: if you wanted advancement you must be available, even if there was scant employment. Taking service on a merchant deck meant no longer being on the active list. His naval career would be as good as over.

"Matters with France do not improve. Davidson maintains that despite the best efforts of the opposition war cannot long be avoided."

"I recall he said the same last year and the year before that, when those *canailles* carried their king to Paris. Now they try him like a common criminal and what do we do? It was ever thus. Those cowards and placemen in Whitehall will do nothing."

"How can you say that after last year's alarm?"

"You would do yourself a kindness not to mention that!"

He might not mention the Spanish Armament, but he thought often of that brief period when his hopes soared with the news of two English ships seized by the Spaniards off Vancouver Island, the crews confined in Mexico. The revolutionary government in France made ready fourteen sail-of-the-line, war was in the air and employment with it. High hopes had been raised, only to be dashed when the Spanish, once the proudest nation on earth, meekly caved in to all Britannia's demands.

"Things have moved on, Fanny. This time it is France. Their king I feel sorry for. But what is more important is that the revolutionaries have gone to war with their neighbours and they are beating them soundly. Britain cannot stand aside and see Europe engulfed."

"Why do you talk to me so, Nelson?" she whined. "Like some Westminster candidate trawling for votes. I cannot abide it."

His reply was designed to mollify her. "I merely seek to advise you, my dear, that matters move our way. War will see the fleet expanded, and I flatter myself that my character is such that they will never refuse me employment."

"They have managed to do so for five years."

"Davidson suggests it would be wise to be in London, that a call on Lord Chatham might serve best."

"Then I hope he has enclosed the coach fare, for if he has not you must needs spend a week out in that wilderness shooting enough food to fill the larder."

He smiled. "I am reliably informed that I'd more likely shoot myself."

Nelson bent down, pulling at the shawl enough to reveal the red end of Fanny's nose. He recalled those pale cheeks in sunshine, where they had been fetching. Now they were pinched and chapped, the lips that had smiled so sweetly likewise. "Are there no words I can say that will bring you cheer?"

A mittened hand emerged to take hold of his. The voice ceased to whine, and instead seemed crestfallen. "Forgive me, husband. The cold shrivels regard as quickly as it does the skin."

"Not in my breast, Fanny."

"Do I deserve such a sentiment?"

"You always will, my dear."

"Little enough have I done to earn it."

Nelson put a hand to her cheek, his fingertips welcome, being warm from the fire. "If I repeat myself, forgive me, but I see all this as a trial from God, a test of my regard for my country. Can I let them treat me so ill and still retain the golden glow of my patriotism?"

"Can you, Nelson?"

"With you by my side, yes."

"All I do is fail you."

"I will not let you think that," he insisted. "You were raised to better things. I met you in sunshine and plenty, and have brought you to this. It is I who have failed you. But believe in my destiny as I do, Fanny. And know that there is a future day when this will be a humorous memory, a tale to tell your grandchildren that they will never understand, being surrounded as they are by everything material a man, a woman, or a child could desire."

She dropped her head to kiss his fingers. "If God rewards a forgiving nature he will surely reward you."

"He has done that already, Fanny, by bringing you to my side."

"Go to London, Horatio. See Chatham, if you can, though don't ask me to hold out much hope, given the way he has abused your requests these last five years. I have seen his letters, don't forget, and read the sentiments that can only be described as cold rejection."

Chatham had never mentioned the King, and neither had he to his wife. He was in bad odour at court, and while the Sovereign had no veto over naval appointments it would be a brave First Lord of the Admiralty who would gainsay his wishes. Lord Chatham seemed far from that. The trouble was that such an attitude denied him the chance to redress the low opinion in which he was held. An annual levee, which was his right as a post captain to attend, did nothing to thaw relations. No chattering king now, instead a mumbled "How d'ye do?" from a cold and distant monarch.

"And," she continued, "I cannot fathom how you can even begin to tolerate the name of Admiral Hood, who does not even deign to reply when you write to him."

Hood had wounded Nelson by his indifference, but he had his

own problems with royalty. "Do not castigate a good man damned by politics," he said.

"Is there anyone you will not absolve?"

"My God would scarcely forgive me if I did not. And I know how deeply my father would chastise me for that sin. I think now, if we pray hard enough, God may answer our submissions."

"The Rector's on his way," shouted Lepée, "looking as cold as charity too."

Nelson stuck the poker in the fire, trying not to think of Frank Lepée, who could scarce be brought to lift a finger to undertake duties he saw as domestic. Five years on the beach had not tamed the sailor in him, just as it hadn't tamed his love of drink, his ability to relate a tall tale, or his less than respectful relations with his master.

"I will fetch my father a posset to heat his bones, and add some brandy to it."

Fanny smiled, though not much, since to do so fully hurt her lips. "You'd best not tell him, husband."

"No. He would see it as a waste of a gift from God."

She clasped his hand. "I'm sorry, husband. I promise, when the sun comes out from behind those infernal clouds, to be a better wife to you."

"I cannot, my dear, see how that is possible." He stood up as the Rector entered, his tall frame shivering with cold. "Good news, Papa. Davidson has written to me to tell me there must be a war."

"With France?"

"Who else?"

"Then God be praised," said Edmund Nelson, raising the Bible in his gloved hand to point at heaven. "The Antichrist will at last be slain."

The sentiment and the way it was expressed made his son shiver.

He had no sooner arrived at Davidson's lodging than he was whipped off to a grand dinner at Hanover Square, home of the Duke of Grafton. Davidson had sent them a note to say he was bringing

Nelson along. The welcome he was afforded did not extend to seating him close to his friend. Indeed, he was so far below the salt that he could barely see the carroty top of Davidson's head. The huge room was noisy with the buzz of a hundred conversations, and introductions were so garbled that he was unsure of the identity of his dining companions.

Nelson was seated between two women, both in their middle years. A fat fellow called Padborne, to whom Davidson had introduced him, sat opposite, so enamoured of gluttony that, once the soup was served, his head hardly lifted from the plate laid before him. When he did look up, his eyes, set deep in folds of flesh, cast a jaundiced eye at other portions, as if he were intent on consuming those too.

"Please, sir," Nelson said, having taken just a few sips, "my appetite is small. If you feel that you can manage it, have what I cannot eat."

That earned him a loud sniff of disapproval from his left. The suggestion had come from five years in Norfolk, five years of care in the avoidance of waste. Nelson had forgotten where he was. Wearing his most pleasant smile, he turned to mollify the offended lady with an appropriate excuse. "Short commons are such a regular feature of naval life, madam, that waste in any form is anathema. Why, if I had any midshipmen here they'd sweep the board like a biblical plague."

"Who would invite a midshipman to an occasion like this, sir?"

"You would be surprised," he replied, still smiling, though curious as to where he had seen her before. "Some of the mites are well connected."

"Obliged, sir," said his fat dining companion, who clearly had no more manners than Nelson. He looked at his naval dining companion quizzically.

Nelson reminded him of his name, and added, "Davidson introduced us."

"Nelson?" said the same lady. "Are you any relation to the Reverend Edmund?"

"Yes, madam. He's my father."

"Then we have met before, sir," she trilled, "in the Pump Room at Bath. I scarce recognise you, sir. You were a skeleton when I last clapped eyes on you, with your dear father, who was quite fatigued by the care he administered. Did I not tell you, Padborne, about that naval officer at death's door after that foolish expedition on the San Juan river?"

The fat head lifted from Nelson's plate for a second. "I cannot recall it, Mrs Padborne."

"His mind extends no further than his last meal, sir," she confided, in a voice that could be heard ten feet away. "Your recovery is remarkable, sir. I take it the Bath waters provided an efficacious contribution."

"That and Norfolk, where I now reside with my wife."

"You were not married on our first meeting. You made a good match, I trust?"

He bridled at the question, but fought to keep his temper at this woman's impertinence. "An excellent one."

He had to look her right in the eye then, because in the sense that Mrs Padborne meant it his marriage had been far from a good one. Herbert had been parsimonious indeed when it came to granting any money to the newlyweds. Talk of a substantial legacy had been just that. Herbert had passed away and only a small bequest had materialised from his estate.

"A woman of means, then?" Nelson was just about to slap her down, to tell her that Fanny had few means, yet was blessed with a good heart, but he didn't get the chance. "The Rector is still with us, I trust?"

"In such rude good health that it puts mine to shame."

"Would I know the lady who is now your wife?"

"Do you have connections in the sugar islands?"

"Never in life, sir." She waved a fan at her fat-faced husband, head still in his soup plate. "Padborne there would speculate in that pit of thieves if I was not there to stop him, sir. But, by God's good grace, I am."

"I was about to add that my wife is the niece of the late president of Nevis, who was himself grandson to the Duke of Pembroke."

"An excellent connection, sir," she replied with insufferable arrogance. "I'm sure you have made a proper match."

There was a snap in his voice when he responded: "I did not wed the lady for either her dowry or her bloodline. I married her for herself."

That earned him another sharp wave of the fan. "How singular, sir."

"I married her," Nelson insisted, "because I esteem both her person and her accomplishments. I must tell you that there is no finer companion for a man's heart than my dear wife. I cannot praise her enough. She is kind, good-natured in the matter of my manifest faults, a rock upon which my house can withstand whichever storm fate throws to test us."

He carried on, all the time knowing in his own mind he was lying because, in truth, Fanny had been a sad disappointment to him. He tried to suppress his train of thought, but it would not go away. Where was the warm anticipation he had anticipated at Montpelier; where were the children he had written of in his Caribbean letters? His longing for physical contact had been broken on the granite of her coldness. What satisfaction was there in sex without even a pretence at emotion; what point if the prospect of procreation was greeted with horror?

"It was a great shock to me, Davidson," he confided later, when they were back in front of his friend's hearth, "as deep as any I have ever experienced. The sudden knowledge of my own unhappiness."

Davidson leant forward to tap him on the thigh. "You will have a ship soon. That will lift your spirits."

"I don't love her, Davidson," he said, pulling himself from his chair to lean on the mantel, his voice choked with emotion. "And when I look backwards I cannot be sure I ever did."

Davidson put his arm around Nelson's shoulders. "You need sleep, my dear friend."

"I feel I've been asleep for five years."

He was just that when Davidson entered his bedroom, to stand and look over a man he admired more than anyone in the world. Certainly Nelson could be trying when he spoke of the follies of other naval officers or the certainty of his own destiny, but though he was full of confidence, he was a mass of inner tribulations—in his relations with his officers and men, his standing *vis à vis* his superiors, and most of all in anything to do with the heart.

In repose, his hair tousled, his face relaxed, those full lips slightly open, Nelson looked so young, still like a boy at thirty-five. He would find out tomorrow what Davidson already knew but was sworn not to reveal. That Nelson would have his ship and the gloom under which he laboured now would be lifted.

Chapter Fourteen

THE NEXT MORNING Nelson arrived at the Admiralty still a half-pay captain. He departed after an interview with Lord Chatham as the commander of HMS *Agamemnon,* a 64-gun ship-of-the-line. Had the First Lord discerned his reasons for turning down a larger ship? Nelson knew that *Agamemnon* was faster than most 74s by several knots, the kind of vessel likely to be sent on detached service rather than tied to purely fleet duties, a ship in which he could individually distinguish himself. She was berthed at the Nore, but there was much to do before he could journey to Sheerness to join her. The next two weeks were all activity as he fired off and replied to endless letters.

Lepée was detached from his celebratory bottle and sent back to Burnham Thorpe, Fanny requested to keep him sober and oversee the way that his servant packed Nelson's sea chest. He added a detailed list of what it should contain. Josiah had to be alerted to join his stepfather as a midshipman aboard his new command. Another letter went off to his brother-in-law, George Bolton, to tell him that if he still wanted his boy, George Junior, to be a sailor, then the time had arrived for him to take up his duties.

Using Davidson's credit he could gather the personal stores necessary to stock his own larder with the wines and combustibles he would need to maintain his station among his peers. He had officers to alert, to take up their duties, from Edward Berry, who would be his premier, to his fourth lieutenant, the faithful Bromwich, made up at last and sent to Norfolk to recruit men around his own locality, using the Nelson name. The parents and relatives of a stream of midshipmen were another group with whom he had to correspond, some to accept, many more to turn away. William Hoste, the son of the Reverend Mr Hoste of Inglethorpe, in Norfolk, he would gladly accept since he knew the boy, and thought his shyness and reserve would disappear once he was serving in a mess. But Mrs Darby's son Henry, despite a connection to his Walpole relations at Wolterton, was, he regretted to say, too young.

There was a stream of missives to the warrant officers, boatswain, gunner, carpenter, armourer, and purser, to report to the premier the state of the ship and stores. When it came to crew, sailors had a communication system that seemed to defy time and distance. They knew before the King's ministers that war was certain, knew before the Admiralty secretaries which captain had been appointed to which vessel. Anyone who had served on a man-o'-war wanted the familiar face at the helm, the face of a man they knew they could trust. Nelson hoped he could look forward to seeing a host of old acquaintances.

He would still be short-handed, even with his strong Norfolk contingent, but at the start of a war that would be made up easily from volunteers. On arrival at Sheerness he put up at the Three Tuns, known to all serving officers as the worst inn in the world. William Locker, who commanded at the Nore, joined him for dinner, as hearty as ever and remarkably well informed, eager to advise Nelson to plump for the Mediterranean fleet, since Hood would command there and not the Channel.

"Forget his cold behaviour, Nelson. Hood was frightened to upset the King, who blames you for his son's failures in the West Indies. He might be devious but Hood esteems you as an enterprising officer. The Channel goes to Admiral Lord Howe. He has his own list of deserving captains whom he will favour, and you ain't among them. And there's more chance of independent action away from the home shore for a ship-of-the-line, a chance perhaps to distinguish yourself."

Locker didn't know he was preaching to the converted. Nelson wanted nothing more than to get away from the shores of England. He was still confused about many things, especially his relationship with Fanny. He felt he needed to be at sea, surrounded by familiar sights, sounds, and faces, to put the last five years of inactivity into some kind of perspective. He couldn't wait to get away to sort out his life.

When the time came to go aboard George Andrews was at the quayside, just as he had been when Nelson took command of *Boreas*. There was no hesitation in Andrews now, a young man of nearly twenty years and *Agamemnon*'s third lieutenant. His orders were crisp and loud, and Giddings, who had arrived to take up his previous station without any form of communication from his captain, carried them out in his usual competent fashion.

"How fare you, Mr Andrews?" asked Nelson, looking up at the young man whose fair hair and blue eyes could still conjure up a disturbing image of the sister who had once been the single object of his captain's affections.

"Very well, sir, very well indeed. All the better for being in your ship."

The sight of his first ship-of-the-line lying at anchor, rising and falling on the slight swell, lifted his heart. *Agamemnon* displaced thirteen hundred tons, carried a crew of five hundred and twenty men and sixty-four main- and lower-deck cannon. Built at Buckler's Hard in 1781, she was as handsome a vessel as he had ever clapped eyes on. The deck was certainly prepared, with every sign of the mess created by a vessel taking on stores hidden for the new commander's eye. Berry knew just what to clear away and what could be let pass. Captain Nelson was not the man to go prying for faults below decks or on the companionways as soon as he came aboard. He would settle for what he could see between the entry port and his cabin door, between the great cabin and the poop where he would read out his commission. And what he saw pleased him.

Then he set to work, to get ready for sea and, Nelson hoped, glory.

HMS Victory, *off Toulon, 1st September 1793.*
To Captain Horatio Nelson, HMS Agamemnon.

Sir,

You are required with the vessel under your command to proceed with all despatch to Naples, there through the good offices of the British Minister Plenipotentiary to press upon the Court of the Two Sicilies the need for troops to hold and protect that which we have gained on the French mainland.

Enclosed is a letter from myself to King Ferdinand, which I require you to deliver personally into his hand.

I am yours,
Admiral Lord Hood

"Are you familiar with the expression 'see Naples and die,' Josh?"

"I believe you did say it to me the other day, sir," his stepson replied, without much spirit. "When we first got our orders."

Midshipman Josiah Nisbet was in titular charge of the Captain's barge, though he would in all respects defer to Giddings as coxswain. Such a duty was part of his training, which after four months at sea was moving along tolerably well. He had been seasick in the Thames estuary, for which Nelson, who was prone himself, could not fault him. He attended to both his duties and his lessons, and had progressed well in all departments. Yet Nelson was concerned for the boy, who did not share with the other mids a seeming delight in their station. It was as though he had come to sea to please his stepfather, not because he himself desired it. Even the sweep of the Bay of Naples, as noble an aspect as nature had ever created, failed to move him.

The six-week voyage to the Mediterranean had done Nelson a power of good. He had spent the time in working up both crew and ship so that whenever the Admiral called for any manoeuvre it was carried out swiftly and with grace. With Berry he tinkered with each watch to balance them out in efficiency. His cannon, eighteen and twenty-four pounders, had been run in and out so frequently that Nelson knew in a fight he would get at least two broadsides a minute from his gunners, a rate of fire that no Frenchman could match. Activity, distance, and the companionship of sailors had eased his troubled mind, and allowed him to conclude that his difficulties with Fanny were more his fault than hers. A sailor, who by his very nature must hanker after the sea, must be a hard companion with whom to spend your life; a poor and frustrated one denied a ship so much worse.

Looking at Josiah, the thought did occur to Nelson that he was in such a buoyant mood that anyone else might appear glum. Since joining up with Lord Hood off Cadiz he had enjoyed an excellent rapport with the Admiral. Hood liked enterprising officers, and being back at sea had cleansed him of politicking. The kindred spirit who was prepared to stretch rules to gain a positive conclusion, the officer who talked about destroying the enemy not merely engaging them, was one that the admiral valued highly.

Hence this vital mission to Naples. The great French naval port of Toulon had surrendered to the British fleet, but Hood lacked the means to hold it against the revolutionary armies marching from Marseilles to recapture it. Nelson's mission, to him, implied that he had his admiral's trust, and it had also given *Agamemnon* the chance to snap up a prize on the way, a fully laden Levant merchant vessel, which Nelson had valued provisionally as worth at least ten thousand pounds. Three-eighths would be his share, less commission to Davidson, who was acting as his prize agent. Letters had already gone off to him and to Fanny, to tell her of the increase in their wealth.

And here in Naples he was going ashore as a man of substance, Hood's representative, to treat with a king and his ministers on behalf of his own sovereign. With his signal gun he had saluted the kingdom, and Naples had replied most handsomely. His launch was surrounded by boats of all shapes and sizes, some with fishermen, others carrying people of obvious quality come to greet a British man-o'-war.

They were not the only eyes on the barge. From one of the higher chambers of the Castel Nuovo, Maria Carolina, using a telescope on a tripod, had both launch and occupants in view. Emma Hamilton was trying to focus on the same with the naked eye, but the distance was too great. The Queen was calmer now than she had been at first light, when she had been alerted to strange topsails on the horizon. Like most of her wealthy subjects, she stood in terror of the arrival of the French who, having chopped off the head of King Louis, would bring with them the seeds of revolution and murder.

That had occasioned panic in her husband and most of her courtiers, to the point where many had a coach and four laden with their possessions ready to flee. The Queen's nerve had held firm enough to stop Ferdinand from leading a Gadarene rush to safety, which was singular given that her own sister Marie Antoinette was in grave danger of following her husband to the guillotine. There were enough elements in Naples, vocal ones these last months, who would gladly deliver her to the same fate.

As a witness to the earlier reaction of the nobility, Emma was somewhat amused at everyone's behaviour since the vessel had been positively identified as British. Inclined to boast without cause anyway, the Neapolitans she met now swaggered in a parody of bravery, and told her how they had spent the time since dawn loading guns, sharpening swords, preparing to repulse the French invader.

"Your British captain is not very imposing, Emma."

"Might I be allowed a look, Your Majesty?"

Maria Carolina stood back from the spyglass and Emma peered through, adjusting the lens to get a clearer view. She homed in on the dark blue naval coat, but could see little of the face, obscured as it was by the crowd in front. The man was not tall, but that was commonplace. Few naval officers were, it being so uncomfortable to have too much height in a ship. Emma swung instead to look at the warship in the bay, twin rows of ports open to let in air, though with no guns run out. The sails were furled now, tight against the yards, but the vessel was still a hive of activity, ant-like creatures running through the rigging and traversing the decks. The tide had turned her near bow on to the shore, showing her as broad at the base and much narrower at the level of the deck, the figurehead a proud bust, coloured gold and carmine, with the royal arms at the base. Her pennants fluttered in the breeze and the boats that had gone out to her, to sell their wares and women, stood a way off, awaiting permission to come close enough to trade.

"It is the ship that matters, Your Majesty," Emma said, as she swung the glass to the quay, fixing her gaze on her husband's back. "That, I swear, is imposing enough."

The reception committee on the public quay was numerous, led by the man Nelson must see first, the Ambassador, Sir William Hamilton, whose bearing identified him easily as an English *grand seigneur*. Nelson examined him carefully: tall, once handsome, now showing the lined face and prominent bones of his age. Nelson knew that Hamilton had been in his post for thirty years, and had become famous not only for his length of service but as a collector. There was also the matter of his marriage, which had occasioned a minor scandal, the ripples of which had reached Norfolk. The bride was thirty years his junior and a lady with a colourful past.

After weeks or months at sea, great self-control is required by a sailor to maintain his dignity when stepping ashore. Motionless dry land can easily make a man whose legs are in tune with the waves appear an idiot. Was Hamilton aware of this? Nelson didn't know, but the Ambassador aided him by grasping his hand so firmly that his natural inclination to sway was choked off. Indeed, Hamilton held him in such a strong grip that Nelson felt he was keeping him upright while they exchanged names and courtesies.

"Captain Nelson, you have no notion what it does to my spirits in these troubled times to see a British man-o'-war anchored off Naples."

Though not yet steady, Nelson had achieved some sense of balance, enough at least to carry off the rest of the introductions without support. In between the exchange of names, speaking rapidly, he brought Hamilton up to date with events: what had happened in Marseilles, which had tried to surrender to Hood only to face the Red Terror. Men, women, and children, whose only crime was gentility, had been murdered in cold blood on a guillotine set up in the main square. The citizens of Toulon, frightened by this, had surrendered their town to the British, along with the best part of the French Mediterranean fleet.

"A great coup, Captain," Sir William cried, just before he introduced the Duke of Amalfi.

"A great burden, sir," Nelson said, acknowledging the greeting of some count whose name he missed. "The Admiral lacks the means to hold Toulon. The Revolution was already on the march to retake the town when I left. We had soldiers aboard in lieu of marines, but no more than two thousand in all. Even with the loyal French and half the sailors from the fleet we cannot hold out against a determined enemy. We must have more men, and Lord Hood has sent me here to request that the Two Sicilies provide them. What prospect have I of an immediate audience with the King?"

"Every likelihood, Captain Nelson. I sent my wife to see the Queen with that request in mind. Since Her Majesty holds her in the highest esteem, I'll take the liberty of assuming acceptance and coach you directly to the palace."

Nelson was surprised, but also pleased. He had little knowledge of British plenipotentiaries abroad, but he had them tagged as a slothful crew. Sir William Hamilton was clearly cut from a different batch of cloth, able to act with despatch even before he was asked, to the point of dragging him away from a crowd eager to press his hand. He got Nelson into his carriage, at the same time issuing instructions that would see the Captain's stepson and the crew of the launch catered for in the article of food and shelter.

"I have sick men aboard, Sir William, who would benefit from being ashore. I require fresh victuals, greens, beef, and citrus fruits. My water is so brackish as to be undrinkable and I have little time for delay."

"Use the credit of my office, sir, to purchase anything you need."

"The expense will be great."

"My credit hereabouts is greater, Captain," said Sir William, without pomposity. "Longevity and a consistency of policy have seen to that."

"I thank you, sir."

"It is I who must thank you and Admiral Hood. My task in Naples is never easy, but these last months since the outbreak of war have been strewn with difficulty. I must confess that, at times, my own conviction that we would see something of a British fleet in these waters has been sorely tried."

They had to talk over the noise of cheering and the endless stream of flowers flung at them by an emotional Neapolitan mob, each man sizing up the other as an aid to those first impressions. Sir William, urbane and dignified, was struck by the seeming youth of this fellow, obviously a senior captain, as well as his application. He was in control of both his subject and his mission. While careful to be polite, Nelson nevertheless had a grasp of what he needed and how he intended to go about getting it. He spoke quickly and succinctly, describing the situation of Hood and his fleet clearly and graphically, explaining the terrain at Toulon and how he, if he were in command, would go about securing it.

"I fear you're wasted at sea, sir, given your grasp of the finer points of land warfare. For my sins I am an old soldier, so I know of what I speak."

"Never fear, Sir William, I have chosen my career well. My name was unknown to you not half an hour ago. That will not long remain the case for our fellow countrymen. Soon they all will know the name of Nelson!"

Such self-assurance would normally have made Sir William uncomfortable, but somehow the way Nelson said it, the lack of artifice and the look of conviction on his face when he did so, rendered it truthful rather than conceited. Then Nelson demonstrated that he also had good sense, in the way he listened intently to his host as Sir William gave him a brief account of Naples, its court, its politics, and the personalities who mattered.

"The Marquis de Gallo, who heads the government, is a man who feels his country is best served by doing nothing. He is the type who would neither support a friend nor oppose an enemy. He has one abiding wish, and that is to stay in his post and increase his already considerable fortune."

"Does the King trust him?"

"It matters not one jot if he does. Flatter the King but place no store by his promises. The Queen matters most but avoid any attempt at flattery with her. She responds to clear ideas simply expressed, and whatever she decides will be in consultation with her favourite minister, General Acton."

"Is he party to our cause?"

"He is an Englishman, Captain Nelson. He cannot help but be so. And it stands you in good stead that he is also an ex-naval officer. The 'general' is an honorific from Ferdinand. Acton knows that he who controls the Straits of Messina controls the fate of the Kingdom of Naples."

Hamilton, too, was under scrutiny, and Nelson liked what he saw. His manner was open and friendly, and he had about him an air of sound common sense. Accustomed still to the social mores of home, he was taken by Hamilton's total lack of condescension, his readiness to treat him as an equal and to defer to him in any area of his own expertise. At the same time he had a certain steadiness about him, and gave the impression that ample time was available even if there was, in truth, precious little. Nelson judged that if he had still been a soldier, Hamilton would be a cool fellow in battle, which was the highest praise he could bestow.

The crowds thickened as the carriage approached the gates to the Palazzo Reale. People were there, Hamilton explained, because they were unsure of what was taking place. "They sway greatly, Nelson, from bellicosity to abject fear in seconds." He indicated the floor of the carriage. "Do not be fooled by these flowers. They're as fickle as they are emotional. Ferdinand fears his own people as much as he fears the arrival of the French—with good cause."

"Then he must be eager for a military victory."

"I daresay, such are his dreams, that he wins one every time he sleeps."

Ferdinand, dressed in black and grubby in appearance, towered over his visitor. He greeted Nelson fulsomely, naming him as the saviour of his nation, and enveloping him in an embrace both crushing and malodorous. That remark raised a round of applause from the assembled courtiers to which King Ferdinand responded with a joyous shout. Then he introduced his chief minister, the Marquis de Gallo.

He looked as slippery as Hamilton had described: bland of feature, with blank black eyes and dry skin, vain in the way he spoke and moved, as if Nelson's presence had interrupted far more important business. It was the royal consort who cut across him. The Queen had a presence her husband lacked, and the wit to discuss with her Minister of Marine and the Army what response Naples should make to the request, which had been communicated to her a mere ten minutes before the audience had been granted. It was Acton who spoke: short, deeply tanned, with sharp bird-like features and a look in the eye that denoted deep intelligence.

"Their Sicilian Majesties are cognisant of the joint responsibility of both their nation and yours, Captain. The plague from France must be halted and thrown back into the gutters of Paris from where it emanated. Both my sovereign lord and his queen have had to bear the tragedy of personal loss as well as witness the turmoil released on Europe by these demons. But they are also responsible to the nation God has given them the power to rule."

"That nation is safe," Nelson replied, speaking somewhat before he should. "The French have no fleet and what few capital ships they have at sea are poorly manned, ill prepared, and blockaded in Hyerés Bay."

"We have a land border as well, Captain."

"You have even less to fear from that source, Sir John. There is no army closer than Toulon to threaten you."

"It could be said, Your Majesty," interposed Sir William, addressing the vacant-looking King, "that the Neapolitan border stands at that very spot. Hold Toulon and France can never menace Naples."

Sir William had warned Nelson not to expect any decisions, cautioned him that the court of the Two Sicilies moved at a snail's pace when it moved at all. Acton replied on the King's behalf. "His Majesty King Ferdinand has already arrived at that very conclusion, and is prepared to put at the immediate disposal of Lord Hood a force of six thousand men, plus the vessels to carry them, which are at this very moment being made ready to sail."

The slight nod between Acton and the Queen, allied to the far-away look in the eyes of King Ferdinand, was enough to tell all present who had really made that decision. The frown on the face of the Marquis de Gallo showed that not everyone agreed.

"I've never known the like, Nelson," exclaimed Sir William, "in thirty years of being here. Somnolence, not zeal, is the common currency around these parts, hunting and whoring excluded, of course."

"I would have wished to decline this feast tonight. Apart from being knocked up from months at sea there are matters aboard my ship to see to."

"It is one of the burdens of my office, Captain Nelson. A royal wish is not that at all. It is a command. And I fear that this means your ship will have to wait. Besides, I would be most upset if you declined to be my guest."

"Perhaps for tonight. But I must get back aboard tomorrow."

"Possibly," replied Sir William, with an enigmatic smile.

Their progress to the Palazzo Sessa was just as noisy and flower-bedecked as their previous journey, it seemed, with every citizen of Naples eager to show their relief at Nelson's appearance. The noise died as the gates shut behind them, and Nelson picked blooms out of the brim of his hat. The cool of the entrance hall was pleasant after the heat of the open carriage, and Sir William was flattered by the attention of his visitor to the classical statuary that decorated the vestibule.

The rest of the palazzo was like that, an Aladdin's cave that he was encouraged to wander, cooling drink in hand, while Sir William went to find his wife, to tell her of their guest, and to forewarn her of the ball at the Palazzo Reale that night. Emma was in her music room, playing an early harpsichord piece by the recently deceased Mozart, from which she broke off as soon as he entered. She stood up, the loose gown dropping to cling to her figure, in a way that still took away her husband's breath.

"How fared our naval officer?"

"Captain Nelson fared amazingly, Emma. He has quite enchanted the King, and Acton has pre-empted the request he was about to make for military help. Six thousand troops promised in the blink of an eye!"

"He must be a magician. I was with the Queen when you came ashore. I'm not sure she had quite recovered from her fear that his ship was French."

"He's a remarkable fellow, my dear, quite remarkable."

That gained him raised eyebrows, for Emma knew her husband to be the least impressionable of men. New acquaintances, if they rated a mention at all from Sir William, rarely benefited from a favourable one.

"You will see in him what I did, I am sure."

"Which is?"

"You know how rare it is, my dear, to meet someone to whom you take an instant liking."

"I have no experience of you ever succumbing to that."

Sir William smiled. "I did with you."

Emma brushed a hand across his cheek, her voice soft and ironic. "It was your breeches, not your heart, that was smitten."

"I protest," he responded, without rancour, his hand reaching out to grab her.

Emma slipped into the seat at the harpsichord again and pressed a sharp key. "So, tell me about your naval officer, and why you're so taken with him."

"It's the oddest feeling. I have not, as you know, been a soldier for many a long year."

"With not a good word to say of the breed in the meantime. Nor do I recall much praise of sailors. I've heard you trounce them as an uncouth menace."

"This fellow is different. He has little height but a commanding presence." Sir William stood with his head bowed in deep thought. "Is it that he looks you in the eye? That there's no feeling of any thoughts harboured other than the ones of which he is speaking?" He looked up again. "I don't know. But I would hazard that he will go far in the service. He certainly thinks so."

Emma pursed her lips, looking doubtful. "How do you know that?"

"He told me."

"What?" she cried, hitting another sharp key. "How vain!"

Sir William smiled, but there was still a look of wonder in his eyes. "Perhaps you'll see what I see, perhaps not. He is to be our house guest. The King is throwing a feast in his honour at the Palazzo Reale tonight."

She stood up. "Then I must shift since I shall require the dressmaker. Shall I ask my mother to have a room prepared?"

"The apartments we had decorated for the Prince will serve splendidly."

Emma could not hide her surprise. Sir William had lavished much money and time on decorating special rooms to accommodate the Queen's sixth son, who even at the tender age of seven was much attached to Emma.

"For a mere naval officer?"

"No, Emma," Sir William replied. "More than that. I think they are fitting for a man who one day may be vastly more important to both us and our mission here than Frederick Augustus, even if he is a prince."

Passing, Emma pecked his cheek. "I fear, husband, that you have been too much in the sun without a hat."

Chapter Fifteen

INSTANT ATTRACTION is such a rare thing that those exposed to it must distrust the immediate onset of the feeling. In seeing Horatio Nelson Emma felt as if some chord had been struck in her breast. He wore the blue naval coat and white waistcoat and breeches that had always given her cause to recall her first, heartbreaking, romantic attachment, when she had been no more than a housemaid, to sixteen-year-old Samuel Linley. Emma had never been able to see a sailor in uniform without being reminded of the Linley House: of Samuel's life, their stolen moments, but most of all of his lingering and tragic death.

But it was not just this visitor's attire and a tweaked memory that engaged her. The near-white hair might be less glossy but it was there in all its abundance. The skin was as clear as alabaster, the odd slight scar an enhancement not a blemish. But it was the eyes that struck her: light, blue, and direct in the way they looked at her.

Nelson saw a woman of great beauty, flowing auburn tresses, startlingly green eyes, allied to a vague notion of recognition. The smile she gave him was all-enveloping, her hand held out to kiss far enough away to demand that he move forward to take it. As he bent over he could barely hear Sir William's introduction.

"My dear Emma, Captain Horatio Nelson of His Britannic Majesty's ship *Agamemnon*. Captain Nelson, my wife, Lady Hamilton."

His fingers were under hers, lifting her hand to his lips, Nelson aware that each tip seemed filled with a tingling sensation. Emma was suffused with a rush of memory—youth, purity, and breathless stolen moments in a corridor. There was a slight constriction in her chest, and her heart missed a beat as Captain Nelson's lips pressed themselves to her flesh with more pressure, and for a longer time than was either polite or necessary.

Nelson kept hold of her hand as he straightened up, looking at her unblinkingly, a stare returned in full measure. "Lady Hamilton, it is a great pleasure to meet you."

"And you, sir," Emma replied, aware that her voice held a trace of huskiness. "I cannot say how relieved my husband and I were to see your sails on the horizon."

He let go of her hand at the mention of the word "husband," turning in some embarrassment to look at Sir William, who had an odd smile on his face, knowing and amused, which led Nelson to suspect that his wife had the same impact on everyone she met. Then Sir William's eyes flicked slightly to his left, which reminded Nelson that he had another duty to perform.

"Lady Hamilton, allow me to name my stepson, Midshipman Josiah Nisbet. Josiah, Lady Hamilton."

Josiah, brushed and powdered for the royal feast, stepped forward smartly, hat under his arm, his heels tapping on the parquet floor. He stopped and bent forward as if someone had slapped him on the back of the head, and missed with his lips Lady Hamilton's hand by the merest fraction.

"Milady."

"Why Mr Nisbet," she responded, gaily, "what a smart fellow you are, a credit to your stepfather and your ship." Accustomed to abuse rather than flattery, the youngster blushed to the roots of his hair as Emma took his arm and headed for the open double doors. "And handsome to boot, in your naval blues. I shall have to guard you well, young sir, for I tell you no secret when I say that the Neapolitan ladies are all rapacity when it comes to fresh game."

William Hamilton laughed, indicating that he and Nelson should follow, his voice near a whisper as he confided, "Damn me, Nelson, she can spot shyness at a mile off. She has every young man in Naples, including the King's own son, in thrall to her."

"Given her beauty, sir, I would hazard it's not only the young men. Your wife could rejuvenate the ancient statuary." Nelson, who knew himself to be the least accomplished of men when it came to repartee, was quite astounded at his own ability to get that sentence out without a stammer.

"Handsomely said, sir," Sir William responded, "and very true. Emma does attract the eye. I allow my wife the degree of liberty her station commands, yet she has never once given me cause for misgivings."

Nelson could not be sure that the older man told the entire truth, given the attention to which his wife was exposed both before they took their places and afterwards. His eye was drawn to Lady Hamilton in a way that he felt sure must be noticed, given that he had been allotted the place of honour at the King's right hand, an exposed position even in such a huge gathering. Ferdinand helped him, not being the type to engage in quiet conversation with a neighbour, more inclined to shout to someone a dozen places distant, with all his courtiers and their ladies hanging on to his every blaring word. He spoke in Italian, which Nelson couldn't understand, and the rare asides Ferdinand made to his premier guest had to be translated, which clearly bored the King.

General Acton was close enough to converse with, as was Sir William Hamilton, and much was exchanged about the need for Great Britain to protect such a stalwart ally as the Two Sicilies. Nelson agreed, with genuine feeling, being of the opinion that holding the Mediterranean without good bases was militarily impossible. He was less sanguine about a quick peace, convinced that, without a major rising of monarchical forces all over France, such a hope was wishful thinking.

"Even if Provence rises in its entirety, General Acton, it will not answer. It is an under-populated part of the French nation, and far from the seat of real power. Lyon, I am told, has suffered the same butchery as Marseilles. A coup in Paris might give grounds for hope."

"I wouldn't hold out for that, Captain Nelson," said Sir William. "My wife and I came through the city on the way back from London, in the time of the Convention, before Robespierre and his regicides took over. Nothing depressed us more than the sheer stupidity of the mob. Parisians are drunk with power, so drunk that every man must fear even to be their leader."

He could not avoid looking at her again. The object of his surreptitious attention was seated near the Queen, able to engage in pleasant conversation with her and her offspring, which made Nelson jealous. He also observed that Josiah, some distance away with the rest of the *Agamemnon*'s officers and midshipmen, couldn't take his eyes off her. But that bothered Nelson not one jot: young swains were supposed to be bowled over by such beauty and charm.

"Then we must fear for Italy, gentlemen," said Acton, dragging his attention back to the conversation. "Lombardy provides a route to Vienna. Let the Revolution defeat Austria, and the wolves will be at our throats next."

Nelson thought Acton unduly pessimistic, but diplomacy forbade him to say so. For an ex-naval officer he showed a scant grasp of reality. France, having murdered its king, was isolated, with even their common ally Spain ranged against them. Their enemies included Austria, Prussia, the Russians, the United Provinces to the north, as well as a substantial number of French émigrés encamped on the Rhine. In turmoil, she could feed neither herself nor her armies. British naval power would choke off a goodly portion of what could be imported, taking ships and cargoes to deny French armies the means to sustain themselves. Defeating France was far from certain, but containing the Revolution within her borders seemed eminently possible.

He stole another glance as he raised his wine glass to propose a toast: "Then let us hope that they murder each other until not a Frenchman is left alive to keep their damned Revolution going."

He felt a delicious thrill as Lady Hamilton, mistaking the purpose of the raised glasses, nodded to accept what she took to be a compliment to her. Rejoining a conversation about fleets, bases, victualling, and the progress of armies seemed to act like a strain on the muscles of his neck.

What Nelson failed to see was that Lady Hamilton was throwing as many glances in his direction as he was in hers, which was why she had mistaken the toast. Too experienced to suffer turmoil, Emma was drawn none the less towards Captain Nelson, without being sure why. His smile, which looked slightly melancholy as he listened to the King's translator, entranced her, as did the way he moved his hands as he ate or responded to a question: slowly, as if each gesture required deep calculation. The slight air of loss when the King made an obscene gesture to one of his subjects contrasted to the certainty that animated him when he made a point to her husband or Acton.

When not talking, listening, or thinking about Lady Hamilton, Nelson was wondering how this monarch had stayed out of confinement. He had heard that Ferdinand was uneducated, his ignorance a source of humour all over Europe. But the King was more than a buffoon, he was deranged, and would most certainly have been removed as the nation's ruler if he had resided in England, as King George had so nearly been when he had gone temporarily mad.

"He is a child, Captain," said Sir William, once they were back in the coach. "No more and no less, with a child's passion for that which pleases him. Hunting and procreation seem to be his abiding traits. The poor Queen is rarely out of the delivery couch, so ardent is he in the bedchamber."

"She confides in me that conception is as painful a chore as birth," said Emma.

Sir William responded with a weary air—but he was checking his wife none the less. "I think that is one confidence that Her Majesty would not wish to be disseminated."

Emma laughed, in a way that showed she was slightly intoxicated. "You cannot chide me, sir, for there is no greater gossip in Naples than yourself. Believe me, Captain Nelson, you must beware in my husband's company for no gaffe will go unrecorded. Few English visitors to Naples leave without adding to his store of anecdotes."

The light of the carriage lamp was just enough to let Nelson see that the rejoinder had been well received. Sir William wore a self-satisfied smile.

"I confess that is true. But I also sense Captain Nelson to be an upright man, my dear, so he has nothing to fear."

"I daresay I shall find out if he has," said Emma, nudging Josiah, who was sitting beside her. "Young Master Nisbet here will tell me all."

"You're in for a dull exchange, milady," said Nelson, without much thought. "Josiah's mother and I hold each other in the highest regard, is that not so, boy?"

"It is, sir," Josiah replied, with such conviction that he made his stepfather, who had had time to consider the statement that prompted the response, feel like a scrub.

"They say she was a whore, sir," Josiah exclaimed, as soon as the servant closed the door to their rooms, "and that she tricked Sir William into matrimony."

"Enough of this!" Nelson was rarely sharp with any of his youngsters and that applied most to Josiah. The evidence of this was plain in the crestfallen expression on the boy's face. "Is that the first thing you can say of someone who has treated you with kindness? Lady Hamilton is our hostess, so you will oblige me by containing the kind of talk that passes for conversation in the mid's berth."

"Aye, aye, sir," replied Josiah, stiffly.

"I suggest that you retire. We have a busy day tomorrow, that is, unless you'd rather not accompany me."

Nelson knew that he was being cruel because his stepson was merely repeating things he too had heard, and which he had believed before making Lady Hamilton's acquaintance. Yet, having met her, how could he give credence to them now? His expectation of some coarse creature had been quite swept away on that first encounter.

The introduction, in her music room, had underlined what Sir William had told him: that she played more than one instrument and sang like an angel. No one had cut her at the Palazzo Reale, quite the reverse: people of both sexes and obvious merit had lined up to greet her. He had heard her speak French to one of the King's guests, German to another, and her Italian appeared close to fluent, accomplishments to make the most aristocratic woman proud. In translating the conversation between him and the Queen she had demonstrated the regard in which she was held in that quarter. No London trollop could attain such a position—surely her reputation was the result of malicious and jealous tongues.

"Well Josh, do you wish to go to Portico tomorrow?"

"I do, sir," Josiah replied softly.

"The company of kings clearly suits you." Nelson put a hand on his stepson's shoulder and smiled. "Well, I can say that your desire outweighs mine. Another royal feast will be the death of me, I'm sure. And I fear we will have to depart at such an early hour that it will afford me little time to visit those of our seamen who have been brought ashore."

"Sir William assured me they were being well looked after, sir."

"It is my duty to ascertain that for myself. The men expect and deserve it. Remember that when you command your own ship. Put the well-being of your crew above all other considerations. Then when they are required to fight, they will do so willingly."

"Yes, sir."

"I will require you to deliver some orders for me while I am thus engaged, so I suggest it is time we both retired." He paused, looked around the well-appointed rooms, his mind full of the image of the lady of the house. "This will be something to tell your mother, will it not?"

Sleep was hard, partly because of the amount he had been obliged to eat, all of which seemed stuck somewhere between his throat and his ribcage. But he was equally troubled by his thoughts. His relationship with Fanny, easy to suppress while afloat and occupied, was now thrown into such sharp relief by the vision of Lady Hamilton that he could not erase it.

There was guilt too, the memory of the relief he had felt when they had finally weighed, the cutting of the umbilical cord to wife and home, a feeling of being released from a prison of his own making. Home was never ashore, it was on a ship in the company of like-minded men: officers commissioned, warrant and appointed; topmen and upper yardsmen, able seamen and even landsmen fit only to haul on a rope. Lepée, for all his drinking and his foul moods, took on the attributes of a saint when compared to the dull, insular servants at Burnham Thorpe.

Nelson nearly groaned when he recalled the first dinner he had thrown for his admiral and fellow captains. He knew he was no drinker, yet he had allowed his normal abstemiousness a night off due to the joy of being at sea and the pleasure he took in the company of men who matched his rank. Naturally at an all-male table, with ample drink, an element of ribaldry had entered the conversation. Instead of diverting it, his responsibility as host, he had actively encouraged his guests.

Admiral Hotham had served with Captain the Honourable Augustus Hervey, famous throughout the fleet for his amatory adventures, twenty years before, in the Mediterranean. It was claimed he had seduced more than two hundred women, English, Italian, Austrian, and French, in a two-year commission, fathering enough bastards to man a frigate. Those who approved of Hervey's record were matched by the number who thought it a disgrace to the service. Nelson had embarrassed several of his guests, including his good friend Troubridge, by the crass remark, "Every man is a bachelor east of Gibraltar."

"Am I that?" he asked himself aloud, before thumping his pillow and throwing himself on to his other side, determined to get to sleep.

Emma left Sir William with a light kiss of his forehead, his eyes closed and face relaxed. Drink affected him badly and tonight's coupling had taken time and effort, with her in the role of a supplicant wife seeking clemency for a condemned husband, Sir William fully committed to his performance as the tyrant who would accede only if granted certain favours.

Her husband made no secret of his need to conjure up images in his lovemaking, yet for all his knowledge and lack of hypocrisy it never seemed to occur to him that Emma might require the same. Every movement she had made tonight, every seemingly enforced submission had been carried out with eyes closed, the vision in her mind a jumble of places: Harry and the cottage, Greville at Uppark and Edgware Road, Nelson and the great cabin of a ship, all three faces blending into each other.

As usual, her mother was waiting for her, dozing in a chair, head lolling forward, jaw slack. When she awoke and helped her daughter to prepare for sleep, Emma was required to recount the events of the night's entertainment.

"So what's he like, this Captain Nelson?" Mary Cadogan asked, removing the ties with which earlier she'd dressed Emma's hair.

"A nice man, but too gentle for the task, I shouldn't wonder. He has none of the brash quality we associate with seafarers."

"The Chevalier seems to rate him high enough. He dislikes seafolk as a breed, I know, for he has told me so more'n once. I could scarce credit it when I was told to prepare the royal apartments for this one."

"Sir William has taken a liking to him," Emma replied, yawning. She was tempted to say that she had, too, but with a mother as nosy as hers it was best to stay silent. "He advises me that Captain Nelson is a fellow to watch, though how he can know this on one day's acquaintance escapes me."

"Happen his servant, Lepée, has been a-tattling to him. God knows, I had my fill of the fellow, as much as he had fill of the Chevalier's claret. When it comes to his charge paragon ain't in it. There's not a virtue going that Captain Nelson don't have in spades from care of his men, the way he sails his ship, to being a terror in a scrap. It's a wonder he ain't the Lord High Admiral of England."

Emma yawned again as her mother began to count off the brushstrokes on her hair. "I can't imagine him fighting anyone. He looks too gentle by far."

Chapter Sixteen

"AN AWNING WILL BE ESSENTIAL, Mr Berry, for us, if not for our guests."

"Aye, aye, sir," Berry replied, wearily. If his captain had been busy, the premier had outdone him, not only obliged to attend the social events ashore but also to oversee the revictualling of the ship: wood, water, flour, fresh biscuit, greens, anti-scorbutics, and meat, both butchered and on the hoof.

"The hen coop will have to be struck into the boats," Nelson continued. "Clear the manger of animals and douse the deck with vinegar."

"Are we clearing for action, sir?"

Nelson smiled. "Worse than that. We're receiving royalty, Berry. I want a special effort below deck, everything shipshape, with every man in his Sunday best, shot chipped and blacked, every rope from the sheets to the gun carriage tackle flemished and snow white."

"Vittels is arrived from the Palazzo," growled Lepée, interrupting without even a pretence at a cough. "Who's to detail hands to get them aboard?"

Nelson looked up at him, the bloodshot eyes and grey face of a man who had spent the last three days drinking and boasting, taking full advantage of his stay at the Palazzo Sessa, a place with ample servants to do what he knew to be his duty and a cellar that was full to bursting with the means to get drunk. Lady Hamilton's mother had mentioned it when they had met, making no secret of the fact that she thought Lepée a poor servant, more concerned for his own comfort than that of his master. The good lady, who had struck Nelson as eminently sensible, didn't know the half of it. Liverish himself from three huge feasts in three days, he wondered how Lepée managed it.

"Should you not see to that, Lepée?"

His servant held out a hand, as proof of how unsteady it was. “Got the marthrambles, don’t know how, your honour. Like to drop most of it.”

“I hazard that wine and rum might have something to answer for.”

Lepée closed one eye, as if to confide in his captain. “I reckon it be the stinking air and the heat. They be a filthy crew these ’politans. Shit where they like and don’t wipe their arse, papist heathens that they are.”

“Ask Mr Andrews to detail some hands,” his master replied, wearily.

“I’ll oversee to it, of course, your honour,” Lepée insisted. “Sir William’s steward promised to send us the finest from his larders and his cellars.”

“It will all make it to the storeroom, I trust?”

“What a thing to say, your honour,” Lepée replied, his protest so forceful he sent a blast of bad breath in Nelson’s direction before staggering away.

“We may have to strike that one into the bilges, Mr Berry,” Nelson said as Lepée reached the doorway. “His breath is enough to clear out the rats.”

“Be better off there than here,” Lepée growled, overhearing the remark. “Slaving like a Barbary capture when it’s not appreciated.”

Berry was looking at him and Nelson knew why, since there was hardly a member of the ship’s crew who could understand why he put up with Frank Lepée. “He can be a sore trial, Mr Berry, I know, but my needs in the servant line are modest.”

“With respect, sir, we have the King and Queen of Naples, their family, and most of the local nobility coming aboard in two hours’ time, not to mention Sir William and Lady Hamilton and every important visitor who happens to be here from England. And your servant, one of those charged with attending to them, is drunk. I suggest that the wardroom servants be left alone to look to our guests.”

“Lepée would be most offended.”

"You don't fear to offend a king?"

"You do not know this king as I do," Nelson replied, with a wicked grin. "He and Lepée will probably get on famously."

Berry knew he would have to resolve that problem himself, since his captain, a man universally held to be one of the most competent officers in the service, could not bring himself to chastise the man. The premier was no martinet; he could not serve with Captain Horatio Nelson and be that kind of officer. He shared his commander's notions of training and responsibility, openly admired a quality of seamanship that he could never match.

He hoped and prayed that when he had his own ship the ease of manner Nelson had with everyone aboard would be gifted to him. The Captain knew the name of every man on the muster roll, where they came from, if they had a wife and children, which ships they had served in and what ailments they were prone to. He liked to talk with them, more to listen to them, his feel for the mood so acute that he could smell a reason for discontent before it had time to manifest itself.

Berry knew how the need to maintain a captain's dignity constrained Nelson. He had seen him itching to go aloft and show the upper-yardsmen, nimble boys all, that he could still set topgallants. When he talked to the gunner about his flintlocks, powder, and guns, the conversation was one of knowledge on both sides, weight of shot, quality of powder, which gun fired best in length and power.

He and the boatswain spent hours discussing the crew, seeking to extract the best from them, to gain them skills that might see them raised to a better station on another ship. Likewise, Nelson spent extra time with the sailmaker, the carpenter, the master-at-arms, and the ship's corporal. His coxswain, Giddings, as familiar as he'd been from their first meeting, acted as an extra conduit of information to a Captain always prepared to listen and learn. After five months at sea, *Agamemnon* was a crack ship, better than most frigates when it came to tacking, wearing, or coming about. Clearing for action, practised every day, was down from twenty-five to seven minutes.

Even the purser, usually the most hated man on any ship, was popular aboard this vessel. Hand-picked by his captain he was allowed to make his profits, but only if it was fair. The provision of double hammocks had done for half a year of potential gain. Once past Gibraltar, Nelson insisted that, in the Mediterranean heat, a single hammock and fourteen inches per man to sleep in was a recipe for sickness. Each man must have two hammocks, one to be used, one to be washed clean each make-and-mend day. It was a fine notion, much appreciated by the crew, and the cause of mixed mirth and fury when, in a sudden squall, all the drying hammocks festooned around the rigging had suddenly been blown into the sea.

Gazing at them floating away, many already sinking below the waves, with no boats in the water to go after them, Nelson had remarked, "The fish will sleep better than us this night, lads, and we'll rest better than the purser."

They had laughed and cheered him for that calm response, their affection open, their faith in Horatio Nelson as their commander, judge and jury for offences, and in some cases father figure of the ship, quite obvious. And yet this man feared to tell his servant that he was a useless drunk.

"The King will want to see the great guns fired, so detail four of our best gun crews to oblige him," Nelson said. "I shall have to turn my cabin into a refuge for those ladies who will be affrighted by that."

"Might I suggest, sir, that since it's royalty, your cabin should be set aside for the Queen's retinue, while the wardroom is cleared for the rest."

"A capital notion, Mr Berry. Make it so."

As the boats set out from the shore, the royal barge commanded the most attention. But Nelson found himself searching the flotilla for the craft bearing Sir William and Lady Hamilton. He had had only limited contact in the previous three days, his duties precluding any form of relaxation: attendance on a monarch who wanted to hog his presence; meetings with General Acton, the Queen, and her council regarding the despatch of troops to Toulon. At the same time he had to look to the welfare of seamen, both sick and well, make sure his ship was victualled, write letters both official and personal, and issue orders to send out to sea a pair of boats. They were to take station in the approaches north and south of the Bay of Naples to ensure that *Agamemnon* would not be caught unprepared should an enemy appear on the horizon.

Fleeting glimpses, a hasty exchange of pleasantries, a view across a dinner table or an audience chamber was all he had been gifted. Josiah had enjoyed the bulk of Lady Hamilton's attention, a match that had benefited his stepson no end. She had brought the boy out of his morose shell and captivated him. No strictures were needed now to stop him traducing her reputation. Josiah was all praise and was given to extolling her numerous accomplishments in a way that made Nelson jealous.

He had spent almost all of the three days with Sir William, who had roused himself in the most admirable way to ensure that what could be done to aid Nelson was carried out with despatch. For a man who termed himself a lazy dog Sir William had great energy. He also had a deep and impressive sagacity, outstanding patience, and a huge knowledge of who was for the British alliance in Naples, and who, fearing French reprisals, was against.

Nelson's initial approval had turned into a deep regard for the Ambassador. He had eased Nelson's burdens not only with his presence and his courteous way of deflecting the King's wilder flights of fancy, but also with his wit and conversation, his consideration, and his open way of letting the naval officer know that he esteemed him personally as well as professionally. It was therefore uncomfortable to be with Sir William, enjoying his company, asking his advice, sharing plans and proposals while simultaneously being unable to get out of his mind the man's stunningly beautiful wife.

He spotted them under an awning, in a decorated *felucca* that was being propelled by a gaily dressed crew. Lady Hamilton, her mother, and her maid all seated, Sir William, with his valet in attendance, standing behind them, hands clasped on the awning poles. Joy and anxiety were mixed in Nelson's breast: the pleasure to be had from seeing her again and in circumstances where, as the host, he could command some of her time, but against that was his desire to impress, and he feared he had failed in that. It might be his ship they were visiting, but it was Sir William's provender they would eat, his wine they would consume, the impression created that the Captain of the *Agamemnon* could not afford to provide such a feast himself.

"The salute, Mr Berry, if you please."

The guns, armed with powder only, blasted out 21 times, wreathing the ship in white smoke, leaving in the air that delicious odour of saltpetre. Eleven guns, the salute due to the ship, blasted out immediately afterwards from the battlements of the Fort St Elmo, which stood on the highest peak overlooking the city. And, in the background, Vesuvius billowed forth an extra puff of sulphurous smoke, as if determined not be left out of this occasion of mutual appreciation.

"Man the yards," was Nelson's second command.

Berry bellowed the order and two hundred men raced for the shrouds—fore, main, and mizzen—going aloft in controlled fashion, the less able at the rear. The older topmen fanned out on the main yards, the more nimble occupying the space between the caps and the tip of the upper yards, while the youngsters, small of build and feet, raced to the upper yards, some to stand in a death defying pose on the twelve-inch circumference of the topgallant poles.

"Three cheers, lads," yelled Nelson, his voice loud enough to carry all the way to the tip of the topmast, where one sailor, with only a finger and toe-hold, had taken his place at the highest point on the ship. The huzzahs roared out, three on three, with every man on the deck, including the Captain, raising their hats as they cheered.

Nelson and his officers left the upper deck and made their way to the maindeck to take station by the entry port. The marines, red coats brushed, belts pipeclayed a startling white, and boots polished, came to attention as the royal barge slid alongside the gangway, the bosun's pipe timed to begin the ceremony of welcome as soon as the first royal foot touched the platform. Two of the most reliable members of the afterguard, the oldest and most experienced seamen, hooked on to the barge, hauling it in tight to steady it. Another pair were on hand to assist the King.

Ferdinand had dressed for the occasion in a Neapolitan naval uniform. Out of his customary black food-stained garments and properly clad like an officer, he was an imposing figure, a man with whom it was a pleasure to exchange salutes. He also had the courtesy to tip his hat in the direction of the quarterdeck, a signal mark of honour from royalty.

It took nearly half an hour to get the entire visiting party on to the upper deck, to where wine and food were laid out under the awning on the wardroom tables: smoked hams, fowls by the dozen, oysters, crustaceans, pastries, and fruits. The wardroom stewards, in brand new duck trousers and wearing their best kerseymere striped jerseys and stockings, moved smoothly through the throng serving wine to nobles English and Italian, women who looked more like courtesans than wives.

"Milady," said Nelson, taking Lady Hamilton's hand to kiss. "You do me great honour by consenting to be my guest."

He had observed her taking the breeze on the windward bulwark, close to the master's day cabin. They were just far enough away from others to have a private conversation.

"I would look a fool, Captain, to ignore an invitation accepted by *tout* Naples."

He looked at her then: his unblinking eyes, which could so unsettle the insincere, fixed on hers. Having rehearsed this meeting he had a whole string of polite conversation all ready to employ, every word sifted through his imagination a hundred times. It all deserted him now, to be replaced by that fearlessness of manner that had caused him so much trouble in the matters of the heart.

"Is that why you came, just because everyone else did?"

Allied to his stare, as well as the expression on his face, it was a bold remark, and she knew it. Her face reddened and she spoke as if she was short of breath. "Why else, Captain Nelson?"

"As the Ambassador's wife," he replied smoothly.

That flustered response, from such an accomplished person, had cheered him. His question and the way he had delivered it had bordered on the outrageous. Nelson knew that, but he simply had to know, too, if there was any feeling in her like the one he had experienced before, and was suffering from now. His chest was tight and his muscles, lower back, and legs had a sensation in them somewhere between an itch and an ache.

"You have made a conquest there, Captain Nelson."

"Have I?" he enquired.

His eyes bored into hers so that she was forced to look away. That took great effort, given that his nerves were jumping and his conscience was heavily pricked by images of both Fanny and Lady Hamilton's husband. He knew he was not good in situations like these, that he lacked the easy wit and charm necessary for seduction; that his habit of speaking direct truth, an asset sometimes, could damn him just as easily.

A part of Emma wanted to put this fellow down, to puncture the air of assurance in those startling blue eyes. Yet she was aware of her own physical reaction to his proximity, for she was trembling and confused. There was anger at her inability to master the conversation as well. In six years in Naples, with a string of male admirers, Emma had become adept at deflection. Why could she not do so now?

The door to the master's tiny cabin was open. Nelson wanted desperately to lead her into that confined space, to close the door behind them, to . . .

"I meant that you'd made a conquest in my husband, sir."

Crashing from such a high-pitch emotion to quotidian reality was like an imagined fall from the rigging, half a second of suspension before his sense of his responsibilities as a ship's captain and a representative of his own king reconnected with the ground. Even so, his breathing wasn't right.

"Then, milady, I can only say that feeling is returned. Your husband is a man after my own heart."

"He predicts that you will achieve great things."

"I flatter myself that I shall, milady, should Our Lord spare me time to do so."

"Your stepson is waiting to speak with you."

That brought Nelson right down to earth and broke the train of conversation, which seemed to imbue every word said with two meanings. Realising he was standing too close to Emma Hamilton he stepped back a fraction then turned to face Josiah, noticing that his stepson was not the only one watching their exchange with interest. Lady Hamilton's mother was looking at him, a quite singular expression on her face.

"Mr Berry's compliments, sir, he asks me to inform you the cutter is approaching at speed, flying a signal to say that the enemy is in sight."

Everyone who had ever served with Horatio Nelson was aware of his absolute decisiveness, a speed of reaction to an event that could sometimes be said to border on the irrational. Most praised it and few damned it. Right now both would have been nonplussed at his reaction. Nelson was looking at his deck, covered in food, wine and guests of the highest station possible. The threat, whatever it was, lay outside any immediate assessment. The pace at which the cutter was approaching probably had more to do with the commanding midshipman's desire to impress his captain than anything requiring panicked response; an enemy close enough to be a threat would be visible from his own tops.

"Tell Mr Berry we will be putting to sea at once. A party to clear the deck while he assembles the men to weigh." He spun round to Lady Hamilton. "Forgive me, milady, but I must request that everyone goes ashore."

"You speak of the King and Queen of Naples, Captain."

"I have a duty to them, I acknowledge. But that includes defending their kingdom as well as my responsibilities as a serving officer of my own sovereign. I fear I must insist."

"Then I suggest you inform the King of this."

"I shall, if you will oblige me by passing on what I say to Sir William."

Emma was forced to observe, as she watched the decks clear into the waiting boats, that if there was one thing the Neapolitans were good at it was panic. King Ferdinand, apprised of what might be in the offing, showed no pique at being unceremoniously ejected from the ship. Indeed, he led the charge, getting away just before the cutter hooked on and a message was passed to the quarterdeck that a French man-o'-war convoying three merchant ships had been sighted to the west of Capri.

No reassurance that the threat wasn't imminent had any bearing on that hysteria, and the sailors who had so courteously helped them aboard now found themselves required to be quite firm about the way the guests departed. The other visitors, English, émigré French, Germans, and Austrians, were more stoical, moving to the poop as they were directed by members of the crew, busy striking everything off the deck. There was a degree of admiration for the sheer efficiency of a ship's company who could steal the food on the table while carrying it below at speed. What could not be transported was tossed into the Bay of Naples.

Eventually the noisy locals were gone, and the remaining guests were led down to the maindeck, Sir William and his wife bringing up the rear, Horatio Nelson stopping them to allow the gangway to clear. Mary Cadogan took the maid by the arm and moved her away from the conversation.

"Sir William, I apologise to you and your wife. I ask you to convey my proper regrets to His Majesty. My cutter, which was placed out as a screen to the west, has been told there is a French ship-of-the-line in the offing."

"A threat to Naples?"

"A threat to shipping, our own and those of the Two Sicilies. My duty demands that I seek to engage and destroy her and that must take precedence over all other considerations."

Emma wondered where that softness had gone. However, what

had replaced it was just as telling, an air of command, the impression of a mind in control of what it observed. Captain Horatio Nelson was the only person, apart from themselves and a midshipman by his side, who was standing still. Everywhere else was movement as men rushed to obey a stream of commands from the Captain's inferior officers. Yet for all the seeming disorder it was far from that, this evidenced by the quiet way in which Nelson himself imposed his presence.

"I would ask you to care for those men I have left ashore, Sir William."

"Leaving them behind will render you desperately short-handed."

"I have enough to tackle a single Frenchman, Sir William, even if he outguns me. Look about you, sir, at these fellows I have the good fortune to command." Nelson smiled then, which to Emma made his face look radiant. "Why, if this Frenchman could just gaze upon them he would strike before I opened my gunports."

"They are a fine set of men, I agree," Emma said.

"Lady Hamilton, when we beat our enemies it is not men in blue coats who win the battle, it is these fellows you see now going about their tasks. All their officers do is get them to the right place."

"Goodbye, Captain Nelson," said Sir William. "I wish you a speedy return to us, and good fortune attend you until then."

Nelson raised his hat to salute the Ambassador and his wife, who curtsied in response, saying, "A happy return."

Agamemnon was hauled over her anchor and plucking it out of the sea before the ambassadorial *felucca* had got more than half a cable's length away from the warship's side. Aloft, the rigging was full of men loosing sails and the Hamiltons could just see Horatio Nelson, who had come to the leeward side of the quarterdeck.

"What a strange man, husband," said Emma.

"An admirable one, my dear, who does not, it seems, worry about offending kings." The ship heeled slightly as the wind took the now tautened sails. The great rudder was hard round to sweep it on a course that would take it out to sea. "Something worthy of praise, I think."

Emma was looking at the single figure on the quarterdeck, diminishing by the second, when she replied, "I certainly have nothing but admiration for Captain Nelson."

The object of her observation was looking at the gaily decorated *felucca,* wondering if his desire to get so hurriedly to sea was the prospect of a battle. Or was it to save him from making a complete fool of himself?

HMS Agamemnon, *18th September, at sea*

My dear Sir William,

You will, I'm sure, already have heard that I missed my Frenchman, which makes the nature of my departure from the Bay of Naples all the more indefensible. I plead duty, which I am sure you will understand, and that you will convey to Their Sicilian Majesties the assurance that Nelson stands ready to defend their country to the dying breath.

My compliments and deepest thanks to your dear lady wife, who has entranced every man aboard my ship, not least my stepson, Josiah. We all look forward to a happy return to the warmth of your hospitality.

I am yours,
Horatio Nelson (Capt)

Chapter Seventeen

1797

HORATIO NELSON couldn't stay in his cabin even if his dignity as a commodore demanded that he do so: he needed to be on deck, even if in the thick haze there was little to see but half the ships of his own squadron. HMS *Captain* ploughed through the grey Atlantic waters. His heart was pounding in his breast, blood racing, none of which altered the tactical situation in the slightest. Somewhere out ahead was HMS *Victory,* flagship of Admiral Sir John Jervis. Beyond *Victory,* between him and the southern tip of Portugal, also hidden from view, lay the combined fleets of Spain, so recently an ally against France, now as much of an enemy.

"Mr Hoste, be so good as to join me."

The midshipman hurried over to join him on the windward side of the quarterdeck as he paced up and down, his heels beating a heavy tattoo on the planking. The prospect of action always excited Nelson. Prone to recurring bouts of malaria, nothing banished ill-health like the sound and fury of battle. In the four years since he had sailed to war he could think of no officer who had been as active as himself: single-ship actions, cutting-out expeditions, the siege of Bastia, and then Calvi, which had cost him clear sight in one eye but had secured Corsica for the natives. To that he could add diplomatic missions, sea chases, and storms that had seen good old *Agamemnon* so reduced that she had had to be sent home for a refit.

Yet for all the success of the Royal Navy, France had been triumphant everywhere on land. Bonaparte, unheard of before Toulon, was now a national hero, his armies carrying all before them in Savoy and Italy until the states who had actively opposed the Revolution sued for peace. But the seas were British, Nelson able to sail where he wished, to support and harry the enemy, to hold Corsica and Elba, and keep a promise to protect Naples.

He was hardly aware that he was talking, using Hoste, whom he counted as his favourite among the mids, as a sounding board to relieve his inner tensions. "The defection of Spain altered everything. Combine the French and Spanish fleets, then place them in the English Channel, and the whole fate of Britain hangs in the balance. It would be the Armada all over again, with no guarantee of the result. That, Mr Hoste, is why the Mediterranean had to be abandoned, even Naples, to counter such a threat."

"Aye, aye, sir."

"You do understand all this, don't you?"

The boy's "yes sir" carried a fair measure of doubt, as did his large dark brown eyes. He gazed at Nelson as if he was of another species, evidence that such patient explanation had only gone so far in clarification. Hoste, like many others, was in awe of him, and while that often had a pleasant feel, it also served to underline for Nelson the increased distance that now lay between him and his shipmates.

That lack of contact he had disliked, as a captain, was even greater now. Ralph Millar had been made post, but was serving with him as the Captain of his flagship, seeing to the day-to-day running of the ship, leaving Nelson free to oversee the rear section of the fleet, an admiral's command entrusted to him. Ralph Millar undertook the midshipmen's lessons now; it was he who took divine service and the divisional inspection. Commodore Nelson attended, of course, but the service over he retired to his cabin. If he wanted company he had to do what he had just done with Hoste and ask for it.

"This could be the most important day of both our lives, young fellow."

Nelson could see the boy didn't comprehend that; didn't know that for all the success his commodore had enjoyed nothing could compare with what was possible now. All his naval life he had yearned to take part in a successful fleet action, the naval might of one nation pitted against another. It was why he had gone to the Caribbean in *Albemarle,* hopes dashed when the French declined to oblige a nation that had already beaten them in those very waters. He nearly had one with Admiral Hotham, the fool who had succeeded Hood, only to find the enemy taking action to avoid an engagement.

Single-ship combats were all very well, and good for a long report in the *Naval Chronicle,* but to take part in a successful fleet action elevated a naval officer to the pinnacle of his profession. Distinguish himself, and that plaque he so craved in Westminster Abbey, next to James Wolfe, his hero, would be possible. Lose? To Nelson the possibility did not exist. The possibility of death however, reminded him that he had yet to write a final letter to his wife, Fanny, and compose a will.

Back in his cabin he picked at his solitary dinner, served by Tom Allen, the servant who had taken over from Lepée. Allen was silent where Lepée had been vocal, sober where he had been drunk, Norfolk bovine instead of London sharp. But he missed Lepée, and would have kept him on if he had not become intolerable. It wasn't so much inebriation that had done for him but his increasingly loose tongue.

Servants were supposed to keep their master's secrets not trumpet them. Lepée, in his cups, had started referring publicly to a dalliance Nelson had enjoyed with Carlotta d'Ambrosio, a Genoese opera singer, not just to his fellow crew members but even at dinners thrown for important guests. Drunk, his voice would rumble on, and what should have been thoughts instead turned to ranting monologue. The time had come for him to depart, not to the lower deck, as feared, but with a discharge from the Navy. He granted Frank Lepée a stipend that would keep him from the gutter and, more importantly, since its continuance was based on silence, keep his mouth shut.

Nelson was back on deck as soon as a sharp ear heard the first faint echo of a signal gun. The haze had cleared enough to allow his one good eye to range over the whole fleet, sailing in line ahead. It looked imposing, fourteen line-of-battleships, but he knew just how long these ships had been at sea; how much wear and tear was hidden by endlessly applied paint. More guns sounded below the horizon that could only come from a Spanish fleet on a working-up exercise that saw no reason to hide itself from an inferior enemy.

Nelson knew from conferences held aboard *Victory* that the plan was to close with the Dons and take them on where they found them and in whatever strength, notwithstanding that they would certainly outnumber the British fleet. The Spanish flagship alone, *Santissima Trinidad,* with four decks, mounted 136 cannon and Don José de Córdoba, the Spanish Admiral, had half a dozen ships carrying 112 guns plus a potential fleet strength of over thirty capital ships. To set against that Admiral Sir John Jervis had fourteen: two 100-gunners, two 98s and two 80s, plus eight 74s.

The afternoon wore on, signal guns booming out to the south, with the wind shifting to blow in from the open sea to westward. Frigates shadowing the Dons informed Jervis that they'd turned for home, on course for Cadiz, their premier Atlantic naval port, halfway between Portugal and Gibraltar. The flags ran up *Victory*'s yards to order the fleet to increase sail. Sir John wanted to be in a position at dawn to bear down on them should the wind favour him.

Aboard every ship they dined that night in full anticipation of a battle on the morrow, 14 February. Wills and last testaments were updated. Final letters to loved ones composed, promises extracted and exchanged so that whatever fate befell the individual someone would see to his effects and his responsibilities. Nelson had written to his wife and his family, father, brothers, sisters, and uncles.

He also penned a letter to Naples, to Sir William and Lady Hamilton, with whom he had enjoyed a lively correspondence these last four years. He assured them that battle was imminent, of his fidelity to their mutual friendship and reiterated the Navy's determination to return to the Mediterranean as soon as the business was done. As he did so, the image of Lady Hamilton filled his mind: those auburn tresses, green eyes, and lively animated face faded through a pang of guilt into that of his wife.

Had Fanny, in the way her husband had praised Sir William's

wife in his letters, discerned the attraction he had felt? He had wrapped his own fascination in kind words regarding her treatment of Josiah. Would that make the mother in her jealous? It was a truism that praising people was as dangerous a game as damning them. Had Josiah seen the attraction? Though he had never mentioned that Genoese opera singer, his stepson must have known about her. Could he be trusted to remain silent? For that matter could Lepée? He went to his cot still gnawing on such concerns, lying in it, swinging softly, well aware that the following night it might not be his bed but his coffin. His favourite expressions, repeated over and over again, served to still the anxiety in his breast.

"Death, damnation, or Westminster Abbey."

"Twenty-seven of the line, sir," called the lookout, who was above the mist and could see the enemy sailing on a parallel course, "and ten frigates."

"Nearly double our number," said Ralph Millar, the twang of his Yankee accent evident.

"I'm sure our admiral will not shy away from that," Nelson insisted.

In every meeting he had had with Sir John Jervis, Nelson had found him full of fight, dancing around in a way that belied his 62 years. Sir John was a scrapper by nature, an energetic little man with the face of a pug terrier and no tolerance whatsoever for slacking, inefficiency, or the complaints of sailors about their lot. Unmarried, he was a martinet in the article of discipline, irascible, poor company at a dinner table, and inclined to rudeness if given an opportunity to rebut an ill-placed remark.

Nelson, when he first met him, had expected to have to defend himself. The opposite was the case. Though Sir John's reputation was proven with other officers, the Admiral was the soul of kindness to his boyish-looking commodore. They thought alike in the article of fighting and, it transpired, shared between them a perfectly attuned blind eye regarding the behaviour of men in their private life, as long as they properly performed their duties.

The Spaniard Grand Fleet had sailed on the wind overnight, a westerly breeze that was waning by the hour. When they spotted the British fleet bearing down on them they were some 25 miles west of the Portuguese headland at Cape St Vincent, and it was obvious by the untidy nature of their reaction that they had been taken by surprise. But they were clearly inclined to offer battle, holding on a course south of the British fleet, their bowsprits facing east and home, seeking no increase in speed, inviting Sir John to make the next move.

But that was based on the assumption that Sir John would attempt to get alongside his enemy on a parallel course, matching them in speed and course to engage in a gunnery duel. Given that Sir John would have to sail south-west in line, then bear up to the east on a converging course that would overhaul them, the Spanish Admiral felt he had ample time to prepare his fleet to receive the outnumbered and outgunned British.

Two things spoiled Don Córdoba's confident assumption. The first was the inability of the Spanish captains to form proper line. Their ships were bunched into two untidy squadrons; the leading group of nine vessels had got well ahead, leaving a gap astern of them of several miles. The main section of the fleet was also bunched in such a way that many of its guns would struggle to bear on an enemy in proper formation. Attempts by the Spanish captains to form a line were not going well.

The second wrong assumption was a belief that no British admiral would disobey the Fighting Instructions, which dictated the tactics the Spaniards anticipated. But Sir John Jervis did, on a course due south that didn't deviate. He held back, timing his approach to let the lead Spanish division cross his bows. As soon as that happened Sir John reacted.

"Flag signalling, sir."

Nelson watched, full of admiration, as his admiral ordered a press of sail, and aimed his van like an arrow at the gap between the Spanish contingents. This action flew in the face of every tenet of British naval warfare. It was a crime by admiralty statute. Jervis, if he lost, would face at least disgrace and quite possibly a firing squad on his own quarterdeck.

Here seamanship told, as each line-of-battle ship in turn, in what seemed to be no more than minutes, got aloft a full suit of sails. The water began to cream down the side of each vessel, as she heeled over to take the west wind on her beam, yards braced right round to catch it. His old shipmate from the voyage to India, Thomas Troubridge, was leading the fleet in HMS *Culloden,* HMS *Orion* in support. Another friend, Cuthbert Collingwood, brought up the rear of the fleet in *Excellent,* just ahead of *Diadem,* which was behind Nelson in HMS *Captain.*

The plan was straightforward: to get between the two parts of the enemy fleet, isolate the greater part to westward then tack into the wind to take them on. Nelson, watching Troubridge, was full of envy, since he would be the first to engage. That feeling deepened as the Spaniards opened fire, which Troubridge chose to ignore, holding his response until it mattered, the point at which he turned to do battle. Troubridge was holding his course to cross the bows of Don Córdoba's flagship, *Santissima Trinidad,* the biggest fighting vessel in the world, leaving the Spaniard with the option to luff up or risk a collision.

"The Spanish van have begun to tack," said Lieutenant Berry.

Nelson looked to the east, following Berry's gaze, to observe the front section of the Spanish fleet coming round to rejoin the rest of their consorts. Into the wind such a manoeuvre would take time. Don José Córdoba suddenly turned to sail north-east, angling his ships towards the rear of the British fleet, calculating that though they'd face fire from the likes of Troubridge, they would avoid the rest and would be able to slip past *Excellent,* last ship in the British line. Sir John, obliged to hold his ships together, would be forced to come round in succession, which would take an age to complete.

Time and the wind would be against the British, creating a chance by which the Spaniards, passing round his rear, could rejoin into a formidable whole. With both wings of the Grand Fleet reunited, Don José could then choose to retire, making for his intended landfall, or come round again to oppose the enemy as a vastly superior force. If he chose to run, Sir John's only option would be to pursue at a distinct disadvantage.

"They're going to get away," said Nelson suddenly. He could see the course they were steering, and could calculate the triangulation and tell where each ship would be in an hour's time. Only Troubridge, and perhaps *Orion,* would fetch even the Spanish back markers. They would never head off the enemy flagship.

"Don José may choose to fight, sir."

"No," replied Nelson, who was wondering if it was already too late to change things. "The Dons are not like us, Ralph. Even with greater numbers they'll run."

Nelson had a sinking feeling in his breast. Ever since he had listened to his uncle Maurice recount his tale of the fight at Cape Francis Viego, he had yearned for a day like this. Whether it was to match his uncle or outshine him, he didn't know, but he did feel that his whole life had been a preparation for this moment: his visions of a brilliant destiny could be fulfilled or destroyed here. There was a solution, but it was so dangerous to his name and reputation that it took several moments of contemplation before he could bring himself to articulate it. Someone had to check the flight of the Spaniards; someone would have to supply a base and create a triangle, to cut them off and make them do battle. Succeed, and he would have fulfilled that vision he had had on the way back from India. Fail and he would be derided for a fool and very likely never command a squadron again. He would be like those sad cases he had seen in Bath, the so-called "yellow admirals," incompetents who had risen to the rank by mere survival, but who would never be trusted with a command. What decided Nelson was the knowledge that, after this day, he would have to look at himself in the mirror. There was no way he could face looking at the reflection of a man he thought of as a moral coward. He spoke very slowly. "Captain Millar, I require you to wear out of the line."

"Sir?" said Millar, eyebrows shooting up, since that was to turn away from the enemy.

"We will come round full circle and slip between *Diadem* and *Excellent.* Once through and in open water, I wish you to put me across the bows of those Spaniards."

Millar realised what Nelson was about in putting his ship in front of the fleeing Dons. He also knew, as much as his commodore, what failure would mean. To pull out of the line to disobey orders, not only those of his commanding admiral but those of the Fighting Instructions. Nelson was putting his whole career on the line, possibly along with that of every officer aboard the ship.

"I feel it is my duty to point out the consequences, sir."

"Do you wish those orders in writing, sir?" he asked Millar, softly, so his voice did not carry to the other officers on the quarterdeck, Lieutenants Hardy and Berry.

"No, sir. I merely wish to make sure you know the hazards."

"I know what I hazard if I *don't* act so, Millar, and so do you. The Dons will get away. You do agree, don't you?" Millar nodded. Nelson put as much into his voice as he could, seeking to persuade a man he esteemed as a friend and admired as a sailor. "Then take it in writing. At least you will have the protection of that if we fail. The blame will fall on me."

"Fail, sir!" exclaimed Millar, in a voice that could be heard all over the quarterdeck. "I never thought to hear that word on your lips. Mr Hardy, hands to man the braces."

Hardy possessed a voice to go with his stocky build. The order roared out and men moved. On the command the ropes holding the yards were hauled round, at the same time as the great wheel swung, the rudder biting so that *Captain* came up to take the wind and clear the line. The sails were then backed to bring her head round, then sheeted home and lashed off to take the wind on her larboard side, pushing the ship forward beam on to the wind.

Nelson raised his hat as HMS *Diadem* sailed past them, then heard Millar order the yards hauled round once more as the quartermaster put down his helm. Now *Captain* was sailing into the wind at an angle that had Nelson looking left into the stern casements of *Diadem,* with the bowsprit and figurehead of Collingwood in *Excellent* to his right. Within minutes Millar was through, sailing away from his consorts, Nelson's hat off to exchange a salute, his ears full of the cheers that Collingwood must have encouraged. He could see Troubridge had tacked at the head of the Spanish line, and was coming up hand over fist to join him.

"Flag signalling," cried Berry.

All the officers watched as various ships' numbers were hauled aloft to break out at the *Victory*'s masthead. Orders were sent to *Excellent, Blenheim, Orion,* and *Prince George*. That was followed by the message instructing them to support HMS *Captain*. Nelson felt a release of tension, of which he had been unaware in the excitement and trepidation of his actions. The responsibility was no longer his: Admiral Jervis had approved.

Nelson allowed himself one more look around at the ships holding their course to follow Troubridge and those moving directly to his support. He felt his heart swell with the certainty that the fleet would be victorious. That he might not survive didn't matter. If he expired in the moment of triumph he would have achieved the single most important aim of his life, making it worthwhile.

"Lay me alongside the enemy, Captain Millar," he cried, in a voice that travelled the whole length of the ship.

Chapter Eighteen

BEFORE THOSE WORDS had died away the closest Spanish ship, *San Salvador,* opened up, her guns aimed forward to take *Captain,* her whole side wreathed in smoke. Nelson was elated, even though some of the balls struck home, making the frame of the 74 shudder. He was in action.

"Note the time," said Millar to Hoste, acting as his signal midshipman, looking at his commodore to see if he should reply.

Nelson shook his head, seeing that *San Salvador* had held her course, more intent on evasion than fighting. "I believe we may lay that ship ahead by the board." He pointed at the towering four-decker that would be unable to avoid them. "If my memory serves me well, she is the *Santissima Trinidad.*"

"Allus the same with little fellers," said one of the quarterdeck gunners, to his gun captain. "They allus want to pick a fight with the biggest bastard in the room."

"An' how many times have you see the big one taken down?" the gun captain replied. "Old Nellie will have her over, you mark my words, mate."

The approach was close to silent, though ropes creaked, timbers groaned, and some warriors whispered prayers. Aloft, men were taking in sail, leaving only the high topsails to give steerage way. Nets were being rigged in their place to catch anything falling from above. Extra chains had been fitted to the masts to stop them going completely by the board, and Pierson, the marine officer, had his men in place, up in the caps, main fore and mizzen masts, with muskets ready to play across the enemy deck.

The Spanish ship, knowing that a fight was unavoidable, had replicated everything that had happened in the British 74, albeit without the same efficiency or speed, the loss of sail slowing her progress. She loomed up, two decks higher than *Captain,* the great gilded poop so tall that the men who stood on it were invisible. It was always like this before the guns spoke, that terrible period of waiting as two vessels designed for destruction approached each other.

Don José de Córdoba could not have ordered the first salvo, a ragged affair that came from the forward lower deck cannon, the only ones that would bear, 36-pounders, the largest calibre on the ship. The side of the *Santissima Trinidad* vanished as the smoke billowed skywards to hide the upper works. Several spouts of water shot up yards from the British hull to blow away on the breeze. Two balls struck home, making *Captain* stagger, but it was a wooden hull, built to take heavy shot, so they did little harm. The four-decker began to turn away, so that her course would run parallel to Nelson's, inviting a gun-for-gun duel that *Captain* would struggle to win.

"*Culloden* has a press of sail on, sir," cried Berry, pointing south to where Thomas Troubridge, ignoring easier targets, was coming up hand over fist to the aid of Nelson.

"Then we shall be more than evenly matched when he is with us, Captain Millar, two 74s to a 136."

"Permission to open fire, sir. I'd like to get the first true salvo in to disrupt the aim of their gunners."

"Make it so, Captain Millar."

Every gun was loaded and already run out, the crews with bandannas round their ears kneeling ready to reload, and the gun captain stood poised over his flintlock, ready to trigger a spark that would ignite the powder in the touch hole. It was the same on the lower decks, in the glimmer of light emitted by a string of fighting lanterns plus a small amount that came through the portholes. It was just enough to show the eyes of the men and pick up the rouge of the planking, which would show no blood.

Marine sentries stood at the companionways so that no one, panicked by noise or the proximity of death, could run. *Captain,* cleared for action, showed a clean sweep fore and aft, right from the peak of the bow to the stern where the cabins had stood, walls, stoves, and furniture, all now struck below. The animals had been heaved over the side into the ship's boats, and were now well away from the noise and fury of the coming contest.

Behind each group of guns stood a blue-coated officer, in command of his division. He had the task of controlling the gunnery, trying to ensure that weapons didn't fire simultaneously. Better rolling fire than a single blast. Underneath their hats they, too, wore bandannas, an attempt to protect their eardrums from the stupefying sound of the blast.

"Fire!" yelled Millar.

They didn't all go off at once, the timbers wouldn't stand it. Instead the fire rolled down the side, each gun firing within two seconds as the one before it recoiled. The ship shook from stern post to figurehead and the smoke blew back over the deck, the acrid smell of powder and saltpetre catching in the throat. But that slowed nothing. The crew was as well drilled as any in the fleet. On the recoil two bars were shoved under the carriage to hold it steady against the roll of the ship. The first thing down the muzzle was the swab necessary to clear the residue of used powder. That was followed by the charge, already pricked by the gun captain so that a small quantity covered and penetrated the touchhole. It was rammed down the muzzle, next the ball chipped and rounded before the battle so its flight would be true. Last to go in was the wad, tamped down to provide a seal that the blasting charge could act against.

The crew hauled on the tackles as one, pulling the cannon into its firing position, black menacing muzzle out of the porthole, carriage hauled right up to the rings fixed to the ship's side. Timing his action to the gun preceding his, the gun captain would lean forward again to trigger his flintlock. If that failed there was slowmatch to ignite the powder, to make it hiss and flame, the fire igniting the charge behind the ball. Within half a second the gun would spew forth destruction, sending out a heavy ball and a streak of orange fire mixed with black smoke, the trail of the exploding powder. The ball, well aimed and properly fired, with the right charge of powder, arced across the gap between the ships, glanced off an open port lid. Unseen by those who had fired it, the ball ricocheted through, taking an enemy gun on the muzzle, dismounting the metal, smashing the wood of the carriage, trapping and maiming half the crew and killing two on another gun crew with wood splinters gouged out from the deck.

The noise was tremendous, a continuous barrage of sound and fury that made verbal orders impossible. On both vessels the officers walked slowly down the line of their cannons, touching each gun captain's shoulder to control the rate of fire, trying to ignore the effect of enemy shot on their own vessel, the way the timbers of the side suddenly cracked open, parts of the wood detaching to fly like spears across the deck. Men screamed and men died, with extra hands ready to take their places at the guns or to drag them away to the less than tender ministrations of the surgeon.

And all the while the ship's boys raced back and forth to the gunner, carrying powder charges. Others, not powder monkeys, were given the task of replenishing shot from the locker, a chain of small hands that kept the racks full by each gun. Some had buckets of water, and ladles with which to try to quench the thirst of the gunners, who, after just a few salvoes, were black from head to foot, their skin and hair singed by hot flashing powder.

Aim as they might on the first salvo, it was rate of fire that counted, the sheer volume of shot coming in from the British ship enough to suppress the Spaniard's reply. *Captain* was making little headway, wallowing on an Atlantic swell. Fire on the down roll and the balls hit the enemy hull. Fire on the up roll and the shot could go anywhere from the bulwarks to the rigging. The Dons laboured under the same conditions, and though they could not manage the same rate of fire, they had more guns and the damage they did was telling.

Blocks and pulleys cascaded down and whole yards were blown out of their chains, falling to rip through the netting and slamming into the deck, careering on to damage flesh and blood as well as wood. Backstay hawsers snapped, ropes parted, and shrouds were shredded, with the foremast the first to go. It snapped above the cap like a matchstick, falling sideways, a creaking, groaning lament that could be heard above the pounding of the cannon, taking with it several men, some to die smashed on the deck, others tipped overboard into a sea from which there was little prospect of rescue.

On the quarterdeck Nelson stood rock still. Having brought HMS *Captain* into action, he was now no more than a figurehead. Others carried the fight to the enemy, but few were as exposed as he. There were several ways to die, and each man aboard knew them well. On deck a musket ball might fell you, or a stray roundshot cut you in half. Every cannon on the deck was a lethal weapon to those who fired it as well as to the enemy. Free of its breaching it would pulverise flesh, blasted from its carriage it could maim and kill. But of all the deadly things to face, splinters were the most lethal, malignant shards of wood, some bigger than the men they struck, some so small they were barely visible, capable of lopping off a limb or inflicting wounds that were nearly always fatal.

Through the smoke it was hard to see, but Nelson knew from what he could hear that *Captain*, with *Culloden* having come up in support, was inflicting as much damage as she was taking, and that was considerable. But the price was high. The mainmast followed the foremast, so fouling the way on the ship that a party with axes had to be formed to cut it away. The wheel was gone, shot away, taking the quartermaster and two of his assistants with it. In the lull that followed the *Santissima Trinidad* hauled clear, this before the next Spanish ship came up to engage. Millar ordered Lieutenant Josiah Nisbet away from his quarterdeck cannon to take an instruction below, to alert the men on the relieving tackles, heavy hawsers that worked the rudder, that the steering of the ship was now their responsibility.

Josiah shot down the companionway, immediately struck by the way the sound was muted. Looking along the open lower decks it seemed as if he was gazing into hell. Smoke hung in the air, illuminated by the orange flashes of firing cannon. There were dead men, and wounded, screaming for mercy, bleeding copiously, unceremoniously hauled away either to die or be tended in the cockpit. There, with only lantern light to work by, the surgeon used his probes, knives and saws, up to his arms in blood, lopping off limbs, rough sewing gashes, with only a swift slop of rum to ease any pain, that and a leather strap between the teeth of his patient. Hardly surprising that the lad took a little longer to return to the deck.

He emerged to find his ship fully engaged against another enemy, trading shot with a crew fresh and prepared. The air was full of missiles, chain, and bar shot intended for the rigging but just as effective in slicing through men. And there, in the middle of the quarterdeck, stood his stepfather, in his uniform coat, one epaulette hanging off and half the rim of his hat blown clean away.

"Hot work, Josiah," he said, clearly happy.

Another almighty crack, another wrenching lament, before the mizzen mast began to fall. It didn't come all the way, but held by the mass of torn rigging that had once held up the other masts, it settled at a crazy angle, the gaff boom jamming into the poop to form a triangle of useless wood. Men rushed to secure it, lashing it to any solid object to stop it doing more damage.

Looking back at *Culloden,* when the wind gusted enough to clear the smoke, Nelson could envisage what his ship must look like. Wallowing and useless, *Culloden* had fallen out of the battle, rudder shot away and not more than a stump of any mast standing. It was easy to imagine blood flowing out through the scantlings by the gallon, but whatever the cost, Troubridge could be proud. He had done his job.

"Enemy approaching on our larboard quarter," shouted Millar. "All hands stand by to engage."

"*Excellent* is coming up to help us, sir," cried Josiah.

She was, too, with enough aloft still to overhaul the enemy. By the time *Captain* opened fire with a ship they knew to be *San Nicolas,* Collingwood had put up his helm to place himself no more than twenty feet from her beam, opening up with a salvo of gunnery that tore the Spaniard apart. Great chunks flew from her side into the air; the rigging was shredded on the second salvo, and on the third the lower ports were smashed in, the clang of metal on metal so loud it was audible across the intervening water.

To the rear of that *Prince George* had engaged the three-decker *San Josef.* One Spanish ship sought to edge away from Collingwood, with what few tattered bits of canvas she still had aloft. The *San Josef* was seeking to get across the bows of *Prince George,* to a point where she could pour fire into an enemy who would struggle to respond. Instead she ran foul of her own consort, checking her way so comprehensively that *Excellent* shot past to cheers from *Captain.*

"Captain Millar," called Nelson.

"Sir?"

"We are useless in the line," he shouted, pointing to the nearest enemy. "Please be so good as to put us at a point where we can board that ship."

"Mr Nisbet, pray return below again and ask Mr Hooper to put the rudder hard a-larboard."

It was agonisingly slow, the way that *Captain* inched towards the *San Nicolas,* both ships firing ragged salvoes. But Millar had done just the right thing, using the run of the sea to put his prow right in line with the poop of the enemy vessel. Men gathered around their leaders, with knives, clubs, muskets, and pikes. Pierson, leading the marine detachment, had his men lined up as if on parade, ready to put their first fusillade into whatever resistance formed itself on the Spaniard's deck.

Berry was already out on the bowsprit, edging on to the spirit sail yard as the two ships collided, sword in hand, yelling like a banshee, preparing to jump. Around him Nelson could see other old Agamemnons: Thorpe, Warren, Sykes, and Thompson, both Johns, and Francis Cook. Beside him, swearing loudly, stood William Fearny, one of his bargemen, normally the quietest soul in creation, now raring to get into the fight.

"Permission to lead the boarding party, sir?"

Nelson turned to answer Millar, his look almost pleading. "We cannot both leave the deck, Ralph, and I cannot stay while there is a fight. My nature couldn't bear it."

The silent exchange lasted only a few seconds, enough for Ralph Millar to impart his opinion that commodores had no right to lead boarding parties. But then neither, really, had captains. Behind them Berry was swinging his sword, driving down the heads of those who would stop him, allowing those behind him to drop on to the poop and take them on. Marine muskets were fired and reloaded to clear the enemy deck of opposition. And the ship was spinning slowly, now locked into the *San Nicolas,* hanging on to the enemy stern. Millar smiled, touched his hat, and went back to his station.

"To me," Nelson called, leading a group of men forward to the quarter-gallery windows, now nestled up against a point where the bulwarks were smashed open. A marine stepped forward and smashed the glass, Nelson immediately leading his party—seamen, marines, and three midshipmen—through. They found themselves in a small cabin with a locked door. That, too, fell to the butt of a musket, allowing his party into the fore part of the great cabin, led by a wild-eyed commodore, repeatedly shouting, "Death or Westminster Abbey!"

"Heads!" Nelson yelled, pushing one midshipman one way, a second the other, then diving himself for one of the bulkheads as a fusillade of musket balls, mixed with the sound of shattering glass, came through the skylight above their heads.

"Marines, clear them!"

That order was aimed at the rest of the party, still exiting from the quarter gallery. The muskets were up and fired almost before the words were out of his mouth, a salvo that killed several men and aided Berry, still fighting desperately on the poop. Nelson was already out of the cabin on to the open deck, heading for a companionway full of Spanish sailors. He discharged his own pistol, before turning it to use as a club, felling a man who had been stabbing his pike towards one of his mids.

He had to step back to get his sword free, then lunged immediately, missing his main target in his haste but taking another enemy sailor in the thigh, enough of a wound to make the fellow collapse in a heap. In a fight that is a mêlée, all the swordsmanship practised on deck counts for nothing. This was hacking, jabbing work, with the hilt just as vital as the blade, close-quarters fighting in which instinct, or a flash of something in the corner of an eye, counted for as much as skill.

It was that which alerted him to the swinging club. Even though his sword sliced into it, the jarring up his arm was painful. Keeping his embedded sword aloft exposed his assailant's lower body and a swift kick in the groin doubled him over. It was his own club that finished him, retrieved and swung by Nelson so hard he could hear the fellow's skull crack open. A pike, pointed and serrated, shot past his nose, missing him by a fraction as he fought to dislodge his sword. Thorpe, who had jammed a hand on to the shaft just in time, unbalancing the pikeman, had disrupted the enemy aim. The blade of Nelson's sword sliced up under the pikeman's throat, cutting through his neck so hard that his head nearly came off.

Fighting their way up the companionway was hard, a compact mass of British facing an even more dense crowd of Spaniards. Willpower won out over numbers, aided by the first sight of sunlight at the enemy back. Jab—cut—jab—cut, slice—parry—jam the hilt into a face, kick, bite, scratch, anything to keep the forward momentum. Nelson was soaked with sweat, his mouth dry and his arms aching. But he was leading his men to a point where the enemy must break, which they did with a suddenness that nearly had him falling on to his knees.

He emerged on to the deck to find Berry in occupation of the poop, in the act of hauling down the Spanish flag. Odd that the lower deck guns were still firing, unaware of what was happening above their heads, still trying to fight *Prince George*, probably convinced that she had stopped firing through their efforts rather than the dropping of the Spanish ensign, unaware that the British ship was now concentrating its fire on the *San Josef;* this while their officers, on the deck, were in the act of surrendering their swords; this while all fighting had ceased on the upper and maindecks.

"God bless you, Berry," Nelson croaked. "She is ours."

"A party below, sir, to still those guns."

"Make it so, Mr Berry."

Berry hadn't made it to the companionway when the fusillade of musket fire swept across the deck, fired from the cabins of the *San Josef,* still stuck fast to *San Nicolas,* scything through a party of sailors and marines celebrating their victory. Several fell in such a way as to make Nelson think them dead. But that was not foremost in his mind.

"To me, lads," he shouted, waving his sword, which gathered every available man. "Marines form up and give them a volley. Mr Hardy, a party at the hatches to keep those below in check."

Pierson had his red-coated bullocks in line and ready within half a minute, their fusillade poured into the area from which the gunfire had come. Nelson followed the musket balls at a rush, jumping from the bulwarks of one Spanish ship, a Second Rate, on to the main chains of another, to grapple his way on to a First Rate three-deck 112-gun ship.

Berry was with him, using main force to push his commodore up high enough to get over the bulwark of the bigger vessel. Nelson was shouting, his cracked voice sounding mad. He emerged on to the deck prepared to kill everyone in sight, only to find a line of Spanish officers, swords extended, waiting to surrender to him. One, on his knees, informed him in stilted English that his admiral was dying. Nelson took his hand to lift him to his feet, and requested of him in even worse Spanish that all the ship's officers should be informed of the surrender.

A salvo from *Prince George* slammed into the side of the *San Josef,* to remind Nelson that a battle was still in progress.

"Berry, the flag, cut it down."

Berry rushed to obey as Nelson took the swords, handing them to Giddings, who, with an air about him of studied calm, tucked them under his arm.

"They've struck already, sir," Berry shouted, from the poop.

"Then show yourself to *Prince George,* but don't get your head blown off doing it."

Thorpe grabbed his hand and shook it, gazing into Nelson's

astounded face. "You don't know it, do you, yer honour, what you've done? I'm shaking your hand now while I has the chance. When this gets out they'll be queuing up."

"*Victory,* sir," cried Berry, bloodstained but unbowed, pointing to the approaching flagship, fast coming down on the three closely entwined warships, *Captain, San Josef,* and *San Nicolas.* The rigging was full of sailors. On the quarterdeck Nelson could see Admiral Jervis, Captain Calder, and all the flag officers. As they came abreast Sir John raised his hat, and led, in the most flattering fashion, the cheers of every man aboard his ship.

Chapter Nineteen

EMMA HAMILTON read Nelson's letter for the third time that morning, trying to imagine the battle that had taken place a month before, not helped by the way her correspondent played down what must have been a bloody affair. The Spaniards had been soundly trounced, those not taken forced to run for the shelter of Cadiz.

Both she and Sir William had had other letters, from London, that told of how the news of the victory had been greeted. The bells had rung, gold medals had been struck, and every civic body in the land vied to give one of the heroes the freedom of their city. Sir John Jervis had been raised to the peerage, and was now Earl St Vincent. Nelson had become both a rear admiral and a Knight of the Bath. And those letters also told of that new raree-show that was enacted in all the pleasure gardens and playhouses: Nelson's Patent Bridge for the Taking of First Rates, in which the feat of crossing one ship to take another, never before achieved, was played endlessly to an adoring, patriotic audience.

Sir William had been right all those years ago, when he had introduced Horatio Nelson as a man of exceptional ability. Emma began a reply couched in warm terms that would, of course, include a fond wish that a British fleet should once more come to Naples, and that Admiral Sir Horatio Nelson would lead it.

Fanny Nelson, staying in Bath with her husband's father, couldn't deal with the letters she received. They were too numerous. Everyone who knew Admiral Nelson wanted to write with praise of his actions. But so did many who had never made an acquaintance: people from all over the country who had read of his exploits in the newspapers, eager to tell her that her husband, by his actions and his application, had saved the nation.

She had letters from him, too, in which she knew he had played down the blood and danger, more eager to tell her that her son had behaved well, that money would flow from the battle: head money for the enemy sailors captured, gun money for the guns, as well as prize money for the ships themselves.

With *Captain* a near wreck he had shifted his flag to HMS *Theseus* and hoisted his blue pennant at the mizzen, the flag of his new rank. It worried her that the acclaim he had garnered didn't seem to satisfy him, and that he was already talking of a new adventure which, if it succeeded, would eclipse the fame he had already acquired. Together with the Reverend Edmund Nelson she pored over maps to locate an island somewhere off the coast of Africa she had never heard of: Tenerife.

There is always a moment before going into action when a sailor faces the prospect of death, convinced that this is his day to succumb. Pessimism abounds at the moment of composition, when it is easy to conjure up images of those you love and cherish: family, friends, fellow officers, and seamen in a world in which you no longer exist. Nelson had written just such a letter off Portugal in February, and he was writing another off Tenerife in July. That pessimism, in Nelson's experience, usually evaporated as soon as he turned his mind to more practical things. But not on this occasion! Not for the recently promoted and knighted Rear Admiral Sir Horatio Nelson KB!

First mooted after the victory at Cape St Vincent by a junior admiral keen to enhance his already glowing reputation, the operation to take the island had been viewed with confidence. Tenerife lacked a full garrison; what forts it had were weak and under-gunned. Land a substantial force, take those forts and invest the main port of Santa Cruz, and it would only be a matter of time before the island fell, there being no hope of relief from Spain who had seen its Grand Fleet soundly beaten six months previously.

Surprise, a vital element of the plan, was lost when the weather turned against him: a strong gale allied to a foul current meant his frigate commanders couldn't land their troops in the dark. The next attempt involved landing forces in broad daylight while the line-of-battle ships pounded Santa Cruz. This was frustrated by a flat calm that had him wearing to and fro off the bay called the Lion's Mouth, unable to aid the progress of Troubridge, who battered uselessly against the hillside forts until he was forced to withdraw, re-embarking his landing parties, weary and unsuccessful.

When proposed, Nelson's latest plan, a direct attack on the town via the mole that protected the harbour, caused even his bravest subordinate to pale, making him wonder if it was a product of his vanity rather than sound tactical sense. With the success against the Grand Fleet he was loath to return to Admiral Jervis, now Earl St Vincent, without a triumph under his belt. The last time he had seen him his irascible commander in chief had been up to his ears in the suppression of mutiny, the tidewash of the insurrections at Spithead and the Nore, which had led to the unpleasantness of two hangings.

Nelson was glad to be away from that, an impossible conundrum. He sympathised with the sailors' demands while at the same time deploring the methods chosen to effect change. And in a fleet at sea, which might face battle at any time, sentiment had to take second place to the maintenance of efficiency. He hoped another resounding success would do more to stifle discontent in the fleet than any number of yardarm ropes.

"Gentlemen, I shall lead this attack. Please be assured that my desire to do so has no bearing on the conduct of any officer in this room. I think you know my character, and will readily understand that I find it ten times closer to hell to be a mere observer, rather than a participant."

The numerous nodding heads reassured him. There would be no jealousies, but he would have been cheered by more smiles. "I intend to anchor off the town and give every indication of my intention to bombard. Conscious of the difficulties, and not wishing to keep his troops under heavy cannon fire, the Spanish commander must assume another landing and I hope will reinforce his forts, thus denuding the town. In darkness complete, which at this time of year will be close to midnight, we will take to the boats and secure the mole. From there we will attack and take Santa Cruz, manning the walls on the landward side to repel any attempt at a counter attack."

Plans for timing, numbers to be employed, which boats to take which parties, marines or sailors, signals, both to advance and retire, used up most of the afternoon, so that when the captains left to return to their own ships it was time to stand into the bay. Now it was dark in his great cabin and, with all his affairs in order, Nelson took his sword and pistols from Tom Allen and went on deck. His sight, once it was accustomed to darkness illuminated by stars, alighted on an officer preparing to board one of the boats.

"Lieutenant Nisbet, a word, if you please?"

"Sir?"

"Do I observe by your dress that you are about to embark?"

"I am, sir."

"You know that I lead the attack?"

"I look forward to the honour of accompanying you, sir."

"Josh, what if we were both to fall? What would become of your poor mother? The care of this ship is yours. Stay, therefore, and take charge of her."

"*Theseus* must take care of itself. I'll go with you tonight if never again."

"I cannot insist," Nelson responded softly, but sadly, hiding his foreboding. "Not for an answer I myself would have given."

He could feel the wind on his face, and the swell lifting and dropping the ship under his feet, neither a good omen for what would be a difficult task even on a calm windless night. At least the Spanish governor had fallen for his ploy. They had observed a great number of men departing Santa Cruz for the forts, lessening the numbers he and his men would have to face.

Troubridge and Waller would be embarking the left flank party from *Culloden*. Captains Freemantle, Thompson, and Bowen would join him in the central division once he was in the boats from *Theseus,* and young Sam Hood and his own flag captain, Ralph

Millar, would take the right. Movement was always preferable to being stationary: better to worry about keeping your footing when getting into a boat than standing on the deck thinking of the ball from musket or cannon that might kill you.

The slight swell on the 74-gun *Theseus* was more telling once he had lowered himself in to the ship's cutter. That and the tide had the boat crews hauling like madmen just to get them inshore, their efforts not aided by the way the boats were lashed together to ensure they maintained cohesion. Off to the left firing broke out where he perceived the head of the mole to be, though he could not be certain of his own heading, a sharp fight with muskets, the yells of hand combat floating on the wind. Suddenly rockets shot up from behind the arc of the mole, illuminating the stone structure, showing in the harbour behind it several vessels warped right into the beach, as far away as possible from any impending harm.

"Señor Guiterrez is expecting us," Nelson called, naming the Spanish governor. "Let us hope he has laid out a decent table for our breakfast."

It was a feeble joke, but enough to make his men laugh, even those who, by the light of the rockets, could see that they were now within gunshot range.

"Cast off," he shouted, adding, as soon as the cutter was free of its rope, "pull like the devil, give a hurrah to let them know we're coming, and when you get ashore remember your orders. All parties to make for the main square and wait."

The water before them was suddenly full of canister and grapeshot, each small ball tearing up its own patch of seawater, so heavy that it looked as though nothing could live through it. Off to his right the boats led by Captain Freemantle had already made the mole and were clambering on to the stonework, engaging defenders. Nelson's blood was racing, as it always did when he was going into action. The thoughts he had harboured in his cabin, that this was an action from which he would probably not return, were suppressed by the sheer excitement that animated him.

Crunching on to the soft ground that lay at the foot of the

harbour mole, he was first out of the boat, the sword that had served his ancestor, Captain Gadifrus Walpole, held out to lead the charge. And charge they did, his men, screaming obscenities, firing pistols and muskets, clubbing, stabbing, jabbing with pikes, driving back the strong defence. Nelson, seeking to get everyone on to dry land, was waving his sword, yelling to cheer on his fighters, one eye noting that Josiah was fighting like a demon.

Then he felt himself spun round so hard he nearly fell to the ground, the sword knocked from his hand by the blow. His reaction, to pick it up with his left hand, was automatic, taken before he realised that his elbow was smashed and that his right arm was hanging at an odd angle. He felt no pain, just the shock of recognising the wound and watching his own blood pump from his arm to stain the stonework, and glisten in the light from the rockets fired by the defenders. Then he fell to his knees, aware that he was going to die.

"Father," said Josiah, taking his upper arm in a tight grip.

That word opened his eyes, the silhouette of his stepson outlined against the rocket-lit sky. Nelson wanted to say to him, "You have never called me that until now and I had wanted so much to hear it these last twelve years." But he couldn't. Instead he asked, "How goes the fight?"

"Well . . ." Josiah said evasively, knowing that all along the mole, even though they had carried it, the British assault was on the defensive from a strong counter-attack launched from the town. Cannons were firing from the streets that led down to the port, while at both ends guns were still in Spanish hands, playing on the flanks of the assault. "We must get you to a surgeon."

"Take the town, forget me."

"To me, Theseus," Josiah shouted, a call that was immediately acknowledged by half a dozen voices. "The Admiral is shot in the arm. Get him down to a boat."

The pain came as they raised him, so acute that he nearly passed out, but they lowered him on to the thin strand of beach, Josiah holding his arm to slow the blood flow. Then they lifted and laid him in the bottom of the boat. A rocket obliged with a strong light overhead, and that showed how much blood he was losing.

"A tourniquet," Josiah demanded.

One of the men pulled off his shirt and, completely ignoring the balls whizzing past his ears, tore it and wrapped one sleeve round Nelson's arm as a tourniquet, the remainder being fashioned into a sling.

"I thank you, Lovell," Nelson hissed, recognising a man who had served him on three ships. "Should I expire take a shirt from my cabin, the best you can find."

"You'se going to be all right, your honour, don't you fret."

"Mr Nisbet, now that Lovell has given up his shirt, do not let the purser dock his pay warrant."

Nelson heard those words, but no one else did. They were too busy heaving the boat off the sand so that it would float, grunting and cursing as they rocked and pushed.

"Man the oars," Josiah said, as they got it into the sea. "Set me a course to go under those guns. We must make dark water."

Nelson was in a state of suspended animation. Yet he was *compos mentis* enough to admire Josiah's thinking. To row straight out to sea, with the sky still illuminated, was to invite every cannon left on the mole to take a shot at them. Josiah had them row under those very guns, so close they could not depress enough to reach, aware that their attention would be concentrated on what they could see far off, not at the water twenty feet below them. Once out of the arc of light, he put down the tiller and headed out to sea, before handing it over to another so that he could attend to his stepfather.

"How fare you?"

It was a weak left hand that lifted his great uncle's sword. "I still have my weapon."

"Your arm is shattered, sir."

"I saw, Josiah." He let go of the sword to clutch his stepson's hand. "I thank you. You have shown great ability tonight. Your mother would be proud of you. I know I am."

"It would be better to rest, sir," said Josiah, taking off Nelson's hat to put it behind his head. "You will need all your strength for what is to come."

"An amputation, at the very least."

"The surgeon may be able to save it."

The shake of the head was firm. "I have witnessed more of wounds than you, and I have looked at this one. Can you raise me a bit, so that I can see?"

Hands got him to an upright position, so that he could look back to the shore, a place of flame and fire, sound and fury. He had only been upright a minute when a great flash lit the sky to the right of the boat. Nelson saw the silhouette of the decked cutter *Fox,* heard the flimsy timbers tear under the sudden weight of the salvo that struck her hull. Her masts, lit by the flares from the shore, immediately tilted over towards the sea.

"*Fox* going down, your honour," called one of the men. "Her larboard bulwark is shipping water already."

The shouts floated across the water, the cries of men, ghost-like apparitions in the blue lights, screaming for salvation as they jumped into the sea.

"Survivors!" cried Nelson. "Steer for survivors!"

"Your—"

Josiah never got a chance to finish his plea. Nelson might be gasping, but there was no doubting what he said. "That, sir, is an order."

Josiah changed course to set the boat in among the flailing figures in the water, his men shipping oars each time they got a chance to haul some poor near drowning soul inboard. The need to save seamen seemed to revive Nelson, so that he could sit up without assistance to ensure that the search was thorough. He took no account of his wound. There were other boats, which depressed him, since they could only be returning from the shore, where the firing was dying away. Men were calling out for those still in the water to alert the rescuers to their presence, but all response had ceased so they began to row again for the fleet.

"Ship ahead, your honour," said the shirtless Lovell, after about forty minutes. "I think it be the *Seahorse*."

"Steer for her and call for a seat from the yard," said Josiah.

The left-hand grip became like a vice, the voice like a whip. "No!"

There was no sound of firing now from the shore, and no *feu de joie* to indicate a British triumph.

"You must have the attentions of a surgeon," Josiah insisted.

"Not the *Seahorse*. The man is a butcher and a drunk. Besides, Freemantle's wife is aboard, barely wed six months and too young to witness this. I could not face her without news of her husband. Get me to *Theseus*."

"Time is not on your side, sir."

"Do as I say, Josiah," Nelson said softly. "Let me be the judge, and if I do expire, take no blame upon yourself."

Midshipman Hoste heard the shout, the hail *Theseus* a strong one, and he recognised the voice as that of his mentor and admiral. Within two minutes he saw Nelson, arm still in a sling, jump for the side, haul himself aboard with one hand to stand on the deck, his eyes bright.

"Tell the surgeon to get his instruments ready, Mr Hoste, for I know I must lose my arm, and the sooner it is whipped off the better."

"Bowen's dead, sir," said Ralph Millar, reading from the list he had in his hand. Nelson was sitting in a chair, one sleeve empty and pinned to his coat, his eyes showing the grief he felt for a lost friend, as well as the pain from his wound. *Theseus* was engaged in a bombardment, beating to and fro in front of the town. "Captain Freemantle is under the care of his surgeon with a wound that may well carry him off."

"Not that, Millar, not with Betsy so newly wed to him."

"She is tending to him as well, sir. If anyone can provoke his vital spirit to pull him back to health, it is she."

"Boat coming off, sir," said Hoste, popping his head round the door. "Captain Troubridge in the thwarts."

When he stood up, Nelson felt weak, grateful that he was in Millar's cabin, which led straight on to the quarterdeck, rather than his own, one deck below. Tom Allen tried to assist him, and was shooed away like a foolish cat. As he emerged, he was aware of the eyes of the crew upon him. Giddings, his coxswain, was close, his gaze full of concern.

"I'm no use for fishing now, Giddings," he said. "I fear if I am shipwrecked like Crusoe you will have to come with me or I shall starve."

"'Twould be an honour to serve you wherever, sir."

Nelson had to turn away then, and it was not the pain he felt that nearly made him cry.

"Captain Troubridge had no choice but to surrender, sir. He was outnumbered a hundred to one."

The Earl of St Vincent managed a grim smile on that pug-like face of his. "No blame attaches to any one of your officers, and I have nothing but praise for your actions."

"The losses, sir."

"We cannot make war without them, Admiral Nelson."

Nelson knew his commander to be a more callous man than he. St Vincent never showed much in the way of emotion, gruff kindness being the best Nelson could expect.

"I have written out orders for *Seahorse* to take both you and Captain Freemantle home."

"Thank you, sir, but I would say to you that, my affliction notwithstanding, I am fit for duty."

"I hope you are, Admiral Nelson. I want you back under my command as soon as you feel up to a return. And I would suggest that the sooner you are gone, the sooner that will be."

Chapter Twenty

1798

RETURN NELSON DID, to the blockade off Cadiz six months later, with his rear admiral's flag flying above HMS *Vanguard*. St Vincent was delighted to see him, matters in the Mediterranean having gone from bad to worse. News had come of a fleet of twelve French ships-of-the-line ready to depart from Toulon; infantry and cavalry being loaded into four hundred transports that this fleet would escort. Bonaparte, who had done so much to save the Revolution from collapse, was on the move, destination unknown. Nelson's task was to take a detached squadron back into the Mediterranean, find Bonaparte, his warships and transports, and sink them, an assignment that had caused a furore at home, where several senior admirals were incandescent with rage that such a task should be given to so junior an officer. St Vincent was happy. He wanted ability, not seniority.

"I am obliged to ask if you are fully recovered, Admiral Nelson."

Nelson could never get over the way he was treated by his beagle-eyed commander-in-chief. It was common knowledge that St Vincent was at the mercy of constant headaches, which partly explained his normal behaviour: orders barked, insults heaped, and professional reputations traduced in this very cabin. Suggested courses of action from his junior admirals or captains were generally met with withering sarcasm, any failure of his exacting standards brutally excoriated.

There were things this 63-year-old bachelor believed with all his heart: that the best way to clap a stopper on mutiny was a swift hanging; that any officer who showed slackness in the way he handled his ship should be sent home; that a man once married was lost to the service and near to useless as a commander; that one Englishman in a ship was worth ten of any enemy. Yet Nelson was shown nothing but kindness, which had preceded the loss of his arm, and he had even heard Josiah, who stayed on the station and now had his own ship, praised for the way he emulated his illustrious stepfather. As a member of the inshore squadron blockading Cadiz he had distinguished himself in three separate small-arms actions.

St Vincent showed a hard carapace to the world, but was more emotional than his visitor knew. He loved Nelson for his zeal, for his determination to fight whenever the opportunity to strike presented itself, for his ship handling which was of the highest, and not least for his own earldom, which would have gone begging had not Nelson risked all at the battle from which St Vincent's title came.

"I am, sir, in better health now than when I left for Tenerife."

"Then the bosom of your family has done you the power of good."

"It has, sir."

"You may have *Alexander* and *Orion,* Captains Ball and Saumarez," St Vincent continued breezily. "They and a squadron of frigates will see you into the Mediterranean, and I will reinforce you as my situation permits."

Nelson pondered those names. Saumarez he knew of old, a good-looking Guernseyman, a fine seaman whose main problem was his own awareness of his appearance. He was always immaculately attired and had a reputation as a man who could paint the whole ship without a speck of it marring his dress uniform. Ball, he was disposed to dislike. He had met him in St Omer all those years before, and bridled for the man's unwarranted attentions to the lovely object of Nelson's affections, Kate Andrews.

"Send me fighters, sir," insisted Nelson, "for I intend to find the enemy and send both Bonaparte and his Italian army to the bottom of the sea."

"Do that, Nelson, and we'll take our seats in the Lords together."

They discussed plans to co-ordinate if it turned out that Bonaparte was heading for the West Indies. With cavalry aboard that was unlikely. But, then, he was unpredictable by reputation, and successful to an astonishing degree. Never one to waste time, Nelson's squadron fired their salutes, formed line, and set their course for the Straits of Gibraltar. With a fine topgallant breeze they entered Rosas Bay under the towering rock, to anchor, replenish their stores before proceeding into the Mediterranean.

In Nelson's heightened imagination, exiting one sea to enter another was like cutting a chord. He was leaving behind one set of doubts to be replaced by another. He knew—despite all the efforts he made to convince himself that it was otherwise, despite all his protestations to anyone close enough to hear him that she was the object of his deepest regard—his relations with Fanny had not been resolved.

The homecoming, or rather his journey to Bath to meet wife and family, had been muted. Nothing Nelson had written to tell Fanny of his wound would have had the same effect as the writing itself, a left-handed indecipherable scrawl that Fanny openly admitted had reduced her to tears. Her husband could not confess that the loss bothered him too, or that the wound hadn't healed properly. He still, mentally, reached for the quill with the missing right arm, was surprised to look and see that, although his brain had issued the command, and he could feel his right arm moving, nothing was there. That and his constant pain had to be hidden from Fanny to avoid another bout of weeping.

Right handed or left, in four years away, none of his letters home ever intimated that his regard for Fanny had wavered, neither from Naples, in that silly infatuation with Lady Hamilton, nor even from Genoa when he had gone further and transgressed his marriage vows. He had always written to her as his loyal wife, bosom companion, and lifelong partner. The simple truth was that he didn't know his own mind, and since he was disinclined to discuss it with anyone he was unaware of how common such a notion could be. He wasn't even sure if the doubts still existed, the mere act of homecoming lending deep sentiments to his feelings. The dread he had had at seeing her again when he had set out four years ago had faded.

Their meeting had been marked by a gentle touch of lips on cheek. Yet that had satisfied him in a way he found hard to define, making him realise that there was more than one strand to his personality. The part that craved action and excitement found Fanny trying: the part that loved domesticity, a blazing hearth, gun dogs, and the idea of rubicund children conjured up an image of her as the perfect companion.

Davidson had done a sterling job as his prize agent, and while he wasn't rich he certainly had enough money to live in comfort. His old friend had also done a sterling job for himself, marrying a very pretty and vivacious lady, who had promptly presented him with golden-haired twins, something to make the father *manqué* in Nelson truly envious.

One worry had been laid to rest: the failure at Tenerife was seen as folly, except by those who actively disliked him. Most people he had met, and all of the press, while they had harped on about the loss of the *Fox* and some hundred members of the crew, had concluded that it stood as a heroic failure, a defeat caused more by poor intelligence on enemy strength and the Admiral in command having been asked to do too much with too little.

He was Nelson of the patent bridge, the man who had captured the public imagination. So his credit stood high, and his fellow countrymen demanded the right to place his image upon their walls. This he knew from Locker, to whom he had given, some fifteen years previously, a portrait of himself by John Rigaud. His old mentor had been approached with a request to make prints from it, for sale to the public. How good it was to be praised instead of damned, to have his knighthood conferred by the King in person, and not just sent to him on some foreign station.

King George, no longer irascible in the face of a man now a hero, had asked for a written history of his Mediterranean service, and Nelson knew that that which he had returned was impressive: four single-ship actions, six engagements on land commanding batteries, the cutting-out expeditions numbered ten, and he had captured a couple of towns. That, and his wounds, won him a welcome annual pension of a thousand pounds.

The best day had been when his doctors, reaching for the string that held the ligature inside his wounded stump, had pulled, and instead of acute pain, the whole affair had come away, taking with it all the poisons that had kept it from healing. That was the day he went to the Admiralty to say he was again ready for service.

So he had said goodbye to Fanny in the same gentle way he had greeted her, a dry peck on a dry cheek, still uncertain of his feelings. But for all that, when he thought of her as he penned his near daily letter, it was with kindness and warmth.

A red-coated band played them away from Gibraltar, the God-speed of an Army garrison who had entertained them royally, soldiers who never felt quite safe unless a British fleet was in the Mediterranean. Having raised his hat to the island, and waited till *Orion* and *Alexander*, with four frigates and a sloop in attendance, had cleared the bay, Nelson turned to his new flag captain, Edward Berry.

"My lucky sea, Captain Berry. Set us a course for Toulon. Let's find this Corsican menace and destroy him."

Berry grinned. "What a contest, you and Bonaparte."

"I long to try him on a wind, Berry, for landsman or no, I wager that the Corsican will ignore his admirals and try to control the battle."

"I take leave, sir, to differ," Berry replied. "I would wager that whatever battle we have will be controlled by you."

Nelson was not one to be haunted by words, but that expression of confidence made by Berry and wholly endorsed by him produced a sickening sensation when he recalled them. His return to the Mediterranean had not been the success he had craved, quite the opposite. Between Toulon and Corsica HMS *Vanguard*, caught in a violent storm, had lost every one of her masts, and had been left to roll so heavily on a menacing swell that Berry had been forced to flood the lower decks just to gain some stability. Lacking steerage way the heavy seas of a week-long storm had nearly driven her on to the rocks of several dangerous shores, only saved by the application of Captain Alexander Ball, who used his vessel to tow the flagship out of danger.

At the subsequent interview, which took place in a placid bay resounding to the clatter of shipwright's hammers, Nelson faced Ball with some trepidation. Having been brusque with the man on the few meetings he had attended, he now had to thank him for his ship and probably his life. If Ball knew that his admiral disliked him, it didn't show, and as they talked Nelson felt his aversion evaporate in the face of the man's modesty. He refused to acknowledge that his exceptional behaviour and courage had been anything but the action any other captain would have taken.

What was intended to be brief extended itself to an invitation to dine, and as the meal progressed Nelson found his feelings growing warmer by the course. Ball was a man after his own heart, a fighter, a sailor, and modest with it. Nelson couldn't understand his previous animosity. How could he have so misjudged Ball? It was an indication to him to be more cautious in future, never to let his heart rule over every emotion. When they parted, he was sure that he was saying goodbye to a friend.

They got HMS *Vanguard* back to sea in an astonishing four days, and resumed the hunt for Bonaparte. Nelson's hopes were lifted off Cape Corse by the sight of Thomas Troubridge in HMS *Culloden,* sailing to join him at the head of ten sail-of-the-line. Now a battle fleet, they sailed north to close Cape Sicié, only to discover from a Marseilles merchantman that the Corsican's armada had already departed Toulon. But there was no information as to where he was headed. At least he could call his captains to meet him, so that they could have no doubt about their commander's intentions.

It was a gathering of old friends as well as new faces: Ralph Millar, Troubridge, of course, dark of countenance and doleful by nature. Tom Foley was there, his friend from his first ever ship, now in command of HMS *Goliath,* tall Sam Hood, the son and nephew of admirals, who had been with him at Tenerife. There was also the round-faced and cheerful Louis, his second-in-command, and Galwey, who was mad, Irish and looked it, with his protruding eyes and unkempt ginger hair, and Darby, another Irishman of a more sober disposition. These were good men, the best St Vincent could send him, fighters all.

"Gentlemen," he had begun, "we will, as a fleet, pay not one jot of attention to the Fighting Instructions."

The faces of his captains betrayed no hint of the import of those words. The Fighting Instructions, as rules of engagement, were not designed to confer outright success on a battle fleet: they were designed to avoid complete failure. A maritime nation like Britain couldn't afford to entrust its fleet to the mere whim of an admiral, especially since the appointment of a commander-in-chief might often have more to do with politics than ability.

It was the bane of the service that a captain became an admiral by mere seniority, filling a dead man's shoes. A promising midshipman did not always pass for lieutenant; a good premier did not always rise to be a competent captain. Nor did a man who could command and manoeuvre one ship necessarily have the ability to manage a fleet. To take a fleet into battle, risking death and destruction and win, required skills granted to few.

So the Admiralty had evolved a set of rules tying the hands of individual commanders. A battle was considered a victory if the enemy withdrew. A stalemate, in which no side could claim an advantage, was seen as a positive result; defeat was unthinkable. Failure had dire consequences. Admiral Byng, after a farce of a trial, had been shot on his quarterdeck for failure at Minorca thirty years previously, as Voltaire, the French sage, had put it, *"pour encourager les autres."*

"Gentlemen," Nelson continued, referring to that disgraceful episode, "is there one of us present who has not wondered if we'd share Admiral Byng's fate at some time in our career? I am the

Admiral. That risk is mine. I would ask you to obey the orders I give you in writing and put aside all thoughts of what consequences might attend upon failure."

Nelson rarely raised his voice in company, his even temper being one of his great qualities, but he did know how to be emphatic. "Why? Because we cannot fail. We have ships and men that have been at sea for years. Our gun crews achieve a rate of fire that will be double that of our enemies. Not a day goes by that does not include practice in boarding. In short, gentlemen, we are professional naval officers. Our opponents have been decimated by the guillotine and politics, and are led by a bullock, a blue-coated one, I grant you, but a soldier nevertheless, and like to be a buffoon on water."

Some applauded, others grinned. Fat-faced Louis cried, "Hear him."

"Our fleet will be split into three divisions. The pair closest to the enemy battleships, wherever we find them, will engage them immediately, the third will seek to destroy the transports. Since the object of the French plan is to carry troops to whatever destination they have in mind, defending those will become a priority. The first two divisions must and will interpose themselves between the transports and the enemy flag. We will make them fight their way through to provide succour.

"My signals lieutenant will give you the outline of a set of flags each, relevant to your own ship. But we all know that flags can be obscured. I therefore expect you to act according to your outline instructions without recourse to a command from me. These, too, will be in writing."

There was more to discuss, a dozen different outlines. Where would the enemy be? Would it be day or night? The sea-state would have a bearing, as would wind direction. Would the French have an anchorage under their lee to which they could run for safety? What if they split their forces? Nelson had to make sure that every one of his inferior officers understood that their ships were instruments of war; that an individual loss was acceptable, given a positive result to the battle. The conference broke up in a happy mood.

What followed was the worst sixty days of Nelson's life, a seemingly fruitless voyage around the Mediterranean. His instructions from St Vincent, to find and destroy the enemy, fell on the hurdle of his lack of frigates. They were the eyes of the fleet, able swiftly to seek likely rendezvous, the bays and harbours where the French might congregate, then report back to an admiral who could mount an attack. He had too few for an expanse of water that stretched from Gibraltar to the Black Sea.

Bonaparte threatened Malta, Tuscany, Naples, the Adriatic, Tunis, Algiers, Egypt, and the rest of the Ottoman Empire. If there was a grand design, it was secret. Nelson sailed to Alexandria, only to find the anchorage devoid of French shipping. On his return to the Straits of Messina he heard that Malta had fallen to the French, but that Bonaparte was no longer there. He had disappeared again! Faced with a frightened King Ferdinand, still at peace with France, he had to use subterfuge to keep his ships victualled, using what frigates and sloops he had to scour the seas while he remained inactive at Syracuse.

Reports came in of sightings at every corner of the Inland Sea. Thomas Hardy, now master and commander of the brig *Mutine,* spoke with a Ragusan trader in the Adriatic who had sighted a fleet heading east. Was this Bonaparte? Had Nelson guessed right about Alexandria, only arriving too soon to catch a slow-sailing convoy of four hundred transports?

Off they sailed again, Nelson sick, so great was his anxiety. Hailed as a hero in England for his exploits at St Vincent, forgiven for heroic failure at Tenerife, he knew that whatever reputation he enjoyed would disappear like a puff of smoke from a chimney if he failed to find Bonaparte. How confident he had been at those early conferences, how foolish his plans seemed now.

And this voyage to Egypt seemed just as fruitless as the first. Two ships had looked into Alexandria only to find its harbours empty, a fact signalled to Nelson as soon as the fleet came in sight. It was with a heavy heart that the Admiral ordered a signal to turn eastwards for what he suspected to be a futile search of the coastline.

"Frigates," he said to Tom Allen, as his bovine servant served him a solitary dinner. "When they cut me open, Tom, they will find that word engraved on my heart. If I had half a dozen, I'd have Bonaparte."

Allen regarded the man he served with an experienced eye, wondering if he should say something. Nelson was so jumpy he daren't knock one salver into another. The slightest unusual noise made him jerk round to look, evidence of the tension he was harbouring in what he thought was a calm demeanour. He had heard that Frank Lepée had never feared to advise Nelson or to tell him he was wrong. But Lepée had been shown the cabin door, which was the last thing Tom Allen wanted. Serving the Admiral was a soft billet, which he was not about to sacrifice. Let the Admiral tie himself in knots, it was no job of a servant to act the doctor.

The food lay uneaten on the plate, to get cold and congeal. Nelson, looking at it, was inclined to see his career in a similar light. He knew from the faces of the ship's officers that they felt the same. They had started out with high hopes under a commander who never missed a chance for action. This was the place to be; he was the man to be with, yet it had all fallen flat. Berry, he knew, would be above him with his officers, eating a silent repast, thinking the same as his admiral, that they had missed the boat.

All those admirals at home, above him on the list, would be crowing now, telling all who would listen what folly it had been to appoint such a junior and vainglorious character to command. People who had treated him as a hero six months before would shun him now, the man who couldn't find an armada of over four hundred ships. And just where was Bonaparte, a man who had taken on the features of a demon in Nelson's mind? He was attacking something somewhere, and the man ordered to stop him was in the wrong place.

Nelson started to shake. Was it a recurrence of the malaria, a disease which always came to attack him when his spirits were low? Or was it just the lack of sleep, endless nights spent lying in his cot gnawing at the problems he faced both professionally and personally? Tom Allen, had he dared, would have told him to eat, which he had scarce done for a week.

The scraping of a dozen chairs, followed by the sound of running feet, distracted Nelson but did nothing to dent a miserable, sickly mood that had him close to seeking rest. Even the peremptory knock on his cabin door failed to rouse him and he left Allen to respond. But the flushed, excited face of Midshipman Hoste, sent to give him a message, set his heart racing.

"*Zealous* signalling, sir. The enemy is in Aboukir Bay, fifteen sail moored in line of battle."

Chapter Twenty-One

AT THOSE WORDS the enervating malaise fell away. The whole ship was alive with cheering by the time he made the deck. From his position in the line Nelson could see little of his leading vessels, but he trusted to the ships in the van to take the appropriate action, Foley in *Goliath* and Sam Hood in *Zealous*. It was after 1:30, and raking the high masts that lay in Aboukir Bay with a telescope, their hulls cut off by a headland, he began to make his calculations. He had already sent a frigate ahead to lay off and repeat signals to his leading vessels, which would attack unless he issued orders to desist. Was that wise?

Hood and Foley would barely make the bay before sunset, and the rest of his ships would engage in the increasing gloom, the last ships in the line going into battle in darkness. That particularly applied to *Alexander* and *Swiftsure,* straining to catch up, having been detached to look into Alexandria. A night battle was always a chancy affair, with the exercise of command impossible. And the French were anchored in a strong defensive position. But Horatio Nelson had laid out his principles, which were based on an abiding trust in his captains and a deep faith in the men they commanded.

"Captain Berry, be so good as to signal to the squadron, prepare for action."

"Sir," Berry replied, beaming.

"My dinner is on the board, and I intend that this day it should be eaten. If you wish you may join me."

Information came in piecemeal over the next five hours: signals from the frigate standing off to pass orders, through speaking trumpets over the taffrail of HMS *Minotaur* sailing ahead of *Vanguard,* through excited midshipmen sent by their captains in boats, and all that was allied to what his own lookouts could see. Nelson perceived that the French Admiral, de Brueys, had anchored with his strongest vessels to the rear of his flagship, the 120-gun *L'Orient*. The vessels closest to the approaching British squadron were the weakest in his fleet.

By the amount of activity on the beach there appeared to be numerous shore parties, some of whom would struggle to get back to their ships before battle commenced. There were also gaps between the anchored ships large enough for a 74 to sail through, so orders went out to all ships to prepare sheet anchors that would hold the warships by the stern and keep steady and true whatever fire they poured on the enemy.

"Monsieur de Brueys is not anticipating a fight today, Mr Hoste."

The youngster fixed Nelson with his huge soft brown eyes. With his now spotty skin, no one could look less the warrior and, indeed, so small had Hoste been that Nelson had worried for him when he first came to sea. He had grown now, and was nearing an age to sit for lieutenant. As for fighting, he was apparently a right Tartar when it came to fisticuffs.

"He will get one, sir, won't he?"

"It would be interesting to know what would prevent such a thing."

Hoste knew he was being tested, just as he knew that there were no traps in the examination. "We lack charts, sir, so there may be shoal water that would run us aground."

Nelson smiled. "There's enough for the French."

"There might also be shore batteries, given all the men that have vacated the ships."

"Well spotted, Mr Hoste." The youngster talked on, mentioning the lack of light, the possibility of the unexpected, as Nelson listened. "And given all this, and assuming you were Monsieur de Brueys, what would you have done?"

"I'd want to fight in open water, sir. I'd have put to sea as soon as I spotted our topsails."

Nelson lifted his telescope then, and fixed it on the Admiral's pennant flying at the masthead of *L'Orient*. "So would I, Mr Hoste, so would I."

Goliath was just edging *Zealous* to be first into the bay, both ships with leadsmen casting for sandbars. Captain Tom Foley could hear Sam Hood over the gunfire exhorting his men to greater efforts as they rounded the headland protecting the anchorage. The cannon fire came from a French sloop inshore, trying by its pinpricks to persuade either of the captains to pursue it into water shallow enough to run them aground. Foley had made his way to the forepeak, to raise his glass and look at the enemy, the sides of the vessels aglow and orange in the light of a sinking sun. In 27 years, much had changed about the midshipman who had challenged his admiral to a pissing contest, but he still had sharp, bird-like eyes and tidy features, even if they were lined with age.

Foley could see men hurrying about the deck of the lead French ship, *Le Guerrier*. He could also see that, with the tide running east, she was straining on her single forward anchor cable. There wasn't much tidal movement in the Mediterranean, a rise of two feet or so, but there was enough. That meant his enemy, when the tide turned, would swing through an arc of 180 degrees. The deduction that followed was simple. *Le Guerrier* had to have enough water under her keel to do that, which meant that ahead of that anchor cable was a whole ship's length of water deep enough for *Goliath* to sail through.

"Quartermaster," he yelled, "bring her head round and point me to the shore. I want to shave that anchor cable." More softly, he added to the midshipman at his side, "Get off a signal to the flag and tell him of my intentions, and ask the premier to take us down to topsails."

The whole bay was bathed in orange light, the tops of the wavelets pink instead of white. Nelson's lookouts had told him of *Goliath*'s change of course. Silently he blessed his luck in having such men along with him, men who understood not only his orders but also his philosophy: that it was necessary to look for all advantage and take it without recourse to a higher authority. Foley was going to sail inside the French line, and take his opponent on a side that was likely undefended.

The first boom of cannon fire rippled through the twilight air, and Nelson heard Berry order that the time, 6:28 p.m., be noted. His nerves were jumping again, worried that Foley might ground his ship and leave himself at the mercy of shore batteries. Hands clenched, he willed his lookouts to yell that he was through, but whole minutes went by without a sound. Looking round, Nelson realised that the whole ship was holding its breath.

"*Goliath*'s through," came the yell, "with *Zealous* in her wake."

"Signal to all captains, Mr Berry, to hoist out distinguishing lights."

Within minutes men on every ship had raced aloft to lash lanterns to the upper masts, combinations and colours that could be noted. Now Nelson knew that neither he nor those to his rear, in the pitch black of a moonless night, would fire into their own. Over the next hour, as darkness fell, he watched the lanterns of *Orion*, *Audacious*, and *Theseus* follow Foley's lead and take the French on the inshore side of the bay, pouring into them a pounding rate of gunfire that sent visible parts of the ships flying into the air.

Sixth in line, Nelson ordered Berry to stay on the open flank, sailing straight ahead to take station of the third ship in the French line, *Le Spartiate,* reducing to topsails just before commencing to fight. High flaring lanterns, clear against a black sky, told Nelson that *Theseus* was bombarding the other flank.

Berry dropped the sheet anchor to hold his stern, *Vanguard* within pistol shot of the enemy, then gave the order to open fire. The Frenchman, with guns that could be put to good effect, had already raked him twice with two quick salvoes but that rate of fire did not survive the first British broadside. It was only by the flash of cannon fire that Nelson saw what damage his flagship did; that and the sound of screaming men.

He saw in one flash that the mainmast was going, taking with it rigging, spars, chains, and men. Parts of the bulwarks of the French ship flew off, exposing those on deck to the withering fire of the next salvo. He could imagine the hell between decks on both sides, so much worse for the enemy than for his gunners toiling below. There would be men here dead and dying, but not as many as on *Spartiate* and that was what counted. Eight ships now battered five Frenchmen. In the flashes of gunfire they could see that *Spartiate* was completely dismasted, its bulwarks in shreds, the deck covered in men whole or in bits, glistening blood running out of the scuppers. Wisely, those to his rear had passed him to seaward to take on unengaged enemies further up the line.

That was where he should be, opposite the largest ship in the battle, and the enemy Admiral. Nelson was just about to request Berry to haul up the stern anchor and move on to face *L'Orient* when he was felled by a tremendous blow to the head that sent him flying backwards into his flag captain's arms. The pain was instant, as was the certain knowledge that he was going to die. As if from a mile away he could hear voices around him, commands to get him below to the surgeon.

"I am killed," he croaked, as Berry lowered him to the deck. "Remember me to my wife."

How stupid those words sounded once he had uttered them, how pointless and futile. But for all that, if he was going to die he had God to thank that it was at this hour. Battle would still rage, but he knew de Brueys would not beat him, that what had happened already presaged a great victory. He could pass on in the heat of battle like James Wolfe, and there was nothing he would have wished for more if he could not have life. And perhaps, if God were kinder still, he too would, like his hero, expire at a moment of triumph.

He did know that he was blind; the eye that had survived the shattering of stones at Calvi, and which had been milky ever since, gave him only a dim view of what was happening around him. The other was just blackness, with warm blood running down to give a salty taste to his parched mouth.

Arms lifted him and he recognised the voice of Giddings in his ear. "You'll be all right, your honour, when we get you below."

Berry reached forward to lift a long patch of skin off Nelson's face, pinning it back to the forehead from which it had been sliced. Other arms took him and, jerking, eyes closed, Nelson was carried below to the cockpit, lit by shuddering lanterns and full of the dull boom of cannon fire and the screams and moans of wounded sailors. Above their heads gun carriages rumbled out, blasted forth, then groaned as they were flung back by the recoil.

"Mr Jefferson, the Admiral," Giddings yelled, lowering Nelson so that he could stand supported on his own two feet.

"No," said Nelson, opening his eyes and realising that he could still see. Jefferson was up to his armpits in blood and gore, the area around his feet awash and shiny red, sprinkled with limbs that the surgeon had already sawn off. "Let me wait my turn."

"Your honour," insisted Giddings.

"There's near a hundred men in here, I fancy, Giddings, all as good as their admiral."

Giddings didn't argue, but by supporting Nelson more fully he allowed the other sailor to detach himself and go to the surgeon. Nelson was laid on some sacks by the time Jefferson came and probed the huge gash. He announced that the wound was deceptive, not as bad as it looked, and that Nelson was in no immediate peril. Unconvinced, his admiral sent for the parson, Mr Comyn, so that messages could be written now, to be sent to his wife and his second-in-command.

Lying on his sacks, with the bleeding ceased but the pain increasing, Nelson listened to a stream of messages, slowly but surely coming round to the view that he was indeed going to live. *Spartiate* struck at 8:30, and here before him, as Jefferson stitched his wound, stood Berry with the French Captain's sword, plus the news that two other Frenchmen had been struck, while three more, including *L'Orient,* would shortly be overcome.

To get him away from the noise of men wounded and dying and the rumbling of cannon overhead they shifted Nelson to the bread room, and there, deep in the bowels of the ship, in a room lined with tin to keep out rats, he heard the depth of his victory increase at what seemed no more than ten-minute intervals. Demanding pen and paper, Nelson began to write his despatch to the First Lord.

Admiral Sir Horatio Nelson KB.
Aboukir Bay off the coast of Egypt

My Lord,

Almighty God has blessed His Majesty's *arms in battle* . . .

The door opened and Berry was there once more, to tell him that *L'Orient* appeared to be on fire. "Her cabin is ablaze, sir, and I can't see they have left the means to check it while they remain under bombardment."

Nelson struggled to get up, but failed. He felt weak, but his voice was strong. "Help me, Berry. We must see if we can save her."

"The doctor, sir—"

"Is not your superior, Captain Berry." Nelson grinned to take the sting out of the words. "I must see for myself."

He arrived on deck to be told that three more Frenchmen had been struck, an almost unbelievable result. Berry took him to the side and pointed out the flames leaping about the stern of the French flagship, a conflagration that illuminated it all the way to the bowsprit and bathed the whole bay in an ethereal light. In the water hundreds of heads bobbed, some clinging to wreckage, others swimming or floundering.

"Captain Berry, get boats out to rescue survivors!"

It was light enough to see *Swiftsure* and *Alexander,* late arrivals at the battle, pouring a merciless barrage into the stern of the French flagship. If they had the means to stop the blaze the pounding of British cannon prevented them from doing so. The poop was a mass of flames but brave men on the lower deck were still working her guns, replying to the two British 74s. Nelson pointed this out to the crowd of officers and mids surrounding him. "Look hard, gentlemen. We do not have an exclusive call on bravery and honour."

The flames hit what rigging was still left standing, shooting up to the tops like a racing squirrel. They could see ships close by, faced with the sailors' greatest dread, a spreading conflagration, cutting cables and sheet anchors to get clear. Only Ball stayed in position, his pumps working flat out to drench his decks and upperworks with water, this so he could keep his guns firing in the increasing, metal-melting heat. But when the decks were alight even Ball knew that the enemy was doomed and hauled himself clear of danger.

Nelson saw the flames suddenly balloon out, mixed with a mass of timber. A wall of air hit his face followed by an ear-shattering boom that pressed in on his flesh. Looking up he saw *L'Orient* disintegrate, even her guns tossed skywards by the force of the blast that ripped out of her magazine, the hull driven down into the encroaching waters so that the flames, which had illuminated the whole battle scene, were suddenly extinguished, plunging everyone into stygian darkness.

It was minutes later that bits of *L'Orient* came back to earth, wood, metal, tattered fragments of sail, and the limbs of men blown to small pieces by the force of the explosion. By then, aboard the ships of Nelson's fleet, the cheering had already begun.

Chapter Twenty-Two

THE SIGHT of a British frigate, beating up into the Bay of Naples, flags streaming from the masts, was enough to cause panic in some breasts, anxiety in others, and hope in a few. Sir William, trusting the eyes of others, received the news at his dressing table and immediately ordered that a boat should be sent out to greet the new arrivals, with instructions to carry to him at speed whatever message they bore.

Standing by the windows of Emma's private apartments, her new friend Cornelia Knight observed the way the frigate anchored, saw the speed with which two young officers alighted into Sir William's boat, and felt a frisson of fear as she contemplated what news they might carry. France had been triumphant everywhere these last five years. The Revolution had humbled all of northern Italy, overrun the Papal States and Rome itself, taken and held the Low Countries and Flanders. Bonaparte, their famous Corsican general, was abroad in the Mediterranean, seeking God only knew what lands to conquer.

The whole world knew he was at sea with a strong fleet and transports carrying the army with which he had humbled Austria. The destination of that fleet had been the only subject of conversation for a month, since the news had arrived that Bonaparte had captured Malta. Had he gone east to threaten the Adriatic or Egypt? Had he gone west to threaten Gibraltar? Or was he coming here, to burn, destroy, and loot Naples?

"They are close enough to see their faces, Emma."

Emma left the writing table to take the telescope from her friend. The first image to fill the glass when she had adjusted it was that of William Hoste, whom she named to Cornelia. The other officer, a lieutenant, was a stranger to her. Then she lifted the instrument to look over the ship, sitting on the still waters of the bay, sails now neatly furled, an image of peaceful intent.

Mary Cadogan entered, wearing her customary apron, tied at the waist by the chain that held the heavy keys to the palazzo. "Sir William asks that you join him in his library."

"He will insist on greeting them formally," Emma said, for the benefit of Cornelia Knight.

"Will my presence affect that?"

"No Cornelia, it will not."

The trio stood to greet the two officers as soon as they heard their footsteps echo on the marble staircase. Sir William was wondering, as he had since they'd been spotted, whether what they said would be a prelude to flight or celebration. If the former, what should he take with him and what should he leave? If the latter, what was the state of his larders and cellars? Years of waiting for news had inured him to over-reaction in either direction. How many times had he anticipated a momentous despatch only to be handed a packet of social letters?

The double doors swung open to admit the pair. Naval officers they might be but they looked absurdly young, no more than boys, two faces that were struggling to appear controlled.

"Sir William," said the one who could barely be said to be the eldest, "I am Lieutenant Capel, and this is Mr Hoste. We bring despatches from Admiral Sir Horatio Nelson."

A second's pause followed, in which both young faces contorted with effort, before breaking into full grins, their voices rising to near shouts as they imparted the news. "A great victory! The French fleet is utterly destroyed! Admiral de Brueys was brought to battle in Aboukir Bay and . . ."

Sir William saw Emma begin to go, but could not react quickly enough to catch her. Neither could his two visitors, though they moved with speed in an attempt to break her fall. She hit the stone floor with an audible thump partly covered by cries from her husband and her friend to fetch the smelling salts. Capel and Hoste lifted her inert body on to a divan, then stepped back to stand like mourners at a wake.

"Months of worry have caused this."

"You may worry no more, sir."

"Admiral Nelson?"

"Bears a wound, sir," replied Hoste, "but though he suffers from the effects of it the surgeon assured us they would pass."

"Tell me what happened," demanded Sir William, standing to allow a servant to administer the salts. "Briefly."

"We caught them at anchor, sir," Capel replied, his near black eyes flashing with the memory, "though they were ranged in line of battle. It has been proposed that de Brueys did not consider the possibility of an immediate attack, so had made no preparation."

"The result?"

"Five ships-of-the-line taken as prizes, two burnt and Admiral de Brueys' flagship, *L'Orient,* blown to bits. Two 74s, we believe under Rear Admiral Villeneuve, escaped, *Guillaume Tell* and *Généraux.* They had with them a trio of frigates, but that is all. To all extents the French menace in the Mediterranean is gone."

"We must tell the King," said Sir William.

The carriage that had brought them from the mole was still harnessed and it was but a short journey to the Palazzo Reale. Admittance to the royal chamber was immediate, and there sat King Ferdinand and his queen, with all of their children, apparently breakfasting quietly as if all was well with the world, as if no frigate had entered the bay that morning. But Sir William knew that this was window dressing, an act designed to demonstrate that they were brave enough to face news good or bad. In truth Their Sicilian Majesties would be in turmoil. Somewhere close by, loaded and ready to flee, would be a line of carriages.

"Your Majesty, I bring you good tidings. Admiral Nelson, on the afternoon of August first, found and engaged the French fleet in Egyptian waters. I am happy to say that he has achieved the most astounding of victories, and that the French menace to your kingdom is no more."

The Queen had a hand to her throat, as though the guillotine blade that had beheaded her sister was on her flesh. Sir William could see that Ferdinand was trying to be regal, trying to play the role his titles and birthright demanded of him. But the natural child in him could not contain his joy.

Suddenly he rushed to embrace the British Ambassador, yelling, "You have saved my kingdom! You have saved my family!"

The elder children were weeping, the younger ones confused. Their mother was on her feet now, moving around the chamber, swaying as if to swoon and looking to various statues for support. Ferdinand was babbling away to Sir William while the two messengers stood confused, not understanding a word. It was ten minutes before the wailing ceased, during which Maria Carolina had sunk to the floor to pray. Evidence that the news was abroad came from the sudden cacophony of church bells that pealed out over the city. Within the hour all of Naples was celebrating its deliverance, an hour during which, with Sir William translating, the two young naval officers described the battle in detail.

"You know, sir," said Capel, "of the chase we had. I have never seen my admiral so vexed and anxious as the thought plagued him that he had missed Bonaparte."

"He so much wanted to encounter him at sea," added Hoste, "to prove that Bonaparte's success on land counted for nothing."

"Nelson said so in his letters," Sir William replied, this while Ferdinand was asking him a question. "His Majesty counts himself a sea officer, gentlemen. Please explain the disposition of the fleet."

Neither Hoste nor Capel was fazed by that request. In the week it had taken them to make Naples they had had precious little else to talk about. They knew that they were privileged to have been present at the greatest feat of naval arms since the destruction of the Spanish Armada. In the week following the action, before they received their duplicate despatches to carry to Naples, every story of every officer, French as well as British, had been condensed into a narrative account of the battle.

They spoke in turns, using maps when Ferdinand produced them, tracing the route Nelson had taken in his pursuit of Bonaparte. East, west, and east again, the information that he had missed them by a whisker twice. They described the disposition of the fleet, the King nodding sagely at each piece of information as though these were decisions he himself would have made, had he been in command.

"We have it from the French prisoners that, seeing the time of day, de Brueys though it unlikely we would attack."

"He should have studied Nelson," said Hoste, eyes alight with hero-worship. "When he did clear for action, he did so only on the seaward side."

When this was translated, Ferdinand looked confused. Capel was busy arranging model ships, ten or so in line with another eight bearing down on them, a cloth rolled up to represent the arc of Aboukir Bay. With his finger he showed Foley's route, looking at the King to ensure he understood.

"They fought well, the Frenchmen," said Hoste. "There was no thought of surrender, and every one of our ships suffered great damage, *Bellerophon* particularly, she losing a full third of her complement as casualties. But they were out-gunned, out-manned, and out-fought. *Le Peuple Souverain* cut her cable and ran aground; *L'Orient,* it appeared, had been painting and some of the residue of that caught fire. The rest, barring *Guillaume Tell* and *Le Généraux,* struck."

The destruction of Admiral de Brueys' flagship had been heard ten miles away. Troubridge, so eager to enter the battle, had run his ship aground at the head of the bay. Later he said he thought that he had suffered some form of explosion below, so great was the force of the blast transmitted through the water. It transpired that the treasure of the Knights of St John, looted from Malta, with sixty ingots of gold to the value of £600,000, had gone to the bottom with her.

"The cost?" asked Sir William. He did not mean in terms of money.

"Some two hundred dead on our side, sir," Capel replied, "with seven hundred wounded. The enemy losses were of the order of two thousand dead or missing."

"This will mean a peerage," said Sir William. A servant entered to give the Ambassador a message. He smiled, looked at the two young officers, and said, "My wife seems quite recovered. She is in an open carriage at the gates and desires, if you have finished your report, that you join her."

Half in love with her already, both young men rushed to comply. They found her as Sir William had described, wearing on her head an embroidered turban that read "Nelson and Victory." Emma Hamilton took them through the streets, singing patriotic songs, shouting that Britannia had triumphed and generally whipping up an already excited populace to a frenzy of celebration. She was aided by two young men who thought her a most remarkable creature, young men who spent as much time admiring her and thinking about bedding her as they did about the victory at the Nile.

The arrival of the *Vanguard* in the Bay of Naples, under tow, part of the trickle of ships that made up Nelson's victorious fleet, came as no surprise. Fishing boats, trading-vessels, lookouts on high points of the southern Italian coast had been searching for her topsails for weeks. The journey from the Straits of Messina to the Bay of Naples had been regal progress as ships altered course to hold some tenuous link to an English sailor who had saved Europe and had placed the most telling check for five years on that monster, the French Revolution.

Hardy had been made post after the battle and had taken over as flag captain, while Berry had been sent home with the despatches announcing the victory, which would surely get him a knighthood. Despite his best endeavours, Thomas Hardy, big, bluff, red-faced, and a bit of a quarterdeck tyrant, couldn't get his admiral to rest. Bandage over his bad eye, in constant pain from the wound it covered, letter after letter poured from Nelson's pen, as he sent what frigates he could muster flying in all directions, promising, pleading, flattering or chastising, depending on who was the recipient. When not writing he was pacing the deck, thinking and planning, as if there were still a French menace afloat to chase, his good eye searching the horizon for the return of his messengers.

Contact with ships from home brought out-of-date news, the despatch of the victory at the Nile yet to reach London. Fanny was pleased with a portrait by Lemuel Abbot, now finished, that he had sat for on his last leave; her son Josiah, previously praised, was for some reason in bad odour with St Vincent, and was to be sent to serve with his stepfather. That troubled him little, since hardly an officer breathing was not in trouble with the acerbic St Vincent. Davidson wrote, creating the usual pangs of jealousy when he mentioned his offspring. He had answers from friends and the Admiralty to the requests he had made for this person or that to be advanced; bills, pleas for intercession, enough to keep him occupied for a week, all of which would have to be replied to. And having discovered his secretary was useless—the man had fainted at the Nile—Nelson had dismissed him and undertaken the correspondence with the help of the parson, Mr Comyn.

Nelson came on deck without his bandage as they opened the bay, hair swept forward to cover the angry scar. He began pointing out the landmarks to a pair of the younger midshipmen, part of a group who never ceased to trail him, as if by touching his hem they could pick up an ounce of glory. He named the two great castles, Dell'ovo and Nuovo, that dominated the approaches, detailing the armament that made it a dangerous place to attempt to take from the sea. There were bastions, too, covering the arms of the bay, full of great guns that could send a ball though a wooden ship's hull. The battery of St Elmo was right above the Palazzo Sessa, and that got a special mention.

"Take note, young Pasco, of the dangers of sailing into such a place. See how, at a mile distant, they will make it warm for any vessel caught in a crossfire. They are cunningly placed so that an assaulting fleet must wonder at which fort to return fire, and the wind in these parts is fickle enough to see you becalmed under the guns."

"You could take it, sir," protested Quilliam, the other young mid, his freckled face alight with faith.

"Not I, Mr Quilliam, but I do reckon that if any men could confound those defences it would be British tars."

"How would you assault Naples, sir? asked Pasco.

Nelson was tired, Hardy could see that, and he moved to send these pests about their occasions. For a moment the expression on Nelson's face lightened, as if the pain and all his cares had dissolved. "Why, I should use charm, young sir, which is what you must do when you go ashore."

"They say the ladies are very fine in Naples, sir."

"They are to heroes, which is what you are. Every man in this fleet is a hero."

"We are about to anchor, sir. Permission to signal our tow."

"Make it so, Captain Hardy."

"Mr Pasco, Mr Quilliam, you must have duties to attend to when anchoring. I suggest that is where you belong."

Anchoring in a bay full of boats come to greet them was a tricky matter, especially since *Vanguard,* having lost her foremast and four seamen with it, required to be towed by a frigate. There were barges with bands playing "Rule Britannia," "Britons Strike Home," and "See the Conquering Hero Come." Everybody of quality in Naples was there to greet the victor of the Nile, and they had banners to prove it, some woven with images that were far from true representations of the man they admired. Behind him, the quays were lined with a mass of people, all cheering.

"Sir William Hamilton," said Hardy, pointing to a barge pushing through the throng to head for the side of his ship.

Nelson leant over the bulwark and saw Sir William, but searched for his wife. Lady Hamilton was sitting down, but her head was up, looking towards him.

"Five years," he murmured to himself, his eyes fixed on the woman who had so made his blood race. As the barge got ever closer so did her face, under a broad brimmed hat and muslin scarf. The pain in his head grew worse as he stared, but it was not the cut that caused it so much as the way his heart was thumping in his chest. He didn't want to go down to the entry port to greet her, that being dark and shaded. He wanted to see her here on his quarterdeck, in the sunshine, perhaps with her hat off, to find out if he felt now as he had the last time they met.

"Hardy, my apologies to the Ambassador. If he has no objection I will receive him here."

Hardy smiled and tossed his square head, as if to say, "He'll damn well see you where you please."

It was a tense five minutes, from the point at which the barge disappeared from his eyeline, to hooking on and the passengers coming aboard. For some reason he found himself thinking of his wife again: the image of Fanny gazing admiringly at that Lemuel Abbot portrait she'd written of induced feelings of deep guilt. He knew that his God could see into his soul, was aware of every thought and every action. How could He forgive him for what he was thinking now?

The guilt evaporated at the moment he saw her. Emma Hamilton emerged from the companionway, smiling, her cheeks red with excitement, followed by a bright-eyed Sir William, who was much aged and thinner than the man Nelson remembered. Suddenly he realised that he, too, must present a very different apparition to his guests.

"My dear Admiral Nelson, you have joined the immortals."

Nelson locked eyes with Sir William's wife, who stood examining him, taking in the empty sleeve and the mist-covered iris of his damaged eye. "I fear I am a much-reduced creature, milady."

"You are very much more substantial to me, sir," she replied.

He almost didn't hear the words, so taken was he with the look in those huge green eyes. They were like a mirror to her soul and carried in them something deeper than mere admiration. Suddenly she flew at him and, in a very unladylike fashion, threw her arms around his neck and kissed his cheeks.

Chapter Twenty-Three

THE PALAZZO SESSA was illuminated by three thousand candles, liveried servants lining the entrance to greet the stream of guests. The King and Queen attended, though not in a fully royal capacity, because Naples was supposed to be at peace with France, even had plenipotentiaries in Paris discussing an alliance. Yet the battle of the Nile had changed everything; France was not to be quite so feared, with no ships and no army, and ambassadors, princes, the cream of the Neapolitan aristocracy mingled with streams of naval officers from the victorious fleet.

Emma Hamilton's entrance was the kind of staged affair she loved. Her dress had been specially made, very low cut, blue and gold with an edging embroidered with the intertwined names of Nelson and the Nile. The transparent shawl with which she preserved some modesty was white, liberally sprinkled with gold anchors, while on her head she wore a cap of victory, which kept her hair high. On the arm of her elderly husband, she entered the room that had once held the bulk of Sir William's excavated treasures. These had been packed ready for shipment to England, there to be sold, allowing the room to be turned into a space that could accommodate the three hundred guests.

Now Nelson toyed with the thought he had entertained when the couple had come aboard *Vanguard:* that Sir William had aged much more than he. Wounds, battle, constantly being at sea, and the strain of command had done for Nelson, implanting lines on his skin and greying his once blond hair, while at sixty-eight, age alone seemed to have altered the Chevalier. He was thinner all over, but particularly so in the legs, which looked spindly in his tight white breeches. The nose, which had always been prominent, now stood out starkly, this in a face that showed an excess of definition due to taut skin.

Nelson was seated in the place of honour, with the King and

Queen on his left, while Emma and Sir William sat to his right. A slightly unusual arrangement, in terms of rank, had him between the two ladies, both husbands outside them, for which Nelson was grateful. Sir William he could abide, but he had eaten enough meals beside the gluttonous Ferdinand to want ever to do so again.

If the food and the setting were magnificent, the proximity of Lady Hamilton was agony. The Queen had no English and his foreign language skills extended no further than the need to ask for an enemy to surrender, so any conversation with Maria Carolina had to be translated by her good friend Emma and, in a room full of noise, she found it necessary to lean across the guest of honour to undertake that task.

Physical contact was constant, on one occasion her hand actually rested on his knee, squeezing it as she made some pertinent point to the Queen. Asked for his impressions of the battle, Nelson obliged, while claiming that his position in the line, followed by his wound, precluded him from being the best-placed observer. But he was observing Lady Hamilton with a proximity that both excited and appalled him. Her head was often no more than an inch from his, a beautifully formed ear enticingly erotic. Nelson had always been attracted to voices, and hers, low, varied, and always with that hint of amusement, entranced him. He could smell her perfume and her hair, and sense the heat of her body, so had to fight to avoid looking down the front of her dress to her alluring bosom. An occasional squirm was required to ease the pressure on his groin, his napkin pressed into service to cover an embarrassment he could do nothing to control.

Such a situation drove Nelson to drink more than was usual, a greater quantity than the Queen, though less than Lady Hamilton, who grew bolder the more she consumed. Any attempt at modesty by her guest was overborne in a flurry of arms and loud laughter, with many a plea to Sir William to intercede and tell Nelson he was a hero, and should behave as such; that he was their shield and must make Naples his Mediterranean base.

"I had intended to use Syracuse, milady."

"Sicily!" cried Emma. "We will not hear of you departing, Admiral Nelson, will we, Sir William?"

The Chevalier nodded gravely. "It would certainly grieve us, sir."

"I won't be off just yet, Sir William. You will have noticed, even with an unpractised eye, that my ship lacks masts. I doubt the dockyard can repair her in less than a week."

"But we wish you here for more than that, Admiral," Emma pealed. "A month, a year, for ever. If you do not promise me, I shall request a royal command."

That had her leaning across to the Queen again, babbling in German, and what ease Nelson had managed was ruined. Emma Hamilton had put one hand behind his back, better to reach over. The absence of his right arm brought her closer to him than would otherwise have been the case. He could see her lips moving even if he couldn't understand what she was saying. He wanted to grab her there and then with his one good hand, but he sat back instead, forcing himself to look right past her to Sir William, smiling at the Ambassador, an expression that was returned in full measure.

He can't see it, thank God, Nelson thought.

Sir William Hamilton, with his acute sense of observation, was thinking that his wife had gone slightly overboard with regard to Nelson. The nautical simile made him grin just as the man in question looked at him. Certainly the Admiral was a hero, who deserved the thanks of half a dozen nations. He deserved this celebration, too, and all those that were bound to follow. Every city in Britain would want to toast him, and since he was such a hero, women by the yard would fawn over him. The fact that this was true did not alter the fact that his wife was one of them.

Emma's husband put it down to the heightened sense of theatricality that was one of her abiding traits; that and her need to be at the centre of things. Nelson might be the nation's hero, but Lady Hamilton wanted him to be her hero as well, somehow to give the impression that she had had a part in the Nile victory.

"Have you thought, sir," asked Sir William, "about your title?"

"I wouldn't wish to tempt Providence."

"It would be improvident of His Majesty King George, if not downright imprudent, to hesitate in granting you a peerage. I dare-say the thanks of the nation, in financial terms, would not be too much to ask."

Of course Nelson had mulled over these things since the morning of victory. He would have been stupid not to. A title was a near certainty, indeed there were those who had insisted he deserved one after St Vincent. He had scotched that suggestion. A peerage required deep pockets to support it. A knighthood cost nothing. But if they voted him a pension as well . . .

"Nelson of the Nile," cried Emma, pulling herself back far enough to look into his eyes. "That should be your title."

"I had thought of honouring my birthplace."

"Which was?"

"Burnham Thorpe, in Norfolk."

"Then, sir, that is the whole of it." She rose to her feet, which alerted all the diners, who, seeing her standing, glass raised, followed suit. The toast she gave was in French. *"J'offre à vous, Monsieur le Duc de Burnham Thorpe et le Nile."*

The roar that filled the room made Nelson blush, which endeared him to the lady looking down at him with unabashed admiration. Even Maria Carolina had raised her glass, though her dignity as a queen forbade her to stand. Ferdinand looked bemused, as if the idea that anyone else could be toasted in his presence, that cheers could ring out for another, was impossible.

Emma's chest was heaving, as if she had taken part in some taxing physical activity, her face flushed with pride and happiness. She did feel that she had a right to some reflected glory. Had it not been she, with her husband's blessing, who had gone to the Queen when Nelson was stuck in Syracuse needing supplies? It had been Emma, Lady Hamilton, who had used every ounce of her credit to persuade Maria Carolina that Neapolitan neutrality, which forbade giving assistance to Great Britain, should be breached.

Had that not happened, Nelson could not have continued his

pursuit of Bonaparte. Without that, no battle of the Nile could have taken place. So, the very fact that this man was sitting here blushing at the praise being heaped on him was, in a large part, due to her intervention. Emma believed that when they toasted Nelson, they inadvertently also toasted her. As she sat down, the cheers still ringing, she saw that Nelson now looked uncomfortable.

"There's something amiss?"

"I wish I had the French for another toast, milady, which would be to my captains, my officers and my seamen, for in truth they are the people who won at the Nile."

"I would not waste your modesty on this crew, Admiral Nelson. They wouldn't understand it."

"Do you understand it?"

"I applaud it, sir, here," she replied, putting one hand on her heart.

Eyes locked for just two seconds, both Nelson and Emma Hamilton were aware only of their own thoughts; that emotion was taking control of them. The noise of the packed room had faded so that they seemed to share a cocoon. Emma suffered a moment of confusion, under the strain of a raft of feelings she had not allowed for years, the kind of sensuous passion she had felt in the company of Uppark Harry and Charles Greville. Her whole life seemed to be encompassed in a thought that lasted no more than a split second before, for the sake of propriety, that mutual stare had to be broken.

She couldn't read Nelson's mind. Looking into his one good eye gave her no clue as to what he was experiencing. He felt the same set of sensations that came upon him as he went into battle, familiar from so many engagements: racing blood, acute awareness, the ability to see things in a detail denied to him normally, access to those juices that made a fighting man aware of a threat and gave him the speed with which to counter it and stay alive. What seemed odd to Nelson, when he realised his state, was that for the first time in his life, he should feel all this in the company of a woman.

However, concentration on each other was impossible in a banqueting hall containing three hundred people. And when the meal finished and they repaired to the ballroom to dance, Emma was engaged by a variety of partners. Never much given to formal dancing, more at home with a hornpipe, Nelson had the excuse of only one arm, as well as a degree of exhaustion, to avoid participation.

It was unlikely that what happened that night would have occurred if he hadn't been quite so fatigued. An added complication was that Nelson wasn't alone in feeling so. When it came to saying good night, Sir William made it plain that he was worn out by the events that had preceded the ball, never mind the assembly itself. Emma wasn't put out by this nor was she surprised: her husband's desires had diminished steadily since he had turned 65. In the last year that had accelerated, since Sir William refused to abandon his other pursuits. He still coached out to Pompeii for his excavations, still climbed Vesuvius, albeit slowly, and he continued to oversee the care of his English garden. He claimed he had scant energy left for copulation. Tonight was one of many in which he made it plain to Emma that her presence in his apartments was not obligatory.

The absence of servants was also due to the night's entertainment: clearing up after so many guests saw everyone busy, with few to spare for lighting candles, warming beds, or seeing to a most important guest. Under the supervision of Mary Cadogan, the entire staff, including those brought in especially for the occasion, was busy washing, drying, and packing crockery or filling hessian bags with linen and breaking down the dozens of assembled tables. Aware of this, Emma Hamilton saw it as her duty to ensure that the hero of the Nile was comfortable.

Illuminated only by the pair of candles he had used to guide himself to his accommodation, the suite of rooms Nelson occupied was in near darkness. A portrait of George III above the mantel of the fireplace in the drawing room rendered a glowering rather than an inspiring image, which reminded him that royalty were a fickle crew. There was no sign of Tom Allen, who'd last been seen heading for the kitchens, which were full to overflowing with local women.

The act of undressing was difficult without assistance, barring his dress coat, with the embroidered star of the Order of the Bath, which slipped off easily. When it came to the heavy brass waistcoat buttons it was a struggle, and he cursed his servant for deserting him. That was until he recalled that Tom had been at sea as long as he had himself and was, like him, a man. The sight of all those olive-skinned jades would have been enough to inflame any red-blooded fellow. That brought back to him the way he himself had behaved, and he recalled the thoughts he had toyed with earlier, which caused him to smile, then frown, then mentally beg forgiveness from his all-seeing God.

When a knock came he assumed it was from a household servant and called that he or she should enter. The breath stopped in his chest as Emma Hamilton came through the door.

She was still dressed in the costume that had been created to flatter him. What light there was, was playing across her face and hair, as well as the gold embroidery of her clothing.

"I came to see if all your needs have been met."

Was the *double entendre* deliberate? Nelson didn't know, and his reply, which was automatic, only added to the confusion. "Without aid and only one arm, I find it difficult to undress."

"Your servant?"

"I fear after months at sea some Neapolitan lady has claimed him, leaving me to struggle with these waistcoat buttons."

Emma was halfway across the room by the time Nelson had said that, close enough for their eyes to lock. "Allow me to aid you," she said.

"That would be very kind," Nelson replied huskily, his mouth as dry as it had ever been in battle.

She stepped up close, so that the faint light from the candles on the mantel shone over his shoulder into her eyes. The green orbs seemed huge, steady, and direct. He knew that any woman with a modest desire just to undo his waistcoat buttons would not look at him like that. She knew that no man making an innocent request would jerk as he did when her hand moved down to the lowest button on the long garment.

Several spasms ran through Nelson's body as each button came loose. He was achingly aware of her long fingers, her smell, a mixture of bodily musk and perfume, the way that her shawl was less than modest and that the breasts it was designed to cover were rising and falling too fast for a woman hardly engaged in anything like exertion. He wanted to touch her but was frightened to move, fearful that even now he was mistaking kindness for passion and that any act on his part would break the spell.

Emma, with much more experience, supposed Nelson was suffering from a mixture of shyness and fear. Ever since her first days at Mrs Kelly's she had known there was a breed of men frightened of their own passions, so unsure of themselves as to freeze when they should act. That this man, a garlanded hero who could board an enemy deck without fear, should show such an emotion when faced with Emma Hamilton, made her hand tremble slightly.

She was also aware that, in coming here, all her excuses of seeing to Nelson's comfort were just that, pretexts to cover an irresistible desire to be close to him. His mere presence set off something she found hard to control, which had existed since their first meeting five years before. Absence made such a thing seem foolish, but proximity made it so forceful it could not be gainsaid.

She knew because of what had happened on first acquaintance that it was the man, not just his fame. Besides that, Emma wasn't the type to dwell too long on wondering. At dinner, all that contact had been no accident. She had known what she was about as she pushed herself close to him, eager to feel the tingling sensation his close presence brought her. She had it now and, in the glow of the candlelight, looking at his hooded eyes, feeling the trembling of his body through the slightest of contact, she knew he had it too.

Taking hold of his stock to untie it, she exerted a degree of pressure. Instead of holding his body tense against it, Nelson allowed his head to be brought to within an inch of Emma's. To kiss seemed natural, a gentle meeting of lips stretching little to touch each other, the increase of pressure as Nelson slipped his good arm round her waist to pull her body into contact with his. At the back of his mind he knew that what he was doing was wrong, sinful, but elemental.

The lips parted and Emma put a good foot of distance between them and Nelson felt disappointment overwhelm him. Then her hands came up, and slowly, her eyes still fixed on his, she began once more to undo the stock, slipping it off slowly and sensually. At the same time his fingers found the edge of her shawl, which slid from her shoulders to the floor.

Emma continued to take the lead, knowing that this man would hesitate at every stage of what was now inevitable. Her body was on fire, she wanted to rip off his shirt, with its one pinned-up sleeve, and her dress with it. Yet there was great pleasure in denial, gratification in lack of haste, in putting her hand behind Nelson's head and pulling it to her bosom. The throaty chuckle that emerged when his lips brushed the top of her breasts was caused by a thought, not the touch; that a man who couldn't undo his waistcoat would probably have trouble with the button on his breeches too.

"How odd," Nelson murmured. "I feel as though both my hands are upon you, even my right. I swear I can feel your skin through my missing fingertips."

His left hand was pulling her hard, and through the thin material of her dress she could feel his cock pressing against her belly. Nelson's head came up and the kiss he gave her this time was crushing and passionate. Suddenly Emma put two hands on his chest and pushed him away. Nelson tried to resist, but with only one hand she spun out of his embrace.

Seeing his crestfallen expression Emma put a finger to his lips, then slipped across the room to the double doors, turning the key smartly, before spinning round to lean against the wood. Her dress, new and for the occasion, hooked at the back where she couldn't reach, gave way at one of the seams as she tugged hard to pull it down. Everything underneath seemed to go in that one swift movement till she stood naked, one foot raised, the flat of her hands on the lower door panels, inviting him to gaze on her.

Nelson's groin was aching. He felt as if he wanted to do ten things at once: rip off his own shirt and the buttons on his breeches, kiss her, fuck her, caress her, worship her, yet he did nothing. He just stood, feeling a little foolish, until Emma, laughing, came back to him, to help her one-armed hero. His shirt was pulled over his head, Emma's hand, then her lips, caressing his chest before wandering to the stump that hung off his right shoulder, to kiss the point where the healing skin had puckered at the base. Her other hand was at his breech buttons. Nelson nearly ejaculated as her fingers took hold of his prick to ease it out of the restraining clothes.

She had to hold up his falling breeches to get him to the bed, making Nelson feel slightly ridiculous, and propriety resurfaced. But contact with cool sheets as Emma pushed him back, the sight of her kneeling to take off his shoes, her head, still in her cap of victory with his name sewn into the band, bobbing at either side of his erection, produced the first feeling of humour he felt he had had for months, a deep chest-heaving laugh. There was a feeling of evaporation as he lay there, as though every thought that bothered him, every difficulty that assailed him, marital and professional, was being chased away by the action of this stunningly beautiful woman.

Emma wasn't at his feet for long. She knelt on the bed beside him, her hand once more caressing that stump. Her lips were parted showing the tip of an enticing tongue, her eyes full of amusement, her beautiful breasts rising and falling evenly in a way that made him want to raise himself up to suckle the nipples. Then she spoke.

"I fear, hero that you are, that I must take command here."

Nelson laughed again. Then, using his good arm, he raised himself up with every ounce of force he could muster, the weight of his body throwing hers backwards. Emma let out a peal of laughter as he rolled her on to her back, his knee immediately jabbing between hers to open them, not difficult since she was a willing victim. Looking up she saw in Nelson's eye a look that only men who had gone into battle with him had seen. It told her without words that no one commanded Horatio Nelson.

His stump was jabbed into the bed to hold his right side, both his legs now between hers, his hips jabbing forward to get inside her, a manoeuvre that had to be repeated several times before she reached down to help him. Nelson had to struggle to contain himself under the coercion of that cool hand. His lips were buried in her neck and in his head it was as though that orb of the vision he had had when he was sick on his return from India came back again to tell him that what he was doing was right.

He tried hard to be the practised lover, to hold himself, but the passion was too great, uncontainable. The groan as he came was a mixture of deep relief, overwhelming gratitude, and the boyish shame that always afflicts a man who feels that he has failed. Emma, one hand behind him pulling his buttocks in tighter, legs lifted from the bed, pelvis writhing and lifting and falling, was laughing, a deep gurgle that Nelson thought was ridicule and she knew was gratification.

He collapsed on her body, his head sinking into her breasts, feeling the chest below them heave as he continued to jerk inside her, small, delicious spasms that slowly but steadily diminished. Her hands were stroking his back, both of them, palms pressed into his shoulder blades and spine as if that alone would convey to him the feelings that racked her body.

As he rolled sideways Emma followed him, so that it was now Nelson who was thrown on his back. She lay over him, to gaze down at him with a mixture of gratitude and wonder. "Have I just been conquered, Nelson?"

"No, madam," Nelson said, softly, "you have just been victorious."

Sir William, on his way to give a message to Emma, had gone to check on his guest for the same reason as his wife. He was just in time to see the door to Nelson's apartments close on that well-lit and unmistakable dress, blue and gold, decorated with entwined embroidery of Nelson and Nile. He stood for several moments, his mind going back to the dinner, to the way that Emma had fawned over her hero. Recollecting what he had observed, he saw her behaviour as different from those times when she had allowed other men to raise in themselves expectations that would not be met. Her reaction to Nelson had been different, more tactile and very effusive.

There was a sobering moment when he remembered the dozens of letters they had exchanged over the last five years, since Nelson's visit to ask for aid at Toulon. Every one had contained a request to pass on kind sentiments and flattering comments to Lady Hamilton, even though she, too, was his correspondent. He had only been in Naples four days, and had left in a rush that seemed, in retrospect, over-dramatic. Had there been another reason, outside the need to engage an enemy warship?

Close to the door, Sir William had heard the muted voices of a conversational exchange. But that was followed by silence, which lasted a long time. Then he heard the faint sound of pressure on the door, followed by the grate of a turning key. A man of the world, Sir William Hamilton could easily deduce what that meant.

They lay together, Emma face down while he lay on his back, talking intermittently, she fondling his limp cock until the blood began to flow again. As soon as he was erect she threw one leg over his body and raised herself up to look down at him. The previous tussling had thrown back his hair, exposing the scar where a piece of langridge from *Spartiate*'s cannon had sliced into his forehead. She bent to kiss it and his lips found a nipple as her breasts sank to his face.

They made love slowly, Emma in charge of both pace and passion. Her own hair, now loose from that cap of victory, would occasionally brush his chest as she bent closer, while her inert lover gazed up in wonder, sure he must be dreaming that this perfect creature was intent only on his pleasure. Sometimes she would sink low to kiss him, pressing her breasts into his, her whole upper body in contact.

Then he was lost again in that mental wilderness of conflicting images; thoughts of what they were doing and might yet do, the feeling of her belly, warm against his, the way her thighs pressed into his side, the texture of one buttock as he held it and squeezed with his one good hand. The groans that seemed to come from the very base of Emma's spine as she quickened her pace, the rising feeling in his own groin.

When Emma Hamilton left, Nelson lay on his back, his mind racing over what had just happened, the pleasure of which made him writhe with recollected memory. The murmured name of his wife turned that to a guilty squirm. Then he thought of his host, a man who had shown him nothing but kindness and consideration, such nobility repaid by a scrub who had just made love to his consort. It made no difference that she had been willing, had in some senses taken the initiative. But that still made him an ungrateful louse when it came to Sir William, a man who had boasted to him of his wife's fidelity.

Regardless of how much he chastised himself he knew in his heart that he wanted what had occurred tonight to happen again. He felt as if he had been struck by lightning, a *coup de foudre* that no amount of self-control could overcome. The word love barely registered, but lust did, of the most unbridled kind. He could try to put his love of God and his regard for Fanny as a shield between himself and Emma Hamilton, but he knew in his heart it would never answer.

Nelson resolved to move out of the palazzo and go back to the cabin on his ship; to put seawater between himself and temptation. The excuses he would use began to form in his mind, based on the knowledge that in such a large establishment, the chances of Sir William being aware of what had taken place were slim. Lady Hamilton would never have allowed it to happen if there was a risk. He would say that he needed to harry the dockyard or *Vanguard* would never be ready. That even if he had defeated the French fleet in Aboukir Bay there were still two capital enemy ships at sea threatening trade. Sir William would understand, and Nelson could get away from Naples, as he had before, without any damage to either his reputation or that of Sir William's wife.

As he knelt to pray for forgiveness and help, he was conscious of his nakedness, of the stickiness of his body as well as the smell, a combination of her perfume, their sweat, and the odour of stale carnality.

Mary Cadogan was waiting when Emma came back to her own suite of rooms, sitting in the chair she often occupied, but awake. She looked her daughter up and down, noting that her dress was not as well fitted as it had been earlier, her hair not as neat, the cap of victory nowhere in sight. And Emma had her slippers in one hand, almost a badge to tell anyone who saw her in the passageways what she had been doing.

"Sir William seems to have recovered some of his ardour," Emma said.

"Has he?"

"I think Admiral Nelson's victory must have inspired him," Emma added, throwing herself into another chair. "He was quite the bull and I am quite exhausted."

"You're a fool, Emma, and what is worse for me is that you think I am too."

Emma leant back and yawned, slightly more elaborately than was necessary to express her tiredness. "What do you mean?"

"I mean, girl, where you have just spent the last two hours."

"With Sir William."

"Your husband called for his carriage about an hour and a half ago. He left a message to say that he had gone to spend the night at Posillipo."

Emma was upright now. "In the name of heaven, why?"

"I daresay it's because he has a fair idea of where you were, Emma." Mary Cadogan's face softened in the face of her daughter's confusion. "Do you realise what you have done, girl? You have gone and thrown away whatever chance we had of peace and happiness in the future. And for what? For a couple of hours with a passing sailor, and not even a whole one at that."

Chapter Twenty-Four

HOW CAN YOU CONTINUE TO FIGHT with a cutlass blade through your heart? Horatio Nelson knew it was there, just as he knew that it caused him no pain, and did nothing to impede him in the assault on the enemy frigate. The approach had been made in silence; guns run out, lower sails taken in and boarding nets rigged, the usual rush of clearing for action—bulkheads knocked out, furniture broken down, delicate plate and glassware packed into boxes, the gunner filling charges that the ship's boys raced to deliver to the gun captains. He had seen mouths move, understood requests made and orders given, but had heard no sound.

Even the enemy cannon, eighteen-pounders firing off the first salvo, had belched smoke but no noise. It lasted throughout the long gunnery duel. Wooden bulwarks were smashed on both vessels, guns dismounted, masts wounded, and rigging ripped asunder until the ships closed for the final act of boarding. Jumping from one bulwark to the next Nelson felt as though he was floating. But cleaving with the sword that had belonged to his naval ancestor Captain Gadifrus Walpole, he cut down those who appeared before him with heavy blows.

Somehow, instead of landing on the enemy quarterdeck, he had slid through the scantlings on to the maindeck as if the great timbers that made up the side of the ship did not exist. That meant he had to fight his way up the companionway towards the daylight of the quarterdeck, just as he had at the battle of Cape St Vincent. Familiar faces surrounded him, swimming in and out of focus, but he could not recall a single name. The fight to remember began to seem more important than keeping himself alive or taking the enemy ship. Yet ahead of him, drawing him onwards and upwards, was a light so blinding it seemed the sun itself was at the head of those open stairs.

Nelson felt fear then; the terror that something not human lay beyond that light, whose heat penetrated the heavy cutlass blade that protruded from his upper body. Suddenly pain seared through him and shapes formed in the radiance ahead. Faces appeared, but this time he could identify them: his father, his brothers, William, Edmund, Suckling, and young George; his sisters Susanna, Ann, and Catherine, all waving, as if in farewell.

Those images dissolved into another. The next face to appear was that of his dead mother, which melted into a *tableau vivant* he had seen as a child, a representation of the death of his hero, General James Wolfe. Only this time it was Nelson lying in the arms of a fellow officer. The image was shattered by a great explosion, which halted his intended flight, as the French ship *L'Orient,* a mass of orange and red light against the night sky, blew up in Aboukir Bay. Darkness turned to daylight, to reveal behind the falling debris not an Egyptian shore but a calm, sandy Norfolk beach dotted with the red brick houses of the North Sea coast. And behind that the green undulating slopes that led to his home at Burnham Thorpe.

He swooped in like a seagull over All Saints, his father's church, still showing an open damaged face to the world at the south nave, still chilly inside even on a summer's day. The trees that shaded the passage down to the Parsonage were in full leaf, reflected in the still waters of the reed-fringed pond that lay foursquare in front of the house. From inside he heard pealing laughter, and knew that he was its object, but try as he might he could not enter to share in the happiness that lay inside.

His eyes opened, one good, the other opaque, and he was faced with a blank expanse of white linen. Someone, probably his servant Tom Allen, had opened both shutters to flood the room with light. He registered that he was lying on his side, the stump of his right arm trapped and numb beneath him. The bed in which he lay was wider than his cot and there was none of the normal swaying motion, nor the creaking of timbers and cables, the smell of pitch, wood and corruption that went with sleeping aboard ship. Instead a familiar perfume, mingled with the smell of his own warm body, rose from under the heavy coverlet.

The vivid dream was still with him: the faces of long-dead shipmates, the family he had not seen for years and the mother who had died when he was seven. The action he recalled was that with the Spanish frigate the *Santa Sabina,* a bloody affair, in which the Dons had lost over a hundred and fifty men dead and wounded, their ship left with not a mast standing.

He recalled the name and dignity with which the captain had surrendered. Nelson had taken in his hands the sword of Don Jacobo Stuart, great grandson of King James II, who claimed to be the rightful king of England and Scotland. Nelson glanced at the mantel above the fireplace, over which hung a portrait of his own sovereign: heavy jowls, hooded eyes, and the thick, disapproving Hanoverian lips of King George III. In Nelson's memory the Stuart pretender had looked so much more princely than his King.

His head sank back to the pillow and again the scent filled his nostrils. It had all begun last night under that portrait. He had spent the night with his benign host Sir William Hamilton, King George's ambassador at the court of Naples, and his wife, the beautiful and accomplished Lady Emma. She had sat by his right hand, wafting that scent, while she led the plaudits at the banquet held to celebrate his victory at the Nile.

Later she had flitted into his room and Nelson recalled the passionate, lascivious creature who had introduced him to a depth of passion and accomplishment he had never before experienced. He felt as if, for the first time in his life, he had truly made love to a woman. He could still feel every touch of her hand as she helped him to remove his clothes; he had an ache in his groin as he remembered their frenzied and prolonged love-making and blushed when he thought of the way he had sinned.

Worse, he had dishonoured a man he considered a friend and supporter. How could he face Sir William Hamilton after he had, under the man's own roof, made love to his wife?

. . .

Emma threw the umpteenth draft of the letter she was trying to write at the basket. It missed its target. She and Sir William often wrote to each other, even though they were man and wife and shared the same establishment. But Emma was more than his spouse: she had become the British Ambassador's helpmate at the Neapolitan court. A close friend of Queen Maria Carolina, Emma had proved invaluable at communicating to the queen her husband's ideas, thus easing his task.

At times their letter writing was a way of clarifying their thoughts, at others a record that would show, should an action be questioned at some future date, proof of proper intentions, and sometimes a way to resolve a disagreement, or express affection.

This letter was of a type that Emma had never penned before. In all the years she had lived with Sir William, both as mistress and wife, she had never strayed in her fidelity, although she had received innumerable offers from potential lovers, including King Ferdinand of Naples. The list of dukes, counts, earls, lords and knights, artists, writers, wits—English, German, Austrian, and Italian—who had tried to bed her was endless. Sir William had taken as much pleasure from observing them fail as Emma did from their flattering attentions.

Emma put her quill to another piece of paper to try again. What to write? That she had always held him in the highest esteem, that they had a bargain which, though unspoken, was obvious to both, that if an attraction proved potent enough, neither party was debarred from the pursuit of pleasure? That she had not exercised such a right did nothing to dent its potency. Emma knew that Sir William was no prude: now in his sixty-eighth year, he had grown to manhood in an age when the present British predilection to rectitude was deemed unseemly in a gentleman. That was why Naples, with its hot sunshine, warm waters, and febrile sensuality, suited him better than gloomy Georgian London.

Part of Emma wanted to pretend that last night had not happened. How could she be sure her husband knew the truth? Her mother, guardian of her bedchamber, who had alerted her, might have been wrong. Sir William might have left the house to go to their seaside villa at Posillipo for any number of reasons—he had done so before. A bilious feeling after the banquet, to fish perhaps, a pursuit he loved, the need for some solitude or a desire to bathe in the warm waters of the Bay of Naples.

The door creaked, and Emma fixed her eyes on the paper. She knew who it was: only two people would enter this room unannounced—her maid, Francesca, and Emma's mother. However, if it had been Francesca, Emma would have heard her since she never stopped singing. Her mother, with a key to every room in the palazzo at her hip, moved silently.

Mary Cadogan examined the back of her daughter's bent head. Her hair, which good Sir William called "Titian," had not been combed and the loose strands picked up the light from the open windows overlooking the bay, making it seem golden. The furious scratching of the quill, she knew, was intended to shut her out. But Mary Cadogan had interfered often in her daughter's life, always—in her own mind—to the good.

"Is that a letter to Sir William?" she asked.

"It is," Emma replied, her voice far from welcoming.

"What will you be telling him, girl? That your time spent in the Admiral's bedchamber was all innocence, or that you gave your Nile hero a fitting reward for thumping the French?"

"I think, Mother, that what I write to my husband is my business."

"That be true, Emma," Mary Cadogan replied, easing herself into a chair beside her daughter. "But I wondered if you might want to speak of it first, seeing as how in the past, you have done yourself more harm than good by flying off the handle."

"Don't you mean you have, Mother?"

There was venom in that, since both women knew that Emma was in Naples due to her mother's influence. It was she who had seen first that her daughter's liaison with Sir William's nephew, Charles Greville, was over; that after six years as his mistress, the man Emma claimed to love had traded her off to secure his inheritance from an uncle he knew to be besotted with her. Maternal persuasion, aided by deliberate coldness from her previous keeper, had convinced Emma that her love for Greville was wasted; that security lay with a man over thirty years her senior.

Mary Cadogan had one overriding concern; that after a life of ups and downs, of widowhood, being a kept woman so that her family would not starve, and a near descent into prostitution, the only thing that mattered was the comfort of a good roof over both their heads. She thought her daughter too romantic to be sensible, too fanciful to see where danger lurked or advantage lay. She had done everything she could to prevent Emma falling into the same traps in which she herself had been snared, only to fall short too often.

There was a child, now grown to womanhood, who had no idea that Emma was her mother. Any number of folk could recall that the present Lady Hamilton had once been a lowly housemaid named Lyons, and as Emma Hart that she had been at best a lady of easy virtue, at worst a whore. She might be at the top of the social pile in Naples, but back in England her title brought mockery not respect. Received at court here, she was debarred from audience with the King and Queen of England and shunned by those who took from them their social cue.

"If you are thinking of penning a confession, girl, I feel I am bound to advise against it," she said.

"I'm old enough to make my own decisions, Mother."

"Old enough, for certain, and you've been that for many a year. But I hazard if you look back and examine some of the decisions you have made, and how I've aided you from being foolish, you might see fit to pass by me what it is you're planning to do."

Emma turned to face her mother, her curling uncombed hair framing what was still a beautiful face. In shadow Mary Cadogan could not see the green eyes and the flawless skin, but she knew them well—indeed the twelve years they had spent in Naples were hardly reflected in Emma's features, certainly not the miserable look of the first year. Good fortune, some hard maternal truths, and Sir William's ease of manner had combined to turn her first into his mistress, then into his wife, gifting them both that life of ease Mary Cadogan so desired. That Emma did not love her husband was of no account: to Mary Cadogan's way of thinking, more attachments survived through mutual respect than ever endured on a diet of connubial bliss.

She could not believe that Sir William would respond to Emma's first lapse by sending her and her daughter packing. Emma was his wife: he would respect that—and not just to avoid public embarrassment. But he was getting on in years and for a woman who prided herself on being longsighted that was a consideration. Old men were as prey to jealousy as the young, sometimes more so. And Mary Cadogan knew that they were entirely dependent on Sir William, even after he was dead and buried. Starting hares that might affect the future was a bad idea if you had no idea to where they would run, so silence was likely to be a better option than confession.

For the tenth time since she'd woken up, Emma was examining her own actions, which seemed to her to have been caused by some force of nature. But to say so to a woman as practical as her mother was impossible.

"All Naples," she insisted, "indeed the whole of Europe, fêtes Nelson as a great hero, a saviour, the man who has finally checked the French abomination. He is the most famous man in the world. Am I to be immune from such . . ." Emma was unable to find the concluding word. "I'm sure Sir William will understand the nature of what has happened." She could not say that the attraction she felt for Horatio Nelson was one that had been with her ever since their first meeting five years previously. He had been a captain then, and whole, with both arms and two good eyes. She had written numerous letters to him from this very desk, never once allowing her feelings to surface in her correspondence.

But then he had returned a hero. Instead of the bright-eyed man she remembered, Emma had encountered a wounded, weary one in need of comfort. At the sight of him her repressed feelings had burst out, multiplied tenfold by tenderness. Every time she touched Nelson she felt an electric charge run through her. She could not tell her mother that what had happened between them last night was no mere fancy. It had been inevitable, and right now she would rather be back in Nelson's suite of rooms than here.

"Then you don't fear that Sir William will be agitated?" Mary asked.

"Why should he be?" Emma replied with an assurance she did not feel. "My husband has hinted often enough that he considers it impolite to enquire into such matters."

"Then why alert him to it?"

"How can you say that, Mother?" Emma snapped. "It was you who told me last night that he . . ."

"Knew you bedded the Admiral? Well, that's as maybe, Emma, but I can't see what good it will do to go rubbing it in. From what I know of Sir William you're right. He won't say a peep. Nor will you know by his face what he's thinking. Being deep is what he's good at. Let him be I say."

She was tempted to add that Nelson would sail off soon, as all sailors did, ending something that her daughter should never have started, and that once that happened, provided a discreet silence was observed by all, life could return to normal.

Naked and without his wig, Sir William Hamilton lay in the warm shallow waters of the Bay of Naples, one hand gently fondling the loose wrinkled skin of his scrotum, ruminating on past scrapes. Like any young aristocrat he had whored his way around London and Europe in the company of like minded individuals, including the present King George, a riotous prince then, a dull-as-ditchwater prude now. Hamilton's first marriage, a sensible match, had been made more to secure his wife's income than for any notions of love—as a younger son of a ducal family he had had little in the way of an inheritance.

He could hardly say that the same sentiments applied to Emma.

He had been smitten by her the first time he had seen her at his nephew's house in London: her beauty, her vivacity, her innate kindness and natural wit. As the past lover of many women he had seen every facet of their behaviour: false affection, outrageous infatuation that could not last, naked greed for a man who had a good post, a reasonable unearned income, a palazzo, servants, carriages, and access to the highest society. Emma loved these things, as any sensible woman would, but her enthusiasm was based on innocent enjoyment not calculation.

It was enlightening to compare his first marriage to his second, his Lady Charlotte to his Lady Emma. The former had been refined, reserved, dutiful, the very epitome of the English rose abroad, a companion of the mind more than the body. The latter, over thirty years his junior, was more Italian than the Italians, high spirited, often gauche, intelligent, instinctive, and an unrestrained delight in the bedchamber.

It was hard to recall the *ingénue* who had arrived here all those years ago, with her comparative lack of refinement. Yet even then Emma had charmed Naples: the peasants hailed her as the living embodiment of the Madonna, while the aristocracy admired her as akin to a Greek goddess, more so when she learned, in four years, to speak Italian, French, and German. Emma sang with gusto if not refinement, while her beauty and theatricality attracted the admiration of every visitor who called upon Sir William at the Palazzo Sessa. An invitation to watch her perform her "Attitudes" was much sought after: her renderings of classical poses were sensual and greeted with much applause. But in the privacy of the bedchamber, he was gifted with attitudes that owed much to pagan rites. And yet, for all the abandon of which Emma was capable, she had been faithful.

Greville, the nephew who had exchanged Emma for a promise of being made Sir William's heir, had on occasion complained about her spirited behaviour. He had also shown an unattractive possessiveness whenever some gallant flattered her, even though Emma had never once caused him to feel he might be cuckolded. At least Sir William could pride himself on never showing jealousy, though he could not deny that now he felt it.

"Why Nelson?" he asked himself, softly. Looking down at his bony chest he knew that his age was a factor; that he was no longer potent enough to keep satisfied a creature like Emma. For some time he had considered it inevitable that Emma would succumb to the blandishments of the kind of man she would have rejected in the past.

The Admiral was a hero, and for Emma that would outweigh wit, wealth, or any common accomplishment. She considered herself part of his victory at the Nile, which had seen, for Britain, an enemy fleet destroyed for the first time since the Spanish Armada. Had it not been her efforts and close connection with the Queen of Naples that had kept the British fleet at sea? Her intercession had ensured that supplies had been forthcoming from a kingdom that was nominally at peace with France, a nation that should, for neutrality's sake, have turned Nelson away. Without Emma, would Nelson have won his battle?

"Once a conqueror, how easy it is to be a seducer."

Sir William tried to imagine the scene. Nelson would not have forced matters, he was sure. For someone so at home in his professional milieu, the man was a sad case in a social setting. Quick to blush, more forthright than was polite, and utterly lacking in that ready wit and *sang froid* required in the circles in which the Hamiltons moved, Nelson seemed always to hover on the edge of embarrassment.

Yet Sir William liked and admired him for many things: his honesty, ironic in the present circumstances, his zealous attention to the needs of his sailors, and that he was prepared to offend anyone, kings, princes, dukes, and sea lords, if he felt it necessary. Sir William had seen him in different guises: the timid social creature who seemed to be a battleground of all the available medical disorders, and the outspoken advocate of any policy he held to be right, which gave a hint of the man he must be in a fight. According to his officers, when danger threatened, afflictions dropped away to reveal an *enfant terrible*. Sir William knew those officers adored Nelson, just as he knew that Nelson doubted he was fit to lead them.

Nelson had been famous and a hero to his profession since his actions at the battle of Cape St Vincent, where, disobeying standing orders, he had accomplished a previously unheard of feat in capturing one Spanish ship from the deck of another already taken. Even his failure at Tenerife, where he had lost both a battle and his arm, had enhanced rather than damaged his reputation. His appointment to the Mediterranean command, with the express task of stopping Bonaparte had caused, according to Sir William's correspondence, much disquiet in the breasts of more senior admirals who felt the duty should have fallen to them. Sir William could easily imagine that while many were anxious about Nelson's failure to beard the Corsican menace, those same senior admirals would have been crowing about how right they had been.

They wouldn't be crowing when news of the Nile reached London. Nelson had done the impossible: he had not only destroyed a French fleet and French ambitions in that region. He had saved the Turkish Sultan, the route to India, secured a breathing space for Italy, and imposed the first check on the insidious Revolution that had made every European nation tremble for fear of France. And then he had come back to Naples and bedded Sir William's wife.

Closing his eyes, Sir William placed himself once more in the dimly lit corridor outside Nelson's rooms. That he had gone to see to the well-being of his guest forced a reluctant smile to his lips. But then there had been the sight of his wife slipping into Nelson's room, and minutes later the grating sound of the key turning in the lock. He had pictured what was taking place behind those double doors: his wife, her hero, both naked and writhing.

Still fondling his groin, Sir William was aware of an increasing and now rare tumescence as the thoughts he harboured flitted through his mind. He knew how unrestrained his wife was: she knew how to arouse a man, and how to tease that arousal until passion could no longer be contained.

He signalled and his valet stepped forward, first to pour fresh water over him to wash off the sea salt, then to wrap a towel round him as he stood up, a trifle unsteady on legs that had grown thin with the onset of age.

"My carriage in twenty minutes," Sir William said. "I shall be returning to the Palazzo Sessa."

"Maestro," his valet replied.

Chapter Twenty-Five

TOM ALLEN knew he was not the brightest of men, nor the best of sailor servants. He hung on to his job because he was quiet and unassuming and his master was benign. This morning, though, as he helped his admiral to wash, dress, and comb his hair, he had the sense to realise that something was not quite as it should be.

First, his master had not asked where Tom had been the night before, or why he had been left to undress himself. All the excuses Tom had rehearsed to cover the truth: that he had drunk too much wine, then spent the night with one of Sir William's female servants had remained unspoken.

From fearful silence, Tom graduated slowly to talking about the ball and the banquet, how splendid they had been, a fitting tribute to such a justly famous man. None of this had produced a smile or even a nod. But when he had told him that Sir William was not at home, that he had departed an hour after the last of the guests to spend the night at his seaside villa, Nelson shuddered.

As he cut up Nelson's breakfast Tom watched him closely, seeing the frown on his master's brow. The Admiral was troubled, and Tom didn't know why. He had beaten the French wholesale, so he could not be fretting about that, especially with the praise he so loved being heaped on him by the bucket load ever since. Happen it was that head wound he'd got at the Nile, still paining him, though he hadn't said anything when Tom combed his hair over it to hide the ferocious red scar. Tom felt it was his duty to know what was upsetting his master. It was also a way of protecting his position: Old Nellie might be kind and gentle, but he had got shot of one servant, and Tom had no desire that the same fate should befall him.

In his mind Nelson was running over a dozen scenarios, none of which brought on a sense of happy anticipation. First he would have to face Lady Hamilton; that in itself would be not be easy—it never had been, given that he could never act rationally in her presence—but now there was the added complication of what had happened between them. A worse prospect was Sir William. That he had left the palazzo to sleep elsewhere might have an innocent explanation, but only a fool would think so. He must have found out, either through his own observations or from his servants, where Lady Hamilton had spent the night.

Thinking back to the banquet Nelson realised that he must have been wrong. He had assumed at the time that Sir William had not noticed the attention his wife was paying him as the principal guest. With the Austrian born Queen on one side of him, Lady Hamilton on the other had been called upon to translate their exchanges. As she had leaned across him to hear the Queen over the buzz of three hundred other guests, the physical contact between her and Nelson had been constant, intense, and for him physically uncomfortable.

That, of course, had been the precursor of what had followed. Could he have stopped it? The fact that he should have done was not in question; he was married and so was she. Looking at his image now in the glass he was torn between knowledge of the sin he had committed and the pleasure he had taken from it. To a man who believed in an all-seeing God it was troubling that he could not decide how much his Maker would have observed. Would He have perceived the depth of the impulse that had led to their coupling? Would He weigh that in the balance against the offence?

The real horror was that he would probably have to face husband and wife together, in a three-sided exchange in which Sir William would be wounded, Lady Hamilton possibly remorseful, and himself unable to be open. This would compound his sin for he would have to add lies to the other broken commandments. Even less attractive was a scene of mutual recrimination in which he would be branded a poltroon, a man who could smile at his host one minute and cuckold him the next. What Sir William would say to his wife scarcely mattered, since Nelson would be obliged for her sake to take upon himself entire responsibility for what had occurred.

That there could be no repetition of last night went without saying. His marriage to Fanny might have withered in the face of a cold English climate, but she was still his wife. He felt another stab of guilt when he recalled the nights he had spent two years before in the amorous embrace of a Genoese opera singer. Yet that had been brought about by loneliness added to the desire, after many comfortless years with his wife, to once more prove himself a man.

Carla d'Ambrosio had been a rather overblown and foolish creature, heavily powdered, plump and given to giggling. He was well known in the states bordering the Ligurian Sea for the way in which he had harassed the French armies invading northern Italy. As the senior officer of a fast-sailing squadron of romantic heroes he was fêted whenever he entered port, and it was inevitable that ladies of a certain type had set their caps at him.

Carla had been just one, and if Nelson had been taxed to admit why he succumbed to her charms when he had refused so many others, he would have been hard put to give an honest answer. He had drunk more than normal, so that her foolishness melted, glass by glass, into attraction. But he could also remember a feeling of stubbornness: in his mind's eye he could see again the faces of his officers as he dined the lady aboard his ship, HMS *Agamemnon*. They would never know how their disapproval had driven him on where he might naturally have stopped. He didn't want to be the paragon they supposed him to be: he just wanted to be a man like any other, with red blood in his veins, salacious thoughts in his head, and the comfort of a hot-blooded creature in his cot. And Carla had been warm and eager, where his wife Fanny was obliging but cold. For a week he had behaved as he supposed a normal man would when separated by a thousand miles from fear of discovery. Whatever remorse he had felt then at the breaking of his marriage vows had been assuaged by the certain knowledge that time and distance would erase the affair. That would happen here too: he had told everyone when he arrived of his intention to sail on to Cadiz within two weeks to report to his commander-in-chief, Earl St Vincent. Yet that thought brought with it a stab of regret.

"This 'ere victuals'll have to go back to the kitchens to be warmed if'n you don't set to 'em," said Tom.

Nelson shook himself and glanced at the food on the table, a beefsteak, quails, and a glass of red wine. For someone who normally took a light repast with the rising of the sun, this was a late and hearty breakfast indeed, yet he could not contemplate eating it. His stomach rebelled and he jerked his head to indicate that Tom might take it away.

That earned Nelson a frown. "It's not for me to tell the man I serve that he's wrong, your honour."

"But you're going to tell me anyway, Tom," Nelson replied wearily.

Frank Lepée, Tom's predecessor, had been just as bad, with the added burden that he drank like a fish and in his drunken ramblings could not hold his tongue. At least Tom was sober. Clearly this was a morning for unwelcome memories. Carla d'Ambrosio had done for Lepée, who could never stop referring to it, in private and before others, as if he was his master's conscience. Nelson had pensioned him off, making it clear that his stipend was dependent upon silence.

"I am that, sir," Tom insisted, "since you need to be telt. I knows you fret, 'cause I've seen you at it, and I do say that it does no good. What's going to happen will happen, and starving yourself won't aid matters one whit."

Nelson could have told him to be quiet, and he knew that most men given unwanted advice by a servant would have done just that. Instead he stood up, tugged at his dress coat, smiled weakly at Tom, and left the room.

Nelson had spent no more than a few nights at the Palazzo Sessa, several years previously, so the layout of Sir William's abode was still a mystery to him. It was a warren of corridors, staircases, and passages, some sunlit, others in near Stygian gloom even in the middle of the day. The building had that air of decay which seemed to go with warm climates, as if the elements combined with the lassitude of the inhabitants to render frayed what should have been noble. In places the marble floors were cracked, as were the walls, and in every corner damp or mould had taken hold, only to dry out and flake, leaving behind a musty odour.

But there was much to admire, not least the wide variety of Sir William's virtu—statues, vases, mosaics, coins—all extracted from the nearby ruins of Pompeii and Herculaneum. There were the stunning views that would suddenly manifest themselves through a window or embrasure: the Bay of Naples, an arc of off-white buildings backed by a smoking Vesuvius or, to the west, purple islands shimmering out to sea. There were ships, too, the few of his own victorious fleet that he had kept here for communications and repair. His own flagship, HMS *Vanguard,* bereft of masts, was hove down in the royal dockyard at Castellamare, next to Thomas Troubridge's ship, *Culloden,* in dry dock with a damaged bottom and stern from running aground at the Nile.

That turned Nelson's mind to the problems of his command, which were many, varied, and worrying, not least because they fell squarely on his shoulders. Advice or approval on what action to take was, at best, two weeks away with Earl St Vincent at Cadiz. At worst, six weeks stood between him and his political masters in London, the people who had the final say of whether he had acted correctly or not.

The Nile victory had bottled up Bonaparte, and left him landlocked in Egypt with his army: hopefully the forces of the Sultan would bury him in the desert sands. But the legacy of his previous victories remained: Captain Ball was at this very moment off Malta, his task to ascertain if the island so recently captured and plundered by the French could be retaken. But Nelson would be expected to take responsibility for progress on land, as well—it was the lot of admirals on detached service to be accountable for things over which they had little actual control.

The northern Italian states, those that had succumbed to the French menace and those that still had cause to be fearful, must renew the struggle. Surely the Nile victory would give hope to the conquered and cheer the free, and encourage those who cared for their liberty to once more take up arms against the invader.

Yet in this, Nelson was only too aware of the limitations on his own ability to effect the outcome. British sea power had created the opening but it would be land armies that would decide the fate of Italy. News of his victory would not suffice—if he was to press home the advantage his fleet had provided, he must get powerful warships, of which he had too few, into the Italian ports to demonstrate to the populace that they had real support. He must overcome in the Italian mind the memory of defeat, occupation, and expropriation and lift their eyes to what was possible.

The crux of that lay here in Naples, a country that was a byword for national lethargy. Nelson needed to persuade the Neapolitan court that the time was right to strike north towards Rome and the Papal States, and hopefully, in concert with the forces of Austria, to take on the French and throw them back over their own borders. Each freed tract of occupied land would add men and passion to France's enemies. There was enough latent power waiting to be unleashed—could he, from the sea and by persuasion, act as the catalyst to harness that strength.

"You are in a brown study, sir."

It was Mary Cadogan, and Nelson's mind leaped immediately from professional to personal matters. Before him was an individual of some importance in the household. The dowdy dress and the heavy bunch of keys identified her as a housekeeper, and even her face, square, snub-nosed, and common under a mob cap, marked her as a servant. Yet the expression in her dark brown eyes was far from submissive.

Mary Cadogan, as mother of the lady of the house, was clearly more than a servant. That Sir William esteemed her was obvious in that he unfailingly included her in any conversation at which she was present, and paid clear attention to her opinions. She gave the impression that she, and she alone, knew everything that was going on in the house. There were questions Nelson longed to ask her—the same questions that had troubled him as he lay in bed not an hour before.

It was never easy to separate rumour from fact, but he had heard that Emma's mother had been both a kept woman and a high-class trollop and that her daughter had followed in her footsteps. It had to be admitted that when it came to the daughter the gossip mill tended to completely race out of control. Messalina and Lucretia Borgia combined could not have committed half the sins with which Emma Hamilton was credited.

"I have much to ponder, madam."

"I daresay you have, sir."

What was in the flat tone of that voice? Irony perhaps, or an acknowledgement of the thought process she had interrupted—that he was the fulcrum on which events five hundred miles in radius would turn. Or was it closer to her home and attachments. His next comment was impulsive, and one he regretted immediately it emerged.

"I am informed that Sir William left the Palazzo Sessa after the ball."

"He did that," Mary Cadogan replied. "He often retires there, thinking as he does that waters are restorative."

"You do not believe them so?"

"Depends what you're trying to mend." There was enough light coming through the window to allow her to see the reddening of Nelson's cheeks, so she added hastily, "He claims it is a help to old bones. I reckon a bit of good flannel next to the skin serves just as well."

Mary Cadogan was thinking that this little admiral was a strange one. She had known hundreds of men in her life and was happy to have no further intimate connection with any of them—but none like Nelson, though there had been sailors aplenty. This fellow had probably never seen the inside of a house of pleasure. He was more the Norfolk squire: God-fearing, church-going, forthright on morality, and drear company. There was a wife, she knew, and Mary Cadogan tried to picture what she might be like. Dry skinned and dry of passion was her supposition, the type to induce guilt, which made this fellow's coupling with her Emma doubly dangerous. This little blusher was likely to confess to Sir William and beg forgiveness, which would never do.

"Rest assured," Mary Cadogan added, "that Sir William mends easy. He never fails to return from his seaside villa in a better humour than when he left."

Nelson couldn't resist fishing. "Which supposes an ill temper when he departs."

"I doubt you would ever see that side of him, sir," Mary Cadogan replied, forcefully. "I know of no man for whom he has more time and no other man to whom he would not gift all he had than your good self."

Mary Cadogan was surprised by his reaction. Nelson seemed to grow before her eyes. She could not know that she had given him the reason for which he had been searching all morning to excuse what he must say to Emma Hamilton. That regardless of his feelings, what had happened last night must never be repeated. He would use the mutual regard in which he and Sir William held each other as a shield to deflect her disappointment.

"I must be about my duties, sir."

"And I, Mrs Cadogan," replied Nelson, in an almost jaunty tone, "must be about mine."

Francesca flitted about in her usual manner, moving much and achieving little, her soft singing for once grating on her mistress's ears. Emma knew that it would do no good to frown at her. She would only respond with a dazzling grin and the singing would continue.

Emma was wondering if she felt different, concentrating on each part of her body in turn to try to discern some fundamental change, without discovering much to either please or alarm her. There was a warm memory in her lower belly, that consciousness of having successfully made love, the recollection of that sated feeling that followed gratification. That induced a whole raft of memories. Mentally leafing through her previous lovers she ticked off first their attributes, then their failings.

The first, an overweight oaf called Jack Willet Payne, whom she could never recall without the epithet "whale," was not recollected with any pleasure. Her deflowering had been painful and unpleasant. Harry Featherstonehaugh had been her first real lover. Uppark Harry, with his overbearing mother, his stunning mansion, his broad Sussex acres, and hearty rustic ways had been an elemental force in her life. Francesca stopped her singing as Emma chuckled, throwing her mistress an enquiring glance that Emma picked up in the mirror. Just fourteen at the time, she could recall the dreams she had toyed with looking across the deer park to the great mansion, dreams that one day she would be mistress of that place, chatelaine of one of the most beautiful houses in the land.

The glow had faded on Harry; he was selfish, vain, boastful, overbearing, violent, and ultimately detached. To him Emma was just a chattel, of less account than one of his racehorses, to be parcelled out to any of his friends who wanted her and to be disposed of the minute she became a burden.

Charles Greville was one of those friends, but different. It was fitting that her thoughts should turn to him now, since that was the only previous time in her life that she had been knowingly and willingly unfaithful to the man who kept her. Of course Greville had known what she did not; that her dreams of a future of bliss with her keeper were nonsense; that at some point Harry would tire of her and he would be there to pick up the prize. Yet he too, having gained her trust and her love, had betrayed her.

There was a gentle knock on the door and Emma's heart missed a beat. She put up a hand, too late, to stop Francesca responding. It could be her husband and right at that moment she wasn't sure that she was ready to face him. She glanced over and saw Francesca take a note from Nelson's man, Tom Allen. The girl brought it over to her, and Emma recognised the untidy left-handed scrawl, familiar to her from all of Nelson's letters since he had lost his right arm.

"The Admiral's man is waiting for a reply?" she asked.

"Yes, Signora," Francesca replied.

Nelson wanted to call on her immediately. Was that wise, Emma wondered, and was it generated by passion or remorse? Matters were at enough of a stand without Sir William coming home to find herself and Nelson closeted in her private apartments. Quickly Emma re-read the note.

> *It is vital, my lady, that we speak without delay. Everything for the future of both our lives, our happiness, and the fate of our nation's arms could depend on it! N.*

It was too dramatic to be romantic, surely, but very much Nelson. Could she risk it?

"Tell Allen to convey to the Admiral that I will be happy to receive him in my drawing room in five minutes."

Francesca rushed back to the door, then returned to the dressing table to brush her mistress's hair.

Nelson stood outside the gleaming double doors that led to Emma Hamilton's apartments thinking that he would rather be single-handedly boarding an enemy First Rate than here. Every word he had rehearsed had deserted him, leaving him without the faintest idea of what to say. His main argument, that the mutual regard between himself and her husband debarred further intimacy, so forceful just a half an hour before, now seemed feeble in the extreme.

All he knew for certain was that they had to call a halt now, that any future departure from the strictest self-control by either party might be disastrous. Sir William could not be expected to sit idly by while Nelson made love to his wife. And Nelson was not stupid enough to think that such an attachment could be kept secret: it looked as though Sir William knew already, and it was unlikely that Mary Cadogan had remained in ignorance.

If the servants had been too busy to notice because of the task of clearing up after last night's banquet, that would not last. And what had his own man, Tom Allen, made of the events of the morning? First a hastily scribbled note to Lady Hamilton, her reply, then Nelson's instructions for him to wait by the front entrance to the palazzo and hotfoot it upstairs should there be any sign of Sir William

Hamilton. Tom might be slow-witted, but even he, Nelson suspected, could make four out of that.

On the other side of the door Emma was composing herself, trying to quell the thumping in her breast, worrying about how the folds of her dress lay, the angle of the light as it played on her profile, and most of all the calm face she must present to her expected visitor, an expression she knew would require all her skill to maintain. She realised now just how dangerous a liaison with Nelson might be, for to her he was not like other men: she had never felt for anyone the combination of tenderness and passion, hope and fear he evoked in her. If he was coming now to declare his undying love, she must send him away miserable.

She had ceased to worry about Sir William, her concern now was Nelson. Her reputation was tarnished, his was golden. He was about to be raised to the peerage, probably to a dukedom. Contact between them could only diminish him. Although, deep down, Emma did not believe this mattered, it was the part she was determined to play and it would be the performance of her life.

"Francesca, the door," she said, when she heard the firm knock. "Then you may leave Admiral Nelson and me alone."

Chapter Twenty-Six

FRANCESCA opened the door, but Horatio Nelson did not enter. He stood looking at the vision in the high-backed button chair before him, feeling the last vestiges of his resolve seep away. He knew, as he looked, that Emma had set out to entrance him: why else would she be sitting so that her loveliness was shown off to its best advantage? He took in the mass of russet hair, worn long and curled, the carefully powdered face that hid the rose-tinged glow of her cheeks. And even at this distance of several feet her eyes were huge and green.

Emma, her stomach churning, was fighting to stop herself smiling. Every feature of the man in the doorway was imprinted on her mind: the deep blue coat with one empty sleeve pinned across; the great star and ribbon of the Order of the Bath; the medal round his neck for St Vincent, held by black silk against his snow-white stock; the gilded epaulettes and frogging on his coat that marked him out as an admiral.

His entrancing good blue eye was on her in a steady gaze. She recalled the scar on his forehead, hidden by his bright silver hair, which she had kissed last night, still fresh enough to be red and angry. In intimate embrace it had been easy to see the scars Nelson bore from a hundred fights. She had kissed them all: cuts, dents, and the stump of his lost arm, all the way to the puckered end that he had used to support his body as he made love to her.

"Lady Hamilton," he said formally, with just the faintest trace of a tremor.

"Admiral Nelson," she replied, in a voice so nervous and loud, it seemed to echo off the walls.

Formality insisted that Nelson kiss her hand, which he feared to do. He did not want to come any closer to her than this doorway.

It was only the presence of her maid that forced him to step into the room. When she slipped out Nelson nearly followed her. It had never occurred to him that they would be left alone. He had no choice but to move forward, stiff-legged, and bend over the proffered hand. The contact did for them both.

"I am undone," he said, his voice anguished, as he raised his head to look at her and saw tears gathering in her eyes. "You're crying?" he said distractedly.

Emma dabbed at her eyelids. "It seems I am."

"Why?"

"Do I flatter myself that I am about to disappoint you?" she asked.

"You would struggle to flatter yourself, Emma, and nothing you could ever do would disappoint me."

The name came unbidden, but truly after the intimacy they had enjoyed it was only natural.

"Last night . . ."

Quickly he put a finger to her lips. He feared that she might say it had all been an aberration and he did not want to hear that: he wanted it to remain as he thought about it, the natural culmination of a shared passion. It might not be love, for Emma had made him wonder if he truly knew the meaning of the word, but it was something to be cherished.

"What I am about to say requires all my strength, more than I would ever need to fight a sea battle." He was looking directly into her eyes, once more gripping her hand. "Because of that I cannot say what I wish, cannot tell you the depth of the feelings I have, for to do so would make the rest impossible. Sir William is a man I consider a friend."

Emma wanted to say, "He is that to me, no more," but desisted: she felt that he had reached the same conclusion as she, that any relationship between them was impossible. To tell Nelson that much as she esteemed her husband she did not love him would hardly aid matters.

"Apart from that, there is my duty . . ."

Tom Allen knocked, then opened the door and called, "Sir William's carriage is coming up the hill."

"Wait outside, Tom," Nelson barked. The door shut with some force. "I must not be found here, you know that, and if Sir William confronts me and refers to last night I must tell you I will not lie to him."

"He won't, Nelson, be sure of that," replied Emma, praying she was speaking the truth.

"And I wish to remain your friend."

"For ever that," Emma replied, a catch in her voice.

He kissed her then, a mistake he knew, but impulse overrode sense. When he tried to pull away her arms prevented him, and when he spoke his voice was hoarse and his head just inches from hers. "You must let me go, Emma."

She did so, feeling as her hands dropped a sensation of utter defeat. Emma had wanted many things in her life, to marry a prince when she was a young girl, to live in a grand house surrounded by children and doted on by an adoring husband. The memories she had reprised that morning flashed through her mind and Emma gave credence to the thought, for the very first time in her life, that she had failed. Nelson backed towards the door. He gave her a last longing look, then spun round and left.

Tom Allen was waiting outside, but he was not alone. At the end of the corridor stood Mary Cadogan. As Nelson passed her, she shook her head slowly and tutted, as if to say that even for a hero, he was living dangerously.

"Mister Tyson is waiting for you, your honour," said Tom.

"Who?" Nelson said, before he collected himself. He had known Tyson since his first command and had taken him on recently as his new secretary. Tom seemed bewildered by his confusion. That made Nelson stop in his tracks.

"Tom. Not a word about this morning to anyone. Do you understand?"

As he nodded his servant tried to look innocent, and failed. A blind man could have seen that his master and the lady of the house were a mite more friendly than was proper. He waited for the Admiral to say more, but the sound of the carriage wheels, rattling over the cobbles at the front of the palazzo, had Nelson scurrying away. The last thing he wanted was to bump into Sir William.

Sir William Hamilton arrived home without ceremony and, having been informed by his major domo that his wife was about to leave for a meeting with the Queen at the Palazzo Reale, made his way to his own apartments. There he dealt with the morning correspondence, mainly composed of notes from various Neapolitan ministries that were empty of anything that could be considered meaningful. More interesting were reports from his own sources on the state of feeling in the kingdom to which he was accredited.

Naples was a city in which it was very necessary to possess two faces. Every nobleman, every person of rank, knew that he was sitting on more than one volcano. Vesuvius might smoke in the distance and erupt from time to time, but the more dangerous fault was political, not geological. Secret groupings abounded, in which the currency of entry was discussion of political change, and everything from peaceful overthrow to regicide was propounded as the best means of toppling the absolutism of the Bourbon monarchy.

Had foolish, childish King Ferdinand grasped, as he hunted and whored, dabbled in his Capodimonte pottery sheds, or received his most prominent subjects, that a good half of them belonged to societies dedicated to his removal? His queen, whose sister Marie Antoinette had perished on the guillotine, was certainly conscious of this. She lived in a state of perpetual terror that the same fate might befall her and her children.

Yet they would not fall victim to the peasantry. It was odd that here, in southern Italy, the only people on whom the monarchy could rely were the uneducated *lazzaroni*. They loved their king for the very same reasons that most nobles despised him: his lack of the attributes normally expected in a sovereign. Ferdinand's elder brother, who should have succeeded to the kingdom, had been harmlessly mad as a child and youth, and declared unfit to govern. It was suspected that the brain of Ferdinand himself might be delicate too, and should not be taxed too severely. Therefore the King had been raised with little education: no lessons in statecraft, finance, or diplomacy, or even the rudiments of dignified behaviour. He was a boor with the manners of a rustic: he ate and drank to excess, preferred the company of peasants to nobles, took pleasure only in the chase and fornication. To men who desired Naples to be accorded respect he was an embarrassment; to those who hankered after constitutional change he was a tyrant. To the *lazzaroni,* unwashed, unambitious, and careless of the future, he was one of them, and nothing less than a hero.

When Sir William Hamilton thought of the components of the kingdom to which he had been the British representative for near 35 years, he almost succumbed to despair. Falsehood was more prevalent than honesty, laziness combined with bombast more apparent than activity and courage. Public revenues, with very few exceptions, were seen as fair game. Thus grand aims were never realised as the money set aside to pay for them disappeared into various deep pockets. Somehow he had to persuade this sclerotic structure to mobilise troops and warships, then attack a nation that had swept all before it in the last seven years.

"Admiral Nelson?" he asked his valet.

"Is in his chambers, Maestro," the man replied, it being his job to know these things.

"A request that he join me," said Sir William. "We have important matters to discuss."

John Tyson sat in the anteroom next to Nelson's bedroom, and noted how different he was from the young, gauche master and commander with whom he had first served on the sloop *Badger* in the Caribbean. It wasn't just the Admiral's uniform or the missing right arm: as always Nelson eschewed a wig, but his hair was silver grey now instead of straw blond, yet still untidy and tied at the nape of his neck in a queue. His face had lost its rosy colour but no lines betrayed the worries that must assail him. His one good eye was still pale blue and direct, the voice remained soft, friendly and encouraging, the smile still warm.

Knowing Nelson and others like him had often caused John Tyson to ruminate on the attributes required for leadership. Just as he knew he did not have such a gift, he had met many who claimed it and a very few who had that ability in varying degrees. But none had those attributes like this man.

"You know your predecessor ran off the deck at Aboukir?" said Nelson, without looking up from the mass of correspondence he was reading—letters and reports from every superior officer in his own fleet, as well as despatches from Earl St Vincent.

"There are those who vie to be an admiral's secretary, sir, and think that being shot at is not part of their brief."

Nelson looked up and smiled. "Not John Tyson, I hazard. I seem to recall you having to be restrained when an opportunity arose for a boarding from the deck of dear old *Badger*."

"I'd be more content to stand still now, sir, since my bones have stiffened somewhat. But it's true I could not rest below with a fight going on above my head."

Since those days as Nelson's first purser, Tyson had watched or heard of his rise in the service. The King's Navy was like an extended family in perpetual motion where news was eagerly sought regarding past compatriots. If Nelson had a ship, Tyson knew of it, and also if he had a success or a setback. His romantic adventures with the opposite sex were the cause of much mingled mirth and concern: Nelson was considered to be extremely unreliable in that department, forever in pursuit of the unattainable. Just as worrying was the passion with which he had imbued his suits in places as far flung as France, Canada, and the Caribbean. The news that he had finally married a widow of good family, a seemingly steady woman with good sense, had been greeted with relief.

The disputes to which he was prone were common knowledge too: he had clashed with admirals and their wives, as with civilian and service officials. Then there had been the disastrous tour of the

Caribbean Islands Nelson had undertaken with His Royal Highness Prince William Henry, the Duke of Clarence. It was generally held that Nelson had spent five years without employment before the present conflict because the King blamed him for allowing his son to make a fool of himself.

But that was all in the past. Now he was at his peak, and a peerage was certain. Tyson reckoned that if Nelson had been famous before, he had merely been one of a dozen others—Edward Pellew for his single ship actions, Jervis for the victory of St Vincent, Lord Howe for the Glorious First of June, and Admiral Duncan for thrashing the Dutch at Camperdown. But after the victory at the Nile, Nelson would be elevated above all other mariners of whatever rank and he, lucky John Tyson, had landed the job of serving him as his secretary.

"I have here more correspondence, sir," said Tyson, pointing to the pile of official papers, "but I hazard of a nature more to your liking than that."

As he handed them across the desk, Tyson reeled off the names of those who had sent these communications: the Sultan of the Ottoman Empire and various beys, deys, bagshaws, and viziers of that dominion. There were letters from Vienna, from the Emperor of Austria and his leading ministers; from French exiles in Germany, the Prussian court, Italian grand dukes, deposed Venetian and Genoese doges; from occupied Rome, with the blessings of the Pope and his cardinals. And they were all, without exception, written in the formal diplomatic language, which was French.

"I fear I am good for no more than one word in three of this, Tyson."

"I will have them drafted in English for you, sir, but if I may give you the gist, they are all fulsome in praise of the Nile victory." Tyson picked up one. "The Sultan, for instance . . ."

"Who sat squarely on the fence, Tyson," Nelson interrupted. "Had his navy been more active I would have found the French weeks before. Were they not his domains Bonaparte invaded, his Mameluke warriors he beat in battle by the Pyramids? The Sultan and his court did nothing, and left us to fight their cause for them."

"The Sultan," continued Tyson calmly, "not only sends you written congratulations, but news that he is to confer on you the Order of the Crescent, as well as the most splendid special reward. An envoy is on his way from Istanbul with the decoration, a singular honour that is awarded only to those who have performed with the highest gallantry to the Ottoman State. It is a decoration known in Turkish as a *Chelenk*, and the correspondent describes it as an aigrette, a plume of triumph made from silver and diamonds, which is to be worn in the turban."

"A turban for all love!" chortled Nelson. "It would shake their lordships if I turned up at the Admiralty in a turban."

Tyson grinned. "I fancy the idea appeals to you, sir."

"Oh, it does, Tyson. It so very much does."

The door opened and Tom Allen announced, "Captain Troubridge, your honour."

"Tom," said Nelson, rising.

"Sir," Troubridge replied, punctiliously.

Nelson hated old shipmates to be so correct: it was just another example of the isolation his rank imposed on him. Right now this man was his second-in-command, yet he was still formal. It was never discussed because that was impossible, so Nelson could not explain how much he missed the easy camaraderie he had once enjoyed with men like Thomas Troubridge. They had served together as midshipmen, and it had been in Tom's company that he had witnessed his first flogging and fought in his first sea action. A series of movements up the ladder of promotion had meant leaving behind those who had once been brutally truthful with him and were now inclined to be deferential.

"How are you, Tom?"

"Spitting blood, sir, since I've just come from the dockyard."

Both men knew that Nelson was not referring to that, and he looked into Troubridge's swarthy face for signs of the grief he must be suffering. They had sailed into Naples on the back of the Nile victory, only for Troubridge, who had run his ship aground and missed the battle, to find that he was a widower: news had arrived from England that his wife had died. Nelson, who had hardly had time to talk to him since, knew that anything other than the most perfunctory commiseration would be unwelcome.

Even as a youngster, Tom had been unsentimental and dedicated to the service, a magnificent organiser and executive officer, trusted if not loved by his crew. He had also been the only one with enough courage to mention his dislike of adultery after Nelson's dalliance with his Genoese opera singer.

The Good Lord help me, Nelson thought, if he ever finds out about last night.

They fell to discussing the shortcomings of the Neapolitan dockyards—requests ignored, work avoided, planking, masts, and spars nowhere to be found—like the money to pay for them. Was Troubridge, or John Tyson for that matter, aware that Nelson was keeping the conversation going to avoid that which he must undertake next?

He had a note on the table from Sir William Hamilton, inviting him to discuss the state of affairs in Naples, and how they must proceed if they were ever to stir King Ferdinand and his ministers into some kind of military action. Tom Allen forced the issue, with a polite reminder from Sir William's messenger that he was awaiting Admiral Nelson, only to receive from his master a look of venom.

"Admiral Nelson," said Sir William, smiling as he came to greet his visitor, who, to his delight, looked somewhat nervous. That a man who had become the nemesis of every Jacobin the world over, who had laid the ghost of Bonaparte and the infallibility of the French Revolution, should dread to meet him was risible.

Nelson's throat felt as though it had a cord round it as he croaked his reply. "Sir William."

"I trust you are quite recovered from last night's exertions, Admiral," Sir William paused just long enough to see Nelson blush, then added, "at the ball."

As he made the short journey from Posillipo, Sir William Hamilton had decided how he would respond to what had taken place. It was out of the question to make a scene; it would be both ungentlemanly and demeaning. Neither could he imply that he knew what had taken place between his wife and the Admiral.

He was determined to see the matter in the context of the city and the state in which he resided. In Naples, it was not just customary for a man of parts to have a mistress, it was considered essential. In fact, it was in order for men and women to have several lovers at the same time, and the shifting sexual alliances provided an otherwise dull royal court with entertaining conversation. Many observed their marriage vows with laxity—and even the prelates of the Catholic Church had their paramours.

The King couldn't be trusted with anything female, even his own wife, whom he had brought to bed with child eighteen times. Maria Carolina's only release was in his multiple affairs, either with the ladies of his court or with beautiful and willing girls from a less exalted background who knew that he would be generous when he tired of them. Sir William and Emma had been the exception to the rule in their mutual constancy, he an amused spectator as nearly every man that entered Emma's orbit tried to break that bond. Even the King had tried, only to find Emma very reluctant to entertain such a notion, and stopping him had taken all Sir William's diplomatic wiles.

Sir William did not wish to embarrass Nelson, who he suspected had little experience with women. He had known that as he grew older Emma might take a lover and could not deny there was some consolation to be had if it turned out to be someone he liked and admired. But Sir William still had a sense of mischief and, without Emma present, he could not resist having a little fun at Nelson's expense.

It was a delight to watch the confusion on his visitor's face as he continued. "I do find balls so fatiguing, Admiral, and I attend a damn sight more of them than you do. Too much food, too much wine, and a surfeit of tedious conversation make it hard for one to get a decent night's sleep. I myself went to Posillipo last night to recover."

He gave Nelson a direct stare then, which from what he knew of the man, would normally have been returned in full measure. This time the Admiral had to look away, his face filled with the kind of despair that might precede a confession. Sir William decided he had teased him enough. Time to get down to business.

"I fear I must inform you, Nelson, that things have changed since your last visit to Naples. Those with whom you treated in '93 no longer have the power they had then."

"Acton?" asked Nelson.

"His wings have been clipped," Sir William replied.

Sir John Acton, an Englishman in the service of the Neapolitan court had proved himself a friend to the country of his birth. Nelson had arrived in Naples in November 1793, just after combined fleets of Britain and Spain had taken possession of the French naval port of Toulon. Nelson had been sent to request troops to help hold the place against the armies of the Revolution. Expecting lethargy he had been surprised when Acton announced that the troops were already being assembled. Six thousand men, with warships and supplies had reached Toulon in record time. That they had not performed very well mattered less than that Naples had provided them with such alacrity.

"He fell out with the Queen, I'm afraid," added Sir William.

"They seemed so close, almost intimates," Nelson mused, and regretted the allusion. It had been rumoured that Acton and the Queen were lovers, which was not a subject he wanted to raise.

"A rumour that Acton fostered, for by doing so he disguised his true inclinations."

Nelson had heard that Sir John was a pederast. Indeed he had smoked a hint of that when they had met. Not that the notion bothered him. Nelson had met too many men of that stamp in the Navy, both officers and seamen, to care a fig for a man's sexual orientation. What mattered was how well they performed their duties, and in that respect Acton had been exemplary.

Sir William laughed. "The irony is that he and the Queen fell out over an object of mutual affection, a young officer from Saxony, a tall blond blue-eyed Adonis. A foolish whim from the Queen of course."

Nelson felt a flash of irritation. Sir William was gossiping, which in the circumstances seemed singularly inappropriate. He speculated that the British Ambassador was not the man he used to be—a fellow who had had razor sharp instincts for the essential. Perhaps age had withered his professional abilities just as it had atrophied his limbs.

"Forgive me for meandering off the point," Sir William went on, making Nelson feel doubly a scrub. "You will recall the Marquis de Gallo from your previous visit."

"I do," Nelson said gratefully, "though I must admit the memory is not pleasant."

"Well, it is our misfortune that he is the person with whom we will have to deal."

Chapter Twenty-Seven

SITTING ACROSS THE TABLE from the Marquis de Gallo, Nelson remembered why he didn't like the man: it was his insufferable air of superiority. Gallo had a bland face and a flat voice. He was constantly evasive and gave the appearance of deep boredom, playing idly with a jewelled snuff box whenever anyone else was speaking.

Nelson wanted evidence that Naples was prepared to take advantage of what he and his fleet had delivered to them. More than anything he wanted a firm declaration of war on France, which would encourage the other Italian states either to take up arms or rebel against the invaders. De Gallo had the ear of the Queen, who was the true ruler of Naples, plus the trust of the King, which implied political dexterity of the highest order. What it clearly did not imply was any predilection to zeal.

Looking at the Marquis, as he accompanied his passion-free words with tiny negative gestures, Nelson was reminded of something that had happened to him as a youngster. A fellow midshipman on his first ship, Tom Foley, who had later become a firm friend, had invited him to partake in a pissing competition, he who achieved the greatest distance to be declared the winner of a silver sixpence. Nelson went first, only realising when soaked how he had been guyed into pissing into the wind. He felt a little like that now as he reiterated once more the reasons why Naples should act swiftly.

"What if the news of Aboukir Bay reaches Paris before I can inform my ambassador there?" Gallo protested.

Sir William translated, then told Nelson of his intended reply: that even the rogues who ran France would respect diplomatic credentials. Then he reminded the Marquis that on his northern border the French had fewer than nine thousand troops of indifferent quality. That was followed by a rapid incomprehensible exchange before Sir William told him what had transpired.

"The Queen's brother, the Emperor, who shows no sign of movement himself, is sending an experienced general from Vienna to take command of the Neapolitan forces."

Evidently Nelson failed to respond with the enthusiasm de Gallo had expected for the Marquis frowned. The Admiral had had much experience of Austrian generals in past campaigns centred on the northern Italian states and nothing he had seen inspired him to expect from them either courage or military skill. All they had ever offered him was prevarication, obfuscation, or a terse note to say they were retreating or suing for peace.

"Baron Karl Mack von Leiberich," Sir William added, "is already on his way."

"When will he arrive?" Nelson demanded. The response from the Neapolitan Chief Minister was a shrug, so he added, "And the Navy?"

What followed was a long explanation, blaming the British for the delay. How could the Neapolitan fleet be fully fitted out when the dockyards were occupied with Nelson's battle-damaged ships? It was a far cry from the time when Sir John Acton had been in charge.

Emma was playing Blind Man's Buff with Prince Alberto, the youngest of the royal children, aware that the Queen was only intermittently watching them as she paced between her work-table and a window overlooking the bay. That was rare for a woman who had such a deep affection for her numerous offspring. Maria Carolina was troubled—indeed her life since coming here as a young girl from Vienna had seemed one whole sea of such. Her husband was suspicious, cunning at the same time as stupid, wont to leave the running of the state to her only to interfere at the most inappropriate time to ruin whatever consistency of policy existed.

Compared to the ordered world of the Austrian Court Naples was chaos. The Queen had never felt comfortable here, and even now was surrounded with a forty-strong cohort of German speaking servants. If Ferdinand was unaware that many of his aristocratic subjects were disloyal to him, his wife was not. She had seen her own sister brought to the guillotine in Paris, and was shrewd enough to know that although the rabble made the noise, it was disaffected noblemen that made revolutions, and weak servants of the state who failed to stop them.

The Queen's nephew, the Emperor of Austria, heading one of the mightiest states in Europe, had been forced into an ignominious peace. If her homeland, which was huge and capable of putting large armies in the field, could not resist, what chance had Naples? Maria Carolina had to take a decision that she longed to avoid: what advice should she give regarding relations with France?

A few years before, the decision would have been exclusively hers, a time when she had leant on the support of Sir John Acton, but no longer. Acton had not stolen money, but he had turned out in his own way to be just as corrupt and disloyal as the others. His successor, the Marquis de Gallo, was too slippery to control, having succeeded in getting Ferdinand interested in the management of his kingdom—mainly by engendering suspicion in him about the true motives and the fidelity of his wife.

That brought an ironic smile to the Queen's lips. Ferdinand could not comprehend that she was not, like him, a slave to physical passion. Maria Carolina had desires, but of the variety of courtly love, that medieval construct by which a lover committed his soul to his paramour, yet suppressed any carnal thoughts. That was the kind of man she liked, and any intimation that matters should go further was instantly rebuffed. She got enough of that kind of attention from the slavering beast to whom she was married.

A high squeal made her turn. She saw Emma mock-wrestling with Prince Alberto, who was six, and third in line to the throne. He still wore the blindfold, yet protested his invisibility, although Emma held him in a firm embrace. If only, the Queen thought, she could emulate that childish ability to believe that if you cannot see, you cannot be seen. Then she could avoid the coming meeting which her husband had insisted she attend because the Marquis de Gallo had convinced him that it was the best way to stop her plotting.

To Maria Carolina, Lady Hamilton was a true blessing, and she regretted that protocol had kept them apart for the first years of Emma's stay. As the mistress of a diplomat, Emma had had no standing in Naples, but meeting her had been unavoidable. She had surprised the Queen by speaking German, which endeared her to Maria Carolina. A bond had been struck and Emma had quickly become an intimate.

But it remained unofficial; protocol insisted that only those who had been received by their own sovereign could be received at a foreign court, and King George III flatly refused to entertain the notion of meeting Emma, even after she had married his childhood friend. But such a ruling could not stand in the face of the needs of a lonely queen or a fearful nation. Good relations with Great Britain had to be maintained and part of that meant that Sir William must be kept content.

Emma was now a *confidante* in the sense that Maria Carolina spoke in her presence about matters of state, her relations with her husband, and what to do with her children. But the Queen was never subjected to a question, never ever probed for motive, because that was forbidden. It was possible for Emma to advance ideas that had advantage for her husband's mission as British Ambassador. But absolute intimacy was impossible: a ruler could never entirely trust anyone.

"Enough, children," Maria Carolina said, waving away a barrage of protests. The various German women who had care of the children came forward to collect their reluctant charges, who would now be taken off to their lessons. The Queen persevered with studious application to their education, not least because she did not want them turning out like her husband. Before departure, each was required to kiss their mother, and none went without a peck from Emma. Maria Carolina felt a pang of jealousy that she received dutiful embraces, while Emma's were given out of affection.

"So, Emma, what onslaught must we to face today from your little admiral?"

Emma started at "your," then realised that the word had been used in innocence. "He will not attack you, madam, but he will try to persuade you to attack the French."

Maria Carolina laughed. "Believe me, Emma, if I were a man, I would need no persuasion. My sword would be stained already with the blood of those swinedogs."

"Why change sex, madam? Perhaps what we need is a regiment of women."

"Look no further than Naples for that, Emma," the Queen replied, bitterly. "A true man in this forsaken place is not easy to find."

There were things about which the two women disagreed, and Naples was one of them. Emma loved it for dozens of reasons, which seemed to be the same ones for which Maria Carolina despised it. The climate was benign in winter and bearable in summer, as long as they went out of the city. Society was frivolous, the peasantry idle but good-humoured, the scenery beautiful, even rumbling Vesuvius. There was the warm sea to bathe in, an idea that made the Queen shudder, and abundant highly scented flowers, which made her sneeze.

The only thing of which they seemed at one was the Neapolitan love of superstition. Maria Carolina was a firm believer in the Evil One, who could damn you to perdition with a look: thus she was covered in charms to ward off the actions of the devil and his acolytes. She had persuaded Emma to wear them too, because their friendship would render her person vulnerable if Emma was not protected. It was hard to argue with a queen, and Emma didn't try.

In fact, she was careful in what she said, though not from weakness. Emma knew that she could speak to the Queen in a manner that would see others put firmly in their place. She didn't try to understand why this should be so, but knew that Maria Carolina disliked falsehood or disguised feelings. Therefore, ever since they had first become close, she had behaved naturally.

"You would oblige me, Emma, by telling your admiral that my inclinations are to oppose France, but I may not be able to say so in his presence."

"He will believe that without any words of mine, madam. He knows and esteems you from what I have told him of you in my letters."

"Do you always write well of me, Emma?"

Intended as a joke, it was taken the wrong way, with Emma insisting, "I keep fair copies, madam, that you are at liberty to read."

"No, no, Emma, my dear," Maria Carolina said. "You have often read to me Admiral Nelson's replies and that will suffice. I am often left to wonder if the person he talks of as Queen of Naples is me or someone imagined, so virtuous does he make me sound. Now, take my arm, and escort me to the door of that nest of vipers my husband calls his council."

That Nelson emerged frustrated from de Gallo's room came as no surprise to him. He had never expected to be greeted with news that the strategic and tactical moves he had recommended had been implemented. But he had expected political action. However, the man on whom he relied to pressure their putative allies had seemed reluctant to press his case. As he had perceived that morning, Sir William had lost some of his fire.

The best interpretation that Nelson could essay was that the Ambassador realised the limitations of what he could do and was determined not to raise Nelson's hopes. But Sir William had been too soft on the Marquis. He had let him control the conversation instead of reminding a man who was a silk-clad scoundrel what he owed to Great Britain; to tell him that, years ago, without the shield of the British fleet, Naples would have been under French control.

That thought was reinforced as they entered the council chamber to face the several men and one woman who ran the kingdom. Ferdinand was there, of course, looking bored, although the proceedings had not even begun. Nelson observed the huge nose and heavy, dark features, the prominent brow made more so by thick eyebrows. The King had near-black eyes that never seemed to settle on any object for more than a second, and a hand that seemed to be continually scratching at his groin.

Ferdinand didn't twitch; he was after all not actually mad, just very strange. A tall, broad-shouldered man who should have looked splendid and majestic in court dress, he was the most unkempt person in the room, with traces of food on his coat front. His wig was poorly dressed and very slightly misplaced which gave him the air of some character from a comedy of manners.

As usual a high cleric was in attendance, a hawk-faced individual that Sir William informed him was Cardinal Fabrizo Ruffo, apparently one of those divines who, rich before his elevation, spent most of his time increasing his wealth rather than tending to the needs of his flock.

The Queen was seated beside Ferdinand and Nelson saw her as no more regal than her husband. She was squat at the hips and narrow at the shoulders, with unhealthy skin, a heavy, gloomy mouth, and a long face that ended in a double chin. Only the eyes betrayed animation and intelligence. What was it that made Emma friends with this woman? In every letter he had ever received from her Emma had never failed to praise the Queen. And it was an attachment that had paid handsome dividends. Without Maria Carolina—and possibly Acton acting in his capacity as Minister of Marine, Nelson would have had to abandon the chase after Bonaparte. Then he recalled that it had been Emma, using every ounce of influence she had on behalf of her country, who had persuaded the Queen to break the rules of neutrality. For that she deserved a medal, and he resolved there and then to move heaven and earth to get her one.

A delegation from Malta was shown in, to tell the King and Queen that their islands, captured by Bonaparte, were willing to submit to the suzerainty of Naples if they could be recaptured. The home of the Knights of St John since the time of the crusades, Malta had been just the kind of prize craved by revolutionary France: rich, undisturbed for centuries, and with an abundance of treasure to steal. That treasure had been sent to the bottom of Aboukir Bay with the French flagship *L'Orient*.

Through whispered translation, Sir William kept Nelson abreast of the submissions of the Maltese delegation and the King's response: that his forces would kick the French out. To Nelson's mind the Maltese could invite away and give credence to Ferdinand's promises if they wished. Valetta was the only place that mattered and Malta would be a hard nut to crack with the French holed up in the main fortress. They were not like the Knights of St John, grown soft and corrupt through decades of luxury, an easy target to a determined invader.

De Gallo had arrived while the Maltese were making their case. After their departure he began to talk as though he was barely part of the proceedings, reiterating what he had told Nelson and Sir William already regarding the arrival of Baron Mack. Equally bored Horatio Nelson looked around the overly elaborate decor of the chamber: painted ceiling panels showed the various stages of some celestial contest; feats of a more modern nature graced the wall panels, with knights slaying everything from dragons to Saracens. He was unable to resist the ironic contrast between Neapolitan art and reality.

He needed soldiers and would have given his one good arm for British regiments that would march to his commands. As de Gallo droned on, Nelson let his imagination run to lines of red-coats advancing under his instructions, taking Rome and the states beyond and rolling the enemy back beyond Nice.

Sir John Acton was called upon to speak. Nelson ceased his meandering and concentrated on what his fellow countryman had to say. Acton had always had an agreeable countenance but age had sharpened his features considerably. Though dressed plainly in a dark silk coat and buff breeches, he was immaculate in a way that others present were not. Everything about his person spoke of a fastidious attention to his toilet, from his short well-powdered wig, to his gold-buckled and highly polished pumps. Nelson could see that his fingernails were even, manicured, and clean.

Nelson had always liked him because he was a positive force in this gimcrack court, too professional to be dismissed. He might not have the power he once enjoyed, but he was still a potent minister.

His information, which was far more encouraging than de Gallo's, revealed that troops were available and more could be recruited. The royal regiments were up to strength and all the noblemen of the mainland and Sicily had been called upon to serve with horse and carbine.

Acton called upon Commodore Caracciolo to speak about naval preparations. An old adversary of Nelson's, Caracciolo, despite his squat and muscular frame, had the same courtier-like arrogance as de Gallo. He declined to be specific—in fact, he did little more than invite Nelson to dine on board one of the Neapolitan capital ships as a guest of the King. Nelson could see what that meant without explanation from Sir William. Ferdinand was telling him that Naples was still neutral. To dine a British admiral on shore would breach the obligations of neutrality, giving the French envoy every right to object. Naples was sitting on the fence.

Which was where Nelson wanted to be on the way back to the Palazzo Sessa, preferably a fence miles away from Naples. The meeting he dreaded, at which he, Emma, and Sir William would be present, was about to take place. He contemplated an immediate return to his ship, but dismissed that out of hand. Even if *Vanguard* had been ready for sea, which she was not, his flight would strengthen rather than allay suspicion.

There would be a brief respite while each party returned to their own apartments, or so Nelson thought until he opened the door to his and found his stepson, Josiah Nesbit, waiting for him. The sight of the young man brought forcibly to mind an image of his wife, which induced feelings of deep guilt. This he tried to disguise by giving the young man a hearty greeting.

"I have come to proffer an apology, sir," Josh said, as Tom Allen took Nelson's hat and removed his cloak.

Stiff, non-familial, typical of the grown up Josh. "An apology?"

His stepson was looking at a point above his head. "For my behaviour last night, sir."

Nelson looked perplexed. "I was not aware that your behaviour gave any cause for an apology."

"Captain Troubridge does, sir, and also, it seems, Captain Hardy. I am here at their express wish."

There was still no eye contact. "Josh, you can come and go here as you like. We are, if not blood relations, family nevertheless."

"Sir."

Nelson wondered what had become of the boy he had once known, whose company he had so enjoyed. In a life in the Navy Nelson had seen hundreds grow from nervous boys to confident men, watched them lose that sense of frolic on taking up an officer's responsibilities. But Josh had surpassed them all. His golden hair had turned dull brown, his happy countenance had soured.

That he drank more than was good for him was obvious from the puffy face, bloodshot eyes, and the protruding belly in an otherwise spare frame. On his desk, Nelson had a letter of complaint from the commander-in-chief that alluded to transgressions without being specific. This was odd, because when they had met at the beginning of the year, prior to the Nile campaign, St Vincent had been full of praise for the same person his letter damned.

"For what offence do Hardy and Troubridge say you must apologise?"

"I made some remarks regarding you and Lady Hamilton, which they deemed inappropriate."

Nelson turned away, with a sharp look at Tom Allen, which commanded him to leave the room. "Tell me, Josh, did you drink much last night?"

"Several of your officers told me I was drunk, yes."

Nelson turned back, smiling. "Was it not an occasion to over-indulge? We were celebrating a great victory."

"You will recall, sir, that I was not present at Aboukir Bay."

Nelson was angry now, but he sought hard not to let it show in his voice. "For God's sake, Josh, stop being so damned formal. I am your stepfather, and while I acknowledge that such an estate is not perfect I hope and pray you believe that I regard you as my own son. I have done everything in my power to advance you in the service and will continue to do so. Now, let us put aside the events of last night for a moment. Tell me what you did to upset St Vincent."

"I became engaged in various disputes with my fellow officers on the Cadiz blockade, sir."

"I can hardly fault you for that," replied Nelson, with a laugh. "I have, as you know, spent half my service life arguing with some of them."

His attempt to lighten the atmosphere fell flat. Nelson had already replied to St Vincent, requesting a more detailed explanation, while at the same time requesting that Josh be given a frigate and the right to serve under his stepfather's command. Better to wait for a response from the Earl than to tax his stepson about his misdemeanours. However, although he didn't want to ask what happened at the ball last night, he knew he had to.

"Tell me what was it you said that so upset Troubridge and Hardy?"

"I complained, sir, that the attentions you were paying to Lady Hamilton were those you should have properly been paying to my mother, and I said so loudly enough for a great number of people to hear."

"She was our hostess, Josh. And I do recall that when you came here with me in '93, she was the soul of kindness to you."

Josiah Nesbit positively spat his next words. "Just as *I* recall, sir, telling you that she was a whore who had tricked Sir William Hamilton into marriage. And I also remember how severely you chastised me for that statement."

"I thought you wrong then, Josh," said Nelson, softly, "and further acquaintance with the lady means that now I know it."

"She's ensnared you too."

The realisation that his stepson was jealous came as a flash of insight, though Nelson had little time to examine it. For five days in 1793, Emma had doted on the youth, flattered him, made him feel special, and broken through his shyness. How had she treated him on his return? As just another naval officer, perhaps, well connected but of less account than the abundant Nile heroes?

"Lady Hamilton has ensnared no one, Josh. I will not lie to you when I say I find her a most pleasant person to be with."

"I doubt you are alone in that, sir," said Josh. "I should think that half the cocks in Naples share that notion."

"How dare you, sir!" Nelson shouted, regretting it immediately. Too stout a defence of Emma could only confirm the young man's suspicions. "How dare you bring your vulgar filth into my presence? Do I have to remind of my rank, as well as my status as your legal parent?"

"No, sir," said Josiah stiffly.

"I have it on very good authority," Nelson went on, "that the lady in question gives no cause for scandal. Have I not written to your own mother these last five years to tell her so, and point out that whatever demeaning gossip she might have heard about Lady Hamilton cannot be true? Do you not know that Lady Hamilton, out of the kindness of her heart, also wrote to your mother to praise you, and to tell her that, having taken you under her protective wing, she felt that you would grow to be a man of whom she could be proud?"

"I am aware of that, sir."

"Then by your behaviour you are denying the truth of that assertion. Captains Troubridge and Hardy are right, you do owe me an apology. But more than that you owe a greater one to someone else who has shown you nothing but kindness. Lady Hamilton, herself."

Chapter Twenty-Eight

As he made his way towards the main reception rooms of the Palazzo Sessa Nelson was seething, yet he sensed that the ground was shifting beneath his feet. Who else had noticed his behaviour with Emma? Troubridge for certain, and his flag captain Thomas Hardy. Did they think the same as Josh? Had they, in fact, sent his stepson to apologise as a way of alerting him to the obvious nature of his behaviour? His own weakness, which he experienced that very morning, would work against him. Proximity to Emma shattered his resolve so he must never be alone with her, nor show her too much attention when they were in company.

The doors opened before him to a room full of people engaged in polite applause. As he bowed he saw Emma glance at him proudly. The look on Sir William Hamilton's face was a combination of admiration and perplexity.

It was easier to avoid being alone with either Sir William or Emma than Nelson had supposed. Few occasions arose in the endless round of balls and receptions when they were not in the company of others. The Palazzo Sessa had always played host to a stream of visitors: expatriate or travelling fellow countrymen, locals and foreigners interested in art, antiquities, music, literature and gossip. Sir William Hamilton's reception rooms were home to wit and malice in equal measure and, over the years of his tenure, they had become one of the focal points of Neapolitan society. With Nelson in residence the number of callers increased and The Palazzo always seemed full. When either the crowd, the contemplation of Emma's beauty, or a stab of jealousy at the attentions paid to her by another man became too much for him, Nelson had his own apartments to retire to, where Tyson waited with sheaves of correspondence requiring his attention.

Most days and every night they went elsewhere to be entertained. In the main, Nelson travelled to these events in a separate carriage with his officers because whenever he appeared a crowd gathered to cheer him. Walking in the streets was impossible—he was mobbed whenever he tried.

The nights were the worst: alone in the dark he half feared, half hoped that Emma would visit him. A man with a lively imagination, he could easily conjure up the pleasure of her presence, just as easily as he could let his mind rip on the consequences. Often he feared to close his eyes, lest the images that assailed him came once more to mind.

He saw more of Sir William on matters pertaining to duty since the Ambassador was his conduit to the Neapolitan government. Slowly and haphazardly his ship was being refitted, the army was being mobilised and trained, supplies and armaments were being stockpiled. And Baron Mack von Leiberich was on his way. The frustration lay in the time it all took, and the way the whole of Naples society seemed more intent on dancing, gossiping, drinking, and eating than war. As he wrote to St Vincent, they were no more than "a bunch of fiddlers and rascals."

Ferdinand and Maria Carolina made good their promise to receive him aboard one of their capital ships, the 74-gun *Tancredi*. His own barge crew, under the watchful gaze of his coxswain, Giddings, rowed him there. A stocky Londoner with a battered face, who had served with Nelson for years, Giddings never looked quite right in the neat blue jacket, white straw hat and gaily striped trews of his office. He looked like what he was: a bit of a brawler, a man who would never shy from a fight be it against a fellow sailor or the whole French fleet.

On coming aboard, Nelson's professional eye was employed in comparing the Italian vessel with one of his own. The ship was dry and weatherly, the rope work neat, and the decks were pristine, all of which testified to time spent at anchor, not the quality of build. The ships of his own fleet were worn, having been at sea for months, in blazing sun, howling gales, rain, sleet, heaving seas, and battle.

Hardly a rope was not spliced or a sail lacking a patch, the decks gouged at the edges where the guns had been run in and out and in other places where shot had ripped out splinters. Even an amateur eye would spot repaired bulwarks and masts fished with spars and gammoned with ropes to strengthen them where cannonballs had struck or a hard blow had loosed them from their seatings.

"What do you make of it, Mr Pasco?" Nelson asked the young midshipman at his side as the ceremony of piping aboard was completed.

Wherever Nelson went he took with him one of the midshipmen, youngsters who alternated between fear of making a gaffe and the even greater dread that should food materialise they might not get enough. It was a means of introducing his young charges to polite society, but it afforded him a chance to get to know them better, and to ensure that their life in the midshipmen's berth was bearable—it could be hellish if it was not carefully supervised. He also felt that contact with these youths kept him young.

He enjoyed their company too. There were exceptions, morose individuals or those too nervous to relax, but in the main, once they had realised that Nelson was not going to devour them, the midshipmen were talkative and informative. He had formed the habit when he took his first command, and malicious tongues had wagged. He had pretended not to care, but before his marriage he had worried that there might some truth in the accusations covertly made against him.

"Tidy, sir, very tidy," Pasco replied.

He was a white-faced youth, whose clear skin seemed impervious to either the ravages of his age or the Mediterranean sun. He was slim, with black hair and lively, dark brown eyes, keen as mustard to do well, bright, intelligent, with the right mix of mischief and capability. Pasco was just the kind of young man Nelson liked: one whom, should he survive, would rise to become a credit to the service.

"And?"

"The men, sir," said Pasco doubtfully. "They seem timid. They fail to meet the eye."

It was true. Smart though they were they lacked the spark that animated a British crew. Britannia's sailors had a way of looking at their officers which let them know that while they would be afforded all due respect, they were dealing with souls who knew how to go about their business. Not insolent—that would only bring down punishment—but assured.

"Well observed, young Pasco," Nelson said, as they were escorted across the maindeck, "d'you know, I quite missed that."

It was good to sense Pasco swell a little beside him. No doubt he would regale the midshipmen's mess with the tale, embellished a trifle, of how he had put his admiral right. As they came up on to the sunlit maindeck, the midshipman fell a step behind so that his commanding officer could raise his hat to the Commodore of the Neapolitan fleet and the flag of the kingdom that streamed from the masthead.

The commodore was Caracciolo, and by waiting on the quarterdeck, the Count had inflicted a minor insult on Ferdinand's guest: given Nelson's rank and what he had just achieved, Caracciolo should have greeted him at the entry-port on the maindeck. He looked at Nelson keenly to see if the slur had been noted, and his disappointment, when he was greeted by a bland British admiral, was almost palpable.

Nelson and Count Caracciolo had met before, when the ships and troops of Naples had been despatched to Toulon in '93. After that unfortunate town was abandoned to revolutionary reprisals Caracciolo, in one line-of-battle ship, had stayed with the British fleet as part of the squadron under Admiral Hotham. Able to speak clear if heavily accented English, he had served in the British Navy as a youngster attached to Admiral George Rodney, a man he admired greatly. At a dinner aboard Hotham's ship, Nelson had questioned Rodney's reputation. There was little doubt that the late, successful admiral had been corrupt. Everyone knew that in every command he had held, he had stretched the rules to near breaking point to line his own pockets and promote his followers, however dubious their abilities.

He soon discovered that Caracciolo would not hear a bad word said about Rodney—nor it would seem, a true one. To the Italian the man was a paragon and any attempt to dent his reputation exposed the critic to contemptuous questions about their own capabilities and honesty. Everyone soon learned, including Nelson, that in Caracciolo's company, Rodney was a subject best left alone.

"The Commodore and I, Mr Pasco," said Nelson loudly, "were at the battle off Genoa in March '95, he on this very 74-gun and I in command of *Agamemnon*."

"Your favourite ship, sir, I am told."

"By whom?" asked Nelson, ignoring Caracciolo who seemed offended that the guest of honour was more interested in talking to one of his midshipmen than to his host.

"All the old Agamemnons aboard *Vanguard* say it is so."

Three things pleased Nelson about that remark: first, that it was true; second, that his old shipmates were not shy of telling anyone; and third, his recollection of the large number who still served in whichever ship he sailed. It was comforting to have around him faces he knew.

"Then while we are waiting for the King and Queen I shall tell you all about that day. I'm sure the Commodore will oblige you with a description as well. Having stayed close to the flagship he was so much better placed than I to observe the whole action."

Nelson knew by the man's pursed lips that he had paid Caracciolo back for the slight, and he took the opportunity to move away from him to tell Pasco of what had occurred that day. It was another Nelson habit to regale his midshipmen with tales of battles, sometimes those he had fought himself, more often those he felt would inspire them.

To call what happened in March 1795 a battle was to elevate it somewhat, Nelson rating it as no more than a skirmish. The French, sighting the British fleet had run for their home base of Toulon, with Admiral William Hotham in pursuit. Yet he had proved timid when a chance came to trounce the enemy, seemingly more afraid of damaging his own ships than those of the enemy. It was a day of high hopes that ended as dust. In the initial excitement he had dashed off a note to Fanny.

> *My character and good name are in my own keeping. Life with disgrace is dreadful. A glorious death is to be envied.*

He could have written a hundred pages as they sailed all through the afternoon and into the night. As the dawn mist cleared, the enemy lay ahead, still running, and Hotham ordered the fleet to give chase on a parallel course in line-of-battle. As one of the fastest sailers in the fleet, *Agamemnon* was soon well ahead, with half-a-dozen other ships who had also out-sailed the main body forming a block between him and Hotham, and a clutch of frigates out ahead almost in touch with the enemy.

One of the rearmost French ships, an 80-gun two-decker, had run foul of one of her consorts, carrying away her fore and main topmasts. The frigate *Inconstant,* with a mere 28 cannon immediately closed with what was identified as the *Ça Ira,* a bold step given the respective firepower of the vessels.

Pasco was enthralled as he listened to Nelson, watching his hands as they traced the various ships' positions on the hammock nettings.

The frigate had received heavy fire and was force to haul off to avoid destruction, but had achieved the aim of slowing the enemy, towards which *Agamemnon* was now standing. The *Ça Ira,* under tow, was vulnerable, unable to manoeuvre, and unable to gain enough speed to get clear. Coming up in the wake, Nelson overhauled the Frenchman under a raking fire from his stern chasers. Nelson had had his own worries—*Agamemnon* was short of men through death, disease and the manning of prizes. He had too few hands aboard to sail the ship and fight the guns, so he resolved that the crew would have to do both.

"Once in range, Mr Pasco, I called the men from their guns to man the braces and let fly the sheets. At the same time the quartermaster spun the wheel to bring *Agamemnon*'s head round. In the minute it took to come broadside on to the *Ça Ira*'s stern we had taken several knocks to our hull and observed a couple of balls nearly nick the mainmast. But those gun crews were soon back at their pieces, in time to pour a devastating fire into the Frenchman. That was repeated several times with our ship being cut up quite badly on the approach. Sailing straight in *Ça Ira*'s wake, we were unable to return fire."

"Hot work, sir," said Pasco.

"Two hours that went on, and though we took a bit of punishment we inflicted a damn sight more. *Ça Ira* was a perfect wreck. The pity is that we could have overhauled her, for she was a sitter, and by passing her to windward taken on the next ship in the French fleet."

"The *Sans Culotte,* sir."

"You know about this?" Nelson asked.

"Yes, sir," replied Pasco proudly. "We mids know of every battle you've been in. We re-fight them on our mess table."

Nelson nodded and smiled, for he had done the same thing himself as a youngster, and every time he and his messmates refought a battle, they always did better than the original admiral: taking more ships, inflicting more casualties, and employing superior tactics.

"I fear to continue this, Pasco, lest you inform me of where I went wrong."

"The opinion is, sir," said Pasco, guilelessly, "that it was Admiral Hotham who went wrong."

"I am forgiven on your mess table for not getting amongst the French laggards for the lack of any ships to support me?"

Pasco replied in the same natural way. "Oh no, sir. You are reckoned brave but never foolish."

Nelson laughed out loud. "Not an opinion you will find unanimously shared in certain high places."

Had he been foolish? Tired of the punishment, the captain of the *Ça Ira* ordered his towing frigate to bring his head round and aim a broadside on his tormentor. The Frenchman had every right to expect his enemy to shear off, but Nelson did nothing of the sort—he sailed on boldly as most of the French shot screamed harmlessly over his head. What had Admiral Hotham seen? One of his smallest line-of-battle ships, isolated and outgunned, racing into battle as if nothing mattered but contact, a sitting duck that lost would weaken the fleet and rebound badly on Hotham's reputation. That was when the Admiral raised his flags and ordered the recall, forcing Nelson to break off the action.

"It would never do, Pasco, to say that Admiral Hotham was wrong that day. I had tested my luck, but it is not a good idea to push that particular lady too far."

The following morning the *Ça Ira* had been taken, along with *Censuer*, a 74-gunner then towing her, another engagement in which his Agamemnons had distinguished themselves. Yet Hotham, instead of continuing the pursuit and trying to bring the French to battle, had declined to agree with Nelson and his own second-in-command, Admiral Goodall. He, supported by the third admiral, Hyde Parker, had claimed "that they had done very well."

As a captain Nelson had strongly disagreed and said so. Now he was himself an admiral he knew that his opinion would have been the same.

His tale was interrupted when a lookout shouted and all eyes turned to the shore, where the royal barge was pushing off. It was so like the day, five years before, when he had entertained the King on the deck of *Agamemnon*—the sun had shone then too. The royal couple and their court had come aboard to be fed and wined by splendid comestibles at the expense of Sir William Hamilton, who had been there too, with him his wife.

And on that deck, close to a woman who excited him like no other, Nelson had very nearly committed the mortal sin of telling her so publicly. Just in time the news had come that a French warship was in the offing, which had given him the excuse to turf the royal party off the ship, Hamiltons included, and sail away from temptation.

Now a whole flotilla filled the sparkling blue waters of the bay, timing their arrival aboard so that the royal party would arrive last. Of course, the Hamiltons were there, Emma in layers of white and cream muslin, a shawl of heavy lace preventing the sea breeze ruffling her hair. As he was not the host, Nelson was not obliged to welcome her as she came aboard, for which he was grateful.

As they approached, the King and Queen were greeted by a 21-gun salute, stamping marines, and whistling pipes. The Queen and her entourage made straight for the cabin where they would remain until dinner. Maria Carolina was not a lover of the sea, and preferred to be surrounded by wooden walls and eager servants than stand on a windswept deck.

Ferdinand arrived alone on the quarterdeck dressed in the uniform of an admiral, splendid for once in dark blue silk coat edged and buttoned with gold, sparkling white waistcoat and breeches, with a fine hat, trimmed with ostrich feathers, on his head. Graciously he tipped it to Nelson, a signal honour from a sovereign to a commoner, before insisting that his guest accompany him on the ritual inspection of the ship.

"I do not believe, young sir, that we have been introduced." William Pasco turned from watching the broad back of the King, to be faced by a vision. Emma was smiling at him, and his heart raced. He knew who she was and snatched his hat off his head. "Midshipman William Pasco, Lady Hamilton, at your service."

"I find myself without an escort, young man. You will observe that my husband, Sir William, is engaged with Count Caracciolo."

"If I can be of service, my lady?" replied Pasco hoarsely.

"You may take my arm, young sir, and tell me about yourself."

Pasco had found that he could talk to Horatio Nelson with ease, but the notion of conversing with this woman rendered him tongue-tied. Like every blade aboard ship, he had heard tales of her past and her beauty, and had speculated with his shipmates by candlelight about the sybaritic practices of which she was capable. He had lain alone in the dark, as well, thinking about that very same thing.

"You are, I would guess, serving on *Vanguard?*" Pasco nodded. "And you were at the Nile?"

That brought out the pride that he, like every other man in Nelson's fleet, felt at having shared in that battle. "I was."

"Good. I wish to hear as much of that engagement as I can. Admiral Nelson has told me about it, of course, as have several of his officers, both *Vanguard*'s and others. But I confess to you Mr Pasco, that I cannot hear enough."

Pasco could talk of the Nile with ease, even to a famous beauty, for not even the potency of his fantasies about her could dent his self-satisfaction. Like all of his shipmates he had thought about it, discussed it, embellished and honed it in preparation for a lifetime of recounting. They all knew they were heroes, and they could not wait to get back to their homeland to bask in the glory their story would bring them.

And Pasco had an imaginative and colourful turn of phrase: he could describe the dying light as they approached Aboukir Bay, the way the sky turned first gold then orange. Even though he had spent most of the battle on the gundeck below, he knew enough to give a good description of the events of the night: of the coloured lights above every British vessel that identified them to each other; of the shot, shell, and fire, the screaming of men in the water, the blasted stumps of masts trailing over the side, and blood running out of the scuppers to stain the sea; of the boy Casabianca refusing to leave his father, the captain of *L'Orient;* then the final great cataclysm as the French flagship exploded, taking father, son, and six hundred crew to perdition.

"Why, Mr Pasco," said Emma, clutching his arm a little tighter, "you tell your tale so well as to render me fearful."

"I will not lie to you, my lady," the boy said, his shyness now quite gone, "when I say that my heart beat as fast as it ever did that day, and there were occasions, seconds only I grant you, when I was frozen with fear. But my need to do my duty saw me through."

As he gazed into those amazing green eyes, Pasco felt pleased with himself. In perfecting his version of the tale he had reckoned that undiluted heroics would never do: humility and an admission of fear would be more believable.

"You are lucky to have such a commander, Mr Pasco, are you not?"

Pasco replied with genuine feeling. "The greatest sailor and the best man that ever lived, my lady, and there is not man in the whole fleet who will say otherwise."

Emma had heard often enough from the lips of Nelson's officers how highly he was regarded, but she felt a warm glow as she encouraged this young fellow to tell her again. An admiral he might be, but Nelson could joke with the lowest swabber on the ship, and talk knowledgeably to every warrant officer about his duties and methods. The gunner reckoned the Admiral knew more about cannon, powder, and shot, as well as range and trajectory, than any man alive. The master, whose job it was to plot navigation and see to the sail plan would never fail to listen if Nelson cast an opinion, and only once in a blue moon advised against whatever course or change of sail he suggested.

Nelson swapped tales with the carpenter about some of the rotten ships they had both served in and discussed changes to the ship's design that would facilitate some fighting task. He even treated the purser as a human being. No man could go further than that, since pursers, in any sailor's opinion, were robbing bastards.

Pasco talked on and on as they circled the quarterdeck and Emma was content to listen. Edward Berry had been flag captain at the Nile, but he had been sent home with despatches and replaced by Thomas Hardy, another of Nelson's protégés. Hardy was nicknamed the Ghost for his way of appearing silently in any number of places on the ship, as well as his disinclination to engage in trivial conversation. His elevation, it seemed, had brought the cat out of the bag for Hardy, unlike Berry, was a strict disciplinarian.

Emma could see the royal head emerging from below, then Nelson's head appeared, and she felt a deep surge of emotion.

"My dear," said Sir William.

As she turned to her husband the admiration was still in her face and it took all of Sir William's self-control not to acknowledge it. The most telling pang came from the knowledge that, while he and Emma had been happy together, she did not love him. The look on her face was one he had never seen. It made him jealous.

"Allow me to name Mr Pasco of the *Vanguard*," said Emma. "He is Admiral Nelson's escort today, and I must say he has entertained me handsomely."

"Thank you, my lady," said Pasco, beaming. He would be top dog in the mess tonight just for having spoken with her. That she had enjoyed his company was a bonus he would admit to with care.

"You will find, young man," Sir William said, "should you get to know my wife, that no one can turn her head like a sailor." He regretted saying it before the whole sentence was out of his mouth. To have spoken with such obvious pique was a breach of his own standards and those of his occupation. And he saw by the way Emma turned her head that his barb had hit home. He could not tell her that he had appalled himself, nor could he apologise, for that would require him to allude openly to what had happened between her and Nelson, which he could never do. He said instead, "I think, my dear, that we are about to dine. I wonder, would Mr Pasco escort you to the great cabin?"

"Delighted, sir," crowed Pasco.

"It would please me too, Mr Pasco," Emma replied, offering him her arm as she threw a forced but sweet smile at Sir William.

Chapter Twenty-Nine

THE BELLS PEALED all over London and within days the news brought by Captain Edward Berry had spread throughout the nation. Strangers stopped each other in the street to ask if they had heard the stupendous news of the battle of the Nile, and it was the sole topic of conversation in coffee-house, home, or place of employment. Disbelief was rampant, because the success of the British fleet, and the Admiral who commanded it, had been so absolute.

Every theatre owner in the land was lashing together a patriotic show to tell the tale, creating an overwhelming demand for the artefacts of Egypt: pyramids, sphinxes, obelisks, and crocodiles. The risk that a whole building might burn down in a massive conflagration was ignored in the interests of re-enacting the climax of the battle: the explosion of the French flagship *L'Orient*. Any one-armed ex-sailor prepared to tread the boards could command his own price to play Admiral Sir Horatio Nelson, the hero of the hour.

Lord Spencer was cock-a-hoop, too overwhelmed with gratitude to notice that the men who had damned him for a fool before Berry's arrival were now praising his sagacity. Even Farmer George openly lauded Nelson: being King no one would dare to remind him of his previous long-held animosity.

In the City of London, meetings were held to decide how such a success should be rewarded, and an already amazed public was stunned by the announcement of an award of ten thousand pounds to the victor of the Nile. Alexander Davidson, Nelson's long-standing friend and appointed prize agent, employed extra clerks for what was sure to be an increased workload, and ordered gold medals struck for the officers of Nelson's fleet, to be paid for out of his own pocket.

The government moved more slowly, which allowed euphoria

to be tempered by time; those forced to disguise their distrust of Nelson after the news had broken began to reassert their malignant opinions. At the same time the King was asking himself why such a victory had not been granted to an officer he liked.

To a nation waiting with bated breath for the announcement of Nelson's elevation to the rank of duke, the award of a barony came as a bitter disappointment. The populace decided that the official excuse, that Nelson was only an admiral in command of a detached squadron, not a commander-in-chief, had been prompted by small-mindedness.

Fanny Nelson had only one wish: that her husband would come home. Who could achieve more than he, who was now styled Baron Nelson? Now that he was the hero he had always wanted to be, surely he would cease to put himself in life-threatening situations and come home for a well-earned rest. If not, she was resolved to join him in the Mediterranean, and she wrote to tell him so.

Even such a spacious cabin as that of the *Tancredi* struggled to accommodate the numbers who sat down to dine, and around Nelson conversations flowed in French, German, and Italian, with little English. As guest of honour, he was seated next to the King, a privilege he had been granted previously, and one that, given the man's boorishness, he would gladly have surrendered.

Ferdinand was not a fellow to talk to his neighbours if he could hold a shouted discussion with someone at the furthest end of the table. This he interspersed with stuffing his mouth with food and wine so that his deep blue nautical garments were soon as food-stained as those he habitually wore. Occasionally he would turn and beam at Nelson then raise his wineglass in a way that forced his guest to follow suit and consume the entire contents. The King's glass was immediately refilled, and so was that of the man he had toasted.

Horatio Nelson knew he had a limited capacity for alcohol and that over indulgence in the past had got him into trouble. But caution evaporates as quantity increases, and even if he had been determined to fight the effects, whatever resolve he had was weakening. He tried to concentrate on others at the table, like young Pasco, who was in an animated conversation with one of Maria Carolina's younger ladies-in-waiting.

When that failed he turned his attention to Count Caracciolo, distrust surfacing. Yet fair-mindedness forced Nelson to consider that just as he was a patriot to his own nation so must be Caracciolo. Perhaps the Neapolitan nobleman experienced the same feelings that surged in Nelson when he thought of his country. His devotion to those things for which Britannia stood made him want to do well for her.

He recalled the vision he had had on his way back from Calcutta as a youth. He had been in the grip of malaria and fever had generated in him a conviction that he was destined for great things: that his love of God and his country would shield him as much as it would raise him. Did Caracciolo hanker for a shrine in the cathedral of San Gennaro, as Nelson dreamed of a statue in Westminster Abbey?

Nelson knew that Britain was far from perfect. Thanks to a survey he had undertaken during his five years on the beach he was well aware of the depths of rural poverty, the despair and fecklessness it engendered, and the lack of alleviation that stood in stark contrast to the statements of concern that issued from the hypocritical mouths of those who claimed to care.

The politics of his country could appear just as venal as those of Naples, and in some cases just as corrupt. Was the Marquis de Gallo any worse than Lord Holland, who in the 1770s had used money entrusted to him as Paymaster to the Forces for private gain, and remained embroiled in dispute till the day he died? Nelson's superiors at the Admiralty were not always given to acting in the best interests of the officers and men of the service. Politics was a constant bugbear: people of little merit were advanced to senior positions in the administration merely through the power of their sponsors. The common seaman was paid sporadically, often by warrants that, for want of cash to feed their families, the men of the fleet had to sell at a discount to the crimps who thrived in every naval port.

Conditions aboard some ships of His Majesty's fleet were downright shameful: rotten food, hard-horse captains too fond of the lash, commanders and pursers who misused their office for private profit, while dockyard workers stole anything that was not nailed down. Abuses abounded, and though he had a care as to whom he voiced his opinions, it was well known in the service that Horatio Nelson had some sympathy for the men who had mutinied at Spithead and the Nore in the previous year. And yet for all that was wrong, the system worked. There were enough good men to see that the fleet remained effective.

Under the influence of the wine, Nelson, every so often, had to look at Emma, and it was not easy to be discreet given that she was seated to his left: any attempt at eye contact required that he sit forward to look past the boisterous King. If he wished, Sir William, seated next to Princess Esterhazy, could observe him. Nelson found that he no longer cared. And Emma met his eye, although she was engaged in conversation with the neighbour to her right.

Things were easier during the ritual speeches: all the toasts—to Naples, Britannia, Ferdinand, King George, the Austrian Emperor, the British fleet, its sailors and, most of all, Nelson himself—required him to gaze around the company. During the toasts news was delivered to Ferdinand that his Austrian general had reached Caserta. Clearly fuelled by the amount of wine in his belly, the King felt the power of his office: in a display of personal braggadocio that made the slippery Marquis de Gallo blench, he raised his glass, said, "Damnation to the French," and drank, breaking in that simple phrase the neutrality of his kingdom. Nelson could not help but be delighted, although he knew that the matter about which he cared so passionately had been resolved by drink, rather than wisdom.

"Admiral Nelson."

He hesitated to turn round. He had been standing on the

windward side of the deck, gazing out at the sea, deep-blue under the late afternoon sun, hoping that the breeze would remove the brassy taste of stale wine from his mouth. Like everyone on board he was waiting for royalty to depart—or, more specifically, Maria Carolina and her suite of German servants. Ferdinand had gone an hour before in the *Tancredi*'s cutter, but the Queen had insisted on waiting till the sun dipped and the temperature fell, which would ease the breeze and the choppiness of the water.

"Lady Hamilton," he replied as he turned.

"I require a private word with you." Nelson glanced around the deck for Sir William as Emma added, "It is on behalf of the Queen. I am, as you know, at Her Majesty's disposal." Emma walked towards a less occupied part of the deck, obliging him to follow her. "If I may refer to something you said when you arrived in Naples."

"Why so formal, Emma?" Nelson whispered.

"You said," she continued, as if he hadn't spoken, "that you would remain here for no more than two weeks, that once your ships were repaired you would sail to Cadiz."

"I have a commander-in-chief to whom I must report, Emma, and St Vincent is off Cadiz. I must look into Malta on the way—that is a pressing concern."

"You also said that you would base the fleet on Syracuse."

"It is the best place to hamper French movements, Emma. You, of all people, know that. From there I cover both the Straits of Messina and the waters between Taranto and the Barbary shore."

She wouldn't look at him. "So that is still your intention?"

Now Nelson adopted a formal tone, because he felt wounded by hers. "I intend to meet with Baron Mack to find out what plans he has to attack the French in the Papal States. Once I have done that I will make whatever dispositions are necessary to support him."

"So Cadiz is not a necessity?"

"I have the trust of St Vincent, who allows me to make my own dispensations. I will do whatever I see to be in the interests of our country."

Still she wouldn't look at him. "And Naples?"

"Thanks to the King's wine-fuelled bravado, the two are now the same, although I will be convinced only when I see the French Ambassador sent packing. I don't trust de Gallo not to change the King's mind when he returns to a state of sobriety."

"Would it help you to know that the Queen feels the die is cast, that Naples cannot live at peace with France, and that she and her husband cannot ever feel secure until the cancer of Revolution is excised from their patrimony?"

"Those sound like her words, Emma."

At last she smiled. "They are."

"I would be happier if you used your own."

"You must be aware that Maria Carolina fears her own subjects as much as she fears the French. Perhaps the army will march now that Mack is here, but you know as well as I how hard it is to beat the French."

"On land," he said, smiling, which earned him a squeeze of his good arm.

"The Queen feels she will not be secure without you anchored in the bay."

"Me?"

"If you are here, the fleet is here."

And the means of escape, thought Nelson, for a royal family who could not be sure in a crisis if their own naval officers would be reliable.

"I cannot decide on any action until I have met with Mack."

"Can I tell her, then, that you will not desert us? It would ease her mind."

Nelson was required, he knew, to say no: he could not hobble himself and his duty to his own sovereign by making such a commitment to another. But neither could he look into those green eyes and say the word. "Yes, you may tell her that."

The royal party, led by the ladies-in-waiting, began to assemble on the deck. Emma breathed, "Thank you," and went to join them, no doubt to tell the Queen what Nelson had said. That she did so was obvious, since Maria Carolina looked straight at him and inclined her head. Nelson wondered at her perspicacity: had she asked him herself he would have been obliged, however diplomatically, to refuse. How had she known that if she used Emma Hamilton as an emissary he would say yes? He was under even more scrutiny, by many more people, than he had assumed.

He felt very much under Emma's scrutiny at dinner that night—a private affair for him, his senior officers, and several close friends of the Hamiltons—from the numerous paintings that lined the walls of this private dining room. Three, he knew, were by Romney, Emma as herself, young and stunningly beautiful, in a classical pose as a *bacchante,* others by Gavin Hamilton and Angelica Kauffman, and the one he liked best, by Madame Vigée Le Brun, of Emma in white, hands clasped in supplication as St Cecilia.

In every picture her eyes seemed to be on him and he almost squirmed to think that Sir William had bought them all. A man who had so many portraits of his wife was likely to be enamoured of her. She was seated halfway down the board with an eager midshipman to one side and a stiffly formal, and hopefully chastened, Captain Josiah Nesbit on the other.

There was much talk of the war, as well as of London and country society: friends, acquaintances, or public figures to commend or damn. Others, once assurance had been given that no person at the table was a cousin or comrade, were condemned outright. Whatever scandals had reached Naples from London were dissected, and compared with the more disreputable local ones.

Nelson was seated at one end of the table next to Emma's friend Cornelia Knight, whose mother, the widow of Admiral Sir John Knight, was on his other side. He liked them both, the older lady for her sagacity, the daughter for her verve, though he found Cornelia's voice a trifle blaring. They had been shunted down to Naples from their residence in Rome by the French invasions of '96, forced to settle in Naples when the armies of the anti-revolutionary coalition made peace with Bonaparte.

Lady Knight was an invalid, yet she swore that, but for her daughter, she would have stayed in Rome and "not given a damn for the consequences." Nelson believed her: you only had to look at her to see that she had a truly steely determination. More importantly, on her last visit to England Lady Knight had become a friend of his wife: she had met Fanny with the Reverend Nelson when his father made one of his frequent visits to Bath.

Cornelia was a writer of books, which to a man who hated to pen a letter was astounding. He could not comprehend how anyone could sit down voluntarily with a quill. As a writer Miss Knight was agog to hear his own experience of the battle of the Nile, and Nelson told her his tale in great detail, concluding, "I believe Miss Knight, that my hand was guided by divine providence."

"God must hate a Frenchman, sir," Lady Knight interjected, "for they are demons and apostates," and Nelson realised how like his mother she was. The words she had used might have come from Catherine Nelson's lips, for she had hated the French with a passion, and often told her little Horatio that when he grew up it was his duty to confound that damnable race.

"You flatter me, sir," Lady Knight responded, when he said as much to her. "I know your mother to have been a Suckling, and I had the good fortune when my husband was alive to meet your late uncle on many occasions. He was an upright man, and modest about his own achievements."

"Apart from my dear mother, Lady Knight, I can think of no person who has inspired me more."

Captain Maurice Suckling had taken his nephew as a youngster into his ship and made sure he learned his trade. He had chaired the board that examined him for lieutenant and used his influence to get him promoted to the rank of post captain. It was no exaggeration to say that, as a fighting sailor, Nelson owed him everything.

"Inspired?" Lady Knight exclaimed. "You surpass him, sir. His actions were splendid, but they cannot compare with yours. Imagine his pride, Admiral Nelson, if from some celestial realm he observed your recent victory. His heart must swell at the sight."

"The Nile, sir," added her daughter, loudly, "must have been the happiest day of your life."

This coincided with a lull in the conversation and Cornelia's voice acted like a clarion. Every eye at the table was now on him, including those of Sir William Hamilton and his wife. Lady Knight corresponded with Fanny on a regular basis, and if Josiah, sitting looking morose, had noticed his behaviour with Emma then others could do so.

"No, Miss Knight," Nelson replied. "I have to tell you that the happiest day of my life was the one on which I married Lady Nelson."

"Bravo, Admiral," cried Cornelia's mother.

That pleased him, although Emma's eyes bored into him with an amused accusation that he lied, while others, embarrassed by such a fatuous and maladroit statement, coughed and looked at their plates. Josiah glared at him.

"Such a sentiment does you great honour, sir," said Sir William.

Nelson had no idea if he had spoken the truth or indulged in deep irony, and had no way to find out—the mood of the gathering picked up and the conversation was flowing again.

Nelson made the journey to meet with Mack, now resident at the royal country palace of Caserta, in the company of the Hamiltons. They were travelling on an oft-used royal highway in a well-sprung carriage, free of attendants or guests, the only bar to conversation being the hum of the ironbound wheels on the smooth *pave,* in an atmosphere that was somewhat strained.

Sir William applied himself to keeping up a flow of witty anecdotes about the stream of English visitors who came to the Palazzo Sessa. He had a great store of such stories, being a man who could highlight a fault or a weakness, recall an attraction or a peccadillo in even the most puissant of his guests, and then recount them with humour. Yet even he faltered at times, obliged by the circumstances to leave out any reference to seduction or adultery, the normal mainstay of his tales.

Nelson's fear of making some revealing remark led him into a rather didactic repetition of the problems he had in his command and in dealing with their Neapolitan allies. Emma took refuge in defence of the Queen, maintaining that if Maria Carolina had her way, none of Nelson's problems would exist.

What was most telling to Sir William was Nelson's inability to meet his eye, for the Admiral was famed for his direct gaze. Emma too, normally a light-hearted companion, was behaving in an odd, stiff way. The question for her husband was obvious; did such manifest guilt spring from mere embarrassment, or did it disguise some deeper feeling that neither party dared express?

Nelson was thinking that with *Vanguard* finally ready for sea, he must get away from Naples, and remove himself from the hothouse of his emotions. In his present circumstances he couldn't think and guessed from the way Emma was behaving that she was similarly distracted. He could not know that she was wriggling with frustration at the restrictions imposed on her. She wanted to speak out, to break the shackles with which she and Nelson had bound each other.

The sight of the guards of the Royal Regiment at the gates to the palace brought an almost audible sigh of relief from all three occupants.

Baron Karl Mack von Leiberich was a pleasant surprise, a Bavarian not an Austrian, a scarred survivor of many battles against the forces of the Ottoman Empire, both as a junior officer and as a commander. Nelson found him refreshing. He was a man who been raised to his noble rank not born to it, which also pleased Nelson. He had met too many officers of the Austrian army who appeared to have achieved their elevated status without dirtying their manicured hands in a fight. The French army might be composed of riff-raff, but at least its men were fighters, who would battle to take what they wanted and hold on to what they had.

The introduction was made by the King and Queen in person, and Maria Carolina begged Baron Mack "to be on land what

Nelson was to Naples at sea," before they repaired to dinner. Given that the royal palace of Caserta was a huge, sprawling edifice built to rival Versailles, the setting of the meal was intimate, taking place in one of the smaller salons rather than the great echoing state rooms. Baron Mack had no English, and Nelson no German, so the conversation was conducted in French, with Sir William and Emma translating.

Baron Mack insisted that the French would grow stronger if Naples delayed, and Nelson agreed. In fact a despatch had already come in to Sir William from the consul at Leghorn hinting at rumours of French reinforcements, but the decision had been taken to keep this information to themselves. It was not confirmed, but the very thought of greater French strength would only give Naples an excuse to delay.

Having assessed the force at his disposal Mack wished to march north within ten days, his aim to drive the French back from the Papal States and take Rome. Then he would attempt to form a junction with the Austrian forces, who would surely break the treaties forced on them by Bonaparte and push down the valley of Adige.

"Please tell the Baron that I will undertake whatever tasks he sees fit to designate to me, but . . ." Nelson paused " . . . I hardly think such a pleasant dinner is the place to discuss our future strategy."

There was stupidity around this table, Nelson was sure, men whose gossip would alert the French. There might even be true disloyalty: people present who would write to the French commander at Rome with an outline of the planned movements of troops and ships.

"And please tell the Baron that while he makes his preparations I will use the time to visit Captain Ball off Valetta to assess the situation of Malta."

His openness about his intentions was deliberate: Malta was no more than a day's sailing on a fair wind. If the French knew he was coming they would expect action, which might unnerve them.

Bonaparte's reputation had helped the French to capture the island; perhaps Nelson's would assist in taking it back.

The Queen enquired anxiously. "You will return, my dear Admiral?"

"Of course, Your Majesty. Did I not give you my word."

Ferdinand's head jerked up when that was translated, his large nose twitching and the black eyes suddenly suspicious, making it very obvious to everyone in the room just how much he mistrusted his wife.

The rest of the day was spent in consulting maps, and Ferdinand boasted about the advances he would make and the Frenchmen he would kill, although he had yet to actually declare war on France. Away from him and the ears of his courtiers, Nelson and Mack, with Sir William translating, discussed various scenarios in which the Royal Navy could assist. Emma was with the Queen, bolstering her resolve and allaying her fears.

On the journey back to Naples, she said, "The Queen wishes me to assure you that de Gallo will not be made Minister of War. That position will be given to Sir John Acton."

"Even though she mistrusts him?" asked Nelson.

"She distrusts de Gallo more when it comes to a conflict with France," said Sir William. "And she knows how highly you regard him. The appointment will be made to ensure that you keep your word to return."

Nelson looked at Emma then. "It disturbs me that she can doubt it."

"Which only goes to prove, my dear Admiral," Sir William responded, with irony, "how strange to you are the ways of Italy."

Chapter Thirty

NELSON FELT CLEAN merely being at sea again, leaving behind his own evasions and Neapolitan chicanery in exchange for his naval command. He had entertained Ferdinand and his second son, Prince Leopold, at breakfast before raising anchor, in part to show them gratitude for the fact that the dockyards had finished the works on *Vanguard*, but also to seek their help in speeding up work on Troubridge's ship, *Culloden*, still waiting for the metal pintles that would hold the rudder in place, without which she was useless.

From Prince Leopold he learned that orders had gone out to the governors of the Sicilian cities of Messina and Syracuse. They were required to send troops to Malta, with whatever stands of arms they could spare, ammunition, and victuals to feed the Maltese insurgents. Sir William Hamilton had attended that breakfast, and Nelson was grateful that Emma had not. An awkward public farewell had thus been avoided.

Their parting had taken place in the vestibule of the Palazzo Sessa, with coachmen and servants scuttling around them. Their words had borne little relation to what their eyes seemed to say. There was a tinge of doubt in hers that, even though he had promised to return, he might sail away for another half-decade. He had tried silently to reassure her that her fears were groundless.

The routine of the naval day soon imposed itself, although the crew seemed a little slack after a fortnight in the dockyard. Every man on board knew that there was prize money on the way for the captures at the Nile, ship money, gun money for the cannon, and head money for the prisoners. Sure that it would be paid without any of the usual fuss, Captain Hardy had advanced his men a portion to make pleasant their Neapolitan stay.

The problem for the crew was that every whore and cheapjack trader in Naples knew they had money, so it was doubtful if many of them left Naples with a single penny piece. The 'tween decks of *Vanguard* this past two weeks had been like Paddy's Market: singers, jugglers, and dancers performing while traders sold everything from sweetmeats, silks, and cloths, to charms and false gold trinkets. Naturally, the local whores had come aboard in droves.

There would be endless sore heads from sour wine, pox aplenty, as well as the odd tar who, in a drunken stupor, had somehow got himself married. The "bride" would emerge at sea, often disguised in male attire, sometimes to remain undiscovered and meld into part of the crew. If he cared to look closely, Hardy might also notice an increase in the number of ship's boys. There were numerous homeless urchins in Naples who would happily swap a damp culvert for regular meals aboard a British man-o'-war. If that involved sharing a hammock to get themselves on the muster roll, so be it: such things happened in every port at which a warship called. In time they, too, would become part of the crew, indistinguishable from the rest, good sailors who could hand and reef with the best.

Like the females their real identity might be known, but unless it was made too obvious their superiors would turn a blind eye. Every ship, unless a captain made a special effort to clear them out, had its portion of such pairings. In the main they kept themselves to themselves, and as long as they showed a proper degree of discretion they would be left in peace. The smooth running of the ship came before unenforceable Admiralty statutes: better to accept and manage the situation, than be forever in front of courts martial.

Tom Allen was happy to be back aboard ship too. At sea he could look after his master with his eyes shut; the pre-dawn awakening, the early morning shave, assistance to dress, and a quick tidy of the cabin as the Admiral took a walk on the windward side of the quarterdeck.

Tom hadn't liked the Palazzo Sessa. There were too many servants, as well as that Cadogan woman who was forever turning up unexpectedly like a wraith, able to make him feel guilty without reason. And things had been going on there between the lady of the house and his master of which he wanted no part. Better to be aboard, where Tom Allen was a somebody instead of a pawn, accosted frequently by his shipmates asking to know how the Admiral was feeling.

The men of HMS *Vanguard,* especially those who had sailed with Nelson on previous ships, had an almost superstitious attitude to the well-being of their admiral. They knew he was prone to bouts of fever, the victim of any ailment that was going the rounds, and was even prey to black moods brought on by doubt. But they also knew he was a fighter; that any disorder fell away at the prospect of action. And the men who sailed with Nelson relished a scrap as much as he did.

Tom could tell them happily that "He's at his very best, his old self so to speak. Wouldn't surprise me to see them guns run out, mate, as soon as we sight the Maltese shore."

Most of Nelson's time was spent in writing letters. He dictated the official missives to Tyson, who could turn a neat phrase, but he scrawled more intimate notes, with his left hand, to family and his wife. When he came to mention Emma Hamilton in a letter to Fanny, Nelson paused. He had referred to Emma many times since his first visit to Naples, and to omit her now would generate curiosity. He had told Fanny that malicious stories about Emma's past could be safely ignored, that she was kind, clever and patriotic, that she and her husband had been, individually, for the last five years his regular correspondents.

Emma had written to Fanny too, to tell her that in Josiah she had a fine son who would one day make her proud. Nelson was tempted to say in his own letter that the young man was a snake in the grass, who had bitten the hand that had been kind to him, but he contented himself with observing that, with his moodiness, Josiah was in danger of ruining his career.

He wrote of Emma uneasily, praising her as he had always done, asking Fanny to let all know that without Lady Hamilton's intervention in securing supplies for the fleet the Nile battle might never have happened. Longing and guilt fought each other as he tried hard to strike the right tone, and he could not be sure he had. The way he thought about Emma had changed so dramatically that his judgement was suspect. He felt a pang of loneliness that there was no one to whom he could turn for advice.

The following day at first light they raised Malta. As well as the masts of his own warships and those of Naples he could see a clutch of Portuguese men-o'-war, a squadron whose arrival he had been anticipating for weeks. That they had made a rendezvous with Ball was to be commended, but he wondered if Malta was the right place for such a force.

"A message to Captain Ball, if you please, Hardy," he said softly, as they approached the main island, "that he repair aboard."

Hardy smiled, which did little to light up his face, and Nelson reckoned that Thomas Hardy hadn't changed from the rather grave midshipman he had taken into his ship. He had always had a heavy countenance, sad eyes, well-rounded cheeks, and down-turned lips over a heavy jaw, which made him appear dull and a touch slow-witted. But he was painfully honest, without guile, as brave as a lion and a very competent sailor. Nelson loved and trusted him for that.

"I think you will find, sir," Hardy said, handing him his telescope, "that his barge is already in the water. Mr Pasco, oblige me by seeing to the arrangements for the reception."

Nelson fixed the glass on the entry port of HMS A*lexander* in time to see Ball, in a boat cloak to keep the spray off his uniform, step nimbly into the waiting boat. The boatswain was ready to pipe Captain Ball aboard at the entry port. That was where Nelson would greet him: by taking *Vanguard* under tow in the most dangerous of circumstances, Ball had once saved him from going down in this very ship. He had been one of his Nile captains, and was therefore one of his "Band of Brothers." The captains had commemorated the victory by the formation of the Egyptian Club. They called each other "crocodiles," had subscribed to a portrait of their admiral and patron, and had presented him with a sword. The Canadian, Captain Ben Hallowell, had had his carpenter make a coffin from

L'Orient's mainmast, and had given it to Nelson so that his admiral could carry it with him wherever he went.

Nelson gazed through the telescope at Malta's splendid natural harbours, backed by the island's barren hard-baked earth. The town of Valetta stood to one side of the choke point that formed the entrance to a secure anchorage, with Fort Ricasoli on the other. The whole was dominated by the citadel and the gun-bristling bastions that stood at the horns, the most potent being the four tiers of cannon, from water level to topsail height in Malta's Fort St Elmo.

Now he recalled the promises Ferdinand had made to the Maltese delegation. The King had assured them that once supplied with guns, ammunition, and troops, the islanders, in concert with the forces of Naples and Sicily, would take it back from the French in a week. With a better eye and a damn sight more experience, Nelson reckoned it too formidable to assault without several regiments of British troops, and Ball agreed. He pointed out that a land attack was fraught with difficulties and major forces would have to be deployed. Nelson could see for himself that no ship could get within range of the main fortress without facing fire from those formidable bastions—and even if the bastions were knocked out the entrance to the harbour would still be under heavy fire from the forts. As only one ship at a time could make the passage, it would be reduced to a hulk before it could even begin to bring fire to bear on the citadel. Bonaparte, with a force big enough to invade Egypt, had bluffed the previous owners out of the castle. The British Navy must either do the same or blockade the place and starve them out.

"Boat approaching, your honour," said Tom Allen, "from the Portuguese flagship."

"The Marquis de Niza," said Ball, his dark and handsome face creasing in a frown. "He will expect a salute, sir."

"Of what kind?"

"The same as that due to you, sir."

"Will he, by damn?"

Nelson was fussy about flags and salutes—who was entitled to fly or receive them and who was not—which had got him into disputes throughout his naval career. On one occasion his objections had led to censure from the Admiralty, creating among certain members of the body that ran the Navy the impression he was something of a pest.

"The Marquis," Ball continued, "rates himself as equal to an English admiral in detached command of a squadron. He has tried to issue orders to me. Naturally I have declined to oblige him."

"I should hope so," said Nelson emphatically, "and so shall I in the matter of a salute. Tell me, do you perceive his presence as an asset?"

"No, sir. His ships are poorly manned, with under-nourished and ill-trained crews. Heaven knows, a Portuguese sailor is as good as any, but their officers are more interested in their rank than their duties. We cannot assault the main island from the sea without heavy losses, as we have already concluded. If I am not prepared to risk my ships, then there is even less point in risking those of an ill-equipped ally."

The Marquis de Niza turned out to be a pompous oaf—who, as Nelson informed St Vincent by letter later that day, "is a complete nincompoop in matters pertaining to the sea." He had to resist the desire to chuck him overboard, either just to the left or right of his barge. It was Nelson's task, as commander in the Mediterranean, to hold together a coalition that included allies who were often more of a burden than an asset. De Niza had ships, which Nelson was short of, so the idiot must be humoured before being sent to Naples.

Nelson's Neapolitan allies were no more helpful. The supplies and troops demanded by de Gallo were nowhere to be seen: no guns, no food, no ammunition, and not a single soldier. Nelson was obliged to supply the Maltese insurgents from his own stores. He also called on the French commandant at Valetta to surrender or face destruction, but the man knew he was bluffing and answered accordingly.

Useless here, Nelson resolved to return to Naples, but first he used the force at his disposal to frighten into surrender the French garrison on the second Maltese island of Gozo. The defenders, without the fortress protection of their compatriots on the mainland, sailed for France with their arms and flags, leaving Ball a safe anchorage from the coming winter storms and good supplies of wood, water, and food on the fertile island, while denying those commodities to the enemy on Malta. It ensured that if all else failed, and no reinforcements got through with supplies, the fortresses could be starved out.

Correspondence between Nelson and Naples was constant, as was the reverse, and Sir William and Emma knew of every step taken at Malta—while Nelson was well aware of what little progress had been made in Naples. Baron Mack talked more than he acted and planned more than he executed.

Emma threw herself into the task of keeping up Maria Carolina's morale. This proved increasingly difficult as it became more and more obvious just how many Neapolitan nobles were in touch with the French. Some were genuine republicans, but others hoped to save their wealth and possessions by appearing to support the Revolution.

What was evident was that the Queen had little support in Naples among the nobility or the peasantry. Through various ministers, she had used spies and informers to root out the more vocal of their enemies. Torture, confessions, several executions, or banishment followed. Called a "White Terror" by Jacobins it was a pale copy of the same regimen that had racked France, but whatever odium resulted fell squarely on the shoulders of the Austrian-born Queen. Ferdinand, as usual, was held to have been manipulated rather than responsible.

Even the peasants who loved him had no time for Maria Carolina. The sobriquet *lazzaroni,* originally applied to the numerous beggars of the city, was a corruption of the name Lazarus. Feckless they might be, but the beggars and paupers were also organised, with strict bounds to territory and a court of their own which handed down harsh punishments for transgression. Since Ferdinand loved them and protected them, it was little wonder that they reciprocated. Neither was it a wonder than when some statute was issued limiting their activities he was never held to be at fault.

Blame centred on the Queen. Good King Ferdinand they would save from his own nobles, his wife they would happily burn at the stake.

The task of reassuring the Queen was made easier by Nelson's return and the fact that Baron Mack finally declared himself ready for battle. He invited Nelson and the Hamiltons to inspect his forces before their move to the north. Nelson stood on a podium with Mack as the contingents marched by, drums beating, trumpets blaring, and flags waving. Bursting with martial pride Mack declared them *"la plus belle armée de l'Europe."*

"And splendid they look," Nelson replied in halting French, while thinking in plain English, "all that glisters is not gold."

His own task was to transport a force of soldiers and artillery to Leghorn, land them behind the French and secure that port. Thankfully *Culloden* was now ready for sea and her captain Thomas Troubridge bursting for action. However Mack and Nelson, alert to the likelihood of treachery, did not even tell the Neapolitan in command of that army their destination. General Naselli was told he was bound for Malta. His demeanour made it plain that the only place he wanted to be was back in front of his own hearth. He was scared stiff and the appalling weather as they sailed north rendered him less than useless, since he was convinced they were about to drown.

He was no better when they arrived. After accepting the surrender of the city, he was more interested in appeasing the local Jacobins than corralling them, and horrified by the suggestion that he might undertake offensive operations. The same applied to the numerous French privateers that filled the harbour: Naselli wished to let them depart, ships and all. Nelson knew he could leave Troubridge to see to that dilemma, so he parted with *Culloden* and sailed south, happy to hear by despatch that the corsairs had left without their ships.

The return from Leghorn was made on the same storm-tossed sea under a low grey sky as the outward journey, yet Nelson ran into a messenger sent by Emma Hamilton, bearing despatches from England. One informed him of his elevation to a barony, an occasion for toasts in his cabin. In her private correspondence Emma wrote that she feared for his well-being at sea: she was worried about the stormy conditions. Unaware that he was on the way back she also begged him not to go ashore at Leghorn, which was home to many a republican sympathiser who might take his life on the blade of a stiletto. The better news was that no one in Naples knew where he had been or when he would return.

Another *felucca* found them off Stromboli, bearing tidings that had Nelson ordering Allen to break open the wine for a second time. "Gentlemen, I have received news that King Ferdinand is in Rome."

It was dour Thomas Hardy who asked, "But is it true, sir?"

That earned him a wry smile. "Lady Hamilton writes to tell me it is, that the French have abandoned the city and retreated north."

On this occasion Nelson could not fault Hardy for being wary. He viewed Neapolitans as grubby, thieving rascals, and the notion that they could beat the French was one of the few things that made the Ghost laugh.

The waters of the bay reflected the grey colour of the sky, even Vesuvius losing its double-domed majesty as its plume of gaseous smoke merged with low clouds, and the mood of the locals was no more cheerful. When Nelson landed he was greeted with none of the usual huzzahs, and the glances he was thrown ranged from anxious to hostile. It wasn't long before he found out why. The "most beautiful army in Europe," sent to eject the French from Italy, had disgraced itself: Neapolitan troops had plundered their own baggage train long before they made contact with the enemy so that their fellows went without rations. The King and his entourage suffered too, spending two whole days without food, their baggage scattered throughout the army. The guns were in the wrong place, the cavalry nowhere to be found and information had come in that a French force of thirteen thousand men was holding a strong position at a place north of Rome called Castellana.

That meant their main force had abandoned the Papal capital as indefensible. The latest information put Ferdinand in Rome, where he was accepting the fealty of the Roman nobility and dreaming of an expanded kingdom. But he was far from master of the city, since the French had left a contingent of some five hundred men to hold the Castel St Angelo, a vital hilltop fortress overlooking the Tiber. Everything depended on Baron Mack beating the French force to the north.

"Your opinion, Admiral?" asked Sir William, looking tired and older than his years.

Like all civilians behind the lines, he had heard rumours of the most depressing kind—that Baron Mack had been captured; that the army of Naples was in full retreat; that half of the Neapolitan commanders had deserted to a republican enemy with whom they were in sympathy. More worrying was information that was not in doubt: the Austrians had declined to move to support Naples. Mack must defeat the French on his own.

"Mack has superior numbers, Sir William, but not the quality of troops, so the issue must be in doubt."

"And if he loses?"

"The road to Naples is open. The French have nothing to fear from their rear, and the Baron does not command a force that will stop running once it is in motion. Their officers are fond of display and boasting but they don't like fighting—and I said that before they marched north."

The next few days were anxious indeed. Nelson saw Emma often but fleetingly, as she hurried between the Palazzo Sessa and the Queen's apartments in the Palazzo Reale. The weather, overcast and dull, seemed to match the mood of the city. Everyone went about armed, fearful of a secret knife, and that applied to those who supported the Bourbons as well as those who opposed them. Sedition was now discussed openly.

Nelson could do nothing but write fulsome reports to his commander-in-chief. He received word from Troubridge at Leghorn, corresponded with Ball off Malta, smoothed the feathers of the Marquis de Niza, and made sure his ships were ready for an evacuation. At the same time he was brusque with the admiral of a Russian squadron that had arrived, ostensibly to assist, but seemed too interested in Malta for his liking.

The news from the north was constantly depressing, the only hope that French sympathisers were spreading false tales. Baron Mack had asked permission to sabre half the army for cowardice; the King had fled south ahead of a retreating army; half of what remained of that army had gone over to an enemy who were on the march, coming south to take and sack a now undefended Naples.

And all the while three people bobbed around each other, Sir William observant but determined to be detached; Emma concentrating on boosting the Queen and keeping her promise to herself about Nelson; and Nelson, who felt increasingly secure that his one transgression weeks before would be the last. Sometimes it was agony to be in the same room as her, but he took comfort from the pain. He longed to ask Emma how she felt but could not, knowing that to do so would open the floodgates of his emotions.

"The rumours are true, Nelson," said Sir William. In his dressing gown and slippers, without the wig that usually hid his wispy grey hair, he looked worn and tired, while his voice reflected the despair he felt. "King Ferdinand returned to the Palazzo Reale in the garb of a common soldier. The *lazzaroni* heard he was back and demanded he appear. The man has no shame. He came out on to the balcony, and when he did so his peasants cheered him."

"God knows, he had little honour when he marched, but he has forfeited that now."

"The concept of honour is alien to Ferdinand," Sir William replied sadly.

Sir William had always rather liked the King for his simple ways, and for being a committed fellow hunter. They had shared many a chase together and many a drunken meal after the sun had gone down. Now, though, he was forced to see him in a new light; not as the fun-loving sovereign at one with his land and his people, but as a coward who, to get here so far ahead of his own men, must have fled at the first whiff of enemy grapeshot.

"The army?" Nelson asked.

"In full retreat. The French beat them at Castellana."

"Tom," Nelson said softly to his servant, who was hovering in the shadows, "raise me Mr Tyson, would you, please?"

"Beat them, did I say?" Sir William continued. "I rather think they beat themselves. They ran away and their officers were ahead of them. How can a man stomach such disgrace?"

Looking at him, Nelson felt a wave of pity—here was a man seeing his life's work disappear before him—but he had much to do, and his head was filled with the orders he must give to get all his ships ready for sea.

Tyson came in, looking as dishevelled as the Ambassador. "You must, I hazard, have matters to attend to Sir William," Nelson said.

The washed-out eyes regarded him vaguely for a moment, then Sir William answered, "Yes."

"I will require an audience at the palace as soon as possible. Perhaps it would be wise to tell their Majesties beforehand that I have three transports available for them and their retinue. Naturally, should it become necessary to abandon Naples, I will take them and the royal family into my own ship."

"Such a thing must be carefully planned. The flight to Varennes looms large in the royal imagination."

Varennes, half way between Paris and the Rhine, was where Louis of France and Marie Antoinette had been apprehended trying to flee with their family to the frontier.

"This is not France," said Nelson, forcibly, "and we have the sea and British sailors behind us. But you are right, Sir William. There are so many traitors in this place that an attempt will certainly be made to stop them leaving."

"Perhaps at your audience . . ."

"No!"

Brusquely interrupted, Sir William was seeing Nelson as he had so often heard him praised: commanding, decisive, the master of his own surroundings. Perhaps this was the man his wife saw?

"No," Nelson repeated. "We must plan it, and they must do what we say. Whatever we decide must be arranged here and not a word of it breathed in the Palazzo Reale."

"You can do nothing without the consent and co-operation of the Queen, and in that, Admiral, you would do well to take advice from my wife."

"Sir William, I fully intend to include Lady Hamilton in whatever plan we devise."

The two men exchanged a look, one which underlined the subtext of what had been said, but it was equally plain, from the sudden breaking of eye contact, that neither party wanted to pursue it.

Chapter Thirty-One

NELSON ADMIRED EMMA for her beauty, and over the next week, as they planned the evacuation, he had more reason to appreciate her application and courage. Only she had the total trust of the Queen—Ferdinand, having seen his martial hopes dashed, had taken refuge behind his stupidity and was now no more than a cipher, doing as he was told, only throwing occasional tantrums to establish that he still had some rights as the king.

Sir William was anxious about his possessions. He had no intention of leaving a lifetime collection to be plundered by looters, who would surely raid the empty palazzos as soon as order broke down. There was a great deal of virtu, even though most of his collection had gone already in HMS *Colossus,* a 74-gun ship so in need of repair that Nelson had ordered it home. Left were the things he valued most, personal possessions with a sentimental or an aesthetic value. It mattered little—when it came to planning a daring escape the skills he had honed as a diplomat were of scant use.

With no force of soldiers to hand, protection must be provided for the King and Queen, their children and the king's ministers—the royal regiments had gone north with Mack and were still fighting. It was suspected the gunners who manned the forts were republicans, while the crews of Caracciolo's flagship and the frigate *Archimedes* were discontented and unreliable. British marines from Nelson's ships would create suspicion—and cause no end of complications when it came to getting them back aboard.

Ferdinand's peasant supporters provided the solution. The leader of the *lazzaroni,* a barrel-chested, moustachioed peasant called Edigio Bagio had acted on his own initiative, sending men to the north of the city to disarm the deserters from Mack's army who were fleeing south. He was busy forming bands to protect his beloved king, with guards outside the Palazzo Reale and armed bands close to the royal person. Ragged they might be, but it worked; if there was one thing a traitorous Neapolitan nobleman feared more than the monarchical state, it was the cut-throats of the streets.

Numbers were another problem, for it was obvious that even with the ships at Nelson's disposal more people would want to embark than he could readily accommodate. Nelson had sent messages off to Troubridge at Leghorn to come back with all haste. He had also requested from Alexander Ball, who was lying off Malta, that he send one of his 74s to Naples. But on no account was he to allow any Neapolitan ships to leave the blockade. Even if the ships requested did come in time, Nelson feared overcrowding.

Priority must go to the royals, their retainers and ministers, in short the government. But Nelson had to get his fellow-countrymen away as well and there were too many for the available transports. His solution was to allot them the Portuguese ships commanded by that nincompoop the Marquis de Niza. To disguise the fact that he would be taking the Bourbons aboard *Vanguard* he told him he intended to remain in the bay and bombard the city as the French tried to take it, which he could not do with a ship full of passengers.

Emma undertook to get a list of attendants and supporters from the Queen, but equally pressing were the royal possessions: clothes, state papers, money, and jewels that would go with them. No one could say how long their exile would last, just as no one could say for certain where they would finally find refuge. Sicily would be their first destination, since the occupants of that island hated anything to do with Naples, and could confidently be expected to do the precise opposite of their mainland cousins and support a King and Queen that the capital city had repudiated.

But would the French leave them there in peace? They might invade Sicily, leading to a further evacuation and an exile at a foreign court. Thus everything must be taken to form a government in exile and that could not be left till the last moment: getting such a quantity of possessions aboard on the night of the evacuation would take too long. Emma again showed her worth. She had all their chattels brought secretly and in small quantities to the Palazzo Sessa. Sir William's virtu, when packed, was loaded into *Vanguard*. No one observing packing cases leaving the ambassadorial residence knew that a good number of them belonged to the royal family.

There was much more: when to evacuate—something that could not be decided until the French threat had been properly evaluated: Mack was still fighting a rearguard action. How to get them from the Palazzo Reale to a safe part of the shore—that solved by the information that there was a secret passage for that very purpose. Every move Nelson made was the subject of intense interest, and that applied equally to his ships. When he transferred them to an anchorage less exposed to gunfire from the forts it caused near panic, the assumption being that he was about to weigh anchor and leave Naples and everyone in it to stew.

And on one day, Emma and Nelson, wrapped in cloaks to keep out the winter chill, walked the shore, he to pick the spot of embarkation, the protection it would need and the number of boats; and she must work out the time required to get the royal party to the chosen spot. And if by walking arm in arm without attendants they gave rise to gossip, so be it. That was enough to keep idle tongues wagging, in the hope that their equally idle minds would not suspect what was being planned.

Proximity to each other was a dangerous thing. Yet they had the excuse of conspiracy to mask what was actually the desire to be together, to talk in an intimate way, without any chance of showing a physical expression of their feelings. The fact that Sir William, preoccupied with his own cares about the forthcoming evacuation, seemed to give them a nod of approval imbued what they were about with false innocence.

Nelson knew very little about Emma Hamilton that was neither impersonal, the stuff of correspondence, or rumour. And she made it hard to extract information about her past, regularly turning the conversation so that Nelson was obliged to describe some exploit or embarrassment of his own.

Thus she learned of his family and his birthplace: of the domestic despotism enforced by his widower father, of a cheerless house in which there never seemed to be enough food for a growing boy or his half-dozen siblings. They had eaten under the eye of a parent determined that they should sit upright, while he told them repeatedly of their noble antecedents.

Edmund Nelson was not a bad man, just a dour one who lacked faith in his own abilities both as an ecclesiastic and as a father. That he had loved his deceased wife could never be in doubt. He had inscribed on her grave, set into the floor before the altar of his church, "Let these alone, let no man touch these bones."

"You were always destined for the navy?" Emma asked.

"I have no idea," Nelson replied, making a mental note of the suitability of the southern mole as an evacuation point, being as it was, protected from fortress gunfire and close enough to the arsenal to make any gunner cautious.

He had been a rebellious child, a scrapper who started many a brotherly fight and a sore trial to his father. He had been a prude to the elder brother, William, with whom he went to school. Not that William had used the word prude. "Pious little turd" had been his expression. Did William now, as an ordained minister of the church himself, remember that and blush?

"I think it was decided upon when my Uncle William came to visit."

"He was a hero too."

Nelson tried a shrug of modesty, but it felt uncomfortable. He was aware that he liked to be called a hero, just as he was aware that the sin of hubris was one he must avoid. There was the other pleasure too, in hearing this woman refer to him thus, that brought an even warmer glow to his being.

"I sailed past the site of his battle at Cap Francis Viego, in the Caribbean." Nelson smiled. "There was nothing to see, of course. That is why we sailors talk of sea battles so much. There are no fortresses to see, no hills or valleys, forests or rivers to point to bold attack or stout defence. The sea closes over our exploits, so they must be retold time and again so that all remember."

"You loved your uncle?"

There was a slight hesitation, because Nelson was forced to admit to himself that he hardly knew William Suckling. A lifelong bachelor, his uncle had been a rare visitor to Norfolk, a larger than life presence when he was there, a distant memory soon after he left. But he was a somebody, a man who had friends and influence enough to keep command of a king's ship in peacetime when many another officer languished on the beach.

"He was an easy man to admire."

"Then it must be in the blood," said Emma. "And what would he think of you now, your Captain Suckling, to see his nephew termed Baron Nelson of the Nile and Burnham Thorpe?"

Emma said that with pride, but her reaction to the news of his elevation had been less than effervescent. In fact she had been incensed. She had railed against her own government, reeling off the titles she would have granted him: Duke Nelson, Marquess Nile, Earl Aboukir, Viscount Pyramid, Baron Crocodile, and for good measure Prince Victory. And she had damned the official reason for such parsimony, that Nelson was not actually a commander-in-chief but a subordinate officer, as sheer jealousy.

"Where does that secret passage begin?"

The Palazzo Reale occupied a frontage of over half a mile on the Naples shore. No point in picking a potential embarkation point that was too far from the point at which the royal party would emerge. There were numerous postern gates leading to the working parts of the palace: kitchens, storerooms, butteries, bakeries, and wineries, but only one led to the private royal apartments.

"It is so secret, that I have not been told," Emma replied.

"Not been told?" Nelson demanded, only to look into her face and observed he was being joshed.

Emma laughed. "I think we have passed it, though I felt it prudent not to point it out."

"Very wise," said Nelson, taking the paper, glancing at it, then spinning round. Those who were following the couple, a dozen middling Neapolitans of an idle disposition, stopped. He surmised one or two would be spies eager to know what he was about. Emma had been quite right to remain discreet under such observation. Nelson pulled out his watch, and said, "Let us retrace our steps to this gate, and count the minutes."

This is how Nelson must feel as he goes into battle, thought Emma, as she watched him receive from the Turkish envoy the Order of the Crescent and the Plume of Triumph aigrette that had been brought to him from Constantinople. Her heart was beating faster than it should, but her head was clear and she felt that her eyesight was more acute than she had ever known it to be. Standing to one side she saw the diamond and silver plume twinkling in the light that filled the salon in which the reception was being held.

Nelson lifted it from the case in which it lay, to hold it up so that those gathered could admire it. Kemal Effendi, the sultan's envoy, had no idea that this presentation had been chosen as the cover for the evacuation of the royal family of Naples. Neither did the cream of Neapolitan society, gathered to watch the Victor of Nile honoured. It had been Nelson's inspired choice to use this glittering occasion to cover the planned escape, aware that a number of the men prepared to betray Ferdinand would be bound to attend the function.

The French were moving south slowly, subduing the Campanian countryside as they went, and were not expected to try to invade Naples for at least a week. Everyone knew the crisis was approaching—some in this very room would be planning what bloody fate to visit upon Ferdinand and Maria Carolina. They would be looking at Sir John Acton and the Marquis de Gallo, and savouring the thought of seeing, in only a few short days, their heads on the block of the guillotine.

Perhaps too they would be relishing the sight of this British admiral taking his leave. Certainly they would applaud politely at the presentation of the aigrette: Nelson was undoubtedly a hero, but he was an enemy to the formation of a republic in Naples, so the sight of him sailing out of the bay was another event to look forward to. There was no doubt he was going and the distrust he felt for the Neapolitans was obvious, he having moved his ships from under the guns of the forts to an obscure part of the harbour.

The Hamiltons would go with him of course, and that to many was a pity. Sir William was well liked, had been here a long time and had many friends, even amongst the seditious. And his lovely wife? In many a male breast there was regret that such a bastion as her virtue had proved unconquerable. And her gaiety would be missed as much as her husband's urbanity. But perhaps there was time for one last visit to the Ambassador's residence, one last chance to enjoy his famous hospitality.

Had anyone bothered to enquire, they would have been told that there was indeed time to visit. The Hamilton carriage was waiting to take them back to the Palazzo Sessa, where, at this very moment the table was being laid for dinner.

Captain Josiah Nesbit had arrived at the reception just after the Hamiltons. In what had become his habitual stiff manner he stood to one side in the dress uniform of a post captain. When the ceremonies were over he would escort Kemal Effendi and his entourage to the ship which his stepfather had prised out of Earl St Vincent. HMS *Thalia*, a 28-gun frigate, was tasked to take the Turkish envoy home. There the stepson could present to the Sultan the personal thanks of Lord Nelson for these gifts. That it would also remove his morose gaze from the actions of his stepfather was a bonus.

At that very moment small parties of British seamen were fanning out through the city, quietly rousing out their fellow countrymen, telling them to make their way to the northern mole, where the boats of the Portuguese Squadron were waiting to embark them and their possessions.

Emma found it hard to be patient while speeches were made, thanks professed, drink consumed in between toasts to every enemy France had, but mostly to Nelson, King George's Navy, and insincere thanks for the protective shield at sea of Britannia. Her calculation was that from the time of leaving this reception, she had at most fifteen minutes to take up her station. In her imagination she could see the boats being lowered from HMS *Vanguard,* each with its component of armed sailors. Nelson's marines would already have secured the mole at the southern end of the harbour, the point of embarkation. She must make her way to the secret passage that ran from the Palazzo Reale to the shore. Admitted to the royal apartments Emma was the one who would have to tell her charges that it was time for them to leave.

As Nelson, Sir William, and Emma emerged, the empty carriage left, to return to the Palazzo Sessa and take on board Emma's mother, the servants of the family and the final load of possessions. The trio, escorted by a party of armed *lazzaroni* provided by Edigio Bagio, hurried down the steep hills towards the harbour, parting with a whispered farewell as Sir William and Nelson continued towards the mole and the waiting marines.

Emma, with her part of the escort made her way to the secret gate. She was aware that the wind was strong, and that the sky above her head, seen between the high buildings, was full of scudding clouds flitting across the moon. It seemed appropriate, as if the gods had arranged for a stormy backdrop to a dramatic episode. One of the Queen's German servants was waiting at the gate, opening it to her as she gave the password in his native tongue. Soon she was following a lantern along whitewashed and musty damp passages, climbing worn stairs to face the door she knew led to the private royal apartments.

Nelson, not for the first time in his life, was cursing the conditions. On a night when he needed calm water the Bay of Naples was choppy, and if his instincts were anything to go by it was going to get worse. The scudding clouds presaged foul weather coming in from the open sea, which would make the task of getting the evacuees aboard that much harder. He could hear the hiss of the waves on the shoreline and smell the tangy odour of sea-spray. Ahead, at the point where the mole joined the shore, the phosphorescence from breaking waves showed a line of shadowy figures, one of whom, by his height and the way his pale skin reflected the moon, looked very familiar.

"Is that you Mr Pasco?"

"Sir," the midshipman replied, rushing forward.

"Take Sir William to my barge," said Nelson, gently urging the Ambassador forward, "then find me Mr Giddings. He has my sword and pistols."

"I'm here your honour," Giddings called, moving forward and unshading a lantern. As usual, he ignored the injunction that no sailor should speak to an officer unless asked to do so. He always had, since the day he had discovered over twenty years earlier that here was one officer who didn't mind.

"This be a rum do an' no error, your honour."

"What is, Giddings?"

"This 'ere rescuing lark," his coxswain replied, speaking as usual out of the corner of his mouth. By that one physical trait Giddings had the ability to make everything he said appear to be a closely guarded secret. The irony was that this time it was just that.

"Comes to a sorry pass when kings and the like can't trust their own. Worse'n than the bloody frogs, I say."

Nelson was tempted to ask how he knew, since it had been a well kept secret just what the crew of HMS *Vanguard* were being employed to do. But he decided not to bother; he had learned from experience that the crew of a man-o'-war always seemed to know what was going on. He took the proffered weapons then, accosting one of Hardy's lieutenants, requested confirmation from him that all was in place. The man could only reply regarding what he knew: that the mole was secure, the boats manned and ready and since there had been no sound of gunfire, the armed parties that had fanned out through the city were going about their business quietly.

"Then," he said, hauling his boat cloak around him to ward off the night chill, "we wait."

. . .

Emma emerged into a brightly-lit chamber to find the entire royal party assembled and dressed for the outdoors. Having curtsied to the indifference of the King, who was determined not to look her in the eye, she did the same to Maria Carolina, seated on a chair, who beckoned her forward. She smiled at the silent children, and mentally ticked off that the numbers in the room, including retainers, tallied with what had been agreed.

"Emma," Maria Carolina said, and proffered her hand, which Emma took as she executed a low curtsy. A folded piece of parchment was pressed into her hand, that followed a whisper low enough to evade the hearing of the Ferdinand. "We have had this note from Commodore Caracciolo."

Emma hesitated to unfold it. Time was short and the danger that their proposed flight would be discovered very real. But at an insistent nod from the Queen she moved over to an oil lamp and began to read, slowly, since her ability to read Italian was not as good as her speech. Not that the message was difficult. In it Commodore Caracciolo, as commander of the Neapolitan navy, stated that the situation was grave, that the royal family could not be sure of being safe in the city, and that he felt their security could be better guaranteed if they were to take refuge aboard his ship.

Her thoughts would be the same as those of Maria Carolina. Was this a genuine offer or did he know of the plan to go aboard Nelson's flagship? If so, was there a trap waiting to be sprung if the King and Queen failed to respond to his invitation? The *lazzaroni* were not the only armed men in Naples. Every disloyal nobleman had retainers to use against them and Caracciolo had half the officer-class of the navy at his disposal, all aristocrats, but how many loyal to the crown? Fortunately, he had few men—the sailors, fearing for their homes and loved ones, had deserted their ships and come ashore to swell the ranks of fearful mobs that had begun to rule the streets.

Emma suddenly felt very isolated. There was no one to ask, no one to consult, and she could feel, by the silent atmosphere in the room, that this letter has been the cause of some friction.

"Your Majesty," she said, addressing the broad back of the King, sensing that to appeal to his more sensible wife would not aid matters. "Do you have complete faith in Commodore Caracciolo?"

"I have never had any reason to suspect him of being disloyal," Ferdinand boomed.

Emma wondered if he suspected a single member of his court. If anyone was capable of occupying cloud cuckoo land it was Ferdinand. Emma saw the Queen's head drop, and knew that she had her support, but she also knew that such support would count for nothing if she could not persuade the King. This was typical Ferdinand: to let matters reach such a stage then to throw in some objection. But he held the ultimate power: everyone else in the room, Francis, the Hereditary Prince, his pregnant wife, the Princes Leopold and Alberto, and the three royal princesses, did not matter.

"I agree with you." Emma said, emphatically. That made Ferdinand turn round, and he aimed a glare at his wife, now reduced to looking at her own twisting and anxious hands. "His ship will, of course be in the company of the rest of the other ships of the Neapolitan fleet at present in Naples?"

Ferdinand frowned as though the question was a difficult one.

"Which means that he will also be in the company of all the officers of that fleet." Maria Carolina looked up, her eyes showing that she knew the route Emma was about to take. The fact that Ferdinand turned away again demonstrated that he was not completely stupid either. "If you can assure Admiral Lord Nelson that you have complete faith in all your naval officers then I feel he would be forced to recommend that you accept Commodore Caracciolo's offer. If not?"

The question was left hanging, but truly it was one that answered itself. Ferdinand was no more certain of the loyalty of Caracciolo than he was of anybody else. Even he must know that the most profound protestations of fealty were often the ones that masked the deepest treachery: the notion that there were no Republican sympathisers amongst his naval officers was patently absurd. Royalty reasserted itself as Ferdinand, with that inability to admit an error, which was a hallmark of his character, said. "Naturally, that is the conclusion I myself have reached."

There was a moment then when no one moved, the enormity of what they were about to do taking hold, at least in the adult minds. Once out of the palace, the royal family was beyond the pale. They were deserting the city and their state, so that even men who had been supporters would curse them for abandonment, the indifferent would hate them, and their enemies would bay for their blood, claiming that only the spilling of that could cleanse their new dominion.

It was the Queen who moved first, she was a woman who expected no clemency anyway. Maria Carolina stood by the door to the secret passage and willed her husband to enter first. Looking at him, the slow way he turned, the look in his eye and the deliberate way he responded, Emma sensed that this was what he wanted. To be able to say at any future date, should his motives be called into question, that he had been reluctant to depart but that his Queen, lacking the same love of patrimony that filled his breast, had forced him.

Maria Carolina held her tears well, not so Francis, the Hereditary Prince, though he was outdone by the wailing of his pregnant wife, which was soon added to by the cries of her first born, still a baby in swaddling cloths. Young Prince Alberto, six years old and Emma's favourite was not crying, but he was pale and shaking as though in the grip of a fever, so much so that Emma requested that one of the servants carry him. She brought up the rear, the last person to leave that well-appointed apartment, the private drawing room of the royal couple, the palace of three hundred rooms were she had spent so many happy times. If she felt saddened, Emma could understand the depth of feeling that must affect her charges. The closing of the door was like a clanking death knell for a whole way of life.

Chapter Thirty-Two

FERDINAND, who knew the exit well, had stopped before the last turning in the passageway, forcing Emma to pass and be the first to risk herself at the postern gate. As she went, she had to impose silence on the party, no easy matter with a princess in the throes of panic, and a baby given to wailing.

The King's self-elected *lazzaroni* guards, who had escorted Emma to this place, still manned the gate, a quartet of swarthy, ragged individuals bearing muskets as tall as themselves. When Ferdinand emerged they knelt to kiss his hand, and were patted on the head like pet dogs. It was noticeable as the party moved off that they did not follow. They had an open gate to the palace: loyal to their king they might be, but with him gone his chattels were there for the looting.

Emma's nerves were jumping as they made their way along the shoreline. It had been her idea that Nelson's men should not venture from the mole: then if the royal party was accosted they could say that they were shifting to a Neapolitan ship, not fleeing into British custody. Now she wished that she had around her a party of Nelson's tars, whom she knew she could trust.

They were on the mole at the point where it met the shore, with Nelson ordering all lamps shaded and his men to make themselves as obscure as possible, most staying in the boats, the rest pressing themselves against any dark object to hide their profile. As always, Giddings, his coxswain, was right behind the Admiral.

"Bit like press-ganging, your honour," Giddings whispered.

Indeed it was, Nelson thought: the dark, wild night, men hiding in wait for an unsuspecting individual to meander into the maw of the naval net. He had always hated that duty, and counted himself lucky that he had only rarely undertaken it. Ships were manned easily in peacetime, and when war threatened his name and reputation provided him with a crew.

"Trade," Giddings added, employing the phrase he had used as a press-ganger.

"Aeneid," said Nelson, stepping forward to give the agreed password, appropriate, since it was the title of Homer's tale, which was partly about the flight of royal survivors from the sack of Troy. He unshaded a lantern as he said it and immediately saw Emma's pale but beautiful face. As their eyes met Nelson reckoned that, for a moment, they both forgot their purpose, but it was fleeting for Emma stepped aside to let the royal party through.

"Your Majesty," Nelson said, raising his hat to Ferdinand with Emma translating. "I have arranged for the ladies to be placed in the cutter, which is the steadiest boat we have. May I suggest that they go aboard first?"

Even by faint lantern light Nelson could see that Ferdinand had to weigh this against his royal prerogative. He looked as if he was about to demur, when Nelson added, "I know you to be a fine sailor, sir, and the waters of the bay, which will indispose the ladies in their present disturbed state, will not affect you."

That mixture of truth and flattery made the King step to one side and Nelson said to Emma, "Lady Hamilton, pray go with the Queen, the smaller children, and her ladies. My own quarters have been set aside for their accommodation."

It was dark enough to take her hand and squeeze it, but in the lantern light he gazed into her deep green eyes, framed by the fur-trimmed cowl of her cloak. In that instant both Emma and Nelson felt everything else fade to insignificance: the presence of their charges, the hissing of the wind as it bent the branches of nearby trees, the crash of a wave against the brickwork of the mole.

"The men are waiting to assist, sir," said Midshipman Pasco, breaking the spell.

Nelson watched as Emma got aboard nimbly and took up station in the prow. What followed was a pantomime of cries, squeals, protests, and entreaties as the rest of the ladies embarked. There was no steady gangplank as there would have been for the royal barge—the boat was bobbing unevenly through several feet of air, with just a sailor's hand to steady them.

Eventually the Vanguards got them aboard, with several marines to provide protection, and shoved off into waters that were much more agitated than those around the mole. That brought forth renewed wailing which turned to near panic as a flash of lightning illuminated the western sky, followed by a deep roll of thunder.

Getting the royal servants into the boats was just as bad—they screeched like banshees, almost outdoing the ladies—but Ferdinand, to his credit, boarded Nelson's barge easily, while Prince Leopold, like the sailor he had always wanted to be, assisted others to take their place. Then he leaped back on to the mole and bent to kiss the soil of his homeland, before boarding again to watch the receding shore as the crew bent to their oars.

The waters were vicious: a cross sea that added to the local currents set up waves that headed the barge, and others that slammed into the quarter to create a corkscrew effect. All the while, to the west, Nelson could see the approach of a storm. *Vanguard* showed just how bad the sea-state was, rolling and pitching at single anchor. If such a swell was prevalent in this relatively sheltered part of the anchorage, Nelson knew that out of the lee of the land it would be much worse. His plan had been to weigh for Palermo as soon as the passengers were aboard and accommodated, but that would have to change. There would be few good sailors amongst the royal party, and seasickness was inevitable.

Could he stay in the bay and ride out the worst of the weather? The royals' escape would not remain secret after daylight, neither would it take much to deduce where they were. How disloyal were the officers of the Neapolitan fleet? Would they, knowing that their King and Queen were aboard the British flagship, attempt to force a change of circumstance?

The scene at the entry port of *Vanguard* was one of utter

confusion. Those Britons in Naples who had been alerted by Nelson's shore parties had hired boats and, even if instructed to head for Portuguese ships, were determined to clamber aboard his. In the cries, shouted curses, and commands that followed, he could hear the voices of many nationalities, including a whole host of French. There were hundreds of *émigrés* in Naples, who had fled the Terror in France. They needed to get away too, sure that any revolutionary army would guillotine them without hesitation.

In the chaos it took an hour longer than Nelson had anticipated to get the King aboard. By then he and every other passenger in the barge was soaked to the skin and chilled to the marrow. Yet still Ferdinand took the salute as he came aboard. Dripping seawater by the bucket-load and shivering, he was still an anointed sovereign.

If it had been chaos in the boats it was even worse on board: there were too many people and not enough room to accommodate them. The wardroom had been allotted to the King, his ministers and the British Ambassador. With *Vanguard* riding at single anchor in a heavy swell it was hard for someone without good sea legs to make any progress from one part of the ship to the other. Most of the passengers had succumbed quickly to seasickness, which rapidly turned the ship into a near cesspool. This mixed with rainwater and spray that forced its way through every gap in the straining planking.

The royal servants, with only one exception, were useless and the lot of tending to the stricken passengers fell to Emma and her mother, both of whom seemed impervious to the tossing of the ship. There were bruises and broken bones, and cries of fear mixed continually with the sound of retching.

Emma took charge of the Admiral's quarters and the ladies, while Mrs Cadogan saw to the men. In this she earned the admiration of Ferdinand, who as a good sailor did not suffer but whose dignity would not allow him to offer help to any of his less fortunate companions.

Nelson's great cabin was a mess, with anything not fixed to the deck sliding back and forth as the ship pitched and rolled. The smell was worse between decks, but not much worse. Emma was comforted by the steadiness of her own stomach and asked Tom Allen to provide warm water to bathe the shivering baby. Meanwhile she comforted the Queen and the Hereditary Princess, and cradled the suffering Prince Alberto, singing to him and telling him stories, while she reflected that those born to rule seemed to lack any resource when the careful pattern of their lives was disrupted.

Nelson appeared at the doorway, one hand on the lintel, swaying easily on well-attuned sea legs, water streaming off the oilskins he had donned on coming aboard. He had come to tell his royal passengers of his decision to wait for the weather to moderate before he set sail, but it was obvious, from their prostrate condition, that they couldn't have cared less.

Emma was thinking that with her clothes streaked with grime and other people's vomit, her cheeks unpowdered and red from seawater, she must look a frightful mess. However, to Nelson, she looked magnificent.

Dawn brought some respite, though as Nelson emerged from the chart room, where he had snatched a much needed nap, the horizon looked just as grey and unwelcoming as it had the day before. The weather had eased slightly, and the low cloud was lifting so that the shore had ceased to be an indistinct line, and had become again a series of identifiable locations. The harbour area was still full of boats, some surrounding the British transports and Portuguese warships as the fearful of Naples sought refuge. Most surrounded *Vanguard*, endless petitioners seeking an audience with their sovereign to persuade him to return to his palace, either to oversee the defence of Naples or to stop the disorder and looting that had already broken out.

This kept the King and his ministers busy, and Nelson, who had concerns of his own, grew impatient. Time and again he sent Tom Allen to the wardroom, with a request that the Marquis de Gallo,

Sir John Acton, and Sir William Hamilton join him in the fore section of Captain Hardy's cabin, but half the day had gone before that request was satisfied.

"Gentlemen," Nelson said, "I have requested you join me so that we can decide what to do about the Neapolitan ships remaining in the harbour."

Acton, who saw himself, quite rightly, as the Admiral of the Neapolitan fleet, looked as though he understood what Nelson meant. Not so de Gallo, who, once it had been translated, looked perplexed. Sir William sensed what might be coming and prepared himself to deploy a degree of diplomatic emollience.

The capital ships of Naples were off Malta with Captain Ball, who had been requested to keep them there, but two heavy 40-gun frigates, commanded by Caracciolo, were anchored close inshore under the guns of the Neapolitan forts.

"They cannot be left to fall into the hands of the French," Nelson said. "Then they must be persuaded to sail with us," said de Gallo.

"Without crews?" asked Nelson. Attempts to bribe the crewmen—who had gone ashore to protect their own homes—to return to their ships had failed, obliging Nelson to send over some of his own seamen to help man them. But Caracciolo showed no sign of wanting to weigh. "I suggest that if we cannot get them away they must be burned."

"Impossible," erupted de Gallo. "Huge sums of money have been poured into creating the fleet, and those are two of the newest vessels."

"It will be nonsense, Marquis, if crewed by Frenchmen I have to engage them in battle."

"Can you not crew them, Admiral?" asked Acton. As the man who had initiated the construction of these very ships he was clearly on the horns of a dilemma, with pragmatism fighting sentiment.

"No," Nelson replied.

His tone was a trifle brusque for Sir William, who winced. But Nelson was not prepared to tell even these men how short-handed

Vanguard was. He had shifted men into Troubridge's ship off Leghorn, which meant the men he had sent to the Neapolitan ships, 25 in number, were all he could spare. Nor was he going to say openly that if his request that *Culloden* return to Naples was fulfilled in time this conversation would be redundant. With Troubridge here he would either take Caracciolo's ships or sink them.

"The King will never agree to this," said de Gallo, "and I doubt even the Queen could be brought to consider it."

"Considered it must be," Nelson replied, "and I would ask that you put the matter before the King."

It was a forlorn hope that Ferdinand would agree, and never had the Queen's indisposition been more unfortunate. Nelson reckoned, as he watched the three courtiers file out, that she would have put aside any considerations of money and ordered them to be taken or sunk—if for no other reason than to tell the traitors in Naples what they could expect of a future restoration of royal power.

He was still ruminating as the cabin door opened to admit Midshipman Pasco, as alert as ever although he had probably been up all night. "Boat approaching, sir," he said, "and Captain Hardy reckons Baron Mack is in the thwarts."

The man Nelson greeted at the entry port bore little resemblance to the glittering white-uniformed general that Nelson had last seen reviewing his beautiful army. That force was now shattered, and so was their leader. Mack's hair was awry, his uniform stained and tattered. He looked as broken as the force he had led to defeat.

Nelson felt sorry for him, although he suspected him to be an incompetent soldier who had led a very inept army. Reports of the deployments Mack had made, and the way he had used his inexperienced troops, had made many question his sanity. But now he was being asked to shoulder all the blame. It was telling that King Ferdinand, his titular commander-in-chief, who had shown no signs of seasickness hitherto, had declined to receive him, claiming illness as his excuse. The Queen, who would certainly have received him was genuinely sick, a fact endorsed by Emma Hamilton, who Nelson had been forced to send for.

"I must entertain him in some way," Nelson said quietly, "and try to restore his spirits. But I cannot commiserate without an interpreter."

Emma used the back of one hand to sweep her wayward auburn hair from her eyes. "Sir William?"

"Is with the King."

Emma fell in with Nelson as he led Mack towards Hardy's cabin for a quiet conversation—there were officers sleeping in the anterooms on each side. Refreshments were served by Hardy's steward: wine for him and Emma, a stiff brandy for Mack. The Baron listed the events that had led to this moment, naming Neapolitan officers, nobles to a man, who when they were not behaving like cowards showed an alarming degree of military stupidity. As he detailed the orders he had issued he was unaware that the Admiral was mentally praising some of those subordinates for showing sound common sense.

But Nelson's mind was only half on Mack. It was delicious to watch Emma in profile as she listened to the poor man, who spoke slowly and deliberately, head bent over, with none of the ardour he had shown before the campaign. Then she would turn to translate, looking at him directly, and he could gaze into her eyes.

Emma was mentally comparing the two men, knowing she would never see Horatio Nelson like this. If her hero suffered defeat, the only thing anyone would have to look at would be his corpse. As they exchanged glances that excluded Mack, Emma felt no danger, or any sense that she was risking her future. The words she translated tripped off her tongue without effort as she held Nelson's good eye.

Nelson was aware that he had a stark choice—the kind of choice he had to make in battle. And he realised that he had known it since he first met Emma Hamilton. Looking at her now, not carefully combed and dressed, a real woman in a real situation, he knew that he must either live with her or entirely without her. There could be no middle way. He knew she was tired and so, too, was he, after a night of almost constant exertion, but that added clarity to his thoughts rather than diminishing them and he sensed that Emma was thinking the same way. He was tempted to say, "I love you," but did not, because he knew it to be superfluous.

As Emma told Nelson what Mack had said, that the last line of defence outside Naples was near to being breached, she could not help but try to impart in her words that she was not talking about the city but herself. She understood suddenly that the constraints she had placed on herself with regard to this man had everything to do with her previous settled existence, her life of entertainment, friends, and routine. The truth that this life had been shattered forever was evident in the disconsolate pose of Baron Mack, who had come to ask the King's permission to surrender so that lives might be saved. Ferdinand being too much of a coward to oblige him, Mack looked like a man who had lost his faith as well as a campaign.

Emma felt as though she was gaining faith: faith in her own judgement, free from the attitudes of her mother and the pain she would cause her husband. There was only Nelson, and a further surge of electricity coursed through her as she saw in his look what was also in her mind.

"The crisis is clearly reaching a conclusion," said Nelson, looking right at her.

"It has already done that," Emma replied, as Mack drained his glass and pulled himself to his feet.

Mack spoke sharply then, with some of his old fire, as though the brandy as well as the needs of his command had restored him. Emma informed Nelson that Mack would return to the shore, and take upon himself the task of surrender. Ferdinand had deserted him and he had the right to do the same, but he would do his duty, and Nelson could only admire him for that. He called for the marine sentry to fetch an officer to escort Baron Mack to his boat.

"I should have gone myself," whispered Nelson, as the door closed.

"He deserves the courtesy," Emma replied.

They were standing a little apart, swaying easily on the swell of the sea, eyes locked, yet there was one final barrier they had still to cross. Nelson knew in his own heart that he had already made the leap. He had never been in love before—he knew that now. All his previous romantic attachments seemed foolish, especially his initial regard for his wife. He was incapable of imagining a future without Emma, and nothing—neither career, fame nor glory—would serve to fill the void of her absence.

Emma had been in love, and knew, too, the heartbreak of rejection. She wanted Nelson to make the commitment that her previous love, Charles Greville, had not. She wanted him to say the words that would break down that final barrier.

"Emma," Nelson said, holding out his hand. His mouth was dry. "I cannot live without you."

"I must see to the Queen," Emma replied.

Nelson smiled, for he had seen what was in Emma's eyes and felt her affirmative squeeze. "Does that make you happy?"

"Yes."

There was no need for more, even though his heart was pounding. He kissed the back of her hand—not the kiss of a courtier, but that of a lover.

Emma had to compose herself as she made her way back down to Nelson's cabin and the Queen, passing officers and men, all of whom tipped a hat or touched their forehead in respect. These were Nelson's men, who were said to love him. So did she. Could they love her too? She felt calm, was not plagued by second thoughts. She was certain that what had just been pledged was right and that the consequences of that decision did not matter. She felt different, too, as she walked into the cabin, as though it was somehow her own.

The sharp tang of watered vinegar tingled in her nostrils. The cabin had been cleaned in her absence, with the furniture in its proper place. The first to greet her was young Prince Alberto, dressed in fresh, clean clothes and it gladdened her heart to see some colour in his cheeks. Alberto, coming aboard shivering in the grip of a fever, had been more violently sick than either his siblings or his mother. Yet now he looked as he always had, black eyes shining and ready for mischief as he rushed over to kiss Emma.

Tom Allen was there, too, standing over the large round table that Nelson used as a desk, a tub of beeswax and a cloth in his hand. "Had a right good breakfast, His Highness did, milady, oats and goat's milk laced with a tadge of the Admiral's brandy."

Emma realised that she was hungry, not having eaten since Kemal Effendi's reception.

"Been helping me put things to rights, has young Prince Alberto," added Tom. "He be a dab hand as a swabber, ain't you, young sir?"

Alberto had enough English to understand that and he looked proud that Tom rated his ability to ply a mop.

"Your mama?" Emma asked, nodding towards the sleeping cabin.

Alberto made a face and moaned, then asked eagerly, "Will I be allowed to go on deck, Lady Emma?"

It was Tom Allen who replied. "Why that comes later, Master Prince." He pushed a cloth in Alberto's direction and aimed a finger at Nelson's mahogany, brass edged wine cooler. "You ain't yet complete here."

Emma exited the cabin to the sounds of Tom Allen's quiet instructions, that, "too much applied was just making work, an' it be best to keep it off the brass if you can."

When Emma went into the sleeping-cabin it was dark, drapes having been put over the casements to keep out the daylight. Maria Carolina lay in Nelson's cot, swaying with the motion of the ship. Her eyes looked hollowed and her skin waxen. She held one hand out to Emma, a damp handkerchief rolled in the fist, her voice weak as she muttered, "Oh Emma, what is to become of us?"

Emma wasn't thinking of Maria Carolina, Naples, or the approaching French when she replied, "Everything will work out for the best, Your Majesty."

Chapter Thirty-Three

ON DECK the weather had moderated, though it was far from calm. Nelson watched as Mack's boat dipped and swayed back to the shore, then lifted his telescope to look at the grey arc of the bay as it ran from the island of Procida to the southern arm at Capri, glowering Vesuvius in the centre. There was nothing more he could do here, Mack had made that plain, and the safety of the royal family meant that he should leave.

A glance at the lowering clouds above his head told him little more than the grey water of the bay. Many years at sea had given Nelson an acute sense of the weather, which allowed him to interpret what might come from what he saw and what he sniffed. The feel of a breeze, steady or gusting, the run of the clouds or the way they masked the sun, or the disturbed state of the water between him and the horizon. Experience also told him that his forecasting was inexact. He had been right more times than he had been wrong but he knew that he had not conquered the art.

However, given that the weather these last weeks had been foul it seemed that any observations should have little bearing on any decision he made. Those of his passengers likely to succumb were sick already, and the sooner he got them to dry land the better. Told by the officer of the watch that the Admiral was on deck, Thomas Hardy appeared silently, awaiting orders. Nelson, as was his habit, asked Hardy's opinion, which was much the same as his own.

"A signal to the transports, Captain Hardy, and to the Portuguese. We may prepare to weigh for Palermo."

An hour after they had cleared the bay, his little convoy of ships was in a violent gale that was worsening by the minute, the screaming of the wind in the rigging increasing in pitch. The bowsprit dug deeper into troughs of waves that grew more and more unpredictable, the stern of *Vanguard* lifting clear of the water then slamming down again. In the wardroom all the men were hanging on to something, pale-faced and fearful—none more so than Ferdinand himself, who was convinced, and prepared to tell everyone else, that his house and his person were cursed.

Above, the Admiral's cabin was in chaos again, and Prince Alberto lay prostrate on a bed Emma had made up for him on the lockers that ran under the stern windows. Strapped in by ropes, with the boy's head on her lap, Emma was talking to him to keep up his spirits, using Tom Allen as a messenger to the Queen, laid too low to nurse her own child, to tell her of her son's progress.

Alberto's black, thick hair was soaking, and his skin translucent, as though the flame of life was struggling to maintain itself. Emma prayed, feeding Alberto sips of the brandy that Tom Allen had fetched at her request, trying to raise him by recalling the games they had played in the royal palaces.

"I's done my best, milady," said Tom, nodding towards the other cabins. Just as in harbour, none of the palace servants, bar one retainer who seemed able to withstand the motion, had been an ounce of use. Yet Emma could forgive them now—the way the ship was heaving even Tom Allen could only make his way around the cabin by clasping on to the ropes he had rigged.

"They're all afeart we're going to drown," Tom continued. "I telt them that as long as the sticks stand—that be the masts like—then there's now't to worry about."

On deck, Thomas Hardy and the Admiral, wrapped in oilskins, were watching those sticks with increasing alarm, as daylight gave way to dusk. Both knew that *Vanguard* had always been a roller, apt to show the copper that lined her bottom, a ship that sat higher in the water than was good for her: a heavy sea made the hull sway alarmingly from side to side. She had rolled out her masts twice before in this very sea, once off Corsica, where only the bravery and application of Alexander Ball had saved her, and again on the way back from the Nile.

"You have a party standing by, I trust?" yelled Nelson. Hardy's response was carried away on the howling wind, but he aimed one mittened hand towards the nearest companionway, to tell Nelson that men were ready with axes to cut away any mast that went over the side.

In truth Nelson shouldn't have been there: this was Hardy's deck, not his. But he could not abide inactivity and, with the wind battering them from west-south-west, they had a dangerous, rocky coastline to leeward that would turn the ship to matchwood if she was driven ashore. He justified his presence on the grounds that he had known Hardy since he was a slip of a lad, had educated him in his duties as an officer and a sailor. Anyway, he knew this ship better than Hardy did.

He did not know that Hardy was glad of his presence. He had had command of a brig and a frigate, but a 74-gun ship-of-the-line was altogether different and his responsibility for the safety of the hero of the Nile was an added burden. Ships foundered, it was part of the risk of life at sea, and the storm was violent enough to send *Vanguard* to the bottom. At least with Nelson here, he had someone to share the responsibility of whatever action he took.

Hardy did not hear the topsails shred, for the wind carried away the sound, and neither did Nelson—he had stepped into the chart room to check the ship's position with the master—but the crack of torn canvas alerted everyone close to the quarterdeck. By the time the driver and the foremast staysail went, bringing down with them a mass of rigging, chains, and blocks that clattered on to the rolling deck, Nelson was back. He could hear Hardy ordering extra hands to the wheel, a party of seamen forward to cut away the debris, and yet more to get aloft to bend on new canvas. Nelson was half intending to go forward with the axe party when Giddings yelled in his ear.

"Best stay put, your honour. With only one pin you can't do owt and keep a safe grip an' all."

The advice was sensible, but it angered Nelson. He never complained about the loss of his arm and how it constrained him, but he missed it, and such situations brought it home to him. He had always been an active rather than a magisterial captain—some rooted themselves to their quarterdeck station throughout a crisis, but he wasn't like that: in a storm or a battle he wanted always to be at the forefront. Fellow-officers condemned him for seeking popularity, but Nelson was merely responding to the way his blood raced. Giddings knew that, which was why he made sure he was always close to Nelson to stamp on temptation that might see him harmed.

The ship was in peril, though not mortally so. But below decks the sound of falling debris and running feet echoed through the planking, and sounded truly alarming. Mary Cadogan saw Ferdinand go white, and all around the wardroom men who had relished power and thought themselves immortal were silently praying to gods both Christian and pagan.

Emma held tightly to Prince Alberto, whose fever had worsened, his small body now racked by convulsions. Emma knew the storm was strengthening, just as she knew that in her arms her charge was sinking. Yet there was no way to bring relief—the sea controlled the motion of the ship, moderated only by the skill of those on deck to anticipate the flukes of the gale and the run of the waves. In the cabin, the howling wind found every crack in the casements beside which she sat, sending in freezing air and water. The floor of the cabin was awash, full of debris, running under the cabin door as the bow dipped, then surging back to splash around the hem of her dress. Every few minutes Tom Allen was there, hanging on to one of his ropes, gazing anxiously at the youngster's face, or exchanging a glance with Emma. His face offered encouragement, but his eyes reflected despair.

From the side cabin the wailing of the other royal passengers was a background din to the cacophony of the storm and a ship that, with groaning planking, sounded as if it might tear itself apart. Above her head, on deck, barefoot seamen, cursing, wielded axes and knives to break wood and ropes or slash canvas, freeing debris which, trailing over the side of the ship, would further endanger them. Men slipped on the water-lashed deck, only saved from perdition by the quick thinking of their mates. Others in even more exposed positions were trying to replace what had been blown out.

Occasionally, through the pouring rain, Nelson caught sight of the topsail yards swinging in the wind. He had served up there as a youngster in weather as foul as this, so he could imagine what he could not see: the bare feet struggling to keep a grip on the drenched foot ropes slung beneath wooden poles, the yardarms that carried the sails as the ship arced forwards, back and sideways through the air. Men with the top half of their bodies hanging over that spar were fighting with freezing fingers, he knew, to bend on a replacement sail so that the way of the ship could be restored and *Vanguard* could haul off the jagged shore that was not far to the east.

Horatio Nelson envied those men aloft: he missed the comradeship that went with being a topman, the elite of the sailing tribe. It was where he had served as a common sailor on his first voyage to the West Indies, and on his first long-service naval commission. He had formed friendships in the rigging that he would have liked to keep, only to watch them fade as he attained higher rank. Those who had taught him his trade would be ashore now, if they were not dead, sitting snug, he hoped, in some warm taproom. They would be telling avid listeners of the places and sights they had seen, with just enough exaggeration to keep the free ale flowing. They could well describe a storm: men overboard in seas from which they could not be rescued, dropped blocks or spikes that scarred the deck or mutilated some unfortunate soul, the exhaustion in the face of toil that could not be avoided, for to rest was to risk damnation. But would they describe the bond that grew between men who served in such a station? Nelson doubted it, because it bred a closeness that could neither be breached nor comprehended by outsiders, with its private language, the cryptic looks, particular jokes, and human intimacies that would seem strange to the ears of a landsman.

As these thoughts ran through his mind, Nelson also admired the quality of Thomas Hardy's calm seamanship. He was in a storm, surrounded by over twenty ships of their evacuation convoy, without much knowledge of where his consorts lay, but he did not appear anxious, nor had he sought advice. Hardy had issued his orders, had ensured that the men on the wheel kept the head into the run of the sea, and waited without impatience for matters to be put right. Hardy trusted his men, and Nelson knew he was right to do so.

Mary Cadogan did not see what Sir William had fetched from the screened-off cabin he shared with Prince Esterhazy, but she noticed alarm in the Hungarian's face, Sir William's furtive air as he staggered out of the wardroom, and the bulge of substantial objects under his coat.

Tottering along the lower deck, Sir William crammed his body between a lashed cask and one of the uprights that held the deck-beams above his head. Using the top of the cask as a table he laid out two pistols, his powder horn, and lead balls. It wasn't easy to load them as the ship pitched: he spilt much of the gunpowder and lost several balls. But he was an experienced hunter, and handy with a gun, so the task was eventually completed. Raising the pistols, long barrelled and gleaming, he opened his coat and jammed them into his waistcoat pockets, then set out with a more determined tread, handing himself off from the obstacles he met on his way, finally descending to the orlop deck.

Emma was approaching despair. She had seen little of death in her life. Samuel Linley, her first love, whose death had wrenched her heart. A neighbour or two in Hawarden as a child, the odd cadaver in the streets of London when she had been a homeless waif with no bed but a pile of rubbish in a stinking alley. She knew Prince Alberto was slipping away—his waxen skin told her that—and several times she had thumped at his heart fearing it might stop. Alberto's breath came in great wracking gasps and saliva dribbled from his mouth on to her hand.

She felt lonely and helpless. Tom Allen's attempts to fetch a physician had produced no one. The ship's surgeon was busy tending the cuts and broken limbs of both crew and passengers, and could not spare time to deal with a child's fever. The court doctor, who had come aboard in the wake of Ferdinand and Maria Carolina, was in a cot groaning, convinced he was not long for this world.

Emma asked Tom Allen to fetch Nelson. She felt that he alone might be able to light in Alberto's breast the spark of life. But when he came, Emma knew that the crisis was upon her. The convulsions were more acute, as was the lack of breath in the few periods of respite. She took strength from Nelson kneeling beside her, as he whispered encouragement into Alberto's ear.

Nelson had seen a lot of death: from sickness and from war, and just as much from the perils of the sea; he had sat beside many a fevered fellow sailor and reckoned to know who was a survivor and who would expire. As he spoke he tried to compose in his head those words he would need to comfort Emma.

The death throes saw the small body stretched to its limit, three massive convulsions that caused deep and terrifying pain that contorted the beautiful young face. The cry that emerged was a scream of agony that grew till it filled both the cabin and the ears of those attending. Tom Allen was openly weeping, Nelson still trying with words to stave off the inevitable, while Emma called Alberto's name. The last paroxysm forced his mouth to expand in a silent rictus. Alberto's eyes were wide open and full of fear as the last breath of his life escaped from his tiny frame in a horrible hiss. Then he went limp, and the light left his eyes.

Emma, through her moans, heard Nelson praying. He was using words he knew too well, learned from his father, who had stood over so many bodies in his time. As he prayed he took Emma's hand and put it to his forehead. Tom Allen had dropped to his knees by the casement lockers and was deep in prayer as well. But Emma, for all the despair she felt at the loss, had a task that only she could perform.

Gently she pulled her hand free, unlashed the rope that held her to the seat and stood up. Nelson stood, too, trying to steady her, but it was he with only one arm who failed to keep his balance and had to clutch at a rope.

"I must tell the Queen," she said.

Nelson heard the keening cry of a bereft mother seconds after Emma closed the door. Maria Carolina had suffered much: eighteen confinements had resulted in the death of more than a dozen of her children, some at birth, some within weeks. Nelson knew this would be the hardest to bear: Prince Alberto had been a favourite with everyone.

It seemed like an eternity before Emma emerged. She left behind her a woman racked with guilt that her own afflictions had taken precedence over that of her child, that another had comforted him through his illness.

"Tom, I leave it to you to tend to the body," said Nelson.

"Your honour," Tom replied, sobbing.

Nelson patted him on the back, and went to Emma, who was still leaning against the door to the sleeping cabin. He took her hand and let the motion of the ship press him against her. "I have no words, Emma, to tell you how sorry I am, nor to tell you how much I admire you."

Her response was to lay her head on his shoulder. Then she began to sob, but even through her tears she could not forget her responsibilities. When she collected herself, she said, "Someone must tell the King."

"I will do that."

The shake of the head was violent. "No. I will."

"Now?"

"Yes."

"Very well," Nelson replied. He turned to see Tom Allen glance surreptitiously at him and Emma, with a knowing expression that held a good measure of concern. "I shall go back on deck."

The first face Emma saw on entering the wardroom was her mother's. It bore the faraway expression of someone under the influence of drink. She sat in a chair set tight against the wardroom table, clasping a goblet, and gave Emma a lopsided smile. That disappeared when Emma told her of Prince Alberto's death, to be replaced by a shocked expression. By the time she had spoken to the King, and seen him drop his head in his hands, Mary Cadogan was crying. The boy had been an imp, but a charming one, a visitor to the Palazzo Sessa as often as his mother would allow. Ferdinand did not lift his head, and did not seem to mind when Emma took his hand in hers to comfort him: for once the king was completely immobile, stunned by his loss.

"Sir William," Emma asked her mother.

"Gone," Mary Cadogan slurred. "Went out an age ago, never saying where to. Had something with him under his greatcoat."

"What?"

"Couldn't see." Mary Cadogan nodded to the screened off cabin. "Happen Prince Hazy will know."

Emma called softly, then pulled back the canvas screen. Prince Esterhazy, normally the most fastidious creature, was dishevelled. He had jammed himself into a corner, and was sitting fiddling with a sparkling object. Emma was close enough to see it was a jewel-encrusted snuff box. Esterhazy held it up to show her the miniature painting on the top, a nude study of his beautiful Neapolitan mistress, the Princess Pigniatelli.

"Do you think if I offer this to the gods of the sea it will appease them?"

"My husband?" Emma asked.

"He took his pistols from his chest and went out."

"You didn't think to stop him?" Emma said, trying to hide her alarm.

"No gentleman can require an explanation from someone unwilling to volunteer it."

Before he finished the sentence Emma was gone, cursing him for a courtly fool. A look at her mother produced no more than a shrug, so she went out on to the lower deck to look for Sir William. In a crowded ship, no one could move anywhere unseen, so Emma found him quickly enough. He was in another screened-off cubicle on the orlop deck, sitting on a tiny cask, his coat wrapped round him for warmth, the two pistols held ready for use.

"The motion is more tolerable below sea level," he said, with a slight scowl to show that he was displeased at being disturbed.

"Those?" asked Emma, gesturing towards the highly polished and decorated pistols.

"For me, my dear," he replied. "I have no intention of dying with the guggle-guggle of seawater in my throat. It is something I have always feared. Should we founder I will blow my brains out to avoid it."

"Would I be allowed to observe, husband, that you are being very foolish?"

"Am I, Emma? Perhaps I will just take this route to perdition anyway."

Emma had never seen Sir William behave like a chastised child before, but now that was what he looked like. His lips were pursed together with the kind of determined look a stubborn youngster might adopt. She felt that if Sir William had looked in a mirror now he would be shocked at his aged appearance. But what she was seeing was the face that greeted him every morning before his toilet: the wispy grey hair, the lined and thin face that needed to be dabbed with powder to be made presentable.

It had rarely occurred to Emma that her husband suffered black moods, perhaps because he was so careful of his demeanour, always the diplomat, able to cover a gaff with a witticism, an insult with professional deafness, and a didactic statement with just the right measure of levity. He would hide his moods from her, of course, that was his nature, but she guessed he had been in one since the night he had spent at Posillipo after the Nile ball.

"Admiral Nelson assured me that we have no cause for real concern."

"Our dear friend obviously feels he can vouchsafe to you things he will tell no one else." That remark was uncharacteristic of him, but instead of regret Sir William was suffused with a feeling of contentment that his pique was out in the open: he might not like to feel jealous—he might do everything he could to disguise it—but he did and it was uncomfortable. Nelson could say what he liked, and try to reassure his nervous passengers. But Sir William knew that the ship was *in extremis,* and so the chance of drowning was high. To dissemble in such circumstances was absurd.

"I would not hurt you for anything," Emma said softly, stretching out a hand to push back her husband's wayward hair.

"For Nelson?" Sir William croaked.

It was as if the words had stuck in his gullet, so reluctant was he to use them: to pose the question was to invite an answer he dreaded to hear. Had Emma shown any signs of dalliance in the past, perhaps the present situation would be easier to bear, but it was her own fidelity that made what had happened so momentous. It was Nelson's singularity that made his attentions a threat.

"You admire him as much as I do."

Sir William could hardly deny that. The day he had introduced Nelson to his wife, five years before, he had told her that Nelson was a remarkable fellow who would go far. Quite why he had been so enthusiastic seemed odd now, although he had been proved right. Until then he had always had a jaundiced view of sailors, never ever offering visiting captains hospitality under his roof. But he had accommodated Nelson in rooms set aside as royal apartments. The man had impressed him from that first day, and still did. Old enough to be the Admiral's father, Sir William wondered if he saw in him the son he had never had.

"Yes, I admire him, but not quite as much as you do, my dear."

Chapter Thirty-Four

EMMA KNELT in front of her husband and removed the pistols from his hands, releasing the hammers to render them safe. She laid them on the floor and took her husband's cold hands in hers.

How to say to him that the pleasures they had shared were now so diminished as to have almost ceased; no man wants to hear such a thing, that the companion of his bedchamber is rarely present, and then only through a sense of duty not anticipation. How to tell him that she didn't admire Nelson, she was in love with him: madly, passionately, uncontrollably, totally. That would be even more unwelcome to a man who had craved that very emotion, only to never have it granted.

"Tell me the truth, Emma."

They locked eyes, she wondering if somehow she had communicated her confusion through touch, the fact that whatever she said would cause him pain and that in turn would make her feel dreadful. Sir William, looking into those green, confused eyes, was reminded of the first day he had clapped eyes on her. There, in Greville's Edgeware Road hideaway, he had seen the beauty his nephew had acquired, a veritable Venus, so alluring that, as a fifty-five-year-old, Sir William was forced to recall his age, which was enough on its own to dampen any fantasies he might harbour about the girl.

Emma was older now, the face a little more full than that of the stunning beauty he had so admired. Yet that recollection produced another memory: of a young woman who had lacked guile, who was so natural and open in her behaviour it was often mistaken by other men for that of a practised coquette. If Emma had lacked one thing it was certainty, being a person who had always seemed to need guidance. Perhaps that was what she needed now.

"Do not fear that what you say will shock me," Sir William

added. "Remember, I have been your intimate companion for a dozen years."

Emma stroked his lined, unshaven cheek. "I never thought I could shock you."

Nor had he. When they had become lovers Sir William had revealed himself to be a proper disciple of the two-faced god Janus: urbane, witty, and formal outside the bedchamber; but a true vulgarian behind closed doors. He was an avid reader of lewd French books, a lover of ribald conversation, a man who relished a robust fart just as much as he enjoyed the private performances Emma kept for his eyes only.

"You have made me happy." He squeezed her hands reassuringly and continued. "Do you believe, Emma, that your happiness is of paramount importance to me?"

She nodded.

"You know, then, that you have made me jealous?"

"Yes." She indicated the pistols. "But I thought not enough for you to see those as a solution."

"I confess, my dear, that I contemplated such an exit when I had them in my hand, and not because of the fear of seawater. But I have always held that those who take their own life for something as paltry as being cuckolded are at best fools and at worst cowards."

"You are neither."

"I am a coward when faced with drowning," Sir William insisted, before adding, "There is some similarity, I suspect, between drowning and jealousy, the one a physical manifestation, the other a submerging of the spirit. I speak as someone new to the emotion. The night I saw you enter Nelson's bedchamber . . ."

"You saw me?" Emma interrupted.

Sir William laughed. "I came to ensure our guest was comfortable. I knew him to be fatigued, and still suffering from his head wound. I arrived at his door just as you entered, and I thought to wait till you came out." He cocked his head then, as if unsure. "Or did I? Was I anticipating what might occur, hoping to beat you to his apartments and so deflect you? I watched you at the banquet, saw how often you laughed and touched our hero. I suspected, even then, a greater attachment to him than to all those other suitors who have pursued you over the years."

"You are making yourself unhappy, husband."

"No, Emma. It does me good to question myself, for I must tell you that jealousy is not a feeling I ever imagined I would experience, and having done so I can also tell you that for a man like me it is damned uncomfortable. I spend all my time watching you and Nelson for signs of your mutual regard, which is foolish, since any I see wound me, and I am convinced and made uncomfortable by the thought that I may have missed more. Have I missed anything, Emma?"

The import of that question was plain: had she and Nelson made love more than once? "No."

"But I sense a craving not wholly satisfied."

"Would it hurt you more," Emma whispered, "if I was to tell you that I cannot help myself."

"The pain, my dear, is acute enough to be beyond augmentation. But tell me, how does he feel?"

"I know he loves me, for he has said so." Sir William's arched eyebrow made her add quickly. "It is not just words. It is in his eyes, his whole being. Yet I think he fears it. He is, as you know, more God-fearing than either you or I."

Sir William, excluding paganism, hated all things religious, and responded sharply. "I should think, then, he anticipates eternal damnation."

"I think he fears more to lose me," replied Emma, with equal force.

"Touché," said Sir William.

"Yet I think he would rather offend his God than you." Sir William's humourless laugh made Emma continue. "It is true husband! I doubt any other man could have caused him a second's doubt."

"The morning after your assignation, while bathing at Posillipo, I was forced to review my life." Emma made to speak but Sir William pressed a finger to her lips. "I have always been concerned about what would happen to you after I am gone. You are so much younger than I, and I have accustomed you to a degree of extravagance that what I will leave behind me cannot sustain."

Having promised his estates and the income from them to his nephew, there would be no comfortable inheritance for Emma. Having used up the best years of her life, he had taken her to a point where she might struggle to find another benefactor, and she would have only a small annuity plus the money left after the settlement of her husband's debts. The style in which she was now wont to live—with three homes, carriages, servants, dressmakers, milliners, and never a thought for the cost—would cease on Sir William's death.

"I must confess," Sir William continued, "that in idle moments I had thought on this before, the possibility that another man should come into your life, who would be able to maintain you after . . ."

"You have many years left, husband."

"Have I, Emma? I am nearing seventy, the allotted biblical span. My bones ache even on the warmest morning. My ardour, which I hold sustains a man against all manner of ailments, has cooled to the point of . . . Well I need hardly tell you that. In conclusion, faithful as you have been to me all these years, I was contemplating the notion of advising you that such behaviour was no longer wise."

Emma smiled. "Yet you did not."

"The diplomat in me, my dear," Sir William responded wryly. "Nothing precipitous has always been my motto. And I must own how different the intellectual pursuit of an idea is from the reality. Is it because Nelson is a hero? Is that why?"

The suddenness of those questions jolted Emma, so that her reply was unconsidered. "No."

"When?"

"The first day I met him."

There was a flash of pain in his eyes, quickly masked. "And you carried your torch for five years."

"I never thought to see him again. We exchanged letters, as did you and he, but nothing in his correspondence or mine touched on anything other than mutual regard."

"And then the Nile."

Emma raised herself up, crouching over Sir William's head, using his shoulders to steady herself against the motion of the ship. "I must go back to the Queen. She is distraught." The look her husband gave her then made Emma realise that she had not told him of Prince Alberto's death. She told him now, ending in a whisper, "I think the King would benefit from your company in the wardroom."

The torn topsails had been replaced with fresh canvas, and although the storm wasn't over, it had eased enough for everyone on deck to feel more sanguine about the ability of ship and crew to ride it out. Their actual position was unknown, but the island of Sicily was too big to miss, and Nelson knew that as soon as they sighted land they would be able to steer for Palermo.

As the night wore on the weather eased steadily, allowing those unused to the sea to sleep. The motion was still greater than they would have wished, but it was no longer violent enough to toss them from hammock or bed, or send them tumbling down a companionway as they made their passage from one part of the ship to the other. Nelson went once more into the chart room and dozed off, half-aware of what was happening on the quarterdeck. His eye would flicker as the bells of the watches tolled, and as he sensed each change of course.

The comatose interludes were punctuated by snatches of vivid dreams: of old faces and strange ones, real battles and imagined encounters, until he heard, "It be coming up dawn, your honour." Tom Allen was shaking Nelson's shoulder. "Time for your shave."

Nelson smiled before he opened his eyes. Routine made the Royal Navy what it was. No matter that the ship was still tossing about on a troubled sea, that his cabin was all ahoo and occupied by others. Tom Allen shaved him at the same time every naval day, and this morning was not going to be any different.

"And may I be the first, your honour," Tom added, "to wish you good cheer on Christmas Day."

"It is that, Tom," Nelson replied, and closed his eyes again. "I had quite let it slip my mind."

What would they be doing in England? Would the family have gathered at Burnham Thorpe for a special Christmas service and a celebration meal? Would his eldest brother, Maurice, with his indifferent health, have been dragged from London and the Navy Office to see in a New Year in Norfolk? His father would be there and Susanna, his favourite sister—now Mrs Bolton—with her seven children; and brother William, now the Reverend, the closest companion of his youth.

There were deaths to mourn: his sister Anne and brothers Edmund and George; but the baby of the brood, Catherine, had married George Matcham, and the couple were steadily producing children. His other brother, Suckling, he had never cared for, and he checked himself for that unchristian thought. But the face that drew his inner gaze was the one he wanted least to imagine—that of his wife, Fanny.

She would play consort to his father and gently scold Susanna's litter as though she was the matriarch of the household, a position she assumed, much to the annoyance of Nelson's eldest sister. Her face filled his mind now: gentle, refined, and smiling as he had first seen it on Nevis; pinched and frozen with chapped lips as she had been in Norfolk, during those five years he had spent without employment.

He fought to keep the comparison from surfacing, Emma's gaiety and abandon with Fanny's reserve and physical coldness. She was his wife before God, and deserved his devotion. But he could not force out the lovelier, livelier face or the memory of the freely offered passion that contrasted so sharply with Fanny's restrained emotions.

His eyes snapped open. It was the best way to blot out dreams. "A Happy Christmas to you too, Tom."

"Wonder what they're up to in Burnham?" Tom said, smiling. He was from Burnham Thorpe as well, baptised by the Reverend Nelson at the font of All Saints.

"A shave, yes," Nelson insisted.

Tom had set up the chair, water bowl, and strop in Hardy's cabin, and had also conjured up a welcome cup of coffee. The cook had got his coppers relit so that there was something hot for all. By the time the razor was under Nelson's chin, the officer of the watch had sighted land, and HMS *Vanguard* had put up her helm on a true course for Palermo.

Dressed and ready for breakfast, John Tyson appeared. He had spent the time since the flight from Naples well out of the way, mewed up hugger-mugger with the ship's purser. But official business could be delayed no longer and that it was Christmas made no odds. Rarely a day went by when an admiral did not have to deal with a mass of correspondence, and Tyson wanted that which was outstanding cleared before the day's work came in. There might be despatches—there would most definitely be lists—of ship's conditions, masts, spars and sails, which would be dire after such a blow. Each would report the state of their water and biscuit, how many men they had left in Naples or lost on the way to Palermo, the mass of detail that was the bane of a commanding officer's existence. And that was before Admiral Lord Nelson must write both to the Admiralty and Earl St Vincent to apprise them of his actions.

Then, and only then, could he attend to personal matters.

Hardy was sensible enough of the occasion to arrange that his officers should gather to raise a glass to Their Sicilian Majesties on the anniversary of the birth of Christ. Yet it was a stilted affair, everyone conscious of the losses that those being toasted had endured: their kingdom and their youngest son. Outside, snow fell in a part of the world usually immune to such a phenomenon, while in the cabin small gifts were offered and graciously accepted, the very lack of intrinsic value seeming to make them more potent than jewelled or golden objects. Ferdinand, for once showing the courtly manner that went with his rank, thanked the ship's officers on his family's behalf. Thomas Hardy then made a brave little speech in which he apologised that more cheer was not possible, but he felt sure, he said, that the protective arm of King George's Navy was there to see them safe, now and in the future.

As he finished the lookout yelled to alert the quarterdeck that the harbour of Palermo was in sight.

Sir William was on deck as HMS *Vanguard* manoeuvred to clear the mole, half of his mind on the way the snow obscured the view, the other on the conversation he had had with his wife. Matters were out in the open now and thus had to be dealt with. The question was how? With another man little would have had to be said, but Nelson was so naïve in matters of the heart that Sir William contemplated that he might need to invite him directly to proceed with Emma.

He balked at the idea. Suddenly, the gruff voice of Mary Cadogan addressing a sailor made him turn. She was so wrapped up against the chill that not much more than her snub nose, reddened by the cold, was visible from inside her closely tied bonnet. But it was enough to remind him that, years before, it was she who had smoothed the way to her daughter's acceptance of him as her protector.

She had challenged him and his intentions in a manner that had made him feel as if she was the master and he the servant. Her attitude had been based on years of experience in dealing with men, and the fact that she suspected he was engaged in a conspiracy with his nephew.

Mary Cadogan had smoked out all the details of how he and Charles Greville had intrigued to transfer Emma from the nephew's arms to the uncle's. And she had known that what had looked simple to the schemers on paper would founder on her daughter's good nature and fidelity. Sir William had anticipated her anger, only to find her eminently practical. Mary Cadogan had deduced one obvious truth: that the chance of Emma's return to Greville's affections was remote. What mattered to her was comfort and security, and once she had established that the best chance of that lay in Naples, she had set out to alter her daughter's mind.

Looking at her now, it occurred to Sir William that she was the solution to his problem. If anyone knew how to alert Nelson to the fact that he might proceed, without embarrassing anyone, it was Mary Cadogan.

Despite the chill December sleet it seemed that half the population of Sicily was on the shore waiting to greet their king and queen, a silent mass of citizens who believed that royal residence in Naples was foolishness. Sicily was loyal where the mainland was suspect, true to the Bourbons, and with a visceral hatred of revolution. There were no Jacobin clubs here, no seditious nobles, only true subjects.

In the calm of Palermo harbour, inching in to tie up at the mole under the great hanging rock and the forts, the ship was now in a ferment of preparation. Ferdinand was berating his valets for the state of his clothes, which had been spoiled by seawater. In Nelson's quarters the Queen was patient, distant almost, as her ladies-in-waiting prepared her to meet her subjects, everyone trying to ignore the plain wooden coffin that had been made by the ship's carpenter to hold Prince Alberto's body.

Emma had found space in one of the side cabins to repair the damage of the last 48 hours. Gazing at herself in a looking glass she saw lines on her face, the result of extreme fatigue. Sir William had already gone ashore with the King's chamberlain and some of the more astute courtiers to secure the best available accommodation at the Colli Palace.

A bed for Sir William in the royal residence could only be temporary; as the British Ambassador he would be required to rent suitable accommodation from which to represent his country, and prices, once the locals realised just how many fleeing royalists had arrived, would shoot through the roof. As an early bird, he might save some money.

The death of the prince was enough to still any cheers from the populace, which would have been inappropriate in any case. As the King and Queen, the Hereditary Prince and his wife, their baby and the royal princesses made their way through the streets, they were accompanied by the quiet murmur of prayers, and the onlookers made the sign of the cross as the cortege bearing Prince Alberto passed.

Nelson, with Hardy and his officers, watched the procession begin from the poop, vaguely aware that the ship was being put to rights around him. The transports and the Portuguese men-o'-war began to unload too, which turned the mole into a mass of gesticulation, as those landing sought accommodation and avaricious monks from numerous monasteries bargained with them.

Some of the faces he knew from balls and receptions he had attended, but he couldn't recall many of the names. He spotted Commodore Caracciolo and wondered how he had got there, since no Neapolitan warship had left Naples. He half considered offering him accommodation aboard *Vanguard*, but the Commodore was not much given to either grace or gratitude, so he might be an unpleasant dining companion. Added to that, he was probably still smarting because his king and queen had chosen a British ship in which to flee Naples, rather than one he commanded.

When he returned with Tyson, Tom Allen had seen to his cabin. The furniture was in place and polished, and when he sat at his worktable it seemed to Nelson as though he could put the clock back to a point where there had been no Nile battle, no Naples welcome, no Emma Hamilton. Then he concluded that the lady had been a presence in his life for a very long time.

"Mr Tyson," he said, "we are required to inform Earl St Vincent, and Captains Ball and Troubridge of our situation."

There was almost pleasure in immersing himself in work.

Sir William felt unwell, sitting up in bed wrapped in blankets and his dressing gown. He had caught a chill on the journey from Naples, which had moved from his chest to his stomach. His discomfort was made worse by the cramped quarters he and his wife had been allotted by the chamberlain. The room was dark, with cracked marble flooring and peeling paint on the walls, and barely big enough to hold his possessions—and that was without the packing cases still snug in the hold of HMS *Vanguard*. The luxury of separate suites that he and Emma had enjoyed in Naples had been replaced by cohabitation, with a couple of his servants forced to sleep on the floor outside the door. It was all very well for the court officials to insist that the Colli Palace was packed to the rafters with courtiers and ministers, but he was, after all, the British Ambassador.

His only consolation was the thought that this setting was likely to be temporary. He was sure his early arrival ashore was about to bear fruit, and a promising villa had been proposed to him, albeit at a staggering rent, in which he could assume once more his usual comforts and the duties of his office. The door opened to reveal Mary Cadogan with a steaming bowl of liquid.

"Not another of your damned possets," he moaned.

"Got to get you well, Sir William," she replied, giving him a hard stare as she approached the bed. "An' if it don't taste like nectar that's all to the good I say, 'cause what seems foul is often best to restore a man's humour."

"The only humour to be gained from that," Sir William sniffed, "is gifted to the person watching the victim consume it."

"Then you won't mind, sir," said Mary Cadogan, positioning herself on a cramped chair, "if I partake of the pleasure."

The temptation to damn her to hell and tell her to get out was overborne by the realisation that he had a chance to engage in a conversation he had been delaying since coming ashore. His high fever and low spirits had been the excuse, but he was aware that procrastination had brought no joy. Emma was absent, Mary Cadogan was here, and it was too good a chance to miss.

"You have a ghoulish turn to your nature, Mrs Cadogan."

Emma's mother discerned the amusement behind that remark, even if it was delivered with a grimace. "You arrange a good hanging and quartering, Sir William, and I'll happily go to that and leave you in peace."

For all his diplomatic skill, Sir William found the next step difficult. "I had a mind to talk with you anyway, but intended to wait till this ague had passed."

"Would it be about matters domestic?"

"No!"

The emphatic response was met with the merest lift of her eyebrows, and since Sir William had no desire to state the details of the matter, a silence ensued. Eventually after what seemed an eternity of a mutual stare, Mary Cadogan spoke. "Would it be about my Emma?"

"I have often had occasion," replied Sir William, "to remark, Mrs Cadogan, upon your sagacity."

There was little doubt in Mary Cadogan's mind as to what he wished to discuss. She had been watching the parties involved with a tight eye since the night Emma had gone to Nelson's room and, sensitive to atmosphere, had noticed the tensions.

"God gave me eyes to see," she said finally, if elliptically.

"And the good grace to be discreet," replied Sir William, nailing the subject.

"Would it ease your mind if I said it were bound to occur one day?"

"No, Mrs Cadogan, it would not."

"If I may speak plain, Sir William."

"I have always found that you do so when matters require it," Sir William observed, in a mordant tone.

"Fidelity has always been one of my Emma's better traits." The Ambassador nodded. "She can be lacking in sense, but even with your nephew, who didn't deserve half the consideration due to your good self, she was true."

The last part of that sentence betrayed a bitterness that Mary Cadogan had never sought to hide and that had remained constant throughout the twelve years since she and her daughter had come to Naples. She held Charles Greville to be a scrub, and made little attempt to disguise this from his uncle.

"I know it," said Sir William.

"It is without a boast," Mary Cadogan snorted, "that I can claim to have not only smoked your game, but made my Emma party for it." It was no time for Sir William to interrupt, since he might open himself to censure, so he stayed silent. "And now you'll be asking me to tell Emma, in a way that you cannot, that this here nonsense with Lord Nelson has got to stop."

There was some comfort there for Sir William in that, with all her natural acuity, Mary Cadogan had not seen just how much her Emma was smitten, had not made the obvious connection between her daughter's natural fidelity and the depth of feeling that would be necessary to break it. For once he knew more of what was happening in Emma's head and heart than her mother.

"Quite the reverse, Mrs Cadogan. I admit to needing your assistance, but it is not to badger my wife into breaking off her friendship."

There was no need to say more. The surprise on Mary Cadogan's face said it all.

Glossary

Aft: The rear of the ship.

Afterguard: Sailors who worked on the quarterdeck and poop.

Bilge: Foul-smelling water collecting in the bottom of the ship.

Binnacle: Glass cabinet holding ship's compass visible from the wheel.

Bowsprit: Heavy spar at the front of the ship.

Broadside: The firing of all the ship's cannon in one salvo.

Bulkhead: Moveable wooden partitions, i.e., walls of captain's cabin.

Capstan: Central lifting tackle for all heavy tasks on the ship.

Cathead: Heavy joist that keeps anchor clear of ship's side.

Chase: Enemy ship being pursued.

Crank: A vessel that won't answer properly to the helm.

Fish: To secure the raised anchor to the ship.

Forecastle: Short raised deck at ship's bows. (Fo'c'sle)

Frigate: Small fast warship; the "eyes of the fleet."

Larboard: Old term for "port": left looking towards the bows.

Leeward: The direction in which the wind is blowing.

Letter of Marque: Private-armed ship licensed to attack enemy. (Privateer)

Log: Ship's diary, detailing course, speed, punishments, etc.

Logline: Knotted rope affixed to heavy wood to show ship's speed.

Mast: Solid vertical poles holding yards (see below).

Mizzen: Rear mast.

Muster: List of ship's personnel.

Ordinary: Ship laid up in reserve.

Orlop: Lowest deck on the ship, often below waterline.

Quarterdeck: Above main deck, from which command was exercised.

Rate: Class of ship 1–6 depending on number of guns.

Rating: Seaman's level of skill.

Reef: To reduce the area of a sail by bundling and tying.

Scuppers: Openings in ship's side to allow escape of excess water.

Scurvy: Disease caused by lack of vitamins, especially C.

Sheet: Ropes used to control sails.

Sheet-home: To tie off said ropes.

Ship of the Line: A capital ship large enough to withstand in-line combat.

Sloop: Small warship not rated. A lieutenant's command.

Spar: Length of timber used to spread sails.

Starboard: Right side of ship facing bows.

Tack: To turn the head of the ship into the wind.

Topman: Sailor who worked high in the rigging.

Wardroom: Home to ship's officers, commissioned and warrant.

Watch: A division of the ship's crew into two working groups for four-hour periods, one watch on duty, one off.

Wear: To turn the head of the ship away from the wind.

Windward: The side of the ship facing the wind.

Yard: Horizontal pole holding sail. Loosely attached to mast.

Yardarm: Outer end of yard.

"An insightful portrait of a man, a hero and his times, and what each of those things, in their essence, truly mean."

—James L. Nelson, *author of the Revolution at Sea saga*

The Eighteenth Captain
The John Paul Jones Trilogy, Book 1

If you enjoyed **Tested by Fate,** and want to read more about the great naval heroes of the Age of Sail, here is an excerpt from another McBooks Press title, **The Eighteenth Captain,** by Nicholas Nicastro. Nicastro's novel probes the complex character of John Paul Jones as he navigates the military, political, and romantic battlefields of Revolutionary America and France. Here in Chapter Two, we join his comrade-in-arms, John Severence, in post-Revolutionary Paris as he strikes a deal to relate Jones' adventures to two new friends . . .

II.

CAPTAIN JOHN SEVERENCE could thank the changes of 1789 for his luck with Mlles. Nathalie-Anne Thierry and Thérèse Gualbert. Very early in their meal together, he placed one of his big buckled boots on each woman's slipper, under the table. He put them there before the soup was served, and had not removed them straight through the veal service. He showed no sign of changing his position as long as the beauties refused to acknowledge the weight on their toes. He was an American.

The condition of the women's apartment could only have encouraged his forwardness. They had struggled to prepare the way for him, cleaning the rooms themselves, curtailing meals to raise money for a reasonable cut of meat, making due with a minimum of fresh flowers. Thierry's outmoded lévite, and the frayed hems of Gualbert's English gown, could hardly have escaped his eye.

With no money to pay night servants, they were forced to serve the food before his arrival and let it sit, waiting for him. The conspicuous lack of domestic help was as obvious a signal as waving a white handkerchief in the face of Severence's scavenging manhood. Sensing their desperate poverty, he peered over the lip of his glass and cast suggestive looks. The women grew bored waiting for the inevitable proposition.

"I accepted your invitation with great pleasure," he finally said. "Might I suggest . . . an unconventional liaison, to consolidate our friendship?"

Gualbert looked to Thierry, who muttered, "*À trois?*" Her friend closed her eyes, nodded. The pressure on the women's feet increased. None of the three would meet the eyes of the others.

Severence imagined it was their modesty he was probing; in fact, they despaired only of their fee.

Mlles. Thierry and Gualbert had, after all, been intimately attached to the persons of Abbé Joseph Jean-Baptiste Abrimal, Second Deputy-at-Court to the Powdered Wig, and Botaniste-Royale Georges Busson, respectively, and had once enjoyed all the privileges, responsibilities and honors of courtesanship in the Outer Court.

Granted, Abrimal and Busson were only members of the *noblesse de robe*, talentless and unremarkable, and, accordingly, had been granted the honor of purchasing government posts at the going rate of one hundred thousand *louis d'or* each. Typically, these honors brought such debt on their two households that the men were obliged to recoup their investments by accepting cash "vocations" for particular services. Abrimal sold access to the treasurers Turgot and Necker, and was even known to drop helpful suggestions into the ear of Louis himself. Busson entertained a relentless stream of requests from gentlemen-scientists bent upon childish researches. In this way, these servants of the state trust became as rich as ever, and set about the project of finding mistresses appropriate to their wealth and station.

This was exhausting business, not unlike the pursuit of public office itself, entailing many hundreds of tiresome dinners, operas, and liquor-leavened anecdotes from notorious libertines. These latter each possessed road maps to the vices of Paris, high and low, and the wise shopper was well advised to seek those places where the maps agreed.

In Abrimal's case, the task was complicated by a peculiar and remarkable condition of abbreviated foreskin that made erection painful and intercourse impossible. The malady was not unknown in France: the King's own case had kept Queen Marie Antoinette herself waiting for seven years before the consummation of the royal marriage. It was eminently correctable, in fact, with a simple surgical procedure, but Abrimal was afraid of both blood and unconsciousness, and would not undergo the cure. His condition therefore called for a *demi-mondaine* of special talents, one versed in the arts of patient, contemplative arousal leading to satisfaction within the bounds of restful detumescence. (His wife, the legendarily devout Madame de Orvilles *(née)*, alas required a more vigorous bucking than he was prepared to mount.)

His relief was suggested to him by no less than Bishop Talleyrand. A tireless epicure, His Holiness referred Abrimal to one Nathalie-Anne Thierry, a small-town draper's daughter of such prodigious beauty she was coveted and deflowered by a local seigneur at the age of ten. Entirely ruined, she was turned out upon her own devices at eleven, and immediately prospered.

Abrimal duly invited Mlle. Thierry to a large and public supper. After slyly encouraging Mme. Abrimal to festoon herself with her most conspicuous jewels, he made certain the former was seated across from his wife, where these advertisements of his worth would shine suitably in the candle flames.

Mlle. Thierry's powers of observation did not disappoint him.

By machinations too lengthy to report, Abrimal supplanted the competition and made his way into Thierry's bed. In the full glory of sensual disarray, his new odalisque's true beauty blazed forth in facets he could only gaze upon in rising exasperation—eyes of almost oceanic greenness, amber ringlets about naked shoulders, an amply graspable bosom.

In minutes, Abrimal was on the floor, his culottes around his knees, squealing with the agony of his rigidness. Mlle. Thierry, a quick study, immediately comprehended the situation. Seizing a bowl of iced fruit, she dispensed with the fruit and poured the ice in Abrimal's lap.

Thus relieved, he then learned the full truth of Talleyrand's praises. Improvising a special method for Abrimal's "release," Mlle. Thierry dressed, powdered, and equipped herself fully, as if for a turn in the garden, then reversed the procedure in a slow and teasing manner. All the while, she kept vigil on Abrimal's member, slowing her progress or making disparaging remarks to control its stirrings. Abrimal achieved a state of gratification without a hint of pain. She was hired.

Thierry was also instrumental in ending Busson's search for a respectable adulteress of his own. Her acquaintance, Mlle. Gaulbert, was such a relentless competitor for their limited market the only peace possible between them was one of tactical friendship. Gualbert's coloring, as black and shining as a blackbird's, made the women chromatic complements to each other. (They had occasionally alternated in the beds of aesthetes rich enough to afford them.) It was not ordinary practice for such businesswomen to help each other, but their equivalent loneliness and ambition gave the women similar tastes. Busson was, in any case, happy for the referral.

Unfortunately, the scheme of their employment did not take into account the untimely Death of Leisure. Abrimal and Busson had taken close notice of the propitiating "reforms" launched by the Crown, from the liberation of the serfs on royal properties to the prohibition of tortures useful in obtaining confessions, to Louis's public stand against the *corvée* tax and his inexplicable tolerance of lies published by trash pamphleteers. They worried when he called the first Estates-General in more than 150 years, then grumbled at his further specification that the bourgeois Third Estate would send as many delegates to the gathering as the nobles and the Church combined.

At length, Mlle. Thierry's special talents became moot. Abrimal's mind could focus on nothing other than what he had heard at the Hôtel des Menus Plaisirs. Sitting with other members of the minor aristocracy on the outskirts of the auditorium, he found himself situated next to a wall, through which he could hear the speeches underway among the rabble next door. Voice after angry voice followed each other, hour after hour, punctuated by joyous yelps of exultation, applause, animalistic growls. The pox-faced Robespierre delivered two- and three-hour oratories fraught with verbs like "strike," "seize," and "universalize," and nouns like "tyranny," "emancipation," and "freedom." Abrimal lost his color for hours at a time; Thierry only had to utter the word *"égalité"* to keep his rising organ in check.

France was already an alien country to them by the time the demagogue Camille Desmoulins ignited the events of that awful July from atop a café table near the Palais-Royal. The Bastille itself meant little to Abrimal, Busson or even to the King, but its violation by the mob rudely deprived them of consoling rationalizations: to wit, the Duc de La Rochefoucauld-Liancourt's reply to the royal question, "Is it a revolt?"

To which the redoubtable Duke replied, "No, Sire, it is a revolution."

As if to underscore this, on the way back from the prison, the marauders happened upon a well-heeled gentleman, kicked him to death and stuck his severed head on a pike. According to horrified witnesses, the victim's clothing was scarcely ostentatious—plain-colored silk frockcoats were hardly seen anymore, and bagwigs were most definitely not *à la mode.* It was frightening to contemplate what the mob would do to a truly well-dressed man.

Suddenly, to the annoyance of our heroines, Abrimal and Busson rediscovered the rising value of their wives' extensive foreign holdings. The decision to take flight from the country was simply out of their hands, the men shrugged, since such important matters were always the preserve of their wise and beautiful spouses. Within two months, Abrimal, Busson, their wives, children and moveable assets were removed, to Austria. Neither man had offered a goodbye to his faithful mistress. Neither left behind so much as a *sou.*

It was a singular position for the two women. Ever since their midteens, they had had little difficulty in supporting themselves, but the atmosphere had changed. Suddenly, the social calendar was less and less marked by affairs at which they could advertise. Had they been practical, they would have fled to the revolutionary salons of Madame de Gondorcet or the Marquise de Chabonas, where they could be pawed by churlish intellectuals and bourgeoisie drunk on new power. Unfortunately, they were not only pampered whores, but patriotic ones, and could not stomach such men. Meanwhile, famine and shortages of available males added competition from the low end of the market. For the first time in the women's lives, their fortunes began to decline.

Stubbornly refusing the attentions of anything less than a Marquis, they tried to make due. Since they would not relinquish their apartment in the well-placed Left Bank neighborhood of Faubourg Saint-Germain, on the Rue des Petits Augustins, they alternated in offering their favors to the landlord's assistant. The carving work on their panelled dining room had to stop short of the completion of the over-door trophies (dedicated to poetry and the marital virtues, respectively). The laurel, peacock, and vole arabesques in their bedrooms were never finished. Instead of crystal, they had to make due with a nine-candle chandelier of plain, patinated bronze. They could not even afford to buy the yards of books they needed to decorate their new shelves.

History continued to turn on its head. Mlles. Thierry and Gualbert were bewildered witnesses as thousands of common women from the bakeries, butchershops, fruiterers and nutsellers marched past the Tuileries on the way to deliver their demands to the King at Versailles. Demands! Our heroines were still more bewildered the next day when these women returned, not only with their necks unstretched, but with the King himself and an escort of National Guard. Parisians cheered as wagons laden with flour followed the royal carriage into the city. Truth be told, Gualbert could not help but be infected by the surging republicanism, and went so far as to pin the tricolor rosette to her bonnet. Later, with the crowd no longer behind her, she threw the device in the trash. Moments later, she reconsidered and fetched it out.

They could not afford their scruples for much longer. Their courtly wardrobes were falling farther and farther behind the new, classically inspired fashion, and they could scarcely meet the expense of buying fresh ostrich feathers for their hats. They fought like common charwomen over the least expenditure, but, in fits of contagious self-pity, bartered jewelry and furs on evenings at the theatre and bouts of boozy despair. They were used to better, after all. It simply wasn't fair.

At last they compromised, resolving that new patrons could qualify for their services merely on the basis of income. Their financial straits eased throughout 1790, permitting them to improve their condition from freefall to merely steady decline. They could eat, stay out of the rain, and purchase what minimal accessories were necessary to their trade, but little else. They began to consider marriage.

Just when they were sure they must settle for either twitchy bourgeoisie or callow Revolutionary officers with manure on their boots, they were reacquainted with the species of true Man. Gualbert saw him first, as he came out of the Hôtel de Ville in a most agreeable green carrick coat and Pennsylvania hat, grasping a cadogan cane not unlike Busson's. Closer, and she spied long black lashes beneath a high and handsome brow, a square chin, and lips curled in a shadowy smile as his rich blue eyes swept over her. More thrilling, he sported a most virile scar, a veritable *gouge,* from the bottom of his left eye down the angular span of his cheek. Who was this man, Gualbert wondered, who dared dress so well, so openly?

Acting on impulse, not calculation, she immediately threw a glove to the ground and waited for this vision to demonstrate his breeding.

"Is this yours, dear Lady?" Captain Severence inquired, caressing the glove as if her hand were still in it. She was careful to reply with a most encouraging blush.

Ordinarily, Gualbert's procedure would have next entailed a precise probing of the stranger's income, cash holdings, stocks, commissions, executorships, bonds, accounts, investments, degrees, associates, real equities, prospective inheritances, outstanding debts, gambling patterns, club memberships, recent invitations received, connections of influence, cut of clothing, and deportment of his footmen (if ascertainable). But these were not ordinary times. In her current desperation, she judged only on the basis of the glad chirping of her own heart—and his perfect manicure.

Without the taste and inclination to mount the barricades in search of the times' finest men, our heroines were starved for reputable male society. Severence was therefore invited to the Rue des Petits Augustins, ostensibly for late supper and conversation. Gualbert allowed her eyes to promise a bit more.

Surging into their elliptically shaped dining room precisely at half past eleven, he took an appropriate unnotice of their still-ungilt beechwood chairs, their console tables topped with second-rate marble, their tulipwood commode with unlaundered doilies. Instead, he reserved his sailor's interest for the Bassement wall clock/thermometer adorned with Cupid astronomers. He even correctly attributed the instrument's decorative inspiration to the 1769 transit of Venus.

"That was the very night of my conception!" Gualbert informed him.

"I understand, in fact, that Venus is at her greatest elongation this very evening," he added with careful indelicacy.

"You surprise me," Thierry chided him, "by hinting at the dessert course before the main is done. Are you Bostonians always such poor guests?"

Severence colored a bit, then smiled.

"Mlle. Thierry, I can't describe to you my astonishment at how often I am called a 'Bostonian' by otherwise educated Europeans. I myself am from New-York—from the green isle of Manhattan, in fact. But I believe the term you seek is American. That is what we are properly called."

"How fascinating!" trilled Gualbert. "A geographical trivium!"

"A trifle," Thierry corrected her.

"Just so."

Severence smiled into his glass. "You ladies speak the English better than most titled ladies I have known."

"Of course," said Thierry. "We are capitally educated. You might also be amused to hear our German: *Wir sprechen auch perfekt Deutsch, nicht wahr, Nathalie?*"

"*Wenn wir mit unseren deutsch Kunden sind,*" her friend replied.

"So you see, we are ladies of quality. You cannot just eat our food and then fuck us."

"He should not," Gualbert amended, her eyes dancing over his.

Severence looked down, thought a moment. The women felt the pressure lift from their slippers. Thierry was relieved to rub her numbed toes against the back of her calf.

"You are most surely in the right, Miss Thierry. My actions tonight have betrayed my rearing, which was in fact quite respectable. You must forgive me—I have been at sea almost constantly for the last dozen years. The trade has ruined me. I have lived with the language, smells, and manners of men. I have slept in bunks no bigger than two chairs lashed together. I have been obliged to see blood and piss through the hawse more times than any man should. My dear mother would not know me. I believe I have entirely lost myself."

His face lacked the slightest hint of irony as he made this admission. Gualbert looked to Thierry, who shrugged. Severence merely sat and drank, adding nothing more.

"Well," said Thierry at length. "It is well you say these things. It has been a long time since we've been regaled with such stories."

"Yes! Tell us of the sea! Tell us how you came by that scar!" Gualbert enthused, clapping her hands together.

"Not just of the sea," Thierry charged him. "In these times—in this age of little men—I want to hear of men of stature. Tell us of the heroes you've known. Tell us well—and you will get everything you came here for."

Severence glanced up, startled by her offer. Even Gualbert was obliged to stare.

"Nathalie! You might have thought to ask me before making such pledges!"

"Your position regarding Captain Severence has been clear all evening," Thierry replied. "Besides, I make no promises. He must first tell his story well. The verdict of the judges must be unanimous." She cast her cold eyes at Severence again, not hiding the quality of haughtiness she had learned from Abrimal. "Tell us then, Captain. Do you take up the gauntlet?"

He raised an eyebrow. "I wonder why I am being challenged to win the prize, when it is widely known to be for sale."

"It is for sale," said Thierry, "but not for money. Not tonight."

The women were staring expectantly at their guest. Severence drained his glass deliberately, as if to pique their impatience, then reached into the Canabas wine cooler beside his boot, lifted the decanter, and offered it to each of the women.

"*Merci, non,*" said Gualbert.

"Yes," Thierry responded.

When she was suitably topped, he sat back in his chair and crossed his legs absently. His recitation began quite unexpectedly:

While o'er my limbs Sleep's soft dominion spread,
What through my soul fantastic measures trod
O'er fairy fields; or mourn'd along the gloom
Of pathless woods; or down the craggy steep
Hurl'd headlong, swam with pain the mantled pool;
Or scaled the cliff; or danced on hollow winds,
With antic shapes; wild natives of the brain?

He stopped, drank some more. Thierry narrowed her eyes.

"Poetry," she said. "Whatever is possible, in English."

"It is from a work of Edward Young, called 'Night Thoughts.' A poem much admired by the only hero I can confess to have known in his person. Have you ladies ever heard of Paul Jones?"

"The pirate?" asked Thierry.

"The lover," asserted Gaulbert. "I walked past him once at Versailles, as he stood at the Bassin d'Apollon looking at the Grand Canal. I remember he was quite gallantly outfitted in a blue uniform faced with white, and a single gold epaulet, in the style of the Bost—American navy. He was legendary at sea and in the boudoir. All the women spoke of him, but he was taken with a married woman—that Bourbon flirt, married to a general, whose name I can't recall—"

"Madame la Comtesse de Lowendahl," Severence reminded her.

"That's the one." Gualbert continued. "They were standing together, looking over the water as the sun set behind it. As I passed, I overheard her telling him there used to be a man o' war afloat on the canal—a frigate of thirty guns—set there just for the amusement of Louis XIV, like a toy. I remember Jones was quite indignant at this. He said something like, 'I spent half my career bringing honor on smaller vessels than that.' Then she laughed at him, and touched his chest with her hand, and he blushed. And that's all I saw."

Thierry smiled at her friend. "No one could see more making a casual pass in a garden."

"Was he wearing that medal of his?" Severence asked.

"It shone quite prominently in the sun."

"I don't doubt it. He may even have calculated the best angle to catch the rays."

"You clearly have very definite opinions of the man," Thierry said, impatient. "Tell us, then."

Severence would not be rushed. Whether it was because of the weight of the story or the promise of the prize, neither woman could say.

"You may be interested to learn that he resides very close to here, on the Rue de Tournon, almost broke and very certainly alone."

Gualbert frowned. "It seems hardly possible he should be forgotten, especially here, in Paris!"

"I'm afraid the years have not treated him well," he replied. Severence inserted a pause here, patently to cultivate an air of mystery. Thierry ruined it for him by waving her hand and insisting, "Well then, go on!"

"Before I begin, a warning. In the main, my association with Paul Jones was early in his career at war. Though there is heroism in those months—as much as in the entire lifetime of an ordinary ship's master—I can't claim to have known him during the cruise on the *Bonhomme Richard,* or in Russia. If you care to hear the well-known stories, you may consult any parlor historian. But at the risk of immodesty, I can say that no one knew him better during his first months in Europe, when the foundation of his fame was laid."

"A fair caveat. As long as you don't disappoint us," said Thierry.

Seeking a more sympathetic judge, Severence rested his eyes on the umbral charms of Gualbert. "A proper introduction to Paul Jones must begin some time before I encountered him," he began. "Even then, my career was influenced by his."